THE SHIELD BETWEEN THE WORLDS

The Second Chronicle
of Fionn mac Cumhal

DIANA L. PAXSON &

ADRIENNE MARTINE-BARNES

AVON BOOKS • NEW YORK

THE SHIELD BETWEEN THE WORLDS is an original publication of Avon Books. This work is a novel. Any similarity to actual persons or events is purely coincidental.

AVON BOOKS
A division of
The Hearst Corporation
1350 Avenue of the Americas
New York, New York 10019

First AvoNova Printing: May 1995
First Morrow/AvoNova Hardcover Printing: March 1994

AVONOVA TRADEMARK REG. U.S. PAT. OFF. AND IN OTHER COUNTRIES, MARCA REGISTRADA, HECHO EN U.S.A.

Printed in the U.S.A.

RA 10 9 8 7 6 5 4 3 2 1

This one is for

Fritz Leiber
and
Elizabeth Marie Pope

foster-parents of the creative spirit.

You left us too soon—may you read this tale
in the tapestry that hangs in the Otherworld.

ERIU

Ulaidh

Ben Bulben

Connachta

R. Sinnan

R. Boann

Midhe

Inber
Colptha

Temair

Almu R. Liffe

Dergdeire

Bri Elé

Druim Cliadh

Laigin

Lamraige

R. Siuir

Mumu

Paps of Anu

D.P. '93

People and Places

CHARACTERS

NOTE: The pronunciations given below are an approximate transliteration of the words as pronounced in a way that can be comprehended by the modern reader. Dh = "th" as in *the*; qh = a guttural "ch" or "gh" sound. A dash indicates a syllable separation, an apostrophe indicates a hesitation. "Mac", meaning "son of", has been left in the modern form (instead of the medieval "magg"). Gaelic is an inflected language, and names may change their spelling in different grammatical positions.

Our thanks to Alexei Kondratiev for correcting spelling and word forms, and to Paul Edwin Zimmer for advice on pronunciation. Any mistakes are the result of artistic decisions or pure ignorance, and are our own.

Characters are listed in alphabetical order. In the course of the story, the personnel of the *fian* goes through many changes. Fian I was that of Cumhal, Fionn's father, a few of whose members have survived. Fian II was that of Crimall, Fionn's uncle, in which he trained in Volume I, and which he inherits. Fian III consists of the men who join during the first years of Fionn's leadership, and Fian IV, taking shape during Fionn's middle years, includes many sons of men from the first two groups. Characters marked by an asterisk belong to the Otherworld, and those whose names appear between parentheses are dead before this story begins.

Achtlan, Airmedb, Ceibhfhionn [AQHT-LAN, AR-VEDH-UV, KAYV-YUN]—priestesses of Brigid

*Aedh mac Fidach [AYDH MAK FIDHAQH]—one of the Sidhe, lover of Élé, the killer of Oircbél

Aghmar mac Donall [UQHMAR MAK DOWNIL]—*Fian 1*

*Aillén mac Midhna [AL-YAYN MAK MEEDH-NA]—one of the Sidhe, a fire elemental who attacks Temair every Samhain

Airt Og of the Hard Strokes [ART OHG]—one of the Sons of Morna, *Fian I*

Aodh mac Ronain [AYDH MAK RAWN-IN]—lord of Gabhair, son of one of Cumhal's enemies, *Fian IV*

Birga [BEER-GUH]—Fionn's spear

*Bodb Derg [BODH-UV DYER-UG]—father of Sadb

(Bodbmall) [BODH-VULL]—a druidess who fostered Fionn

Bran [BRON]—son of Tuireann, in dog form in our world

*Brigid [BREE-ID]—goddess of healing, smithcraft, and poetry

Cairbre mac Cormac [KERBRUH MAK KORMAK]—son of the high king

Caoinche [KWEEN'HE]—Dithramhach's daughter, second wife of Goll

Ceallach [KYEL-LAQH]—the Swift-Footed; a *fennid*, *Fian IV*

Cethern mac Fintan [KETH-ERN MAK FIN-TUG]—master of a school of poets

Cnú Déroil [KNOO DYER-U]—Fionn's dwarf, *Fian IV*

Colgain mac Teine [KOL-U-GUN MAK TYEN-NYE]—high king of Lochlann (Scotland), half-brother of Laigne

Conain [KONAN]—the Swearer, one of the sons of Morna, *Fian I*

Conain mac Luachar [KONAN MAK LOOAQHAR]—the Grey Man's son, *Fian IV*

Conn mac Feabhal [KON MAK FYAW-IL]—*fennid, Fian IV*

Cormac mac Airt [KORMAK MAK ART]—*Ard Ri* of Eriu

Crimall mac Trenmor [KRIVUL MAK TRENVOR]—Fionn's uncle, leader of Fian II

Crimthann [CREEVTHAN]—one of the first young men to join Fionn's *fian, Fian III*

Cruithne [KRUTH-NYE]—daughter of the smith Lochan, Fionn's first wife

(Cumhal mac Trenmor [KOOWEL MAK TRENVOR])—Fionn's father, dead before his birth, *Fian I*

Dáire Dáirfhinel [DAW-RYE DAW-RIN-YEL]—Fionn's fosterling who raped Lugach, *Fian IV*

*Daireann [DAR-YEN]—daughter of Bodb Derg, half-sister of Sadb

Diarmuid mac Duibhne [DYEEARMID MAK DWIVNYE]—a protégé of Fionn, *Fian IV*

Dithramhach mac Cumhal [DYEETH-RAW-AQH]—Fionn's half-brother *Fian II*

*Donait [DUNATCH]—a woman of the Sidhe, Fionn's protectress

Dubh Droma mac Seanchach [DUV DROMA MAK SHENU-QHAQH], *Fian IV*

Dubhtach [DUV-THAQH]—a member of the fian, *Fian IV*

Dubhtach Blackmane [DUVTHAQH], *Fian II*

Duibhne [DWIV-NYE]—one of Crimall's *fian* (once the cupboy), *Fian II*

Eargna [ARGNA]—daughter of Aodh

*Echbel [EQHVAYL]—son of Bodb Derg, brother of Sadb

*Élé [AYLYE]—a fairy woman courted by Cethern

Ethne Taebfada [ETHNYE TAYVADA]—a Leinster princess, queen of Eriu

Faolchú [FWAYLQHOO]—"of the hard-tempered sword", *Fian IV*

Fearghusa [FERQHUS] and **Faobhar** [FWEEVAR]—twin

sons of Muirne by king Gléor Lamraige (Fionn's half-brothers), *Fian IV*

Ferdhomhonn [FERDHOWON]—Fionn's son by a crofter's wife, *Fian IV*

Fergus [FERQHUS]—the poet attached to the *fian*, *Fian III*

Fiacail mac Conchinn [FEEAKIL MAK KON'HINN]—once of Cumhal's *fian*, Bodbhmal's husband and one of Fionn's first teachers, *Fian I*

Fionn mac Cumhal [FYONN MAK COOWEL]—*rigfennid* of Eriu

(Fionnéices) [FYON-EY-GUS]—master poet, Fionn's first teacher

Gaoine [GWAYNYE] **mac Lugach**—"the Joke", son of Fionn's daughter

Glas mac Dreamhan [GLAHSS MAK DRYAWIN], *Fian II*

Gléor Lamraige [GLEE-OR LAMRAYUH]—Fionn's step-father, husband of Muirne

Goll mac Morna [GOL MAK MORNA]—chief of clan Morna, second-in-command of the *fian*, formerly Fionn's enemy, *Fian I*

Guairire mac Reiche [GOORYE MAK RAY'HYE], *Fian II*

Grainne nic Cormac [GRON-YUH]—daughter of the High King

Grimthann [GREEVTHAN]—(dog boy in Crimall's time), *Fian II*

Laigne mac Mor [LIE-NYE MAK MORE]—a shaman and warleader from Alba

The Liath Luachra [LIATH LOOQHRA]—a warrior woman, one of Fionn's fosterers

Lomna [LOM-NA]—Fionn's fool, *Fian IV*

Lugach [LUQH-AQH]—Fionn's daughter by Cruithne

Miogach mac Colgain [MIAQH MAK KOLUGUN]—son of the king of Alba and nephew of Laigne the Shaman, failed his test for the Fian IV

Mongfind [MONGEEN]—chatelaine of Almu

*The Morrigan [MOR-REE-AN]—raven goddess of battle

Muirne nic Tadg [MURRN'YUH NEEK TADH-UG]—Fionn's mother

*Nuadu [NOO-A-DHU]—king of the Sidhe, father of Tadg (Nuada in the genitive form)

Oircbél [ORUKVAYL]—Fionn's friend and fellow student, killed by Aedach

Oisin [O-SHEEN]—Fionn's son by Sadb

Reidhe [RAYDHUH]—*Fian II*

*Sadb [SADH-UV]—daughter of Bodb Derg, a Sidhe woman transformed into a doe, Fionn's great love and mother of Oisin

Sceolan [SKYOLUN]—son of Tuireann, in dog form in our world

*Scena [SKAYNA]—a Sidhe woman jealous of Tuireann

Suibhne [SWIVNYE]—Spear-bearer, smiter of hosts, *Fian IV*

Tadg mac Nuada [TADH-UG MAK NOO-A-DHAT]—a great Druid and Fionn's grandfather, lord of Almu, later called Fer Roich, the "Dark Druid"

Ullan [UL-LAN]—a man of the Sidhe, husband of Tuireann and father of Bran and Sceolan

PLACES

Alba [ALAPA]—Scotland

Alma [AL-VOO]—a dun on a hill overlooking the Curragh, won by Fionn from Tadg

Ben Bulben [BYEN BULUBEN]—a promontory in Connacht, home of the Dark Druid

The Boann [BO-AWN]—the Boinne

Bri Élé [BREE AYLYUH]—a fairy mound near Cloghan

Connachta [KUN'AQHTA]—Connaught

The Curragh [KURRAQH]—plain surrounding Kildare in Wicklow

Druim Cliadh [DRUM KLEEADH]—Shrine of Brigid on the Clay Ridge, County Kildare

Eriu [AYR-YOO]—Ireland

Inber Colptha [INVER KOLUPTHA]—estuary of the Boyne

Laigin [LAYIN]—Leinster
Lochlan [LOQHLAN]—Scotland
Mumu [MOO-VOO]—Munster
Paps of Anu [ANOO]—twin mounds in Munster
The Sinnan [SHINUN]—river Shannon
The Siuir [SHU'UR]—the river Suir in S. Leinster
Sliab Bladhma [SHLEEUV BLADHMA]—Slieve Bloom Mountains, Kildare
Sliab na mBan [SHLEEUV NA MAN]
Tailtiu [TALTCHOO]—Teltown, in the valley of the Boyne
Temair Brega [TCHEVER BRAYQHA]—the hill of Tara
Ulaidh [ULADH]—Ulster

TERMS

Ard Ri [ARD REE]—High King
bendrui [BUN-DROOEE]—woman-druid
bodhran [BODH-RUN]—flat drum
corrbolg [KORBOLUG]—magic craneskin bag
drui [DROOEE]—druid
dun [DOON]—a group of dwellings fortified by a palisade, usually on a hill
fennid [FENITCH]—member of a *fian*
fian [FEEAN] or *fianna*—like a national guard, recruited from the subject tribes
fidchel [FISCHELL]—a board game
fili, filidh [FILEE]—poet
filidecht [FILJECHT]—the poets, poetry
geasa, geas [GAY-US]—a taboo
grianan [GREEANUN]—sun house, usually reserved for the women
ogham [OH-AM]—a system of writing with vertical lines
ollamh [OLAVE]—a poet of the highest rank
rath [RAWH]—a single dwelling, sometimes with palisade
rigfennid [REEGFENNITCH]—"king" of the fian
tuath [TOO-AH]—a people, clan

Beltane [BAL-TEEN]—May Day
Imbolc [IMBULK]—Feast of Brigid, beginning of February
Lughnasa [LOONASAH]—Feast of Lugh, beginning of August
Samhain [SOW-IN]—Hallowe'en

Prologue

"**F**IONN MAC CUMHAL MUST DIE. . . ." THE OLD DRU-
id leaned forward, staring into the flames. The fortress of Almu stood on a hill. Outside, the wind was
rising, and the hearthfire leaped and wavered as the
draft plucked at the edges of the hide stretched across
the door of the hall.

"He is your grandson, let you be killing him," said the
warrior, lounging back on the bench. Firelight glanced
across the hard planes of his face, glowing in his good
eye and veiling the ruined socket of the other, bringing
into bold relief the lines of humor around his mouth
and the brutal curve of his jaw. The *rígfénnid* of Eriu
was in the prime of his strength, and every movement
showed his awareness of physical power.

"Do you think this a matter for laughter?" The old
man's face had been carved by harsher passions, his
nose hooked like an eagle's beneath the winged white
brows. "He is dangerous, Goll mac Morna, to you above
all, now that the high king who helped us to destroy his
father is gone."

"Conn Hundredfighter may be dead, but young
Cormac knows better than to upset the order of
things," said Goll, "And you need not fear that the

1

young ones will ally against us. When Cormac and Fionn met at Tailtiu they nearly came to blows." Now the warrior did laugh. Then he went on.

"Fionn may become a trouble to you, Tadg, when he has mastered all the *fili's* wordcraft, but why should he challenge me for leadership of the *fianna* of Eriu? Did not you know they call him Fionn of the Poets now? The boy is set on the *fili's* path." Goll held out his meadhorn to the serving girl to be refilled and drank deeply. "Six years he has been with Cethern mac Fintan, studying, and shows no signs of leaving him."

"You killed Fionn's father," Tadg mac Nuada said heavily. "And he has seen twenty-four winters. He is a man, now. He will have to challenge you." His robe of bleached wool looked red in the light of the fire.

"Will he satirize me to death?" Goll grinned sardonically. "Surely you have arts to protect me, old man!"

The druid's brows bent, and the embroidery on his mantle glittered as he trembled with the effort to keep control.

"Without my help you could never have brought Cumhal down. You will need me to deal with the son as you dealt with the father. You should have killed Fionn at Tailtiu, when he was a boy."

Goll snorted. "I do not slay children. If you wanted the boy dead, surely you had more chance to kill him than I. He grew up in the Forest of Gaible—you might have hit him if you had cast a stone westward from the walls of Almu. You must have known he was there!"

The dull flush that darkened the old druid's face owed nothing to the flames.

"It was the women who deceived me—" His voice grated as he said the words. "Always the women, and my own daughter worst of all. The bitch defied me, and Bodbmall and that warrior-woman they called the Liath Luachra abetted her. It was women's cunning

that hid them when I learned that Muirne was carrying Cumhal's child. Bendrui though she was, even
Bodbmall's arts could not have protected them if it
had come to open battle. But she had the cunning of
the mouse that hides beneath the eagle's eyrie. Do you
scoff at me? The warriors in your *fianna* had no more
success in tracking them than I!"

"But no woman's cloak hides Fionn now," said Goll.
"Do not you owe him an honor-price for your part
in his father's death as well? If the boy is fated to
seek revenge, surely he will come one day to claim
Almu—" The warrior's gesture took in the breadth of
the roundhouse and the other buildings within the
stout whitewashed walls of the dun.

"Cumhal stole my daughter," muttered the old man.
"I will not let his son steal my stronghold. . . ."

"But that is what he is destined to do!" Goll laughed
and threw back the fringed folds of his crimson mantle
as if he were too warm. The gold torque of a chieftain
glinted from his neck, gold gleamed from his armrings
and bracelets and the plates riveted to his broad belt as
well. "That prophecy frightened you enough to deny
Muirne a husband. Do you not fear it still?"

The wind shook the thatch above their heads and the
druid pulled his mantle, striped in all the colors, more
closely around him. It was nearly Samhain, and away
from the fire the air was chill.

"The cloak of the *filidecht* protects him. . . . My vows
forbid me to touch him while he is in the keeping of an
order that is brother to my own," the druid said reluctantly. "That is why I have summoned you."

"Am I to help you for the sake of the past?" asked Goll.
"If Fionn had wanted to be a warrior, his uncle Crimall
would have given him the headship of Cumhal's old
fian! You will have to do better than this if you want
my aid!"

"Goll mac Morna, hear me!" Tadg's voice deepened,
and the warrior shivered. "You jeer because I could not

find Cumhal's son when he was a child, but by my arts I have learned how he became a man! When you have heard the tale you may judge more surely whether you are in danger from Fionn mac Cumhal!"

Goll sighed, but something in the druid's voice held him still.

"You wished to spare Fionn at Tailtiu because he was a boy," said Tadg. "But he was a killer already. When he was not yet twelve years old he came out of the woods like a wild beast and killed a hand of lads who were playing ball. He took the old warrior-woman with him when he fled from that deed and dropped her into a lake when she discommoded him. Then he slew four of the grown men who were pursuing him. Even at Tailtiu Fionn was a troublemaker—surely your nephew, Dael mac Conain, must have told you so."

"I thought that Dael brought it on himself," muttered Goll. "I would not speak ill of the dead, but he was ever a contentious child."

"Was that why you were so clumsy in getting rid of Fionn?" the druid asked. "I believe that it was Aonghus mac Conal who warned him, not knowing he was aiding the slayer of his own brothers. But Aonghus is dead too—strange, is it not, how many of those who have helped Fionn themselves soon die? Perhaps that is why he fled from place to place after leaving Tailtiu, as if he were an outlaw in name as well as in deed."

"In the west he stayed a year with a smith, and ran away after getting the man's daughter with child. But before he did so, he killed the Grey Man of Luachar. Ah—I thought that would touch you!" Tadg said as Goll sat up, staring. "Fionn has killed the man who first wounded his father at Cnucha, and whether it was fate or revenge, I think the pattern is clear!"

"And then?" asked Goll mac Morna. "We heard he had been with Crimall in Connachta, but when we came there the boy was already gone."

"It was from one of Crimall's men that you heard it," said the druid, sneering. "Even his father's old *fian* would not protect him!"

"I don't know about that," answered Goll. "They certainly seemed upset that he had gone. But whether they were glad or sorry, we lost his trail. And so long as he is not building strength against us, why should I care?"

"He apprenticed himself to Fionnéices after that, Goll—and that is a name you ought to remember well—" Tadg's voice had deepened, and the warrior eyed him uneasily.

"Fionn the Poet?" asked Goll, "Cumhal's *fili*? He went blind after the Battle of Cnucha, and became very strange. The last I heard, he was still playing hermit, trying to pull some magic fish out of the Boann!"

"He caught it," said Tadg softly. "Fionnéices caught the Salmon of Wisdom, and the boy stole its magic and killed his master. Perhaps Cethern does not know that, or perhaps the boy has spun him some lying tale. But I know what he is. Have I said enough to prove the danger, Goll? Or are you as blind as Fionnéices still?"

"You make him sound a monster," the warrior said slowly. "But every *fili* in Eriu would curse me if I attacked him while he is with Cethern. Can you keep watch on him through your arts and warn me if he becomes a danger? Can you tell me what he is doing now?"

The druid stared at him and his eyes glowed red as those of some night beast surprised by torchlight. The grief of all the world was in the howling of the wind outside the walls.

"Do I need to prove myself to you?" he asked harshly. "Very well. Holy gods, here is my offering. . . ." He poured the last of his mead into the fire and the flames blazed up suddenly. "Nuadu, my father, grant me the gift of true seeing—sacred sight . . . speed through the night . . . make darkness light . . . lend me your might . . ." he murmured as he lay back on his bench, wrapping his mantle around him so that all that showed above the cloth was a wisp of white hair.

Goll mac Morna sat up straighter, watching him twitch and mutter. The folds of the mantle rose and fell as the old man's breathing grew deeper and harsher, then stilled. From the shadows above came a sound like an eagle's cry and the warrior's hand went to the hilt of his sword. He ducked involuntarily as great wings seemed to beat the air above his head. Then the sound faded away.

"Wind and darkness . . . wind and darkness . . ." came a whisper from beneath the mantle. "Across the land the spirit paths are brightening. The mounds of the Sidhe glow like coals. Soon their doors will open onto the world. Southward I seek, to Femen's plain, but the huts of the *fili* are empty and cold. Yet the life force of the one I seek has left a track in the darkness. I can follow it northward along the Siuir to its head-waters and northward still. . . . Ah, it brightens! He is close now! I can feel his presence."

"There is great magic here—the Hill of Élé hums like an angry hive. . . . Cethern and his gaggle of baby poets are huddled around their fires in the woods below the hill. There's a haze of light around their campsite. Cethern has sung up a warding. Fool! Does he think that will protect them now?"

For a few moments there was silence, but the air in the room had become perceptibly more chill. Goll huddled into his own mantle, but he never took his eyes from the shrouded form of the old man.

"The hour comes! The Hill of the Sidhe is crack-ing like an egg. Ah . . . ah . . . how the light of the Otherworld blazes through! But only a single shape slips through the gap. It is mantled in darkness, and around it the bloodhunger is a red glow. The door closes, but the dark hunter is free, and the forest grows sleepy as he sings his dark song. . . . He senses the lives within Cethern's fragile circle as points of brightness. Go quickly, dark brother, feed on the fairest. He is there—can you see him?"

The eagle cried in the shadows, the cloaked shape jerked convulsively, and the exhaled breath came out of it in a long groan. Then there was only the harsh gasping of the old man.

"Lost . . . lost . . ." came speech at last, and now it was recognizably the voice of Tadg that Goll heard. The folds of the mantle were thrust back by a trembling hand. "I wanted to see too badly, and I lost him. But the hunter is on the trail. He will kill Fionn, or he will kill one of those puling brats that the boy calls friend, and that will hurt him even more."

Presently the druid sat up. Despite the chill in the air, beads of sweat glittered on his brow. Goll was already on his feet, reaching for his gear.

"This is uncanny and I will have no part of it."

Tadg replied with a bark of laughter. "If you try to leave here now you will see things that are more uncanny still! At night this hill is triple warded by powers you do not dream of. Your body might still be living by morning, but your mind would be gone." His eagle-gaze caught that of the warrior, and very slowly Goll put down his weapons and seated himself once more.

"If the dark hunter does not kill Fionn, you must do it," the druid said. "Will you promise me?"

After a time, Goll sighed. "I cannot touch him now, any more than you. But this much I will promise you, by my honor and my name—to kill Fionn as I killed Cumhal if ever he goes back to his father's fian."

"Do not forget it. If he lives, Fionn mac Cumhal will take the leadership of the *fian* from you, and from me he will steal Almu. He should never have been born."

Like an echo, the Samhain wind howled around the hall.

Chapter 1

⚜

ACHILL WIND SWEPT IN FROM THE EAST, SENDING DRY leaves whispering across the fading grass. Fionn shivered and peered into the darkness. Beyond the flicker of firelight where Cethern and the poets were camping, treetops netted the dim sky. Above them he could just make out the dark silhouette of the Bri Élé, the fairy hill. To the eye there was no movement but the swaying of the trees, but the earth beneath him brought Fionn a deeper pulse of magic, growing ever stronger as the season turned towards Samhain, when the door-ways opened between the worlds.

But as yet, nothing stirred in the mound. It was the wind's whisper that had alerted him, an ancient voice that spoke within his soul.

Once more Fionn shivered, and this time not from cold. He had reason to fear Samhain. This year would the spirit of his friend Bran mac Conal visit him, with the surprise of his death widening his eyes? *Forgive me*—Fionn's spirit cried. *They were attacking me! I did not know it was you!* Or would it be the fili Fionnéices, with the sword with which he had tried to kill Fionn still stuck in his side? That death, too, had been unin-tended, like the taste of the Salmon of Wisdom that had

8

changed his world, But if that had not happened Fionn would not have come to Cethern, and the first time of uninterrupted happiness he had known since he was a little child.

"Fionn!" A much younger voice summoned him back to the world of food and firelight. "You look as if you were seeing spirits! What is wrong?"

Fionn looked up, pushing back a lock of heavy, flax-colored hair that had escaped from its band, and summoned an answering smile.

"Is it not enough to make a man shiver, Oircbél, to have to look at your goblin face across the fire?"

Oircbél's grin widened, and for a moment he did indeed look like a goblin, with his sun-browned skin and angular bones. All the fili wore their hair long and flowing. But only Oircbél's was dark. He came from Dun Canon on the southern coast, and in him the blood and magic of Mumu were strong. But he was Fionn's friend, the first who had warmed to him when Fionn turned up at Cethern's door armed like a *fennid* warrior, with his grief for Fionnéices still shadowing his eyes. Fionn had been braced to fight for acceptance by the poets as he had been forced to fight everywhere else he had gone. But Cethern's benign patronage and Oircbél's laughter had made the school of the *filidecht* a home.

"If I am a goblin, then you must solve me a riddle to go free—" said Oircbél. "Say then what meat was served in mac Datho's hall, and who ate the Champion's Portion there, and what concealed the outcome?"

Fionn frowned and set down the pork bone that was still in his hand. He knew the answer, but the sense was only half of the solution, The form must be fair as well. "*Ni ansa*—not hard to say—" he answered finally.

> "The meat of heroes was a noble hog;
> That was devoured by mac Datho's dog;
> The dust of battle the concealing fog!"

"I suppose that was too easy," said Oircbél, "with the sweet savor of the pig you killed for us still in our mouths, and the strength of its meat in our bellies. My thanks to you. I had not expected to eat so well upon the road."

Fionn swallowed. The few bites of pork he had eaten sat uneasily in his gut and he wondered if he were going to be ill. *Is it some geasa that no one ever told me of?* he wondered, remembering how he had killed the sow of Sliab Bladhma and the Otherworldly boar of Sliab Mis. *Pig meat is always unlucky for me.* The menace he had felt before was returning more strongly, but it was the earth song that was changing now.

Fionn tried to shrug his unease away. Oircbél did not deserve to be weighted by his foolish fears.

"By the time I was twelve I was killing all the meat to feed myself and the two old women who fostered me," he said simply. "I know the creatures of the forest as you know your father's cows. But this close to Samhain I could wish it had not been a pig that I found."

"Poor Fionn. You worry over your successes as other men do over their failures. Do you think the Sidhe will grudge us a beast taken so close to their hill?" Oircbél turned to gaze at the darkness beyond the trees, and the emotion that leaped in his dark eyes was curiosity.

"It is not the pig that they will grudge us, but their daughter!" Fionn exclaimed. "Were Élé as beautiful as Etain, she would not be worth a man's life, and that is the price that those who come to woo her must pay!"

"Warriors!" scoffed Oircbél. "Every hero in Eriu has failed this testing, because human weapons are no use against the Otherworld! The *filidecht* know better. We shall ward ourselves and win the girl with song!"

"But why seek the danger?" asked Fionn. "Were we not happy at Cind Curraig on the Siuir?"

"If happiness consists of sitting by the fire and telling over old tales," said Oircbél. "But why should Cethern let the warriors have all the glory? Especially when the very name of the maiden is an incantation. Clearly she was meant to be the wife of an *ollamh*. When her magic is mated to Cethern's skill there will be no greater *fili* in Eriu!" He gestured expansively, and Fionn looked towards the largest fire where Cethern was sitting with some of the younger students.

That is how Fionnéices spoke of the Salmon of Wisdom, he thought dismally. But Cethern was a solidly built man with only a little silver in his wheat-colored hair, shaven like a druid's across the brow. And Cethern knew how to laugh.

"No good can come of this quest," he said aloud.

"So you have told us—" answered Oircbél. "Several times. But whether or not the maiden will have him, think what a song it will be!"

"But Cethern mac Fintan is already a master," argued Fionn. "He needs no charms from the Otherworld to make a poem."

"So are you, or very nearly," said Oircbél. "You had the spirit of *filidecht* when you came to us, and it was only the forms you had to learn. In another season they will give you the *ollamh's* blue mantle. But have you ever drunk your fill of Beauty?" asked Oircbél. "I would risk my life gladly to gain a kiss from such a woman or to hear her song."

Fionn took an involuntary breath, for suddenly it was not roast pig and wood smoke but the scent of apple blossom that weighted the wind. *It is true . . .* he thought, remembering how he had jumped the chasm to reach Donait of the Sidhe. *And I would walk through fire to see her once more!* For a moment understanding seemed to open within him like a bright doorway, then it slammed shut once more.

"Fionn—" Oircbél's voice seemed to come from a great distance. "Where are you wandering? For days you will be just like the rest of us, struggling to remember your verses and complaining about the chores, and then something happens and your eyes go strange. Are you some changeling escaped from the Otherworld? Where do you go?"

Fionn closed his eyes. It was true, but he had not known that it showed. He tried to swallow past the hard ache in his throat. He would never be like the others. Even with his best friend in the world sitting beside him, he was alone.

But he must not hurt Oircbél further by inflicting his pain. With an effort he made himself smile.

"I go looking for new riddles to stump you, of course," he said lightly. "If you cannot answer this one will you pay a forfeit to me?"

"Very well, but I will set the price if I win!"

"What are three times when less is more?" asked Fionn.

"That is not hard to say," answered his friend.

> *"When words are fewer, more meaning there be,*
> *When cows are fewer, more grass they see,*
> *When friends are fewer, more ale for me!"*

He burst out laughing, and his merriment carried Fionn along.

"And my cup is empty!" Oircbél yawned and held it out to Fionn. "Here's an easy forfeit for you! Go beg us both some bedtime ale!"

Fionn was glad enough to take the cups and go to fill them. Oircbél knew him too well; his questions bit too close to the bone. He had guessed so much already—one day Fionn might even dare to tell his friend the full story of his past. He uncoiled his long limbs and strode out, stretching muscles that had stiffened after the unaccustomed exertion of his hunting, glad to be moving again.

Fionn's steps slowed as he crossed the darkness between the fires. The wind had fallen, but the pulse in the earth was throbbing like a great drum. *Can they not feel it?* He looked at the laughing group by the fire. *Cethern knows so much—can he not feel the doom that hangs in the air?* Suddenly the firelight seemed pitiful, the people beside it puny as folk about to be engulfed by a rising tide.

Bare branches rustled sleepily around him and he could see that several of the students were already curled in their blankets by the fire. Fionn's fingers tightened on the ale cups, and he realized that it was not the past and its demons that were disturbing him tonight, but the future, and hoped that the change he felt coming was only the turning of the year.

WHEN FIONN RETURNED WITH THE ALE, OIRCBÉL HAD SUC-cumbed to slumber, and all his friend could see of him was the curve of his cheek and his smile. The wind had died, but the sudden stillness of the forest made him as uneasy as its sounds. The power he had felt flowing from the Sidhe mound had diminished. There was a week yet until the actual eve of Samhain. Perhaps what was to come would not be tonight after all.

Fionn sighed and drained his ale cup at one swallow, and then, after a moment's thought, drank down Oircbél's share too. He hoped that the ale haze would soothe his nerves enough to let him sleep as soundly as his friend. Then he spread his cloak beside Oircbél and wrapped himself snugly, rolling close so that his friend's warmth would warm him as well. The ankle-length tunics of bleached wool that all of them wore were awkward for hunting, but warm to sleep in. The earth song was slow, soothing. One by one his weary muscles unknotted. His long body accommodated itself to the humps and hollows of the ground beneath him.

Sleep . . . said the music around him; *sleep* . . . said Oircbél's soft snoring in his ear. *Sleep* . . . said his own tired body, as the soft glow of the ale spread from his belly through his limbs and walled him away from the world.

Fionn dreamed of a river flowing through orchards where the apple trees filled the air with heavy perfume, gathering rivulets on its way to the glittering plains of the sea. He dreamed of Donait's hall and of royal duns with crystal walls, He dreamed of fair women who sang with the voices of birds, but when he pursued them they turned into swans and flew away.

Then his dream grew darker. The orchards became a tangled wood whose branches trapped him when he tried to reach the fortress within. And the river flowed red with blood; he could smell the cloying stink of it like the breath of the Red-Mouthed Woman he had slain. And the swans all turned into ravens who argued in the trees.

"*Blood . . . dead . . . food!*" one cried.

"*Alive . . . moves . . . fear!*" the other replied.

Fion had never heard anyone speak so loudly in a dream.

"*One lives . . . one dies . . . we wait!*" the third raven cawed, and Fionn turned over and opened his eyes.

Three ravens were looking down at him from the holly tree. At his movement, two of them croaked loudly and flapped away, but the third continued to fix him with its beady black gaze. Dawn mist still hung heavy in the upper branches, and the clearing had the blanketed stillness that moisture in the air will bring. Other birds were beginning their dawn songs farther away, but the sound came muted, as if only the immediate surroundings were real.

It must be dawn, or very nearly. The others would not be waking till the sunlight burned through the mist and stung their eyes. And in any case it was too cold to be up and doing. The fire had burned down to ash, and a fine frost silvered the fallen leaves. Fionn sighed and closed his eyes and rolled back to let Oircbél's body warm him.

But Oircbél was cold. Fionn poked him and felt the other youth's back stiff and resistant. He held his breath, but there was no grunt of protest or soft whisper of breathing. And the stench of blood from his dream still filled the air.

Fionn felt the anguish building in his throat even before he struggled free from the folds of his cloak, knowing already and not believing what he would see.

A river of blood had flowed from Oircbél's neck to freeze in a translucent garnet-colored pool. But the head had disappeared.

Fionn found himself on his feet, staring. Pain paralyzed his chest; he fought for breath, and suddenly the grief, the disbelief, and the outrage burst from him in a howl that blasted the frost from the tree trunks and rayed cracks across the frozen blood on the ground.

"*Oircbél!*" Again he called the name, and again.

From the one he had summoned there was no answer, but Cethern and the poets popped from their cloaks and blankets like squirrels, chattering in outrage.

"Stop there!" Fionn shouted as the first of them stumbled towards him, and the command in his words held them still. His stunned mind was beginning to function again. "Look around you—do you see tracks in the frost? Are there any tracks on the ground at all?"

The night's chill had laid a veil of glittering frost across the entire clearing, already beginning to fade as the air grew warmer with day. But enough remained for Fionn's trained sight to see that except for one irregular line of footprints where someone from the other fire had staggered towards the privy trench, there was no mark upon the ground at all.

Fionn brought his hand to his mouth to keep from retching, and as the thumb that had been burned when he touched the Salmon of Wisdom reached his lips, suddenly he understood what must have happened as clearly as if he had seen it all.

"Cethern! Cethern!" Fionn's cry was terrible. "See what your pride has won! The doom was that one man of every company that came to woo the maiden

Élé would be taken, and it is Oircbél that they have taken, and he was the best of us all!"

"Oircbél . . . dead! Murdered! Terrible . . ." Boys' piping voices and the deeper tones of the young men wavered between horror and glee.

"Fionn lay beside a corpse all night without knowing," said one.

"He must have heard something! Maybe it was Fionn who killed Oircbél!" came the reply.

"Be still—everyone, stay where you are." Cethern's trained voice silenced the babble. Still rubbing sleep from his eyes, he shouldered his way through the lads and picked his way carefully forward, looking at the ground. "No one came this way after the frost, that's certain."

The *fili* came to a halt beside Fionn and his face worked as he looked down. Fionn saw it and felt just a fraction of his own anguish ease. Cethern had many students, and Fionn only one real friend, who now was gone. But at least he would not mourn alone."

"But Oircbél was killed after the frost covered the ground," he said quietly. Cethern's eyes narrowed, but Fionn pointed to the pool of blood. "There are half-melted crystals of frost beneath it, do you see?"

"I see—" said Cethern quietly, Biting his lip, he drew back the cloak wrapped around Oircbél's body, tugged it free, shook it, and cast it aside. Then he did the same with the one in which Fionn had lain. After a moment's outrage, Fionn realized that the *fili* was making sure that the missing head had not been concealed.

"You lads there, spread out into the woods around us and search them." He waved his hand, and youths sprinted off in all directions, chattering excitedly once more.

"Why put them to the trouble?" Fionn said dully. "They will find nothing. This is the answer to your wooing, Cethern! This deed was done by one of the people of the Mound. . . ."

"I do not doubt it—" The *fili's* voice was edged with strain. "This is meant to clear you, lad."

"How can you clear me?" Anguish tightened Fionn's throat once more, "I did not do this deed, but I blame myself for it all the same! I bring death to everyone I love!"

The headless body looked like a pile of rags, tumbled where it had fallen when the cloak was removed. Fionn's breath caught on a sob, he snatched up the cloth and laid it tenderly across the body once more,

"Oh, Oircbél, Oircbél, I have failed you! I should have known our paltry wardings would not be sufficient. Last night a spell of sleep was on all of us and I did not even suspect it. Not a one of you knows fighting but I, and I should have shielded you all! I should have known I was weary with more than the hunting. I should not have drunk the ale!" Fionn bent over the body, his shoulders shaking with a grief that would not let him give voice after that first great cry.

"It is I that will bear the blame with you, lad." Cethern's strong arm was laid across Fionn's shoulders. "If I had listened to you we would never have come."

The others were beginning to return from their futile searching, voices faltering as they drew near.

"Gerrcind, Ildanach, go you to cut branches for a litter to bear the body home. The rest of you, build up a fire. We'll need food to march on." With a sigh that seemed to come from the roots of his chest, the *fili* rose.

"Come—" He squeezed Fionn's shoulder. "There is nothing you can do for him here. But we will not skulk away like beaten dogs. Let us say farewell to our foes."

When Cethern had combed his hair and arranged the deep blue mantle of the *ollamh* over his white robe,

Fionn followed him through the woods to the clearing before the hill where only yesterday they had chanted the praises that were intended to win Élé's love.

The hill looked quite ordinary in the first glimmer of sunlight, covered with heather and bracken and scattered stones. The Sidhe had veiled their magic, and to mortal sight it was only a hill. Just so had the slope that led to Donait's hall appeared when he looked back after she had sent him away. But at Fionn's feet a drop of blood stained one of the stones. The blood trail continued up the hillside and disappeared. He pointed, and the *fili* sighed.

"On my own head, lad, I did not suspect you. I have not eaten of the Salmon of Wisdom, but when my nose is rubbed in a thing, I understand! Oh Élé, Élé," Cethern shook his head sorrowfully. "You were all the beauty in the turning world to me. Was there only deception in your song? But now there is blood between us, and I will never know if you thought of me at all. . . ."

After a few moments the *fili* sighed and took a few steps forward, leaning upon his staff.

"People of Danu, hear me! It is Cethern mac Fintan that is calling you now. People of Bri Élé, there is a life between us. The blood of a man with whom you had no quarrel is soaking into the soil. And this is the curse that I call down upon you: that as death struck my lad from the night without warning, so destruction shall fall upon the one who took his head, unexpected and without mercy, in his turn. As we mourn, so you shall mourn; as the mother of this young man will weep when she hears of that I lay this binding upon your deed, so will your own women wail. It is with the authority of a mantled *ollamh* and the power of a *fili* of Eriu that I lay this binding upon you—" Then he continued:

> *"Thus the finding, thus the binding.*
> *That mind and magic now have bound*

> *To this ground,*
> *by this sound,*
> *to the people of this mound!"*

Cethern struck his staff three times against the stone and turned away. But Fionn stood staring for a little longer.

And by this mortal blood and bone—he raised his clenched fist and shook it at the hill—*Let the deed so sworn be done!* But if a mantled *ollamh* could not force the dwellers in the mound to open their doors, then he had no craft to do it, and he did not speak aloud.

THEY WERE A DAY UPON THEIR HOMEWARD JOURNEY, AND in sight of the blue hills of the Sliab Bladhma, when Fionn roused from his mourning enough to think once more. The *filidecht* had given him words for his grief, but they could not give him vengeance, and for the first time in his life, Fionn dreamed of seeing the blood of an enemy upon his spear. He had never really hated any of his own enemies, but he wanted to kill the unknown warrior who had slain Oircbél.

The curse of the *fili* was a weapon, useless unless some hand should direct the blow. For seven years Fionn had been trying to think his way into the mind of a poet, but now he remembered how he had raced through the woods and dodged the *fian*'s spears. How would the Liath Luachra have solved this problem? It had seemed to him sometimes that the old warrior-woman who had taught him could track a leaf upon the breeze. But she was lost to him, and there were none left alive with her skills.

Except for Fiacail mac Conchinn.

That night Fionn went to Cethern to say farewell.

"But where will you go?" asked the *fili*. "And what will you do? You are so near the end of your training. I still grieve for the loss of Oircbél. Must I lose my other best student as well?"

"Before I was *fili* I was *fennid*," answered Fionn. "And a *fennid* I must become until the price for Oircbél's blood has been paid in full. After that I do not know. But one of my old teachers dwells in the Sliab Mairce to the west of here, and if anyone can show me the way into the fairy hills it will be he."

"Then go with my blessing, lad," said Cethern, "and with my word of warding upon you. And you must promise one day to tell me all the tale!"

"*Ni ansa*—" whispered Fionn. "That will be easy—" And then he could say no more because of his tears.

IN FIONN'S THIRD YEAR WITH CETHERN, THEY HAD SHELtered a guest one winter, a wandering bard whose specialty was tales of the *fianna*. Fionn had pulled his long locks over his face and hidden himself among the other students, but he had always managed to be in a position to hear. And one piece of news was that Fiacail mac Conchinn, grown fragile as Roman glass but still lively, had settled at last in a house on the slopes of Sliab Mairce with a milk cow and a few goats and a little lad to herd them out to grass. This was the place he sought now.

Fionn came up the path to it in the evening, when the smoke of the cook fires smudged the fading sky.

"And what have we here," said a dry voice from the doorway, "a tall young man, maned like a poet and bare-legged as a farmer's boy?"

Fionn flushed and pulled down the skirts of his gown, which he had kilted up so that he could run.

"Now it looks like a *fili*, except for the spear. . . ." Fiacail pushed past the hide and came out into the yard. "Is this someone that I used to know?"

He is like a withered leaf! thought Fionn, staring. *A good wind would blow him away.* But the watery eyes were bright, and the young man had no doubt that Fiacail had recognized him as soon as he came into view.

"Chastise me as you will for running away from the *fian*," Fionn said stolidly. "I was afraid the men of Clan Morna would destroy you all because of me. But that is no matter—"

"Are you in trouble?" Fiacail interrupted him.

"My friend is dead," said Fionn, "and my spear is thirsty for revenge."

"Tell me—" said the old man, and it seemed to Fionn that he smiled.

"So TONIGHT THE FOLK OF BRI ÉLE ARE LAUGHING AT HOW they bested the *fili* of Eriu, and the trophy on their gate-post is the head of a lad who did not even know how to use a sword!" said Fionn as he finished his tale. "Tell me how I can force the gates of the fairy mound—"

A woman of the Sidhe called Donait had opened her doors to him, long ago, and come to him once when he lay lost and fevered, but even if he had known how to find her dwelling, it would not have been honorable to enter it in order to kill her kin.

Fiacail looked Fionn up and down. "Well, you have surely gained the size for it, despite your silly robes. You would seem to have your father's strength. If you have the control to go with it, there may yet be a way for you." He frowned. "Let me think on it. And while I do so, go and fetch me a bucket of water from the well. Old bones creak at such tasks, and since you are here you might as well make yourself useful!"

Fionn laughed and got to his feet, feeling suddenly as if the years had fallen away and he were ten years old once more. If he were still a warrior, he might have objected, but they had all continued to do such chores into manhood in Cethern's school.

The spring was down the slope from the huts; the willows that grew around it had told him its location when he arrived. It was easy enough to shoulder the beechwood buckets, he only hoped that his questions could be answered as easily. But suddenly he was full of doubts. The old man had spent his life as a *fennid*. He might know how to get into a king's *dun*, but would he know how to deal with the Otherworld?

As Fionn began to trudge back up the hill with his filled buckets he realized that he had come here because Fiacail had been married to Bodbmall. The *fennid* and the wisewoman who fostered Fionn had not often lived together, but surely, in all the time of their marriage, some of Bodbmall's druidry must have rubbed off on him. . . . Bodbmall, surely, would have known what he must do.

Old woman, he thought ruefully, *I would bear all your scoldings with patience if I could only have you back again!*

As he came up to the hut it seemed to him that he heard Fiacail talking to someone. But when he set the buckets down in the shed and went back inside, he found the old man sitting by the hearth alone.

"I have brought you sweet water straight from the spring," said Fionn. "Do you have a draft of wisdom for me?"

Fiacail grinned. "There is no way to force entry into a mound of the Sidhe during any day of the year. The folk of the Otherworld come and go at their pleasure, not ours." Fionn felt his heart sink, but the old man put up a warning hand. "But the festival of Samhain lies between the old year and the new. The doorways between the worlds open then, and nothing can be hid."

"Then I can enter Bri Élé!" exclaimed Fionn.

"You can go in," said Fiacail mac Conchinn, "but I do not think you will find your enemy there."

"What do you mean?" Fionn stood up, fists clenching.

"There is a price for all knowledge. Are you willing to pay?"

Fionn stared down at him. Through the thin strands of hair across the top of the old man's head he could see the pink gleam of scalp. Surely one blow would

smash that fragile skull like eggshell. . . . Gasping,
Fionn brought his fists up to cover his eyes and
turned away.

"What is your price?" His voice came muffled through
his hands.

"When you have killed your man, you must come
with me back to the *fian*. . . ."

Fionn let out his breath in a long sigh. Even without
touching his thumb to his mouth he could glimpse the
shape of his fate reaching out to him. And he could still
evade it, refuse Fiacail's counsel, turn away. But not
back to the *filidecht*, where at every turn he would see
Oircbél's smile and remember that he had not been able
to shield the one he loved. There was no choice, really, not when he smelled his friend's blood with every
breath of air.

"I will do what you ask. . . ." Fionn squatted down
on his haunches and gripped the old man's bony knees.
"Now tell me what I must know."

"The mounds of the Sidhe are open at the turning of
the year, as I told you," said Fiacail. "But the greatest of
their courts are in the two hills called the Paps of Anu.
This, Bodbmall told me long ago."

"I know the place," said Fionn. "When I journeyed
northward from the lands of the king of Benntraige I
passed it by."

Fiacail nodded. "Just as at Samhain all the kings of
Eriu keep court with the high king at Temair Brega, the
great ones of the Sidhe journey southward, to the realm
of magic, Mumu. The folk of Bri Élé will keep the feast
with their kindred in the south, and if you follow my
instructions you will have your vengeance and come
to no harm. . . ."

Chapter 2

❧

WITH HIS FAIR HAIR FLYING AND HIS WHITE ROBES flapping around his well-muscled thighs, Fionn mac Cumhal ran through the plains and forests of the land of Eriu. Westward across Laigin to the headwaters of the river Siuir he raced, and then west and southward into Mumu. Where the footing was good, he loped like a hound. At other times he slowed to a jog, sucking in deep breaths of the crisp autumn air. He sensed the earth song with his feet, not his ears. He could not stop to listen, but he ran within it, drawing strength as its rhythms became his own.

Fionn's own two legs could not bear him as fast as a running horse, but they could go for far longer, and with a more consistent speed. A horse would not have known why it was necessary to force himself through the first days when every muscle protested its agony, or kept on when his body cried out for sleep whenever he paused. To the folk of the Sidhe, all times were as one, and their steeds rushed along the paths of the air like the wind. For the folk of Bri Élé, the journey to the Paps of Anu might be but a night's riding, but when Fionn left the house of Fiacail, there were but five nights left until Samhain Eve, and his mortal feet had to stumble every yard of the way.

Folk who saw him pass watched in wonder, but there were not so many abroad at this time of year, with the crops all harvested and the cattle gathered in from the hills. A few weeks earlier the forest would have rung with the sweet singing of hounds and the shouting of men chasing the red deer, but it was a bold hunter indeed who would range far from home so close to Samhain Eve. The time was not evil, but it could be uncanny, when the Tuatha Dé Danaan rode out from their mounds and remembered that once they had ruled in both the worlds.

Fionn was slowing by the time he came to the hilly lands of Lamraige and the plain beyond them, but he pushed onward, munching the hard journeybread Fiacail had given him as he ran and sleeping for a few hours a night in a hazelcopse or the lee of a hill. On the day before Samhain Eve he crossed the Aban Mor. As he came over the next rise he saw, less than ten miles off, a long ridge from which swelled two hills as round as breasts.

The Paps of the Goddess Anu.

Fionn's smooth pace faltered and he reached out as if he could cup those smooth mounds in his hands. His manhood quivered in instinctive response to the shape of the land before him, and, shaking his head ruefully, he came to a stumbling halt and crouched down beside a clump of broom where a few golden flowers still glowed. If the Sidhe were emerging from their hill already, there was no need to make them a gift of his presence here. He sank his fingers into the sandy loam and gasped as awareness of the land flared through him.

Forest lapped the plain to the skirts of the hills, growing scrubbier as the ground rose and the granite flesh of the earth poked through the soil and gorse and bracken replaced the trees. But the stone was not solid.

Through his fingers Fionn sensed its hidden layering and stresses, and his flesh tingled at the energy that flowed through the land to its upwelling in the two hills.

The milk with which the Goddess nourishes us is power.... thought Fionn. He trembled with the need to cast himself upon the sweet curve of the hillside and press his lips to the earth like a suckling child. But at the same time as he felt the secret shape of the land, he could sense another reality like an overlay upon it, becoming steadily more apparent with each moment that passed.

The song the earth sang here was like the music he had heard at Bri Élé just before he slept and Oircbél was killed, but far, far stronger. There was a shimmer like harp music in it, but these harps were strung with silver; there was a calling of horns in it like liquid gold. And these were only an accompaniment to the pure beauty of the voices. Fionn listened, and remembered how Donait had sung him to sleep when he was a boy. She must have tempered her power to his weakness. He could bear the music he was hearing now only because the worlds had not yet drawn completely together.

Fionn stood up, trying to mute his awareness of the song. It no longer mattered if the Sidhe saw him. It was not their swords and spears but their beauty that was the most terrible weapon of the Otherworld. He wondered why Fiacail had not warned him, then realized that perhaps it was because he had eaten of the Salmon of Wisdom that he was so vulnerable.

And he understood another thing as well. Cethern had told them of a dream in which he heard the maiden Élé singing. It had not been pride but the irresistible attraction of that unearthly beauty that had driven the *fili* to court her. It was the same need that had driven Fionn himself to study the arts of poetry, that he might become part of the song by putting it into words. The final testing of a *fili* was to sleep out all night upon a fairy mound. They said that a man with no understanding would die, and one with the awareness but not the skill to control it would be mad by morning. But the one whose skill gave him words for the visions he saw there would be a *fili*.

They are dangerous because they are beautiful, thought Fionn, looking at the fairy hills with narrowed eyes. *Do they even understand why we fear them but cannot stay away?* It was quite clear to him that the most sensible thing he could do would be to run home as swiftly as he had come.

But the pain of longing that the music had awakened in him was being burned away by a rising anger. The Sidhe had not even troubled to slay the man who was actually courting their maiden. Oircbél had been struck down at random, as one might stone one crow of a flock in order to frighten the others away from the corn.

Fionn's grip tightened on the shaft of his spear. "Birga, Birga," he whispered, "you have drunk the blood of the Otherworld before. Are you still hungry? Fly true for me tonight and you will feed well indeed. . . ." His calloused thumb carressed the sharp-honed spearhead, glinting with the hidden wave-patterns that he had beaten into the steel when he forged it so many years ago. And as he fell silent, it seemed to him that he heard an answering hum from the blade.

Smiling grimly, Fionn set himself to make the final approach to the gap between the two hills.

AS DAYLIGHT FADED FROM THE LAND THE AIR GREW EVER more chill. Fionn unrolled his cloak and wrapped it around him. Its chequerings of grey and brown would have made him invisible to mortal sight, but his lifelight would blaze like a spark in the heather if any of the Sidhe should be on guard. He dared not build a balefire, but he cut himself a wand of rowan and scratched oghams of concealment into the trunk of the oak tree beneath which he was sheltering.

With darkness came a restless wind that carried strange echoes—song and laughter, and the clash of battles fought in some other age of the world. Fionn shuddered, knowing that the time of the Otherworld and his own were drawing together now. An hour or two before midnight the world's wind faded, but in the distance to the north he heard a sound like the roaring of the sea. It grew louder, like a great wave coming, or the galloping of many horses, though the earth was still. And now he heard hoofbeats distinctly, and a sweet jingling of metal. He shinnied up the oak tree and peered into the darkness.

The sky glimmered with points of light where the clouds had been blown away. From the corners of his eyes Fionn glimpsed other lights that danced and glimmered on the hillsides and among the trees. When he looked directly at them, they disappeared, but their frequency was growing, and now from the north came a glimmer of brightness that ran like a storm across the fields. Fionn held his breath, staring, as the radiance rushed past him, and for a moment then he thought he saw horses and riders, flowing mantles and glittering spear points, and in the midst of them a woman fair as a song with flowing, moon-colored hair.

The haze of light passed into the gap between the fairy hills and disappeared, but now it seemed to Fionn that the hills themselves were faintly glowing. Surely Fiacail had been right, and when midnight came all their secrets would be revealed. He waited, and presently from the south another faerie host came riding, and then another one from the east and one from the west as well. And with every minute that passed the radiance increased, until he could see a spirit shape of light surrounding every bush and tree. Across the earth itself flowed shining tracks of light, and through the skin of the two Paps of Anu he began to see walls of interwoven tree trunks thatched with their own foliage like Donait's hall.

And ever more clearly from within he heard the music, the silvery piping, the shimmer of harpsong, and the resonant heartbeat of the drums. It did no good to muffle his head in his mantle, for he was not hearing it with his mortal ears. He clung to the oak tree to keep from running towards that music, and the trunk trembled as his body swayed to its rhythms despite his will. To keep his mind from that spell he began to repeat to himself the ogham list of trees and the ogham of birds and the others, and from there he passed to the lists of tales and riddles, and all the other minutiae that he had had to learn in Cethern's school. With one hand he clutched his rowan wand and with the other he gripped his spear, and, still reciting the *fili*'s knowledge, he watched until the wheeling world paused at the moment of midnight and the halls of the Sidhe that were within the two hills of Anu blazed clear.

Then at last Fionn allowed himself to creep forward, coming to rest behind an outcropping of rock a long spear's cast from the causeway between the two sets of arching doors.

Light streamed out from within the hills. Inside, Fionn glimpsed a confusion of movement and color. He blinked as a shining figure moved into one of the doorways.

"The hour is come," the faerie warrior sang. "The feast is laid—"

"Within our halls a welcome's made—" came the reply from the other hill.

"How does it fare with your sweet food?"

"Our hospitality is good!"

Fionn closed his eyes, fighting the compulsion of those fair voices. Beyond them he saw men and women in bright colors, all aglitter with gold, and the sound

of the harping made all harps he had ever heard sound
like the twanging of a hunting bow. He tried to remember how Oircbél's blood had reddened the ground.

"What shall we bring into your hall?" sang the Sidhe.

It was death that the Sidhe had given to Oircbél.

"What you have given, to you shall fall—" was the
reply.

*And the same gift you gave Oircbél shall you receive
from me!* thought Fionn.

The singing from within the hill was so beautiful
that he was weeping, but he dashed the tears from
his eyes and the pain of resisting it fueled his rage.
Then something stirred in the southern hill. A man
was emerging from the doorway with a broad wood-
en tray in his arms. Fionn could see quite clearly that
there was a piece of beef on it, and a roasted piglet
cooked with wild garlic.

You will feast, but where is my friend feasting now?
he asked. *Listen, Birga, remember how you drank the
blood of the Grey Man of Luachar when he ranged the
hills in the form of a boar, and how you killed the
Red-Mouthed Woman when she came after me. Here
is more blood for you. More blood of the Otherworld!
Are you thirsty, Birga? There it is—if you will only fly
true!* With a sob, Fionn rose from his hiding place, and
in a single smooth motion, threw his spear.

"This gift is from Oircbél the Poet! And so he is
avenged!" Fionn cried aloud.

The spearhead flared suddenly in the light of the
Otherworld as it arched between the hills. Fionn
thought he saw the man with the trencher turn as
it drove down at him. Then the entire scene broke
up into shards of dizzying light like a reflection in a
still pool disturbed by a stone and all the sweet music
became a jangle of disharmony.

A woman's voice shrilled out, "Aedh mac Fidach
is dead!" and at once it was echoed by a cacaphony

of lamentation. "The spear!" they cried. "Look at the spear!" And another voice intoned dolefully.

> *"Poison is the fatal spear,*
> *Poison, he who brought it here,*
> *Poison, him by whom it's thrown,*
> *Poison to him who is brought down!"*

Louder and louder grew the wailing, and the light and the colors were a dizzying whirl. Fionn stared, clinging to his rowan wand, until they merged into a maelstrom that sucked him down into the dark.

WHEN HE CAME TO HIS SENSES, GREY MORNING WAS COLDLY illuminating a world from which all the magic seemed to have disappeared. Mist lay like a damp blanket upon the hilltops and glittered from the ends of the dead grasses that poked through the bracken. Mist had soaked Fionn's hair and mantle and he ached in every bone. He blinked, trying to decide whether he had the energy to move, and something behind him sneezed.

Fionn whirled, reaching for his spear, and saw standing in front of the grey rocks a grey mare. On her back, wrapped in a cloak almost the same color as her hide, was Fiacail.

"If I meant to kill you I would have done so," said the old man. "What were you about, to let me sneak up on you that way? In any case I am not the sort of enemy to be warded with a rowan wand—"

Fionn looked down and dropped the stick he held in his hand. It had not been a dream. But the space between the two hills was empty and bare.

"My spear—" he said helplessly.

"You attacked, then?" asked Fiacail, and when Fionn nodded, smiled. "Then I think that you were successful, for if you had missed, the weapon would be still there upon the ground!"

"Do you think so?" Painfully he got to his feet. A crow flapped heavily past on its way to some rendezvous, but nothing else stirred. The two hills seemed solid stone, but beneath his feet, Fionn thought he sensed a humming, like the trunk of a hollow tree full of angry bees.

"Things do not happen by chance in the Otherworld," said Fiacail. "The warrior whom you have killed here was the one who would kill every man who came to woo the maiden because he himself loved her."

"I am glad of that, then," said Fionn. "But I want my spear." He ought to feel exultant, but there was only this emptiness. Was it because he had not seen the body, or because he had lost the Otherworld? Or was something wrong with him that he could never feel things like other men?

"Was it the spear that you had when you were with the *fian*?" asked Fiacail. "With the fire patterns on the blade?" Fionn nodded, and the old man sighed. "I had hoped to get you away from here, for the People of Danu will be angry over the death of their man, but that spear of yours has power, and you will need it in time to come. We must not leave it in their hands."

"Your advice was good before," said Fionn. "What must I do?"

THE SECOND NIGHT OF SAMHAIN WAS CLOUDY, BUT THE glow of the Otherworld made up for it, bright enough to see by, if not quite so distinct as the night before. At midnight, the door within the southernmost of the fairy hills was flung open, and a great procession began to emerge. Once more there was music, but this time the discordance of pipes wove an anguished strain against the keening of the women, and the deep, slow drumming made the skin prickle like distant thunder.

More and more of them emerged from the hill, and Fionn knew that, like Donait's hall, it must be far bigger inside than it appeared. In the midst of the procession came men carrying a bier with a warrior upon it. Beside it walked the maiden with hair like the moon, with her head bent so that her long locks trailed upon the ground. Where they touched the earth it glistened, but Fionn had no eyes for her beauty. Next to the body of the slain warrior he thought he saw the gleam of his spear.

Fionn felt the anguish of that grief and knew that Oircbél had been avenged according to the curse that Cethern had pronounced upon the people of Bri Élé, for the music was the song of his own sorrow. But still, he wanted his spear.

As the Sidhe wailed and tore at their clothing, Fionn worked his way forward. By the time he reached the gap between the two hills, the leaders of the procession had already disappeared into the other mound. He crouched behind its entrance, waiting until the last of the mourners emerged from the first hill.

The last of them was a woman. As she passed, Fionn leaped from his hiding place and bore her backward into the bracken on the hill.

She did not cry out, but she struggled like a wild thing. Fionn felt the strength in the soft limbs writhing beneath him, and put forth his own power to restrain her. A sudden quickening in his own body made him acutely aware that it was female flesh that struggled in his arms, and then he caught the scent of appleblossom and the strength went out of him.

"Donait!" he whispered as she pulled away. "Donait, is it you?" She got to her feet and looked down at him, radiant in the pulsing light of her own anger as he had never seen her before.

"Have you not done enough evil, Demne,"—she called him by his childhood name—"that you should attack me, too?"

"It was justice," he answered, catching his breath. "Aedh mac Fidach killed my friend and many others, and for no other cause than that they were entranced by Élé's song. I did not know you, Donait—I need a messenger to the folk of the mounds. Let her people take the maiden to the western isles where her music will not be a danger, and give me back my spear, and I will trouble you no more."

She stood in silence regarding him, and around her the angry color began to fade.

"You have grown," she said finally, and there was a puzzling undertone of bitter amusement in her words. "I had forgotten that mortals change so quickly. I thought you would still be a little boy, but you have the shoulders of a hero, and it was not the arm of a boy that cast that spear. . . ."

Fionn stood up, brushing himself off to cover his confusion as he remembered how she had felt in his arms. For years the night he had spent in her bed as a child had haunted his dreams, and then he had decided it was only a dream, and thrust the memory away, but now he remembered the softness of her breast and the fragrance of her bright hair, and his body's response was not that of a child at all.

"You have not changed, Donait," he said hoarsely. "You are just the same. . . ."

"Am I?" Now the bitterness in her laugh was clear. "Perhaps, but in other things there are changes, even here."

He took a step towards her, and felt her nearness like a tingle of light against his skin. She held out her hand, perhaps to stop him, but he took it eagerly.

"I will get your spear for you," she said then, "for I think you will have a use for it soon. But you must pay my price in return—"

Fionn felt his blood chilling, for this was the second time he had been told he was going to need the spear, and he felt the red path of the warrior rising to sweep him away. Was it the fault of his fate, or the spear, or the thing within him that would not accept the death of his friend?

"Do not be afraid," she laughed softly. "I do not think it is anything you will not want to pay. My requirement is only that when I call you shall come to me. . . ."

Already she was moving away from him. Fionn stared after her, and almost forgot to hide himself until the door opened in a flood of light for her to enter in.

For a time nothing moved, but it was not peaceful. Fionn could feel the tension in the earth beneath him. He waited, not distrusting Donait, but wondering about her place in the councils of the Sidhe. She had kept secrets from him when he was a child. Did she keep secrets from others as well?

The night had wheeled halfway towards its dawning when the doorway opened once more.

"Poison you have named this spear," came a voice from inside, "and a plague and a poison it shall be if we keep it, both to us and to the land. Cast it out, and let it do its evil in the lands of men!"

And at that there was a flash of motion. Fionn dropped to his belly as something flared in the air above him and dug itself into the rocky ground a man's length from where he lay. The door to the Sidhe mound closed with a rumble, as if the earth had shifted on its foundations, and the glimmering vision of the walls within it abruptly disappeared.

But in the darkness one thing was still shining. Fionn crawled back down the slope towards the cheerful glow of his spear.

THEY JOURNEYED NORTHWARD WITH FIACAIL RIDING THE grey horse and Fionn running by his side. As they left the Paps of Anu behind them Fionn found himself relaxing. After a time, he even began to wonder what had happened to Crimall's *fian* after he had left it, and Fiacail was happy enough to chatter as he rode.

"If you had to leave the *fian*, why choose such a furtive way? To depart just as they were celebrating having accepted you was an insult that some have still not forgotten. They had begun to love you, lad, and it hurt to have that love flung back in their faces that way."

"It was because I had begun to love them in return that I had to go—" Fionn replied. "If I had tried to leave openly they would have argued and persuaded me, and I would never have got away. I knew that the men of Morna were coming, and dodging a few spears and running a race had not prepared me to lead those men against our enemies. The *fian* would have been destroyed, Fiacail, because of me!"

"Perhaps it is so, and I can understand that it would have been hard to make those hotheads understand what your reasons were."

"It was hard enough to tell Dithramhach, and he was my brother and my friend," said Fionn, remembering a tall shape in the shadows, and the warmth of the amber bead that his half brother had given him. He wore it on a thong beneath his tunic still. "How does he now?"

"He is well enough," answered Fiacail. "He has grown into his strength, and he keeps his temper better than he did. We have taken in a dozen youngsters over the years, and he does a good job of managing them, but for every new man we train, another of the old band is gone. Coll mac Dermot died of a flux three years ago, and Mongan Mael was killed hunting wild boar. Reidhe mac Dael is still with us, but he has grown stiff in the joints and spends most of his time by the fire."

"Not many left from my father's old band, are there?" said Fionn. "The *fian* is what Crimall has made of it. It was not the old ones who had known Cumhal who hated me, you know. It was the younger men who knew only the tales of days that grow more golden with every retelling. My father was only a man, like me. You and Crimall and Reidhe can remember how it really was if you put your minds to it, but those others think of Cumhal as the leader who lost them their chance at glory. And they will transfer their resentment to me. Why then are you so set on forcing me to return?"

Fiacail rode for a time in silence. "When we reach the Sinnan we are not going to cross it, Fionn," he said finally. "We must travel north and eastward through Laigin and along the Boann down to the British sea. There have been changes since Cormac mac Airt became high king. I think he would like to curb the power of the mac Mornas at last, for he has begun to make use of the other *fians*. He has given Crimall's men the honor of guarding Inber Colptha, where the trading ships put in. If the *fian* does well, the days of glory could return."

"I am glad to hear it," said Fionn patiently. "But Crimall has earned that honor. Why not let him enjoy it? Why bring me?"

"Because your uncle is dying, Fionn," Fiacail said gently.

It changed nothing, thought Fionn as he slowed his pace to keep from getting ahead of the grey horse, for the old man had loosened his rein and the animal was taking advantage of it to amble along. But since he had eaten the Salmon of Wisdom, he had heard the meaning in men's voices as well as their words, and he knew that Fiacail was grieving for his old friend.

"Do you think this absolves you from your promise to me?" Fiacail asked sharply, and Fionn realized that his own silence had been eloquent too.

"I will not go back on my oath to you—" he said slowly. "I will come to Inber Colptha, and if the *fian* will accept me, I will stay. The only thing that might hinder me is the other promise that I made to the fairy woman in order to recover my spear. And even if I must go to her, I promise that I will return when I may."

But as they moved northward through the peace that the high king's law imposed during the month of the Festival, Fionn dreamed of Donait, and wondered what she might need him for, and did not know if he feared or desired her call.

FIONN SAT UP ABRUPTLY, FIGHTING FREE OF THE FOLDS of his cloak. What had wakened him? Tense as a questing hound he listened; from the darkness on the other side of the fire came a snort and a long whistle, repeated as regularly as breath. Fionn's lips twitched as he realized it was only Fiacail, snoring. But that would not have disturbed him. . . . He realized abruptly that the past days had reawakened his love for the old warrior. Everyone else he loved had perished; was he going to bring death to the old man now?

As he leaned over to tuck Fiacail's blanket more securely around the old shoulders, a warm breeze brushed his cheeks. Fionn stiffened; that was no wind, but a breath, and a second later he felt the slight weight of an invisible hand upon his bare shoulder.

"Brother, come! Donait has need of you!"

The flesh roughened where the hand had rested, and he felt a chill that had nothing to do with the night, remembering the fairy woman's voice low in the darkness, and the sweetness of her body in his arms. Her call had come! Fionn flung the cloak aside, pulled on his worn boots, and reached for the short warrior's tunic that Fiacail had given him. Then he paused, listening to the old man's snores.

How could he leave him? Would Fiacail be safe here in the wild?

Safer alone than with you, most likely! his heart replied. Then he stifled a laugh. Fiacail had been roaming the forests of Eriu when Fionn's own mother was a child. There was not a beast or a tree that was not the *fennid*'s friend. His fear was an insult to the old man. *He will guess that Donait's message found you,* he told himself. *He knew you must go if she called.*

Swiftly Fionn belted his father's sword about his narrow waist. His clumsy *ollamh*'s gown lay folded for a pillow; it had been weeks since he had worn it. He hesitated then, looking from the sword at his side to the dim folds of cloth, but the *filidecht* of Faerie would sing a half-fledged *ollamh* like himself to shame. It had to be for his mortal strength that Donait wanted him. He sighed, scooped up his cloak and reached for the gleaming spear that leaned against the tree, and looked into the night for direction.

In the silence of the woods he heard only the short squeal of a field mouse as talons struck and the rustle as invisible pinions brushed the leaves. Fionn peered into the darkness and glimpsed the silhouette of the owl, lifting skyward on silent wings. And something else—a wisp of silver light like a single thread winding across the moldering leaves. With the light step Fiacail had taught him, Fionn started towards it. His sword hilt chimed against his cloak pin as he moved and he muffled the metal.

Then his foot touched the shimmering light. Fionn shuddered as power surged through him. *Run!* clamored his body. *Run, or explode!* Fionn took a deep breath and let the power take him.

Light swirled through Fionn's body in a shimmer of power. The Otherworldly track unwound before him. Was he running, or was it the light that whirled him along? Even when he raced the turning year to the Paps of Anu he had never moved with such speed. He understood now how the fairy hosts had rushed across the land. This was like the ecstasy that had swept his mind when he tasted the Salmon of Wisdom, but this delight was of the body. His feet hardly touched the earth, and his bones seemed to have no weight at all. His spear was a rod of light ending in a mouth that screamed for blood.

Time lost all meaning as he ran, until at last Fionn saw before him the yawning blackness of the chasm. He did not hesitate as he had when pursued by the men of the rath of Fidh Gaible so many years before.

Muscles bunched in perfect coordination; power flared through him in a final surge, and then he was flying. The darkness of the abyss flowed away beneath him.

Then, with a bone-rattling thump, Fionn landed on the springy grass that surrounded the fair hall of Donait.

Chapter 3

STEADYING HIMSELF WITH A QUICK STEP FORWARD, Fionn stared into the shimmer of twilight. The thick grass was trampled, and he coughed at the sickening scent that corrupted the air. Had Donait betrayed him? The smell was like the rotten flesh of the boar he had slain on Sliab Muicce long ago. He crouched, spear swinging to guard. Shadows stained the shimmering brightness, closing in. Shapes grew more solid as his eyes focused. A grotesque head turned, and a single great eye glared at him. Then there was a grunt that chilled his blood, and the things rushed him.

Fionn's leap carried him over the first of them. For a moment he glimpsed Donait's hall, rising above a seething mass of the misshapen monsters. Fury flared through him, all the sharper for his moment of suspicion. Donait was in danger!

Birga surged in Fionn's hand. He felt the shock as it struck deep into a hairy breast. Fionn jerked the spear back and saw a sluggish trickle of darkness seep from the wound. The creature swayed, its form dissolving even before it fell.

The spear whirled in Fionn's hands, thirsting for prey. The howling barb pierced eyes like dead coals;

the butt end smashed chests and rebounded to send the blade slashing sideways. He struck out at squat hairy shapes like crippled spiders; he spitted spindly giants with writhing arms. Glaring eyes, distorted limbs, fanged heads sprouted in unlikely numbers. There were no two of them the same. Fionn fought in a flickering ring of light as the spearpoint spun. Rage gave him power.

Battle fury boiled in his blood, released for the first time against a foe whom it was right to kill. His spear was an extension of his arm; this was the work he had been born for. He might never have eaten the Salmon of Wisdom; his years as a *fili* might never have never been. But for every monster Fionn downed, two more erupted from the shadows before him. There were so many—too many! Even Birga could not kill them all. He raged, knowing that all he could do would do nothing against such hordes.

Beyond the heaving mass of his foes he glimpsed the wall of Donait's hall. For a moment Fionn stilled. Then, roaring, he charged three bogles with warty, green-scaled hides. Their clubs whirled towards him, but before they hit he struck Birga's butt end into the ground and let the impetus launch his long body upward. While their goggle-eyes were still staring, Fionn flew over his foes.

As he landed, he heard the thud of clubs smashing the ground where he had been. But before the bogles could turn, Fionn was halfway up the slope to the hall. Six or seven of the uglies gave chase, howling. A spear missed his shoulder by a whisper and he seized the shaft as it flew and pivoted to hurl the weapon back again. His turn brought him a man's length closer to the hall.

For a moment a thin line of gold seemed to wink between the interlaced tree trunks that formed the wall. Fionn caught his breath, coughing as he realized that his body was slimed with the stinking blood of his foes, and loped towards it. Howling, a wave of monsters surged after him. The hall loomed over him suddenly and he slammed violently into a solid wall of trees. Rebounding, Fionn fought for air. He fell back against the wall, thinking that it would defend his back even if he could not get in.

A spear flew at him. Fionn snatched it as it bounced against the tree trunk beside his head and hefted it to throw. The balance was odd, and Birga jerked in his right hand, unbalancing him. The attackers were a dark mass in the twilight; from their midst another spear shot towards him. Ducking, he hurled the strange spear into the midst of the churning huddle while Birga howled for blood in his other hand. Then the shaft of the attacker's spear smashed against his skull, and bright dots danced before his eyes.

Fionn roared with pain and raged forward. Screams of anger and anguish tore at his ears and he wondered who, or what, his cast with the strange spear had found. The stench of rotting flesh almost felled him as he closed, ramming Birga through the torso of a thing with distorted antlers, yanking the spear out and plunging it into the single glowing eye of another. The creatures that could fled his fury, and the rest fed his spear. Then, suddenly, there was nothing in front of him. Fionn stood blinking, knee-deep among the heaped bodies that, even as he stared, wavered and faded and disappeared, leaving only smears of stinking slime upon the grass.

Before the pulsing shadows down the hill could regroup for another attack, Fionn dashed back to the hall, seeking the golden gleam of light he had spied before. Once more it flickered, no thicker than a thread wound into the bark of one of the trees that made up the walls of the hall. His probing fingers stroked the rough bark of an oak tree, then brushed the shimmering strand.

A surge of power ran along his arm and exploded in

his pounding skull. For an instant the world blazed, and his body was made of pure light. Distantly, he heard screams and knew the light was real, and that it had hurt the terrible one-eyed beings who waited behind him. Then the wall opened before him, and Fionn fell forward. Dark and light spun before his dazzled eyes, drawing him into the swirling patterns of the floor.

FIONN LAY STUNNED FOR WHAT SEEMED AN AGE OF THE world, too weary to stir. The smell of apple blossom mingled with the stench of his body. *Donait . . .* his pulse pounded. For a moment he could not move. Then he summoned the strength to get up on one elbow, and in that moment she was there, bending over him. But before he could speak, Birga surged in his hand like a live thing. He fell back, clutching the shaft, and the fairy woman sprang away, terror darkening her blue eyes.

Furious, Fionn shook the spear as one might an ill-behaved child.

"Blood! More blood! More blood!" came the spear's uncanny song.

"You have drunk deeply, Birga," he cried. "Now be still."

"Not enough. Never enough. Give me more!"

Fionn thought of the hideous creatures outside the hall.

"Patience, Birga," he said, more softly. "I think that you will drink again soon." Leaning on the spear shaft, he pulled himself to his feet and faced Donait. Though the blade's fury still sent tremors down the wood, he could sense his own battle fury subsiding. He drew a long breath and shuddered.

Now that the fight was over, every muscle in his body was beginning to scream. Fionn flexed his aching leg muscles and felt the stone of the floor beneath his feet. Surprised, he lifted one foot and saw that the leather of his boot had been worn through. How far, he wondered, had he run?

As he moved, a wave of the foulness that stained clothes and skin reached his nostrils and he gagged. It was like the fetid odor of the Red-Mouthed Woman. He had longed to see Donait once again, but not like this! Stinking like a charnel house and clutching a screaming spear, he seemed to himself no better than the creatures outside. His very presence profaned the beauty around him. Shamed, he felt himself coloring beneath the grime and looked at her in mute appeal.

But those few moments had restored to her the composure he had lost. Donait made a sweeping gesture towards the back of the chamber.

"A hard road you had to answer my summoning. A hero's bath awaits you, son of Cumhal."

Seven years of poesy seemed to desert his tongue at the sound of her voice, and he felt that he was little Demne still.

"And a bucket of water to cool the rage of that battle serpent in your hand!" she said then, smiling.

Do you hear that, Birga? Fionn thought, his grip tightening. *She is likening you to Lugh's spear!* He did not think the point would set the wood of the hall afire, but he had never borne the spear in such a battle before.

He swallowed hard and squared his shoulders and his jaw. "You are as gracious as ever, Donait. I fear that I have tracked a great mess into the hall."

Donait laughed softly. "Is that what disturbs you? Fighting is never a tidy business, even among my own people. Come, now. Remove your garments and cleanse yourself. There is much to do, and you have need of refreshment."

The helpless sense of being a boy left him. Suddenly Fionn was very much aware of being a man, and with that knowledge he recognized that Donait, however different in flesh than dark Cruithne who for a time had been his wife, was female. A wave of warmth rushed through him, focusing in his loins, and he knew that he was blushing again. If he undressed before her, those sparkling blue eyes would see how she stirred him.

Reluctantly he bent to take off his boots. But their condition drove out all thoughts of arousal. Where the blood of his foes had spattered, they were eaten almost through. What sort of folk had blood that destroyed leather? he wondered as he unbuckled his belt and pulled the tunic off over his head. Ugly red weals were rising on his arms and chest where the venomous stuff had eaten through the wool.

Still wearing his reeking breeches, Fionn followed Donait across the spiraled mosaic floor. As they neared the bath, the scent of apple blossom grew stronger. *Donait's scent . . .* thought Fionn. His body was beginning to respond again and he fought to control it. But each breath made him more conscious of the way his manhood was rubbing against the coarse cloth.

They reached the tub, a great basin of gleaming stone from which the steam rose in white curls, and he sighed with relief as Donait turned to the glowing hearth. He could see only the curve of her cheek, but it seemed to him that she was suppressing a smile. Was she laughing at him, or had she taken pity on his confusion? While her slender back was still towards him, he struggled out of the breeches and scrambled into the water.

He sank into the bubbling liquid gratefully, and rubbed his sweat-soaked hair between bruised fingers. When he came up for air, Donait's beautifully formed hand was holding out a round of soap. He took it, glad that the water concealed the way excitement leaped in his loins at her touch, and began to scrub himself vigorously. He had thought the heat of the water would solve his problem, but what was he going to do if he was still stiff as a post by the time he finished his bath?

Perhaps focusing his attention on the myriad pains and aches that the heat of the water was awakening would distract him. Wincing, he probed a bruise along his ribs. But Donait was draping a great drying cloth across the wide lip of the bath. Fionn's water-blurred eyes followed the graceful curve of her back, and the sway of her long, golden braids across her shoulders as she drifted away, singing softly. . . . Hastily, he looked away and went back to scrubbing.

The heat of the water was soothing away his aches and healing the cuts in some magical fashion. Fionn peered into the water and watched the weals on his chest fade into small white scars. Donait was busy at the hearth, and for a time, Fionn was content to let the warm water caress the last of the pain away. At last, he plunged his head beneath the water one more time, and after a quick glance to make sure that her back was still turned, clambered out of the bath, clutching the towel around him. Water from his long hair streamed across his shoulders and dripped to the floor. He grabbed a trailing corner of the towel and tried to pat it dry.

Donait was returning, holding a robe of deepest blue across her arms. The apple-scented odor of her body overwhelmed his senses as she drew near, and the resulting shudder of desire almost made him drop the towel. Her face was grave now, but her eyes held an unmistakable gleam, as if she was perfectly aware of what sweet torment her nearness gave him. He accepted the garment with nerveless fingers, and breathed a sigh of relief when she turned away once more.

Fionn finished drying his body and rubbed at his silky hair until it was merely damp. Then he donned the robe. Its soft folds caressed his limbs and brushed the tops of his bare feet. With more assurance than he felt, he crossed the chamber and joined the fairy woman beside the undying hearth. Donait nodded as he sat on a stool and handed him a finely made bone comb.

After he had spent a few silent minutes worrying at the tangle of his locks, Fionn cleared his throat.

"It is from afar you called me, Donait, but I have come. I suppose those creatures I met outside are the reason? What are they, and why are they troubling you?"

Donait laughed, and fire flared through his body at the sound. "You come to the matter at hand very quickly, son of Cumhal. Are you not glad to see me?"

The heat reached Fionn's cheeks. "To be sure, Lady, I delight in the sight of you," he said stiffly. "But that will not save you from your foes." It had become a contest between them, in which Fionn must conceal how he ached for the merest touch of her long fingers, let alone how his body was reacting beneath the loose robe, while she tormented him.

She sighed and pursed her rosy lips, and he thought of the sweetness of berries and swallowed.

"The world has made you hard then, son of Cumhal?"

His hand jerked and he winced as he yanked out a snarl of hair. Had she meant that double meaning? Why must she tease him? Was it because, fairy or human, she was a woman?

He would never understand them. He jerked his head in a nod and continued struggling with his hair. Let her think him hard and uncaring—it was better than betraying his desire.

"Much has happened since I first came to this hall, Donait, and I am no longer an ignorant boy. The flames of Brigid Herself have seared me."

He sounded pompous, or as if he were boasting. Suddenly Fionn felt like the child who had jumped the chasm to escape the angry men of the rath so long before.

"True, you have gained a wisdom far beyond your human years."

"Wisdom!" The word was bitter on his tongue. "Men seek it, strive for it, suffer for it, for years and scores of years. I got it in a flash, like a summer storm, and in the next moment slew my master!"

He remembered the day when Fionnéices had drawn the Salmon of Wisdom from the waters of the Boann, and the mingled smell of hazel smoke and cooking fish overwhelmed him anew. Fionn felt the pain in his thumb where he had burnt it on the roasting salmon, and the explosion of terrible inspiration that had shaken him when he thrust it into his mouth. Worse, he felt himself reliving the breathless struggle with his blind teacher, and the wrenching mixture of sorrow and certainty as he had slain the man who had killed his father on the field of Cruthna. But there was no joy in vengeance. Once more he mourned his inability to escape his destiny, no matter what path he trod.

"It is a fine thing that you grieve for Fionnéices, son of Cumhal. A lesser man would boast of that deed." Donait's voice sent his thoughts flying.

"A better man would have found another way!"

"It was your master's fate to die as he did. It was a fate made when the world began. There is no blame to you. And you will have need of your hard-won wisdom in times yet to be."

"So you say, Donait. So you say." His muscles cramped with weariness, and at that moment, he did not even feel desire. "Just now, living through the next moment seems enough for me. You have unwelcome neighbors. Who are they?"

The fairy woman coiled the end of her braid around a long finger, frowning. "My foes are of the *tuath* of the Red-Mouthed Woman and her foul son, Beo, whom men called the Grey Man of Luachar. I thought that would stir your interest—" she added as he stared, wondering if somehow his deeds had caused this disaster as well. "Your blood-keening spear is not sufficient to prevail against them. You need protection of another sort, a shield that was prepared for you at the beginning of the world."

Fionn glanced around the hall, but the only shields he could see were borne by the warriors fighting in the dazzling hangings upon the walls. They had seemed wonderful when he was a child, but now he could appreciate their artistry. The magic in those moving images drew him into their world. In his ears, ancient battles resounded, and passionate courtings sent sweet fire through his veins. Then Donait moved, and Fionn blinked, rubbing at his tired eyes, trying to remember why he had been looking for a shield.

"Why are they attacking you, Donait?"

"The Fomorians wish to destroy these hangings, and I am their guardian."

The hangings? Fionn stared, found himself being once more enchanted by their transformations, and dragged his gaze back to Donait.

"Out of malice, or are they having some purpose in the deed?"

"Both. These weavings are the record of my people and all that we have done. If they are destroyed, it will be as if we never were, and our name will go out of the land. The warp of the Otherworld runs through every strand of it. Indeed, it may be the thing that keeps this land alive. Long as I have lived, I do not know all things, son of Cumhal."

Fionn swiveled on the stool and examined the hangings on the long wall behind him. The figures there were very like the hideous creatures that had attacked him outside the hall. They were being slaughtered by the bright-faced children of Dana. He closed his eyes, and for a moment an awareness of depths and interweavings beyond human understanding made him tremble. Then he shook his head and looked back at Donait. It was hard enough to understand what was happening now.

"But, Donait, if these folk destroy your pictures, will they also not cease to be?" He gestured towards the hanging. *And if the Otherworld changes, what will happen to Eriu?* He forced the thought away.

She nodded. "You have the matter in a nutshell, son of Cumhal. But the Fomor have never been famed for their wit, only for their ferocity."

"Very well. What must I do to drive them away?" He heard his own words with a dim wonder, but what choice did he have?

"Come." She led him towards the far end of the hall and showed him a hanging that portrayed a sunlit glade dominated by an enormous hazel tree. The tree seemed to hold up the sky itself, so great was its girth and height. But it was scabrous along the trunk, and the leaves were sere with some blight he had never seen before. The sight of it made Fionn's skin crawl, and foulness seemed to reek from the threads of the weaving. As he looked, dribbles of some sticky substance fell from the boughs, and where they struck the earth, small puffs of mist sprang up.

"What ails the tree, Donait?"

She faced the hanging and he heard a whisper of melody that distilled at last into meaning.

"The Seed that in the depths of Time was sown,
Grown to a Tree whose branches link all lands,
Stands here as both answer and the need. . . ."

As she sang, Fionn saw the seedling sprout and grow, its branches interlacing into a pattern as complex as the weavings on the wall. All the lands where he had wandered were there, and other places, strange almost beyond his imagining, through which figures moved, clad in garments whose like he had never seen. Understanding came to him—*The Tree and the Tapestry are the same.*

"This is the Mother of Hazels, which the bards call the Ancient Dripping Hazel Tree, but twined among her roots is a venom-breathing monster. It poisons the tree and taints all her children, in this world and in yours, so that no wisdom is without stain. If you can slay the dragon, you will gain a shield that will protect you from those who now beseige my hall."

"And if I cannot?"

Donait ignored his question. "First, you need rest."

She turned and waved a slender hand, and Fionn's heart stopped once more at the singing sweetness in the line of her arm. A great bed appeared where the bath had been before. Fionn longed for the comfort of its softness even as he shrank from the fear of what would happen when the woman was so near.

"And I must prepare your raiment," Donait added, smiling, and Fionn sighed, realizing that neither his hopes nor his fears would be rewarded just now.

FIONN, HALF-ROUSED, GAVE A SPINE-POPPING STRETCH, and looked up. For a moment the intertwining branches above him made him think he was in the forest. Then the ease of the bed beneath him told him he was indeed in the house of Donait, that he had not dreamed the call of his invisible sister, that he had truly run the bottoms of his boots away. But there was something wrong with the light. On his first visit here, it had been clear and golden. Now it was dim—tainted, as the terrible creatures outside seemed to foul everything they were near.

The fleecy wool blankets released a sweet scent of lavender as he pushed them aside. Fionn swung his long legs over the side of the bed and got up. Near the hearth he saw Donait, perched on a low stool, a stout needle in one hand and some thick stuff across her lap. She did not lift her head at his movement, but continued to ply her needle so rapidly he could hardly follow it. He had never imagined Donait engaging in so domestic a task, and found himself charmed at the sight. It made her less remote and more human, somehow. He waited, silent, until she bit the thread off between her strong, white teeth.

Donait rose and shook out the folds of her work. The garment she held was unlike anything Fionn had ever seen, until he recalled the scaled hide of the Liath Luachra after he had cast her into the lake. When the ancient warrior woman had transformed into a great aquatic beast, her body had become just such leather as the fairy woman now clutched to her shoulders, eyeing her handiwork critically.

Fionn found that the leather was not the only unique feature of the garment. It was made in a single piece, legs sewn to tunic, and there were no openings at the bottoms of the trousers. Instead, they were footed like boots, and the sleeves likewise ended in hand coverings. Fionn turned and glanced at the hanging of the Ancient Dripping Hazel, a finger of fear chilling the base of his spine. The monster that dwelt in the roots of the tree must be terrible indeed to demand such garb.

When he looked back, Fionn found Donait standing beside him. For a moment the warmth of her body dizzied him, but her face was grave, and his heart began to pound to a more sober rhythm. He drew a careful breath, and this time her sweet scent brought peace.

"You slept well, son of Cumhal."

"I did—and you slept not at all!"

Donait shrugged. "That does not matter. You must hasten now. Put this on. It will not protect you completely, but it will be better than nothing. Any cloth would be rags in a flash, from the vapors of the worm, and I sought long to secure a leather that would withstand it."

Fionn's belly rumbled with hunger. "The worm has been at the roots of the tree forever. Why must I attack it right now?" What he really wanted was breakfast, but he felt ashamed to say so.

"In this hour, the Worm, which never sleeps, is less active. This is the best chance you will have to slay it." Her voice, usually soft and serene, sounded sharp and uneasy, and a long habit of obedience to female voices made him nod.

The garment was heavy. How had she carried it, and how was he going to move in the thing? But he had to trust her. Fionn pulled the blue robe over his head and quickly thrust his long legs into the lower portion of the strange garment. As he started to pull the sleeves up over his arms, he heard the gutteral shouts of the beseigers, followed by a dull thud against one wall. Donait sped down the length of the hall, her hands glowing with radiance. As Fionn tugged the top across his shoulders she pressed her glowing hands against the wall. There was a scream from outside, and words of fury in some unknown tongue.

Fionn fitted his hands into the ends of the sleeves and found there were slots for his long fingers and thumbs. He flexed his hands, feeling the odd texture of the garment against his body, and wondered how to close the front, which hung down against his sides. If he twisted his head down he could see little knobs of bone set across each shoulder. The triangular flaps of the garment seemed intended to cross over his chest. There were little slits in each one that slipped neatly over the knobs. It was an awkward business, and the thing was hot and uncomfortable.

Ignoring his growling belly, Fionn clumped down the hall and retrieved Birga. The spear grumbled questioningly as he lifted it and he grinned sourly. Birga, at least, would be feeding soon. Donait looked at him solemnly and rose from her post near the wall. She reached up and drew a hood he had not noticed up and over his head. Tightening the cords made it fit snugly around his face. Sound came faintly through the dense hide. So close, he could see hints of darkness beneath Donait's blue eyes, and realized she was weary in a way he could never have imagined. She slipped her arm through his and drew him towards the hazel hanging.

They stood for a moment together and looked upon the Ancient Dripping Hazel Tree. But through the armor he could feel only the pressure of her body, and he had a moment to regret the loss of his torment. Then she placed a swift kiss on his mouth. Power jolted through him, and in that moment she put her hand between his shoulders, and with more strength than he would have thought possible in so slender a woman, propelled him forward, into the weaving.

Beneath the spreading branches of the tree, it was stifling, and in moments sweat beaded Fionn's brow. The withered leaves rustled, though there was no hint of a breeze. Shining droplets of venom slid down the bark and vanished into the vapor that wreathed the roots of the tree. Its stink made him giddy. Taking short breaths, he moved cautiously around the huge trunk.

By the time he had circled the tree, Fionn had observed that the noxious mist rose and fell in regular rhythm, and he guessed it must be the breathing of the worm. Blinking sweat from his eyes, he moved cautiously towards the trunk, trying to locate the source of the steam. A little wisp spurted midway along his spear arm, and he saw his protective garment pitted where a drop of the venom had fallen from the boughs. Faint through the leather came a hissing. Fionn jumped, his heart pounding against his ribs, but nothing moved.

He squared his shoulders, took a firmer grip on his spear, and began to circle once again. The vapors coiled and curdled around him, but there—surely they moved more quickly. What should he do? He flogged his fuddled mind, trying to think, but each breath he took seemed to confuse him further, and he knew he must act quickly or perish in the poisonous air.

Grasping Birga in both hands, Fionn rammed the yew butt against the trunk of the tree with as much force as he could muster. There was a booming reverberation, as if the Hazel were hollow, and the ground shook under his strange boots. Then the air trembled to a roar like living thunder, and above the mist reared a head, wedge-shaped, huge eyes gleaming redly and a gaping mouth that sent searing venom splattering round. The head swung to and fro, questing for the being that had disturbed it. Fionn stepped forward, poising his spear.

His foot came down where a drop of venom slicked the soil, and he staggered. In a moment the worm was upon him. A long, dull-hued body whipped about his legs and pulled him down. As the mind-numbing vapor closed over his head, Fionn held his breath. Already his lungs screamed for air; he kicked feebly, and to his surprise, the coils slid away, unable to gain purchase on the strange garment he wore.

Fionn struggled up and nearly banged his head into the worm's descending skull. He dodged and slammed into the trunk of the hazel, numbing one shoulder. As he fought for breath, the worm arched, and the grey coils pinned him against the tree.

Birga quivered in his grasp. *Thirsty! Let me drink! Let me go!*

With consciousness drowning in the fetid vapors that swirled around him, Fionn forced up the spear. Caught between the trunk of the tree and the tightening coils of the worm, he could not throw. The worm wound round and round, its colorless scales cutting into his armor as he struggled to get free.

His head dropped back against the tree as the spear jerked in his hand, unable to reach its food. Through his bones came the moan of the great Hazel, poisoned by the worm, and the song of earth below. He reached deep and felt endurance tingle along his shinbones, quiver up into his thighs, and, as the song entered his blood the tightness in his chest eased. It was a new music, and yet he knew it. The strength of earth and rock surged in him, while the venomous mouth gaped closer still.

Grunting, Fionn swung Birga back as far as he could. The butt end struck the trunk of the tree again, and there was another bone-rattling boom. Then he thrust the spear forward with all the power that earth had lent him. Time slowed before his aching eyes. The quivering head seemed to creep through the air; the skull of the worm moved downward in minute advances.

The patterned point of the spear touched the body

of the worm just below its head. There was a blinding flash, and the scales of the beast flared from dull to bright. Then they began to fly off in all directions, a mothflight of terrible, sharp shapes. Birga burrowed into the beast, screaming bloodlusting delight, but the worm's shriek of agony seemed to go on forever. Fionn's head pounded; behind him the tree rumbled deafeningly.

The worm burst in a flash of blinding light as the tree exploded, sending Fionn hurtling through the air. As he crashed to the ground several spear lengths away, the earth shuddered and heaved beneath his bruised body like a vomiting drunk. He tried to rise as great limbs of hazel began to rain down around him, but the rippling earth gave his feet no firm place to rest.

Surely the world was ending, for even through his confusion Fionn sensed that this seizure of earth was not confined to the area around the tree. The Otherworld must be rattling down to its roots. What had he done? Dimly through the hood covering his ears he could hear cries of terror, the crash of rare glass breaking, and the sound of some fair harp that never would sing again. He dug his bleeding hands into the heaving earth and curled defensively, weeping and cursing himself.

After what felt like several lifetimes, the shuddering began to cease. Fionn rose to his feet on trembling legs, amazed to discover he was alive, too weary to be glad. The air was clear now, and sweet-smelling, and somewhere a bird began to twitter. Beyond the bird, he could hear the shouts of the hideous foes around Donait's hall.

Fionn could see nothing of either the monster or the tree. There was only a dark hole two man-heights across, which seemed to go down to the heart of the world. Even the deadly scales had vanished, though branches lay strewn around. Birga lay a few feet away, quiet for once, as if it were only an ordinary spear. He picked his way across the torn earth to retrieve it.

Something steamed among the debris, and Fionn, curious even in exhaustion, turned. With the butt of the spear he cleared the fallen branches and gazed down. Something lay there; it seemed to his tired eyes both crafted and grown, as if the flying branches had plaited themselves into the oblong shape of a shield, covered by a glowing red skin resistant as bronze and flexible as leather edged all around in gleaming metal. Across the face nine spiral coils curled in and out of one another, and a vapor wafted from their centers.

Fionn reached out a bloody hand and touched the rim. Even through one fingertip the song of the wood thrummed through his flesh. It was strange, old and fierce, wise and mad all at once.

> "I am the root that held the stone,
> For ages of the world alone;
> I am the branch that blazes bright,
> I am the leaf transforming light!
> I am Hazel, hallowed Tree
> Between the worlds I ward the way!"

It was the shield destined for him from the beginning of the world . . . the shield Donait had promised him. And it sang. With the shield on one side and Birga on the other, both yammering, Fionn thought he might come to be grateful that his leather coif deadened sound.

> "I shielded Manannan's stout arm,
> I kept fair Cairbre from all harm,
> The Dagda in delight me bore,
> I rout the wights who wage red war!
> I am Hazel . . ."

With a deep sigh, Fionn leaned forward and picked up the shield, and the song faded. The straps slid over his left arm as if the shield had been made for him; it moved as if it had grown there, no weight at all. Experimentally he hefted it. In that instant, the world whirled away, and before he could blink twice, he was on the greensward before the hall of Donait, blinking in a light like dying day.

Dark shapes struggled in the dusk. Before Donait's hall, distorted imp shapes howled and hurled some long metal thing against the wall, while others howled and ran in circles. Fionn shook his head to clear it and dashed towards the hall. The shield, Hazel, boomed against his side, and Birga quivered to life in his hand, as if it had been napping since it drank of the worm.

The goblins that bore the battering ram gibbered with glee, so fixed on their task Fionn was within a spear's cast before one turned and shrieked alarm. The two creatures hindmost on the ram looked up. Fionn saw their single eyes widen with horror and their mouths round to scream. Then Birga claimed one, and the other was blasted backward by the power of the shield. The end of the ram sagged and the others dropped it, grabbing weapons and leaping towards Fionn, while those who had been capering mindlessly came howling after.

In seconds, both groups surrounded the man, shrieking and waving their weapons. Fionn staggered beneath the weight of the heavy garment he still wore, leaning on the shield in his exhaustion. He heard a murmur and saw a strange mist swirling from its bosses. The war cries of the nearest foes changed to horrid gurgles, but in moments they were dropping to the ground, their weird shapes dissolving away.

Fionn laughed bitterly and staggered forward, leaving a swathe of destruction behind; he slew, and loathed himself almost as much as his enemies. Mindless, he sent Birga flying towards fleeing foes, watching remotely as they fell before the spear. Each time he trudged forward to recover it he saw the misshapen bodies melt into a slimy trickle as they died. The grass beneath them was sere and burnt. Birga slew, and Hazel slew, and at last he was alone, except for his dreadful arms.

Fionn leaned against the spear and let the shield swing away from his body. Without that contact, the mist that came from the spirals ceased to swirl. He flexed his aching shoulders and felt the heavy hide of his garment begin to crack. The scales of the worm had slashed it, and it was a wonder that it had stayed intact so long. Now it fell away from his body in flakes and tatters, until he was unclad. Dazed, he looked down at thin cuts on his chest and thighs, still bleeding slowly. He wanted nothing more than to lie down on the burnt grass and never move again.

Instead, he turned back towards the hall and began to trudge up the slope to the opening door.

Chapter 4

"**D**ONAIT! DONAIT!"
Fionn stopped short, and his spear slipped from his hand and clattered on the mosaic floor. Somehow the slope up which he was trudging had become the faerie hall. Donait stood in the midst of it, her blue eyes blank and staring. The echoes of his call faded, but still she did not move.

Fionn forgot that he was naked and bleeding, forgot the ache in his arms and the terror of the day. Heart hammering, he stumbled towards her, but something held him back—the terrible shield still weighted him. Swearing, he wrenched his arm from the strap and cast the thing aside.

The hazel shield boomed hollowly as it settled to rest. Donait jerked, the only ungraceful movement he had ever seen her make, and blinked several times. Moisture sheened her brow; beneath her eyes the skin was shadowed as if she had smeared charcoal there, and the bones of her cheeks were suddenly shockingly clear. She was still beautiful, but for the first time since he had known her, Fionn was able to believe that she was old.

The blue eyes focused, and with an effort, Donait bent her lips into a smile.

"I'm back," he croaked. His throat felt like a scraped hide. Had the vapor from the worm done that, or had he screamed? She looked at him and he colored. Obviously she knew he was here.

"Indeed you are, son of Cumhal, and once more in need of a bath!" Donait managed a smile.

She waved at the floor and the steaming tub began to shimmer into existence, but this time the image came slowly, and through its outlines Fionn could still see the wall. Donait frowned and raised her hand, pointing. Her arm trembled, and Fionn looked down so as not to shame her by watching her struggle. Her battle this day must have been as desperate as his own.

His feet were black with the slime of the creatures his shield had so ingloriously slain. His nose curled at the smell.

"More muck," he muttered. "All I do is drag in filth!" In his exhaustion, he felt as if he were still Demne, still ten years old.

A new sound brought his head up. Donait was giggling. The kitchen girls had laughed like that when he was a fire boy in King Gléor's hall. For a moment then she seemed only an ordinary woman, and Fionn forgot to be afraid.

And he was not about to stand still so that she could laugh at his nakedness. The tub was quite solid now. He took a quick step towards it, banged his knee hard, and blinked as dots of light swam before his eyes.

Fionn plunged deep into the bubbling waters, frantic to wash away his dirt even though the water stung his many cuts like a swarm of angry bees. Then it began to heal him. He watched, fascinated, as the weals on one arm closed, scabbed up, and turned to gleaming scars. Was it the healing, or his own time sense, that had speeded up? He thought of Fiacail, whom he had left sleeping a night before, and wondered how much time had passed in the world since he came to Donait's hall. He shivered. How long had he slumbered in the fairy bed and battled the venomous worm?

Fionn shivered again for a different reason and looked at the hanging where he had first seen the Ancient Dripping Hazel, bracing himself for the devastation he had left there. But the weaving showed a verdant mound, rich with summer bloom. Rising from its crown was a slender new hazel, whose leaves rustled in an unseen breeze.

How much time had that required? What would Fiacail think if Fionn was gone a year or more?

Fionn had no answers. Instead, he grasped the lump of soap and scrubbed his skin clean. His empty belly rumbled. He understood now why Donait had insisted he meet the worm unfed. Surely he would have spewed from the stinking vapors otherwise. At last, satisfied that he was as clean as he could get, he clambered out and drew the great towel around his body, suddenly aware that Donait's dancing eyes were noting every move.

The time of Faerie had worked its magic upon her as well. The bruises beneath her eyes had faded, and the fluid grace that made her movement like a song was there once more as she came to him.

He felt cool rivulets running across his shoulders from his wet hair. Dimly he knew that he ought to be drying it, but he could only gaze, trembling, as she reached up to him. *Now . . . it is now . . .*, drummed his heart, and he could not run away. He stared at the rise and fall of the full breasts so clearly outlined through the silk of her gown.

Donait was tall, but by almost a head Fionn now was taller. She tilted her face back slowly, and her mouth was like a cavern of roses. Her hands slid smoothly over his wet skin, and Fionn lowered his lips to hers.

He had never known such sweetness; it was as if he had never kissed anyone before. The towel dropped from his grasp and he reached out to cup one breast.

A grip like iron encircled his wrist. Donait's lips released his, and she shook her head. "Not yet, dear one. Not yet."

Fionn felt the blood rise in his face, as anger and lust and frustration battled. Abruptly he was conscious of his damp hair and the towel around his ankles.

She was teasing him! He caught his lower lip between his teeth and grabbed the towel. Women! Sidhe or mortal, they were almost more trouble than they were worth. Almost, he thought, remembering the sweetness of that kiss. Ideas for a savage satire on the subject of females began to come to him.

Finding the words for it occupied his mind quite happily as he rubbed himself dry. But by the time he had finished with the towel, weariness was dragging at both mind and muscles, and all he wanted was to collapse for a week. Donait had been right to push him away—if they had lain down together surely he would have been asleep before he could be any use to her at all.

He knuckled at his eyes to keep them open. If he slept in this place, how many years would pass in the lands of men? If only there were two of him, one to keep his promise to Fiacail and the other to pursue the promise he thought he had read in the fairywoman's eyes.

The robe Donait handed him this time was a glowing gold. He pulled it over his damp hair and let her lead him towards the glowing hearth. The couch sparkled into existence before his aching eyes, and a table appeared. Foolish thoughts chased each other through his fatigue-fuddled brain. This was surely easier than the meals he had helped with when he served kings. No need to worry about mice in the larder, and no dirty plates to scrub clean.

Fionn grinned, bemused, as food began to appear. First came a bowl of milk, foaming as if it had just that moment come from the udder of some great lowing cow. Then a warm loaf of bread appeared, brown and soft, and a comb of dripping honey, golden in the soft light of the hall. A plate of apples and ripe hazelnuts shimmered into being, and a small tub of yellow butter.

His belly growled, and he resisted the urge to seize the loaf and cram it into his mouth with both hands. Donait sat beside him and took up the cup of milk. She held the cup while he drank a long draught. It was the richest milk Fionn had ever tasted, and it refreshed him deeply, even as he wondered what sort of cow produced it. In moments, the bowl was empty.

Donait broke off a piece of bread, spread it with butter and honey, and fed it to him, so the smell of the loaf and the scent of her slender, long-fingered hand became one. As he chewed, she caressed his damp hair with her other hand. His muscles were still immobilized by a pleasant lethargy, but his loins were reawakening. He twitched as the tingling grew, trapped between hunger and desire.

When Fionn finished the bread, the woman leaned forward and licked a drop of honey from the corner of his mouth. He clenched his big hands to keep from seizing her shoulders and bearing her down against the couch. Dimly he remembered how the Liath Luachra had taught him to be patient when he stalked the beasts of the forest. Hesitantly, he brushed her mouth with a quick kiss, and felt her hand coil in his hair, pulling enough to hurt.

It was maddening to be fed like a child, to be teased by the woman's softness, but powerless to *do* anything. His skull seemed filled with wasps, buzzing and stinging. She had been willing enough to let him act when there were enemies to kill!

But as he bit into a piece of apple held to his mouth, he realized that perhaps to Donait he was a child, even though she no longer showed her years. He crunched resignedly and forced himself to concentrate on the sweetness of the fruit, not the honeyed odor of the breast that pressed against his arm. Long ago she had told him that he bathed well, his first acknowledged triumph. More and more, as his strength returned to him, he sensed that this meal was something more than sustenance.

The thought soothed the stinging in his mind, and he focused on the taste and texture and scent of the fruit in his mouth. There was a wisdom to be learned here, if he could grasp it. No, not grasp. It was not a thing to be seized in haste or greed. The apple must be sensed, must be accepted gently.

Donait gave a little smile, as if she were pleased with what he was thinking. She lifted a nutmeat to his mouth, and he tasted the slight bitterness of the hazelfruit. This was not the first time she had fed him nuts and apples. Suddenly Fionn remembered the Samhain when, hunted and burning with fever, he had taken refuge in a tiny cave. The fairy woman had come to him in his world then, and had fed him just these things.

If wisdom had a taste, he decided as he chewed, it was the sweetness of the apple and the slight bitterness of the nut. He had eaten the flesh of the Salmon of Wisdom, which Fionnéices had said was fattened upon hazelnuts, and a bitter feast it had been indeed. But he had not understood the gift he had received, though he had used the insight it brought him. Wisdom was a greater thing than insight. For an instant he almost *knew*, and then it was gone.

Fionn turned his head away from Donait's knowing gaze and looked towards the wall he had passed through to win his eerie shield. Now the subtle living picture contained a youthful hazel, and beneath its slender boughs he caught a glimpse of water. He knew that a pool lay at the roots of the tree, and another salmon swam there, waiting to nourish itself upon the nuts of wisdom. It would be years, perhaps centuries, before that fish would be ready to be caught by some new seeker. He wondered who it would be.

Then he looked again at his new shield. Even in the serene hall of Donait, a subtle aura of evil surrounded it. Beside the shield stood blood-singing Birga, and he knew with a dread certainty that they spoke to one another in some tongue unknown to man. Wisdom, he realized, could be both good and ill, and beside that realization, all that Bodbmall had taught him of the way of the wise seemed a small and shabby game.

As Fionn swallowed the morsel of hazelnut, his throat ached with the weight of the wisdom he had ingested. He felt both solemn and oddly joyous, as he did in the presence of the Goddess.

Fionn closed his eyes as tears filled them. He *was* a child, a babe still wet from the womb. How could he hope to understand Donait when he hardly understood the gifts locked within himself? Soft fingers brushed the tears away from his cheeks, and through a mist he saw Donait lap the moisture from their tips. The movement of her pink tongue against her flesh sent all thoughts of wisdom rolling away in a rush of desire that ran along his bones, searing him within.

His cheeks dried in the heat that swept through him. Donait leaned forward so that her breast pressed against his pounding chest. Their breaths mingled for an endless moment, so Fionn could almost taste the sweetness of her essence.

Donait took his hand and drew him to his feet, a grave smile illuminating her perfect features. She had never seemed more beautiful, and he trembled. While they ate, the bath had been replaced by the great bed, and now it was only a few brief steps away.

Suddenly valorous or mad, Fionn encircled Donait's narrow waist with a steady arm, and pressed his lips to hers. The fairy woman seemed to melt against him, and Fionn felt her tongue press against his teeth, seeking entrance as eagerly as that of any girl. But when their tongues met, she tasted unlike any mortal woman, as if wit and will could have a flavor all their own.

Her gown vanished without effort as she fell backwards onto the welcoming bed, and the same magic misted his own robe away. Donait stretched out luxuriously, displaying her high breasts and long limbs. Even in a daze of lust, Fionn realized that somehow she was not naked, but simply unclad, as if some invisible garment surrounded the sweet-scented flesh that beckoned to him.

Fionn lowered his face to her breast, rounding his mouth upon a stiffened nipple, and heard a moan of delight rise from her throat. He was shuddering with the effort to go slowly, afraid that even now she might stop him again. He stroked the graceful fullness of one thigh, reveling in the feel of her skin beneath his fingers, and felt his way towards her secret place. The soft hair between her thighs was like spider silk, and his loins throbbed.

He felt long fingers seize his manhood, softly but firmly, and nearly screamed as she caressed him. Fionn was caught between wishing she might never stop her tender touching and the desire to be enfolded by the incredible richness between her widening limbs. It was as if he had never touched a woman before.

Donait gave a little gasp, then a whimper of desire that made his nape bristle. Fionn lifted his face from the mounds of her breasts and looked into eyes wide with desire and a mouth that begged for kissing. He plunged his tongue into it, reveling once more in the strong, sweet taste of the woman. She pressed his hips with her hands, arching towards him.

It is now, whispered his blood. *She will not stop you this time. Take her now. . . .*

His body knew the moment as the hunter knows the instant when he and the prey are one. But which was he? Fionn shook all over as his flesh brushed the silky mound between the graceful limbs, and then she opened to him, and he entered in. The rhythms of love took him like a strong current as he moved upon her, a salmon leaping upstream. His blood was coursing in sweet surges, at once familiar and unknown. Her nails pressed the skin of his shoulders, but did not pierce. Her legs wrapped around his like the entwining spirals all about them, and she half-crooned, half-shouted her delight.

The smell and feel and taste of her turned his blood to a river of fire. The pressure was beyond bearing; he must stop or die of it, but he could not. He wanted the unendurable moment never to end. For a moment he hung above her; the salmon above the waterfall. Then one of them drew breath, and he fell, ever and end-lessly, into the whirlpool of Donait's exploding desire. They cried out, breath mingling, in the last instant of ecstasy.

Entangled, they lay together for a time, breathing as one. His tangled locks spilled across her cheek, and she murmured delicious nonsense into his ear. Fionn's hand still cupped the firm sweetness of one of her breasts. He thought about caressing it, but his eyes were growing heavy. Still, he fought against sleep, unwilling to break the perfection of the moment in which they lay joined in a content beyond passion.

He felt as if they were floating at the still point of the world.

He thought he was still awake, but presently he real-ized that the peace in which he floated existed in some dimension of being as removed from Donait's hall as faerie was from the world of humankind. A golden mist swirled before his eyes. As he stared, it began to coa-lesce, and a well-remembered face shone down. Fionn gazed at the stern but beautiful countenance of the God-dess for what seemed a long time. Then she gestured with her graceful hands.

Fionn saw a vista open beside the swirling hem of her gown, and he drew his eyes from her lambent face to look. To one side of her skirts he could see the shining Hall of Donait, and beyond it, the whole of the Otherworld. The raths of the Sidhe glowed in the gloaming. For a long time he marveled at their beauty, saddened for some reason he could not quite define.

At last he looked to her other side, and found Eriu laid out there. Some of the places he knew and others were strange. He could see the soft hills where he had hunted as a boy, and the kingdoms where he had served. The shining fortress of Aonghus Og stood close to the place where he had eaten the flesh of the Salmon of Wisdom and slain the murderer of his father. He could make out the Hill of Almu, where his grandfather waited, plotting some mischief.

The landscape shifted, and he saw a dun on a hill above the sea, and knew it was the new holding of his uncle Crimall. The faces of the men who came and went from its gates were drawn with grief. Then he was within the hall. His half brother Dithramhach sat beside the fire, turning a spearhead that Fionn remembered forging in his hands. His red hair was streaked with ash, and his face was tear-stained. A dog came scampering up, and he kicked at it, then flung the spearhead away. He shouted something then, but Fionn could not hear the words.

He looked up at the face of Brigid, and knew he must choose between the two worlds. He felt very small and helpless beneath her stern gaze, and angry too. He did not want to choose, or perhaps it was that he did not wish to leave the comfort of Donait's hall. But it seemed he would have to. He looked back to his furious half brother, who was still trying to destroy the forge hut with his bare hands. *Very well*, he sighed silently. *I will go back to the fian*.

When he glanced up again, the curve of Brigid's lips and the merriment in her blue eyes told him he had chosen rightly. The Goddess was pleased, and Fionn's heart swelled with delight.

*   *   *

FIONN LAY ON HIS BACK, STARING UP AT THE INTERTWIN-
ing roof and the soft light behind it. He was only half
awake, still caught in the splendor of his dream, and
aware that he was alone in the great bed. Although his
body longed for the touch of Donait's hand and the
smell of her flesh, he was glad for some solitude in
which to contemplate his dream. Even recalling it filled
him with more pleasure than poetry or even the delight
of coupling, and he would have thought that the greatest ecstasy even a few hours ago. He scratched his tangled hair and sighed, wondering if he were ever going
to have the same sensible reactions as other men.

When he heard soft footfalls, Fionn sat up. Donait
was robed in blue, her shining hair combed and braided
neatly. He looked at her, felt the heat of fresh desire
sweep him, then, as if from a great distance, watched
it vanish in the need to relieve himself and a ravening
hunger. It pleased him that he still possessed simple
human needs, that he had not overnight changed into
another person.

Fionn rose and washed, dressed in a fresh linen robe,
and, whistling under his breath, combed out his silky,
tangled hair. He felt no need to speak, no compulsion
to find words for the love that sped along his veins.
It was enough to perform the most ordinary of tasks
with complete attention. Peace permeated his whole
being, and that was strange enough in his life that he
was reluctant to disturb it.

They broke their fast on foaming cups of milk and
bowls of cooked oats, sweetened with honey, sitting
together on the couch in companionable silence. He
had never known a woman who had such a gift for
silences, and it made him think of Cruithne, who chat-
tered from dawn till dusk. He wondered about the child
she had borne. The contrast between the two women
was overwhelming.

Fionn's arm brushed Donait's, and there was no

arousal at the touch. He was puzzled at this, for just the night before the mere scent of the woman sent him nearly mad with lust. Then he remembered that first visit to the hall of Donait again, and how what had seemed to him a single night had been a year and more in Eriu. Fionn concentrated on eating, on stilling the ravening beast in his belly. Four bowls of oat porridge hardly touched his hunger, and this disturbed him, remembering the small amount of faerie food that usually satisfied him.

"I seem to have quite an appetite today."

Donait sipped a little milk. "That is not surprising. You have dreamt for nearly three nights, Fionn mac Cumhal."

Three nights! His mind began to spin, and it hardly mattered that for the first time she had called him by his name. *Fionn! Fionn!* The name had a sweetness on her lips as on no other.

"We have guests, Fionn."

Donait's voice stilled his swirling thoughts and distracted him from the terrible puzzles that swarmed there. Was it more foes? She did not appear alarmed. He turned.

Three people appeared in the doorway, silhouetted against the light. He stood as Donait rose to greet them, squinting above the glow of the hearth. A slender young woman wrapped in a short tunic of brindled hide came towards the fire with two young boys, one very fair, the other dark.

The woman smiled at his look of puzzlement and laughed. He knew that laugh, like a ripple of silver bells in the silence! This was his invisible companion, who had warned him of so many dangers! His sister . . . As she encircled his waist with her strong arms, Fionn felt her tremble. He hugged her, searching the upturned face intently. She was fire-haired, and her features reminded him of someone, though for a moment he could not quite think who. Then his serious stare faded her smile, and he realized she looked rather like that sad queen of Gléor Lamraige, Muirne.

"Greetings to you, Brother. Are you glad to be seeing me at last?" She had the piping voice of the wind, and she smelled as if she had been running with the hounds. He was not alone!

"Surely, Sister, glad I am to know more of you than the whisper of your voice, and the sound of your laughter teasing me. I never even learned your name!" He kissed her brow and smelled wind and earth.

"I am called Tuireann." She laughed, chucked him beneath the chin, and pulled away, restless as a brand. "You are such a solemn stick," she laughed again. "It must be all the years with those old women. I used to wonder how you bore their scoldings." She stepped away and back again, as if she could not bear to stand still. "These are your nephews, Bran and Sceolan," she added casually, waving at the boys, who sat up alertly, watching him.

Fionn glanced helplessly at Donait. How could his sister have children of her own? He was out of his depth with this flighty fire-haired girl whose glass-green eyes slid over the wooded walls of the hall so uneasily. But the faerie woman only smiled at her.

"Which is which?" he asked Tuireann.

His sister pivoted on her heel as if about to take wing. "The fair one who looks like you is Sceolan, and the other is Bran. They were twins, as we were, and I have brought them to you for fostering. I lack the gift of mothering, I think."

Fionn studied the boys, who seemed seven or eight summers, and wondered if he had looked like Sceolan when he was small. His throat tightened as he remembered another Bran, his first friend in the world, and his first victim. As he looked at the dark child he had such a strong sense of foreboding that he nearly missed the import of Tuireann's words.

"What? In my charge. But, but . . ." he sputtered help-lessly into silence.

"You are their uncle. It is your duty."

It was true that in all the lands he had lived, a man had a special responsibility towards his sister's sons. Fionn crouched down, reaching out to the boys. Shyly, silently, they huddled against him, nuzzling against his shoulders and sniffing at his neck. What was he going to do with two lads? A faint smell of dog rose from their strong, young bodies. When Fionn was dog boy to the king of Benntraige he had smelled that way. For a moment he smiled, remembering the king's kindness, and how he had sent Fionn away to save him from the wrath of his grandfather Tadg.

A bit clumsily, he stroked their heads, and they snuggled against him trustingly, dark eyes closing in content. They looked so young and so vulnerable. A fierce yearning to protect them surged within him, even as he wondered if he would be able to do so. Their mother was pacing about the far side of the hearth with increasing restlessness. Tuireann eyed the tree-girt walls of Donait's hall with a shivering anxiety he could not really understand. What an odd creature she was.

"Tuireann, shall we walk outside and speak of this?" he asked quietly.

She gave him a look of gratitude and darted towards the doorway, and Fionn left the boys with Donait and followed her. The greensward was smooth, unmarred, and empty, with no evidence of the conflict that had raged there so recently. As he caught up with her, Fionn wondered about time once again.

A small, familiar hand slipped into his. "Stop wor-rying. You are the most worrying person I have ever seen." Tuireann smiled at him, all traces of her rest-lessness gone beneath the soft sunshine.

"Am I? All the spying you've done must make you the expert. You have come to my aid so many times." His throat closed with gratitude.

Tuireann giggled and gave him a light punch on one arm. "You saved yourself. I just encouraged you." She slipped her arm around his waist and pressed against his chest affectionately. Fionn could almost smell the wildness in her. He put his arm around her slender shoulder and hugged her tightly, enjoying the feel of her delicate bones under his hand, and the brush of her warm breath against his chest.

"Tell me of my nephews, then." Fionn felt a small shudder wrack her body at these words. "They seem good boys."

"They are, but I have no talent for rearing them. And even to look at them reminds me of my great loss."

"Your loss, Tuireann?"

She gave a sigh that gusted against his robe. "I chose my husband badly, and I have paid. Ullan was most fair to look upon, and I was so blinded by his beauty that I forgot he was not my equal in the race. I did not know how it rankled him that I could outpace him easily, for I have no way with folk, brother. Soon he started to take comfort with another, a *bendrui*, Scena, and she used her powers to turn me into a bitch-dog, not realizing that I carried Ullan's sons." She gave an uncharacteristically bitter little laugh.

"I whelped them when you were tending the hounds of the king of Benntraige, which might make a fair poem, were it not so painful to recall. At last Ullan heard of my transformation, and he promised Scena he would wed her if she would release me from the spell. So I regained my human form, and the boys too, but I lost fair Ullan, and unless I find a man who can best me in the race I will never love another."

Fionn held her close and kissed her brow. "They sound as if they deserve one another, Tuireann."

"Perhaps. But that thought gives me no comfort. I know only that I must be free."

Fionn stared at her, wondering how the lives of two twin-born could so diverge. It seemed to him that from the moment they left their mother's womb more than distance had parted them. Fionn had always been bound to someone's will, whether it was Bodbmall or Donait or the kings he had served in his wanderings. Tuireann came and went like the wind.

"Free?" He laughed bitterly. "It seems to me you have used up all the freedom for both of us. How did that happen, Tuireann? Where is our mother? How did you survive?"

The green eyes clouded as she looked at him. "I never knew her. I can remember only the halls of Nuadu. . . . He is Tadg's father, but he has more care for his descendents than our grandfather ever did. Our mother told Bodbmall to take you and flee, while she waited with me to face death or Tadg's wrath. But before the druid could come, Nuadu reft us both away into the Otherworld." A cool wind whispered in the treetops and Tuireann stirred restlessly.

"My fosterers say that Muirne was sent back to the lands of men as soon as she was healed, but I belong to Faerie. No man of the Sidhe can match me in racing, but I have no substance in mortal lands despite my speed. Take care of my children. I can run with the wind, brother, but I cannot craft words or swords or walk between the worlds. Which of us is truly most free?"

Fionn closed his eyes, struggling with dim concepts of gifts and the obligations they implied. It had seemed to him that each skill he mastered had only taken more of his freedom away. Wind brushed his brow, or perhaps it was a pair of soft lips, kissing him. His eyes flicked open, but Tuireann had disappeared.

WHEN FIONN EMERGED FROM THE HOUSE OF DONAIT, MIST was curling along the ground and veiling the trees. His young nephews trailed behind, silent lads with large, round eyes, and he felt the weight of their need settle across his shoulders. Bran, the dark one, reached a small hand towards him, and he took it in his own. Fionn watched the roof of the hall dissolving into the mist and tightened his grip. They had not whimpered when their mother left them, but he could feel them wondering if this strange man would abandon them too.

Donait followed them, her beauty and vigour restored as if the battle had never been. Fionn let go of Bran and reached out to her. As she rested her proud head against his shoulder, the warmth of her body flooded him with memory—but it was sadness he felt, not desire.

"Donait, I do not want to leave you."

Her eyes were like the depths of the well. "You are my champion, and you have saved the web of the world from destruction. If you choose to remain here, I cannot say you nay."

He looked down at her, memorizing the perfect features. Donait would never change. If he stayed with her, neither would he. But he was responsible for these two boys now, and he had made a promise to Fiacail.

"But you believe that I should go—" he said then.

"You are destined for greater deeds than sitting in my hall. The *fian* defends Eriu as you have defended me, but only you can walk in both worlds."

Tuireann had said the same. Did the bonds of love and loyalty against which he chafed imprison because he was fighting them? Even his sister could not run against the wind.

"Will there ever be a time when you do not send me away?" he whispered, and knew in that moment what his choice must be.

"Perhaps, but I may not tell you when that will be."

"Donait, I love you."

"And I you, sweet Fionn. That is why I am letting you go." She kissed him lightly on the lips and moved out of his arms, and he felt the wretchedness welling within him once more. "Hasten, beloved, for events in the world await your coming. Walk into the mist for forty paces, and you will arrive where you began."

Fionn grimaced. Then he lifted the hazel shield from beside the doorway and slung it across his back and took up his spear. For once Birga was silent in his grasp, and he was grateful. "Farewell, Donait, for now."

The silk of her gown rippled as she sighed. "Until we meet again, Fionn mac Cumhal." He took no comfort in her sorrow. He was still leaving her.

The boys moved closer as the mist closed around them, pressing against him anxiously. Fionn wished he had the words to reassure them, but neither Bodbmall nor the Liath Luachra had believed in explanations, and he did not know how.

After he had gone five paces, he looked back. The hall of Donait was transparent, and the woman herself only a wavering shape in the light. He hesitated for a long moment then, but his word was given.

The mist deepened with each step, and fear lifted the hair on his arms as Fionn remembered the great chasm that twice he had leapt to reach the Otherworld. He used the butt of his spear to feel out the path. Ten paces, and twenty, he picked his way. By the time he had gone thirty paces he could see nothing except his hand before him, but something was tugging at his tunic. He looked down, and found his nephews clinging to the cloth of his garment. He took Bran's hand and held out his spear to ward Sceolan.

Another few halting steps, and he caught the scent of woods and rain. Fionn halted, testing the air. The mist was thinning; he saw dim tree shapes and took another careful step forward, then stopped, for the small hand in his had let go.

"We are almost through, lads," Fionn whispered. "Stay by me—"

He felt something press against his leg and looked down. Bran had disappeared. It was a half-grown black wolfhound pup that leaned against him, gazing up with wide, imploring eyes. A cold nose poked at his other side and he saw another, with silky pale fur. The pup whined softly, and automatically Fionn reached down to fondle the silky ears.

"Tuireann?" he whispered, gazing blindly into the wind. "Tuireann, you bitch! Why have you done this to me?" The words died as he realized the word was literally true. Was this why she could not bear to raise the boys she had borne? At Donait's hall the children had been silent, and he had thought them well behaved. . . . But perhaps their canine forms were the true ones, and the images of children the spell.

"Bran? Sceolan?"

Both smooth heads came up, and plumed tails began to beat at the grass. *We love you*, said those bright dark eyes. *We are loyal to you. We will follow you, whatever the trail.* . . .

Fionn felt tears sting his eyes. In his confusion and sorrow he understood one thing at last. He was no longer alone.

Chapter 5

❧

FIONN BLINKED THROUGH THE DRIZZLE, IDENTIFYING familiar shapes of rock and tree. This was certainly the spot from which Donait had summoned him. But branches that had been bare when he left were lush with leaves, and in the hazel copse the nuts were ripening. He took deep breaths of sharp-scented mint and rich odors of oak mould released by the rain, and with a desire deeper even than his response to the apple-blossom scent of Donait, felt his whole being yearn towards the land of Eriu.

Bran and Sceolan were scampering in ecstatic circles, snuffling at trees and stones and poking their noses into the wet grass. They had known only the Otherworld; the smells of common earth must be inebriating for a creature that thought with its nose. Suddenly Sceolan stilled, head up, pointing. Fionn turned and frowned as he caught the scent of wood smoke on the upper air.

Instinctively he whistled and the two hounds came to heel. Children or pups, at least Tuireann had trained them. As Fionn started towards the smoke, Sceolan coursed ahead of him while Bran roamed behind. He felt his heart lightening as he watched them run. The

80

prospect of raising children had scared him, but he knew all about dogs.

Where he and Fiacail had camped stood a hut of withies thatched with brushwood. Smoke swirled from an open shed beside it, carrying the aroma of cooking meat from the skin boiling bag that hung above the fire. Fionn grinned at the familiar smells of squirrel and hare and hedgehog and wild garlic with just a hint of thyme, for it was Fiacail mac Conchinn who had taught him that recipe for hunter's stew.

Bran gave a sharp bark as he caught the man-scent, and Sceolan's white hackles rose. The hide stretched across the doorway of the hut was thrust aside, and a wrinkled face peered through the mizzle. Fionn stepped nearer so that Fiacail could get a better look. The old man let out his breath in a snort and let the hide fall behind him. As Sceolan began to growl Fionn reached down, feeling the fine tremors stir the fur beneath his hand.

"Back in time for dinner, I see," said Fiacail. His gaze moved from the dogs to the hazel shield. "How was your hunting?"

"My obligation is fulfilled. . . ." answered Fionn, and only then did the old man let a smile crack his seamed features.

"Ah, lad, lad, I was afraid—" Fiacail took a step forward, and Fionn felt Sceolan stiffen and saw the hair rise on Bran's neck as he crouched to spring.

"Back, both of you." Fionn's voice cracked across the growling. Tails down, the two pups scrambled behind him, but he could still hear an ominous rumbling. "Shame on you—this is a friend!" His voice must have been sharper than he intended, for Sceolan cowered in the grass and an acrid stink of dog piss wafted from Bran. "Let them get your smell," he said to Fiacail. "They are not used to men."

The older man grimaced as he bent to reach out to the hounds. They sniffed him cautiously, and the growling ceased. Bran gave the hand a lick and Fiacail stroked the hound's rough hair. Clearly the old man was curious, but Fionn did not feel ready to explain.

"Talk to them as you would to children. They are very intelligent," he said ambiguously, "but remember, they are young."

"Faerie beasts—" Fiacail nodded, as if that explained everything. Fionn lifted the old man to his feet and Fiacail embraced him fiercely, the easy tears of age spilling from his eyes.

"Lad, do you know the year has gone three-quarters round! I've worried myself witless waiting!"

"For me," Fionn said simply, "nine nights have passed. I am no longer a boy. Could you not trust my word?"

Fiacail snorted and spat into the grass. "Why else am I here? Come—the stew will boil dry if we stand here talking. Your uncle Crimall died a moon ago, and they say the *fian* is buzzing like an unqueened hive. You have no time to lose."

"Crimall would have been glad to see me." Fionn blinked rain from his eyes, or perhaps it was tears. "But do you think the others will open their arms? Anyhow, they'll surely have chosen a new master by now."

"Your half brother, Dithramhach, is buzzing the loudest, but do you think he has the wit to preserve the *fian*?"

Fionn's hand went to the chunk of amber his half brother had given him, which still hung around his neck from a thong. Dithramhach at least had been sorry when Fionn left Crimall's old *dun* in the hills. But that had been nearly eight winters ago.

His nostrils flared as Fiacail began to dish out stew, but his appetite was gone. As he took the wooden bowl, Fionn sighed.

"I said I would come with you, and I will, but they will not be pleased to see me back again."

*   *   *

CRIMALL'S *DUN* AT INBER COLPTHA STOOD ON A HEAD-
land within sight and smell of the sea. The air seemed
full of light after the secrets of the forests through which
they had come. Fionn tipped back his head and let the
salt wind lift the hair from his brow, thinking that he
could have liked the place very well if a different purpose had brought him here. Fiacail, for all his seeming
fragility, was already halfway up the hill. With a sigh,
Fionn tugged at the strap that held the hazel shield
across his back, hitched up his *fili*'s gown, and followed him. It felt odd to be wearing the poet's robe
while bearing arms. The weapon of the *fili* was words.
But Fiacail had thought it might be as well to remind
the *fian* why Fionn had gone away.

As they passed through the gate, the sound of men's
voices raised in argument carried clearly from the hall.
A growl from Bran and Sceolan silenced the dozen
mangy dogs who came yelping across the yard, but
no guard challenged them. If the *fian* had a new leader, he was either very stupid or very secure, and the
piled refuse and general disrepair within the *dun* were
confirming all Fionn's fears.

But at least someone had noticed the barking. Men
boiled out of the hall, skittering to a halt when they
saw who stood there. Fionn's gaze went from scarred
warriors he had drunk and hunted and fought with
eight years before to the faces of smooth-skinned young
strangers with angry eyes. A few poised their spears, but
clearly they were puzzled by the poet's robes and the
way the older men greeted Fiacail. Bran and Sceolan
whined and bristled, and Fionn motioned them behind
him.

"You two, stay with Fiacail," he said to the hounds.
"Whatever happens, stay still where you are until I give
the word!"

Dithramhach strode out of the hall, his cheeks red
with either drink or rage, and stopped short, glaring.

His body had thickened in eight years, but above the ruddy forehead his fair hair was growing thin.

"I told you they would not be glad to see me," Fionn said quietly, and the old man grunted.

"What are you doing here?" Dithramhach spoke at last.

Fionn stared back at him. *Why am I here?* he wondered. *Because I told Fiacail I would come? Because of the futures the Goddess showed to me?*

Nervously he began to chew on his thumb, but the first touch brought a dizzying flood of vision. Fionn saw the eagle-features of his grandfather contorting with rage as he spoke to Goll mac Morna, and the face of the *rigfénnid* darkening as he heard. Then the scene changed, and he saw the Men of Morna striking the warriors of Crimall's *fian* down. Fionn opened his eyes, swallowing bile. Had there ever really been a choice for him?

"I have come to claim the place my uncle meant for me."

"Why? So you can run away at the first sign of trouble as you did before?" Dithramhach's face contorted with an old sorrow that wrenched Fionn's heart.

"It is because I see trouble coming that I have returned . . ." he said quietly.

"And you expect us to believe that," said Dithramhach with painful mockery. "Since you have showed so much care for the *fian* in the past!"

Fionn winced. That one had bitten too near the bone.

"Just a moment, Dithramhach. You are being hasty, as usual," said one of the older men. Fionn struggled to identify him. *Aghmar . . . mac Donal,* he found the name at last, and matters must be serious indeed if the man was defending him, for Aghmar had never liked him at all. "Let the lad at least tell us why he ran away!"

Fifty pairs of eyes fixed on Fionn. He looked from one to another of those he knew, seeing how he had hurt them, wanting them to understand. Reidhe mac Dael's face creased with mixed hope and anger. Grimthann, who had been the *fian*'s dog boy, was more interested in Bran and Sceolan. Fionn recognized Duibhne the cup-bearer, grown to a warrior now, Dubhtach Blackmane, and Guarire mac Reiche, always wise for his years, who were once his friends. But the sons of Oillil of Eadar were glaring, and Glas mac Dreamhan would not meet his gaze.

"Eight years ago, I was a lad indeed—" he spoke softly, but his bard-trained voice carried clearly. "Not fit to lead the *fian* against the foes who would have come against it if I had remained. Dithramhach knows why I went away. Leaving was the only way I could protect you from Clan Morna's wrath."

"A noble deed for sure!" Dithramhach spat upon the ground. "At the time, I believed you. But I am wondering if it was not an insult to judge the *fian* so weak in war then, and a greater one to think us in need of your assistance now! We can see from your garments where you went and what you learned—" He gestured at the *fili*'s robe. "Since my tenth year I have studied nothing but war!" he proclaimed to the others.

"Reason enough to seek a different leader for the *fian*—" came Fiacail's whisper. Fionn nodded. He suspected that had been Cumhal's failing as well, but did not say so. He stiffened as Dithramhach turned to him again.

"Well, bardling—do you intend to defend us from Goll mac Morna with words?"

Fionn looked at him until his half brother's gaze faltered. *I could sing your remaining hair from your head . . .* , said that stare. *I could wither your balls! Do you have any idea what the words of a trained* fili *can do?* He realized that he could defeat Dithramhach easily, but would the men understand, and would it be fair to so use his power?

"I have weapons other than words," he said grimly.

"I have faced foes whose very sight would freeze your bones!" He unslung his spiral-patterned shield, and a soft humming throbbed in the air.

"*I am Hazel, hallowed Tree. . . .*" Only Fionn heard the song, but in the faces of the men around him he could see the flicker of unease. As if in response, Birga pulsed in his hand. "*Thirsty . . .*" came its whisper. "*Drink blood now?*" Fionn shuddered. His own rage had betrayed him into killing friends too often. It would be better to die himself would than to loose his mindless magic-cursed weapons on the *fian*.

"Here—" he said to Fiacail. "You hold these!" He thrust shield and spear into the old man's hands, and their singing faded to a disappointed whisper of sound.

"Weapons such as those are for my enemies," said Fionn, "and I do not count you among them. . . ."

Empty-handed, he faced the other man. He knew his own skills. Even with ordinary weapons he could probably master Dithramhach in a duel, but it would be far too easy to do serious damage if they fought with steel, and his half brother must not die.

"But I accept that you cannot acknowledge me without a battle," he came to a halt. "Dithramhach, I challenge you! Will you fight me body to body, bare-handed? Will you wrestle me for the leadership?"

Dithramhach gave a short laugh, looking at Fionn with eyes that could not see the long muscles hidden beneath the loose robe. "Little brother, I will break you in two! You do not deserve to lead the *fian!*"

And that, thought Fionn as he unlatched his belt, was undoubtedly true. But against the threat he had seen coming, he was the best defense these men had. . . .

Gabbling excitedly, the warriors gave way. Soon the two combatants stood in the middle of a circle. Dithramhach pulled his chequered mantle over his head without bothering to unpin it. The day was warm, and he wore no upper garment. His belly bulged a little over the wide belt that held his trews, but beneath lay hard muscle. Dithramhach's grey eyes had gone still and steady, and Fionn knew his brother had meant every bitter word. He looked to be a powerful fighter. If Dithramhach were fated to lead their father's *fian* after all, at least he would have a fair chance to win. Dithramhach yanked open the belt and stepped out of the trews, and Aghmar picked up the discarded gear.

Sighing, Fionn pulled the white wool over his head. Smiling shyly, Duibhne took belt and robe and carried them back to Fiacail. When Dithramhach flexed his muscles to loosen them, there had been a little murmur of pride from the men. But when Fionn stood naked before them there was silence. Fionn looked from one man to another, wondering what was wrong. The eyes of some of the older were misting with the pain of memory, as if they saw Cumhal reborn. But the young ones stared at him in simple awe.

The seven years he had spent covered by a *fili*'s robe had leached the brown from his skin, and he supposed he must be nearly as pale as the wool of his robe, for two days on the road had not produced enough dirt to undo Donait's cleansing. Perhaps that was it—Fionn looked down at himself, seeing skin healed of every blemish except for a few pearly scars that he had won in Faerie. Did the glow of the Otherworld cling to him still?

Dithramhach was staring at Fionn's chest. After a moment Fionn realized that the one thing he was still wearing was the piece of pierced amber that his half brother had given him. In the sunlight, the lump seemed to glow like molten gold. He supposed he should take it off—in a wrestling match it could be a danger—but it would not hurt to remind the other man how close they once had been.

Dithramhach was binding his long hair into a fighter's knot atop his head, and Fionn did the same.

Aghmar drew a circle around them with the butt of his spear.

"Two throws out of three shall give victory!" cried Fiacail. "Let the combat begin!"

Dithramhach settled into a fighter's crouch, legs braced, hands open and ready, glaring up at Fionn. He frowned in surprise as Fionn scuffed his bare feet in the dust and advanced his left leg to protect the other. Most wrestlers led with the right leg, but the Liath Luachra had taught Fionn to use either. He smiled sweetly, holding his brother's gaze. Often a wrestling bout was won before ever the fighters touched, in the first clash of wills.

I have worked for the fian all my life—do you think I will let you walk away with it now? said Dithramhach's glare. They settled a little farther, standing nearly knee to knee.

I have stood all night one-legged in an icy pool reciting the Law of Eriu . . . , Fionn's stare replied. *I have endured the embrace of creatures that crawl through your dreams. Can you stop me?*

Dithramhach growled deep in his throat and grabbed for Fionn's arms. As the hard hands closed Fionn brought his own hands up in an identical grip, just where the great muscle of the upper arm slides into the bone. Together they swayed, hard muscles bunching beneath the clutching hands. Dithramhach's arm was like an oak branch; his spirit as sturdy and enduring and hard to bend. Fionn allowed the other man to press his arms downward, bending like the willow until Dithramhach realized he was overbalancing. In the moment when he started to shift his grip, Fionn broke free.

Both were breathing faster now, but they were barely sweated. This had only been an opener, a chance for each man to try his strength against the other. Fionn's pulse quickened with interest, not anger, and he smiled in satisfaction, for far more than Dithramhach, he feared his own killing rage. Still smiling, Fionn assumed a defensive crouch. He doubted that his opponent could outwait him. Would Dithramhach go for an easy neck grip next, or try for a leg dive?

Then he straightened a little as if his back were tiring, tempting him.

He saw the other begin to bend, and hooked his hands under Dithramhach's arms as his brother grabbed his legs just behind the knee, dropping to his own knees, drawing him down. He thought he had gauged his opponent's strength, but that hard grip took him with surprising force. Before he could counter, his left knee was bending. As it slammed into the dirt, Dithramhach drove forward, twisting, and Fionn saw the sky wheel crazily as he went down.

The fall knocked the breath from his chest. Through the roaring in his ears he could hear cheers.

It's all very well to play fair, lad, Fionn thought muzzily, *but don't be forgetting that you're out here to win!*

He blinked and saw Dithramhach standing over him, lips curling in a complacent grin. As he saw Fionn focus he extended a magnanimous hand to help him rise.

"So, Brother—the first fall goes to me!"

"It was a fine throw—" Fionn forced out the gracious words, strangling a surge of anger that was as much for himself as his foe. He had been overconfident. It must not happen a second time. He shook out the tension from his limbs and got into position again.

Earth was his strength. He set his feet and let out his breath in a long slow stream, awareness reaching deep beneath the dust. He heard the dull drum of his heartbeat and trembled as that rhythm was answered by a pulse of power from the heart of the world.

"Tired already?" mocked Dithramhach. "I'll be happy to help you lie down!" This piece of wit produced

a burst of laughter from the men, but Fionn continued
to sway.

Do you not hear the music, brother mine?

Fionn knew his gaze had gone unfocused when he
saw Dithramhach's frown, but his expanding awareness was taking in his opponent and the men around
him and a gull winging out to sea, and the sound of
breath in fifty pairs of lungs, and in Dithramhach's, and
his own.

Dance, Brother, dance!

Dithramhach feinted a grab and Fionn wove aside.
The music surged through him, and like an echo he
heard a simpler harmony. It came from his brother—
how could the man not know it? But Dithramhach's
narrow gaze was fixed on his enemy. Fionn grinned
suddenly and danced around him, grappled, and broke
free. He foresaw Dithramhach's every move as a bard
knows the melodic progression of a song. Dithramhach
began to swear softly as he realized that somehow he
had lost control of their interaction, but he was bound
now to the dance.

Now Fionn sank lower, his neck a tempting target for
the other man's hands. But as Dithramhach's fingers
locked behind his head, forcing him to one knee, Fionn
grabbed his brother's elbow with one hand and with the
other reached for his shoulder, swinging him around.
Instead of fighting Dithramhach's answering shove, he
got his hand around the other's neck and in the same
instant grabbed his ankle. It was Dithramhach's own
strength that drove him downward, arms flailing, as
Fionn jerked his foot out from under him and he
slammed into the ground.

Still on one knee, Fionn pinned him. Dithramhach
made a desperate grab, but caught only the thong
around Fionn's neck. For a moment it bit into muscle and skin, then the overstressed leather snapped
and the chunk of amber flew in a glowing arc across
the yard. Dithramhach's fierce gaze was caught by the

vanishing brightness, and all the fight seemed to go out of him. Fionn lay across him, their twinned breathing wheezing like a bellows in his ears.

"The second fall goes to Fionn!" Fiacail shrilled triumphantly.

"Now we are even..." Fionn whispered into Dithramhach's ear. "Come, Brother, let us show these gawkers how the sons of Cumhal can play!"

He felt the tension leave his brother's limbs and let him go. They got up rather slowly this time, testing each limb. Dirt was stuck to Dithramhach's back and all down one side, and dust had dulled Fionn's white skin. Perspiration cut rivulets through the grime and glittered in Dithramhach's beard.

Slowly they circled. The earth music was slower and deeper now, no more a dance, but the half-heard rumble of power that heralds a storm. Now Fionn moved to the attack, reaching for a lock and allowing his opponent to carry him down. But he was scissoring with strong legs and rolling even as Dithramhach broke the grip, careful to keep his shoulders from touching the ground. It was not strength that mattered here but momentum and leverage. Each move had its counter, locking and breaking, hooking and riding and sliding free. Some separate corner of Fionn's awareness told him that he had never wrestled so well, and that it was his brother's strength that was enabling him to do so.

As move followed move a murmur of appreciation rose from the men. The first two encounters had been merely a warm-up for this unfolding of skill, each man in turn unlocking the grip in which the other bound him. Time and again Dithramhach bore his brother down only to have the supple strength of Fionn's long limbs turn his own force against him. Earth-colored bodies slid from one hold to the next in a sequence of ascending complexity like the spirals on Fionn's shield.

Fionn's fighting had gone beyond calculation; his body reacting from instinct deeper than learned skill, always striving towards some ultimate consummation that drew from the other's opposition its power. He did not want it to end. And then, dimly, he felt the first hesitation in Dithramhach's response. His own breath sobbed in his chest as he dipped and feinted towards the other man.

End it, came a distant voice. *End it now*.

Fionn's arms went around Dithramhach's waist and the other man pulled free, thrusting away with feet and hands, but Fionn continued the movement, forcing his brother down on his belly. Dithramhach rolled, grabbing for Fionn's right arm. Fionn moved with him, seizing the other's left arm above the elbow as his own shoulder hit the ground. His lean body contracted, he arched and swung both legs high over Dithramhach's hips, landing across his brother's body with such force that the other was brought down on his back. For a few moments Dithramhach's steely belly muscles bowed him upward, holding his shoulders away from the dirt. And then, as Fionn's grip tightened, one by one the rigid muscles let go, and he bore Dithramhach slowly backward until he lay quiet, gazing at the sky.

The air shivered to wave upon wave of sound as the combatants sprawled in exhausted embrace, awareness of separate identities slowly seeping back into stressed limbs.

"Fionn! Fionn!" The syllables began to make sense at last. The warriors were cheering for *him*, as men had cheered him on the field of Tailtiu, as they had cheered him after the spear-testing eight years before. But he had fled from those victories.

Now it begins . . . , Fionn thought numbly as he lifted himself from his brother's body. *And whether the end be death or glory, I will run no more.*

But when he reached to help Dithramhach rise, it was the glory that shone in his brother's eyes.

"What happened?" whispered the other man. "Why don't I hate you for defeating me?"

"You fought *with* me, not against me . . . ," said Fionn. A glimmer of foreknowledge dazzled him. "That's how we must train the others; each man's strength challenging the next to put forth the best that is in him until every man of the *fian* is a champion. . . ." Shakily he bent to pick up the piece of amber. With stiffening fingers, he tied it around Dithramhach's sturdy neck.

"All the years I was away your love went with me," he whispered. "Will you accept this as a token of my love now?"

"By all the gods, Brother, the Sons of Morna had better tremble," said Dithramhach hoarsely, reaching out to grip Fionn's hand, "for when the Sons of Cumhal stand together, we can take on the world!"

AS THE LONG DAYS OF SUMMER RIPENED, THE HARVEST they reaped at Inber Colptha was heroes. If Dithramhach had been sullen, even the splendor of Fionn's victory would not have been enough to win the men, but Fionn's half brother bullied and cajoled with all the fervour of infatuation, and Fionn used his *fili*'s skills to inspire them as he strove to adapt the disciplines the Liath Luachra had taught him to the training of the *fian*. They were not in all cases successful. Some of the warriors were too old for the exercises, and Fionn set them to supervise where they could share their experience, or settled them in raths where folk would welcome their tales. And some of the younger ones, unable to live up to the empty boasting that had marked Crimall's slackening rule, slipped silently away. Their stories, full of self-pity and exaggeration, were intended to make Fionn out a monster, but those who understood fighting men found a different meaning in their words.

Other tales began to stir the countryside, carried from

one rath to another by the pedlars who sold embroidery thread and knife blades and beads of Roman glass from across the sea. Fionn's name was heard in the markets, and in forests where the smoke of burning charcoal filtered through the trees. The poets heard the story, and added tales of Fionn's years among the *filidecht* with a kind of rueful pride. Sometimes it seemed the stories were carried by the wind.

The son of Cumhal, the one for whose begetting his father had died, had returned to his family's *fian*, ran the tales. A man called Fionn, gifted with as many arts as Lugh of the Sidhe, was training up a new kind of *fianna*, whose every man should have as many skills as he. Fionn mac Cumhal was coming, and "Death to the mac Mornas" was his war cry. The stories were whirled through the land like chaff on the autumn wind. On the plain of Brega, the farmers were finishing their threshing when the first youths appeared before the newly whitewashed walls of the *dun*, begging admission to the *fian* of Fionn mac Cumhal.

THEY HAD KILLED A BULL TO CELEBRATE THE END OF THE harvest. The sweet savor of boiling meat billowed from the great cauldrons in the yard. Clean straw had been strewn between the hall and the huts they used for sleeping, and the men took their ease on spread cloaks or hides, downing horns of barley beer and ale. It was a calm, clear evening, with scarcely a hint of salt breeze from the sea. Fionn listened to the piping cries of the gulls winging homeward, wondering why he could not rejoice with the rest.

"It reminds me of the old days," said Fiacail, seated on a low bench to spare his old bones. "Soon enough it will not be skins and straw but fine linen and goosedown where our men lie, and the high king's cooks will boil their meat for them and brew their ale!" He belched emphatically and drank again.

Fionn's lips twitched, but his gaze continued to flicker across the crowd. In the lonely days of his child-hood, when his only problem had been balancing the demands of the Liath Luachra and Bodbmall, he could never have imagined what a strain it would be to deal with over half a hundred men. Leading the *fian* was much more like handling the hound pack of the King of Benntraige. There was never a moment, it seemed, but someone was wanting his approval or his judgment, his opinion on a new sword grip, his decision on how much corn they would need to see them through till spring.

As if they had sensed his thought, Bran and Sceolan poked their cold noses against his hand. The dogs belonging to the *dun* were squabbling over the offal by the midden, but Tuireann's children had settled them-selves at his side. Only sometimes, when a particularly delectable morsel came in view, did they give way to their longing with a faint whine.

"Very well—you have been more patient than most men!" Fionn cracked the joint on which he had been gnawing and tossed one half to each of the hounds. They caught the bones in midair and drew apart to worry at them, eyes half-closed in content.

A cheer went up as the serving lads rolled out anoth-er vat of ale. He had not done too badly, thought Fionn. Every man's hair was oiled and braided, and they were all clean. Sun-gilded skins glowed with exercise, and it seemed to Fionn that they were more at ease in their bodies than they had been a moon ago.

"I'll worry about the king's hall when I see if our discipline holds through a night's drinking," he said to Fiacail.

Fionn had dipped into the treasure in Cumhal's crane bag to give the men their festival. Another rea-son why the *fian* needed him, he supposed—the spirit who inhabited the *corrbolg* would not even open it to Dithramhach's hand.

"Well, lad, you cannot be putting it off forever," said

the old man. "If you do not go to Temair soon, the
high king will be sending Goll mac Morna to fetch
you. . . ."

"I had hoped to spend the winter training—" Fionn
began.

Fiacail shrugged. "Words have wings. Those lads
who came in this morning were from mac Morna's
fian. Do you think One-Eye will sit still while you
bewitch his men?"

"It was all one *fian*, in our father's day," broke in
Dithramhach, hunkering down at Fionn's side.

"And will be so again—" agreed Fiacail.

Fionn frowned. Several of the other men had over-
heard and were moving closer. He felt himself being
pressed for a decision he did not want to make.

"Is this the time to be discussing it, with the men's
bellies drum-tight with ale?"

"No time better," the old man said softly. "The decision must be yours, anyway. Speak to them now, when
they are mellow, and they will be convinced they persuaded you. You can manage that, surely, or what were
your years with the poets for?"

Seeking truth, thought Fionn bitterly, *and bringing
beauty from beyond the circles of the world*. But he had
sought revenge, and so, he supposed, had proven himself a man of battle after all. *Have the choices ever been
mine?* he wondered. Once his life had been ordered
by others; now others sought orders from him, and it
seemed to him that all their lives were being shaped
by a doom that moved them like players on a *fidchel*
board.

"Eh, then, Fionn, he's right," said Aghmar, who had
heard Dithramhach's words. "Ye want to go to King
Cormac and demand your place back, lead the *fianna*
of Eriu for him as Cumhal did for his grandad Conn."

"We need a home," added Reidhe soberly. "Not just a
dun we hold on the king's word or a refuge in the hills,
but a strong place of our own—of *your* own, Fionn.

Cumhal never had any place but what the king gave him, and when he ran off with your mother, nowhere to take her except the wild. Conn might have thought twice about siding against him if he had had a refuge."

"But where could we go?" asked Dithramhach bitterly. "It is only because we are a subject people that we are a *fian*. If the Gaelic kings allowed us fortresses, they would not allow us arms to defend them!"

Fionn looked at his half brother with respect. Clearly he was not the only one to whom Fiacail had tried to explain things. The old man was smiling now.

"That was true for Cumhal," he said slowly, "but for Fionn there is a stronghold, destined to be his before he was born. The white fortress of Almu is his by right of blood and prophecy. When you stand before the high king"—Fiacail's rheumy stare stopped Fionn's words— "you must claim your blood-price for his part in the slaying of your father from Tadg mac Nuada. You must ask for Almu."

You do not know what you ask, old one! thought Fionn, remembering his visions of that terrible man who was his grandfather. Those who tried to take things away from the druid died. They did not know the terrors they faced if they went against him, or the strength of Goll. And yet, even in vision, Fionn's first glimpse of those white walls had stirred in him a painful recognition. He did not need to touch his thumb to his tooth to know that what Fiacail had said was true. If he was ever to find a home in the lands of men, it would be Almu.

Abruptly he realized that they were all looking at him.

"We are not ready," Fionn said slowly. "But it is also true that we cannot wait too long. Let us spend a few more weeks in training, get those mac Morna men whipped into shape, decide whom to take and whom to leave on guard in the *dun*."

As grins began to blossom on the faces of the men around him Fionn's heart sank. One thing about having his choices made by others—he had not had to bear the pain of responsibility.

"When will we be ready?" asked Duibhne, as eager as one of the dogs. "Fionn, when will we go?"

"At Samhain—" he answered. At least at the Festival the high king's peace would keep the mac Mornas from attacking them openly. "When the people gather for the Samhain Fair, I will lead you to Temair!"

Chapter 6

❧

A T SAMHAIN, THE HEIGHTS THAT LOOKED OVER THE eastern edge of the Plain of Brega were all aglimmer with lights like some hill of the Sidhe. Even to Fionn, who had seen the Otherworld, there was something more than mortal in the beauty of the royal *dun* of Temair. Folk said the Old Ones had lived there long ago, and he thought that some of their magic must cling still. He had seen Temair from a distance when he travelled with Bodbmall to Tailtiu as a boy, but never yet come there, for all his wanderings. As he looked at the hill Fionn felt his pulse quicken despite his forebodings. It was right for him to be here, at this place that was the center of Eriu.

The palisaded walls that crowned the hill were set with torches, and more lights flickered from the great encampment on the plain below. At Samhain all the *tuaths* of Eriu sent their chieftains to Temair for the Lawgiving and the competitions and the cattle fair. The friendly scents of cows and wood smoke drifted up on the west wind as the *fian* marched down the road towards the fortress, and with them the hushed murmur of many voices, like a distant stream.

"The whole world must be camped down there!"

exclaimed Duibhne. "I cannot count the fires!"

"Lad, you cannot count at all!" put in mac Reiche, and everyone laughed. The men were excited, most of them as new to Temair as Fionn, eager to listen to the old-timers' tales.

Fionn cast a critical eye back down the line. Fifty men marched behind him, the best-trained and most disciplined warriors in the *fian*. No doubt the mac Mornas would be resplendent in embroidered tunics and fringed mantles of dyed wool, for the high king had been generous to them over the years. There was no way his *fian* could compete with them in display. Better, then, to make a virtue of difference, and present themselves as working warriors of the Galéoin, clad in a hunter's close-fitting leather sark and tight short trews. But though their gear might be simple, it was spotless, not a hair escaped their many braids, and the last of the light gleamed balefully from the heads of their well-honed spears.

Fionn wore the same gear as his men, for except for his *fili*'s gown he had no other. The sea whose tides surged within the *corrbolg* did not preserve garments, but the treasure bag had produced a handful of golden bands to finish Fionn's braids, whorled discs to rivet to a broad fighting belt, armrings, and a torque of twisted gold.

Back along the line somewhere men were arguing whether the size of the encampment was less than in Cumhal's day.

"To hear you, Aghmar, the cattle are smaller, the horses slower, even the girls flatter-chested than they were when you were young!" exclaimed Dithramhach. "That still seems a great gathering of folk to me!"

"Ask Fiacail!" said someone. "What use," came the answer, "it is too far for him to see. . . ."

"I do not need to see to know that it is smaller," the old man said evenly, and Aghmar snorted in satisfaction. "It is smaller than it was when Conn reigned here, for the new *Ard Ri* has not been proven, and the Sidhe will be trying to take the Hill back again. What has shrunk the encampment this Samhain is not time, but fear!"

Fionn stopped short in the road and had to leap aside as young Criomthann bumped into him. He could feel Fiacail's gaze upon him and realized that it was by design that the old man had not mentioned this until now, when the presence of the *fian* prevented Fionn from arguing. He let the line pass him and fell into step beside Fiacail.

"And just what form has this attack been taking?" he said with a bitterness that only the old warrior would understand. It was a pity he had not been able to bring Donait's magical armor with him from the Otherworld. But at least he had Birga and the Hazel Shield.

"Aillén mac Midhna is their champion," said Fiacail, "and his method is to lay sleep upon all who would face him, and then to burn the hill with fire. . . ."

"Good time to be visiting—" said someone into the sudden silence.

"Good time to be telling me," said Fionn into Fiacail's ear.

"Well, I've told you now." Fiacail wheezed and Fionn realized he was laughing. "And there's one thing to consider. For all his boasting, Goll mac Morna's attempts to fight this creature have all failed. . . ."

Fionn was still considering it as the *fian* marched through the gates of Temair.

THE MAN IN THE HIGH SEAT OF TEMAIR WAS YOUNG, AND with the springy strength of a young pine tree. His broad shoulders were round with muscle, his springing, ash brown hair barely confined by the golden band. Fionn blinked, realizing that he had somehow expected the old man who had been kind to him at Tailtiu all those years ago to be sitting there. But Conn was dead. This king had never known Cumhal, and for once Fionn regretted that his father's ghost was not going to come between them. The history that lay between him and Cormac mac Airt was his own doing. As Fionn passed through the doorway he wondered if the high king would remember a boy called Demne, who had run away with his glory one year at the games. . . .

Surely Cormac must have forgotten, Fionn told himself as he let the press of men who followed push him forward. And if he had not, surely they had both learned something in the years between. But remembering how furious Cormac had looked as his rival came up to receive the prize, suddenly Fionn wished very much that he had stayed in his *dun*.

For a moment, his mind full of memories, he had lost sight of the scene around him. Dithramhach jabbed him in the ribs and he became aware that a murmur of speculation was stirring in the hall as an oncoming storm stirs the leaves. Ahead of them, folk were turning. The *Ard Ri* sat above the hearth in the center of the hall like the kingpiece in *fidchel*, with his houseguard around him, and suddenly Fionn had the feeling that king and guard and the leather-clad warriors of the *fiana* who were spreading out along the edges of the crowd were all pieces in a game.

They had started serving the feast already. Fionn's belly cramped involuntarily at the rich smell of boiled pork and beef and the yeasty breath of ale and mead. Old Aghmar had been right, the high king fed his people well. Then a space opened before him and he recognized the big man standing next to the *Ard Ri*.

As if he had called his name, Goll mac Morna's head turned. The years had set frost in the fiery thatch of his hair, but the grey eye that fixed Fionn had the keen edge of good steel. Helplessly Fionn gazed back and saw in that single eye first astonishment, and then, as once long ago, fury and something that might have been guilt, or fear. Cormac was still scanning the hall, but some movement in the man beside him focused his attention on Fionn as well, and he frowned.

"It is the *fian* of Crimall—" said someone into the deepening silence.

"It is the *fian* of Fionn mac Cumhal!" Fiacail's voice corrected him surprisingly loudly. Abruptly, the last murmurs ceased. Now everyone was looking at Fionn.

"Say something, lad!" Fiacail hissed in his ear. "What use was all that time you wasted with the poets if you cannot get out the words?"

What can he do to me? Fionn thought wildly as he strode towards the high king. *His own law forbids any bloodletting at the Festival!*

He paused before the high seat, ignoring Goll's baleful glare, and stared up at Cormac, watching as the blue eyes clouded with returning memory. Then, very deliberately, he bowed.

"*Ard Ri*, I have come," he said in the time-honored pledge of loyalty, "to offer you my company. . . ."

The high king's mouth opened, then both he and Fionn jumped as the air exploded with bitter laughter. It was Goll mac Morna who was laughing, and in another instant his men began to bellow like bulls, hiccuping and hawking and pointing at Fionn and his men. The familiar anger leaped in Cormac's eyes, but Fionn thought he also saw uncertainty there.

"*Be still!*" said Fionn, in the voice he had learned among the *fili*, and they caught their breaths, gaping, even Goll. "It was to the high king I spoke; it is for himself to reply!"

Cormac's eyes widened at the sudden silence. There was doubt there now, along with the anger, and Fionn remembered how too much excellence had betrayed him before. But apparently blood and training were worth something, for in a moment the high king straightened, quelling any temptation to resume the laughter with his own gaze now.

"A generous offer indeed," he echoed mockingly,

looking from the splendidly dressed mac Mornas to the drab leather of the *fian*. "And what would the son of Cumhal be wanting in return?"

"What is due me—" Fionn replied, stung by the sarcasm. "The honor price for my father's blood, and my inheritance. I will serve you, *Ard Ri*, as my father served Conn. Give me rule over the *fian* of Temair!"

Fionn sensed movement and had already whirled aside before he understood it was Goll mac Morna whose grip was closing where his throat would have been. He faced the other man from the fighting crouch the Liath Luachra had taught him as Goll's bulk turned.

"You murdering cub! I'll kill—"

"Mac Morna, beware!" Cormac's voice cut through the older man's rumbling, "you know that death will be yours if you break the peace of my hall!"

Panting, Goll paused. One of his brothers took his arm, whispering, not Conain the Swearer, but another, perhaps Airt Og of the Hard Strokes. He looked like a man any warrior would think twice about facing on the field.

"I will keep your peace," growled Goll, "for now. . . . But this is the treacherous cub of a treacherous sire, and do I have the chance, I've sworn to deal with him as I did with Cumhal!"

Fionn straightened as he remembered how he had seen the battle in which Cumhal died through Fionnéices's memory, and suddenly he understood the guilt in mac Morna's eye. Goll believed that he, not Fionnéices, had killed Cumhal. Cormac looked from one to the other in exasperation, and Fionn felt a twinge of sympathy. *He is used to taking Goll's advice* he thought, *and he is angry at being forced to choose.*

"I have no wish to cause trouble—" He loaded the words with all the calming overtones he could manage, suppressing the awareness that invariably trouble was what he brought with him, and the better his intentions, the worse they seemed to go wrong. But he had tamed Dithramhach. Dared he hope that his luck was beginning to change? "I honor all warriors in this hall. . . ."

"D'ye take me for a fool or are you one?" barked Goll, looking him up and down. "Or perhaps—" He began to grin nastily. "Ye've brought your quarrel where ye know I can't touch you because you're afraid!"

Fionn felt the hot blood stain his face as a growl of fury began among his men.

"Be quiet, all of you—" said Cormac tiredly, and Fionn gave him a quick look, only now seeing the shadow in his eyes. "For the fool is any man who threatens death to another at Samhain in Temair. It is sunset. Have you all forgotten the other uninvited guest that we are waiting for here?"

Looking around him, Fionn could see the memory shadowing their faces as dusk was darkening the land. Eyes that had been hot with fury flickered uneasily, and for the first time he noticed the black charring on the beams where the hall had been burned and repaired. His reluctant sympathy for Cormac grew deeper. The high king was learning now what fate had taught Fionn when he was still a child—that the hard decisions always must be made alone.

"Hear then my judgment," said the high king. "All old wrongs shall be pardoned and old possessions returned for *whoever*"—his gaze raked Goll and then rested curiously upon Fionn—"will go out to the walls of Temair and slay the evil creature who has been attacking me!"

At that, astonishingly, Fionn saw Goll's furious gaze fall, and he began to rub at a mark like an old burn on his arm. *He is afraid!* he realized in astonishment. This monster must be terrible indeed to make the chief of the mac Mornas fear. But Goll had never seen the things that Fionn had faced outside Donait's hall.

"*Ard Ri*, I will fight for you—" said Fionn.

Cormac's blue gaze flickered back to him, vivid with

reassessment. Was he replacing at last his memory of the nobody who had bested him at hurley so long ago with the man that Fionn had become? Fionn, meeting that gaze, saw in it the beginning of a tempering that would turn the wilful pride with which Cormac had begun his kingship into royal steel.

"It is cold out there on the hill," the high king frowned with sudden decision. "Have you a cloak to keep you warm?"

"I do not, *Ard Rí*," Fionn replied.

"My grandfather gave you a cloak when you won at the games. Can I be less generous?"

Cormac tugged at the pin and lifted the great ring-brooch that held his own mantle away. It was a wonderful garment, woven with glowing bands of color and embroidered in silk and gold, with fringes of purple yarn a hand's span long. Men began to murmur once more as the significance of the gesture sank in.

It is a king's cloak, thought Fionn as he gathered the warm folds into his arms, and then, *the rigfénnid stands for the king. Cormac must really want me to win. . . .*

FIONN MAC CUMHAL SAT UPON THE EDGE OF THE HILL of Temair, just outside the palisade where the ground began to slope steeply down toward the plain, and remembered how he had waited outside the Paps of Anu only a year ago. One year! To him it was an age of the world, but to the Sidhe, he supposed, it would seem scarcely a day.

Then he had been the stranger, skulking outside the gates of the Mound and hoping to harm one of those within. But this time he was defending the sacred hill. There was some significance in that, but he lost himself trying to find it, and found that he was listening to the soft sounds of nightfall, with no notion what the thought might have been. It was very peaceful here, after the close heat and conflicting scents of the hall.

The smell of wood smoke and cattle drifted up to him from the encampment around the Fair site laid out below. Shouts of revelry grown sweet with distance echoed softly. Closer, there were only the scents of damp earth and grass from the hill, and underlying them all, the earth song, growing steadily more powerful as the night drew on. . . .

Abruptly Fionn realized that he had been falling asleep. He let the warm folds of the high king's mantle fall open and took a deep breath of chill air. Perhaps he should not have accepted that parting drink of mead! He got to his feet, moved a few paces along the rim of the hill, then turned back again. By the stars, the world had moved halfway between sunset and midnight. The noise from the plain and the hall had lessened, but the earth song was louder, a deep, insistent pulsing that made him at once uneasy and expectant.

The fires on the plain glowed like fallen stars, but it seemed to Fionn that on the hill the edges of each leaf and grassblade were beginning to glimmer with another kind of radiance. A red flicker followed the spirals on the Hazel Shield he had leaned against the wall; the spear, Birga, appeared as a sickly green glow. As the world moved towards the holy hour the earth energies were strengthening. By midnight, he thought, he should have no trouble seeing his enemy.

Using his spear as a staff, Fionn continued to pace, afraid of falling asleep again. He was no stranger to wakeful nights; they were part of a *fili*'s training. Could he still remember the lore that he had spent such nights learning? As he walked he began to name the tales of cattle raids and courtships, of feasts and frenzies, the stories of youthful exploits and violent deaths and all the others that the *filidh* must memorize. With Cethern he had mastered most of them, and it would not do to be forgetting. Perhaps when the *fian* lay by the hearth at nightfall he should tell them the tales.

He missed Bran and Sceolan. He had left the hounds

at the *dun*, thinking they would only have added to the confusion, but they would have been useful after all. Well, he would have to be his own watchdog now, and play Cuchulain to Cormac's Conchobar. Now that he thought of it, Cuchulain also had once had to fight a one-eyed man nicknamed Goll.

The night grew colder and more silent. At this hour, in this place, even folk without Fionn's training could feel the thinning of the barriers between Eriu and the Otherworld. He wondered what manner of being was lurching towards Temair. He wondered what his *fian* was doing, and felt suddenly very much alone.

At midnight the stars stood still above Temair. Fionn froze, eyes widening at the blaze of unearthly light that limned each stone and tree. On the Hill of Temair the air glowed where werelight danced on the ancient mounds. Light blazed from the faerie hills strung across the plain and glowed suddenly in the leys between them. He could even see the glimmer, dulled and broken in places by men's workings, of the pathway between Tlachtga and Temair. From the distance came a rising rush and a whisper of hoofbeats and he knew that the Samhain Riding of the Sidhe had begun.

But here there was no sound but his own heart's beating. Fionn forced himself to draw breath, awareness drawn inward by that hypnotic rhythm. *Dub, dub . . . dub, dub . . . dub, dub . . .* he heard it . . . heart drum, earth drum . . . all existence pulsed in a single dance as that drum beat on. When he was a babe in the womb he had heard it; when he was a pig in the forest; when he was a salmon in the stream. His thumb burned in memory, and unthinking, he set it to his mouth to cool it once more. . . .

Brightness blazed as a different dimension sprang into being around him. *Dum, dum!* throbbed the drumbeat. *Dum, dum!* Blinking, Fionn stared at the figure that was striding up the glowing road, fire-colored cloak streaming out behind him, the glitter of gold on breast

and arms and waist less brilliant than his eyes. In one
hand he held a little *bodhran* like the one Bodbmall
had used sometimes when she sang her spells. He was
beating out that compulsive rhythm upon it with what
looked like a human bone.

"*A song of sleep . . . dreams dark and deep . . . thy
souls shall keep. . . .*"

The drumbeat carried a whisper of song. Even knowing what he faced, Fionn found himself swaying. He
had been prepared for terror, but this being was fair
beyond the strength of mortal sight to see.

"*No man shall know . . . the road I go . . . nor see nor
show. . . .*"

"*I* know!" his protest croaked across the music. "I see
you, Child of Danu!"

"Dost thou indeed?" The singing ceased, but the
drumbeat continued, and in the Other's speech there
was scarcely less music. "And who art thou, to separate thyself from the song?"

Fionn's mouth opened; at the last moment he stopped
himself from saying the name he had finally come to
know as his own.

"I am the Child of the Hollow Tree—"

"*Root and tree . . . All I see . . . hark now to me. . . .*"
The singing fed Fionn's thirsty soul like sunlight and
springwater. "I am the music of the Forest . . . sleep and
dream. . . ." His voice grew softer.

Fionn swayed, his feet sinking into the ground as if
he were rooted there. He was a man, he must think like
one. . . .

"I am the *Gilla* of all crafts—" he whispered. "I have
the craft to defeat you, man of the mounds!"

The glowing figure grew larger as it approached,
or perhaps it was simply growing, like the Red-
Mouthed Woman, until it blazed above him. "Only
Lugh Samildanach can make that claim . . . and thou
art not he!" The music merged into soft laughter.

"I am Béo's bane—" Fionn protested, but he was

finding it hard to focus on the colors that shimmered before him. At his answer, they seemed to intensify. He had seen that rainbow radiance before; his senses resonated with echoes of ecstasy.

"*Fall . . . all . . . shall . . .*"

The blood roared in his ears and fire blazed up before him, whirling the world away. Fionn *remembered* that fire.

"I am singer of the Salmon of the Boann—" he cried. "*Samhain! Samhain, sacred season, frees the ways between the worlds!*" As once before, the poetry poured through him, reordering reality. His mind was his own once more but his body stood stupid as the champion of the Sidhe drew closer.

"*Hurled is the Spear its prey pursuing, through all illusion cutting clear!*" he cried, and the spear in Fionn's hand quivered like a live thing. The touch sent sensation surging through his bones.

"*Sidhe blood! Need blood! Feed blood now!*" clamored Birga, drowning out the shining song. Fionn took a deep breath and brandished the spear.

"Halt here, Wild One! This time you shall not pass! I am the speeder of the poisoned spear—"

"Birga! Birga!" thundered the faerie warrior. "Thou art the slayer of Aedh mac Fidach, and I have thee now!" He brightened blindingly, the fair form lengthening into a serpent of flame. From its jaws shot fire. Fionn flinched, flailing with the king's cloak in an instinctive attempt at protection, and the bolt tore it away and buried it, stinking and sizzling, twice a man's length in the ground.

Sound battered Fionn's ears as the serpent swayed above him and he could not tell if it were drumming or laughter or the roaring of a fire. The sinuous coils brightened; in a moment it would blast him again. Fionn leaped and rolled towards the wall, knocked over the Hazel Shield, and came up again with its strap in his hand.

Fire washed over him, but the shield deflected most of it. A sudden mist of light blazed from its bosses, surrounding him and the grips seemed to mold themselves around his arm.

> *"I am the hero's true ally*
> *The shelter of the strong am I;*
> *Whatever weapon's willed at me,*
> *In striking sets my own force free!*
> *I am Hazel, hallowed Tree—*
> *Between the worlds I ward the way!"*

Poetry pulsed from the shield, adding its bitter harmony to the keening of the spear until Fionn could no longer hear the fire serpent's song. He staggered to his feet, peering over the shield's rim, and it seemed to him that his foe swayed backward.

"You know it, don't you?" he muttered. "You recognize the Hazel Shield. Go back to your mound, Bright One—I will not let you pass!"

"This land was ours," hissed the fire serpent. "Ages past, the Sons of Mil stole the sovereignty. . . ." The flame shrank, consuming its own color in an intensification of brightness. Fionn blinked, blinded, then curled into the shield's shelter as flame billowed over him once more.

"This is the center. Who holds Temair holds Eriu . . ." the sibilant hiss continued, "and each new high king must defend his right to rule." Once more the flame contracted, but this time Fionn was ready. As the fire rolled towards him he thrust up the shield and deflected it in a shining wave that arched above the hill.

"For six years neither the king nor his champions have been able to withstand me. This is the seventh year—with this victory we win Temair for the Sidhe, and the dominion of men will be done!" The serpent shape became a concentrated rod of light and Fionn braced himself, knowing that the fire this time would be more furious than ever before.

And then the world exploded in light and sound whose intensity crushed Fionn beneath the shield as it went on and on. Even with that protection the heat was an agony, but anger filled him with its own flame. Gasping, he jabbed upward with his spear.

There was a sound as awful as the one that had overwhelmed him, but thinner, and a sudden relief from pain as the fire recoiled.

"Creature of Chaos, you shall not pass!" Fionn rasped through a throat scraped raw by a scream he had not even heard. "It is the Champion of Eriu who tells you so!"

It seemed to him that the flame was wavering. He took a stumbling step forward, brandishing Birga, and wonder sent new strength surging through him as the serpent shape withdrew.

"*Blood and fire . . . feeds desire. . . .*" whispered the spear. "*Blood and fire . . .*"

Fionn felt the first twinge of regret as he brought Birga back into position and the flame recoiled once more. He had been angry when he killed the murderer of Oircbél, but there would only be sorrow in destroying this bright being, even though he was a more terrible enemy.

"Go back, Flame of Inis Fáil. You shall not enter here." Spear poised, Fionn strode forward, and the fire serpent gave way before him.

They were on the shining path now, the road of the Sidhe that led away from the royal hill. Pursued and pursuer moved ever faster as Fionn pressed harder; swift as the Sidhe sped Fionn on the path between the worlds. Faerie folk swirled like sparks around him, but with each step Fionn felt his power grow. The fire serpent rippled like a ribbon of light before him, seeking the safety of a glowing hill.

The gold-bound doors of the *sid* began to open. Fionn

lunged forward, felt the shock as his spear tip pen-
etrated his foe's brightness and pinned it against the
side of the mound. The fire serpent flared wildly, but
it could not move.

"It is Fionn mac Cumhal who speaks for the *Ard Ri*
of Eriu. Swear!" he said hoarsely. "Swear to me that
you will never again attack Temair!"

A sighing like a ring of untuned bells went through
the glimmering hosts that had gathered. The flame grew
incandescent, pulsing with such pain and fury that
Fionn almost dropped the spear.

"It is Aillén mac Midhna who replies . . ." came the
answer, and Fionn was transfixed by the beauty of his
glowing eyes. "The Champion of the Tuatha Dé will
never take oath to a mortal man! How dare you threat-
en me?"

"*If you release him,*" said a still voice in Fionn's soul,
"*he will come back as soon as you are gone. . . .*" But
this was no goblin like the things Fionn had fought
outside Donait's hall, but one of their great ones, and
who, after all, was he?

Fionn's fingers tightened on the shaft of the spear,
and then, with a groan, he thrust it into the flame.

Fire flared outward like an exploding sun as two
mutually exclusive realities tried to occupy the same
space. But as vision fled, Fionn saw dissolving into the
light the radiant features of his enemy, and through
the clap of thunder that destroyed all sound, heard a
woman's wail: "*Aillén, oh my son . . . he has killed my
son!*"

WHEN FIONN CAME TO HIMSELF ONCE MORE HE WAS
sprawled upon the damp grass of the Hill of Temair.
He was not dead then, though when he rolled over,
his aching muscles made him wonder if perhaps he
should be. Then he smelled something burning, and
tensed, wondering if he had slept after all while the
monster burned the hall. But the logs of the palisade

rose unmarred above him. It was the spear, Birga, that was singeing a black spot in the grass.

Grimacing, he pulled himself upright. The sky was still dark, but he could smell the damp wind of dawn. He pulled the Hazel Shield towards him, then the spear. He could feel the heat of the spearhead without touching it, and in the gloom the smooth metal had a dull glow.

"Are you wanting to be the spear of Gorias, then, with your head in a bucket of water to keep you from burning up the world?" He gave Birga a shake, then used the shaft to haul himself to his feet again. "I am not Lugh, you know." For a moment he listened, but could hear only a deep, satisfied humming from the spear. "So—" Fionn sighed. "At last I have found something to content you. Enjoy it—you'll not get such a meal again!"

He lifted the spear butt and banged it against the gate of Temair. This time he had not failed, he thought numbly, and knew himself at last released from his grief for Oircbél.

It took a few minutes for someone to answer. From enchanted sleep the folk of Temair had passed to normal slumber. As Fionn walked through the *dun* he saw others, as stiff as he but not nearly so sore, rubbing sleep from their eyes and staring at him as if Aillén had conquered after all.

The high king reached the meadhall just as he did, for he and his men had abandoned it, no doubt expecting their new champion to fail.

Fionn stepped aside to let Cormac precede him.

"Did you win?" The high king frowned.

Fionn grinned in response, and wondered why the warriors backed away. The embers in the long hearth were dead. Still grinning, he stuck Birga into a charred log, and almost instantly, it burst into flame. Suddenly the meadhall seemed full of people.

"It was Aillén mac Midhna who tormented you," he answered. "But Birga has eaten his fire."

"What proof have we?" asked someone, not in the first row of men.

"What proof do you need?" said Fiacail. "For the first time in seven years you've wakened on Samhain morn without your meadhall smoking about your ears."

"That I succeeded is no dishonor to any who tried and failed to meet this foe—" Fionn said then, looking at Goll. "No mortal courage would have been sufficient for this battle. I was able to resist him only because I am both *fennid* and *fili*."

"Do you want me to make you *rigfénnid* now?" asked the high king. In his face Fionn could see fatigue, and relief that warred with a dawning awareness of all the problems that keeping this promise was going to cause. Behind Cormac, Goll was glowering balefully, and for a moment Fionn almost pitied him.

"I thought that was why you sent me out there—" he said slowly. "I thought that was why I agreed to go."

Fionn looked around him, and saw them all wondering what manner of man could defeat the champion of the Sidhe. But all that had happened to him had begun to make sense when he looked into Aillén's glowing eyes, and even for Dithramhach and the men of his own *fian* he could not dissemble anymore.

"It hardly matters what title you give me," he went on. "Cormac mac Airt, you are the soul and the center of the land of Eriu. But I have walked in the Otherworld. In the forge of knowledge have I been tried. Of smithcraft and wordcraft and warcraft I am the master, and against all foes that may come against you, I"—he hefted the Hazel Shield and felt it murmur softly beneath his hand—"am your shield. . . ."

Chapter 7

❦

THE WINDS OF THE YEAR'S TURNING HUNTED GREY clouds across the sky as the *Ard Ri* of Eriu and his warriors chased the deer. But the wind blew unhindered from the west while the human hunters soon found themselves struggling in scattered groups through the thick woodland. Fionn could have sped from one end of the forest to the other and killed his deer as he passed in the time it had taken the men of Temair to pick up their first trail. If he had been hunting deer, their clumsiness would have angered him. But Fionn's quarry on this grey autumn day was the laboring pony he was pacing, and the man who urged her through the trees.

"My grandfather never told me about the challenger," said the high king, reining the mare around a fallen oak. "I knew to watch out for the chieftains of the Ulaidh, and . . ." Cormac paused as the pony buck-jumped tangled branches, "rebellion from Laigin. Conn never told me to fear the fire of the Sidhe."

"Perhaps it was something else, in his day," said Fionn, leaping the tree in turn and lengthening his stride to catch up with the king. Cormac had offered

116

him a mount for the day's hunting, but Fionn had only laughed at him. "The poets say that he used to walk each day upon the ramparts of Temair, watching for the Fomor and the Sidhe. . . ."

The chill air was heavy with the scents of wood smoke and wet leaves and oncoming rain. Fionn strode out eagerly, feeling new strength flow into him with each breath. He had been spending too much time within walls.

Cormac reined in suddenly, frowning. "My grandfather certainly walked the walls at Samhain. Now I remember. He must always have wondered if the challenger would come back again."

Branches snapped as horsemen crashed through a thicket ahead of them; from farther away came the yammering of hounds, and fainter still, the rattle of leafless upper branches in the wind. But here, in the lee of a great oak tree, it was suddenly very still. Without even thinking about it Fionn noted the gouges where a pig had rooted for oak mast a day ago, the trail where a fox had passed beneath the holly, a field-mouse tunnel in the frost-killed grass.

"Aillén will not return. . . ." Fionn answered the question in Cormac's gaze. What he read in the high king's face was not fear, but anger at a situation he could not rule. He remembered that Cormac had always wanted to be in control. In a boy among boys it had been exasperating; it sat better in a king. "Nor will his kin. The challenge was defeated. They know now that to reach you they will have to go through me."

"Why?" Cormac asked baldly, and the pony pawed nervously at the ground. "You were not exactly eager to help me at the games of Tailtiu."

Fionn felt himself coloring, remembering how he tried to bury his grief for Bodbmall by walloping the hurley ball between the goals, regardless of teamwork or the wisdom of deferring to the high king's heir.

He hoped that they both had learned something since then. In the distance a hound gave tongue as it caught the scent of a deer and the mare moved restively, but Cormac held her still.

"At Tailtiu, both of us were after the same thing," Fionn said carefully. He grounded his light hunting spear and leaned on it, looking up at the king.

Cormac straightened, tension going out of him visibly as he exhaled with a long, gusty sigh, and the pony began to nose at the dry grass.

"You belong out here, don't you?" He gestured at the woods around them. "When you stop moving you seem to blend into the branches, and I can see the relief of it shining in your eyes. On the playing field of Tailtiu, we were nearly"—he grimaced—"even. In my hall I am your master. But out here, I am in your power. Why do I not fear you, Fionn mac Cumhal? Is it because I sense that even could you attain it, you would not want the high seat of Temair?"

Fionn stared at him, dizzied by a new awareness. He touched his thumb to his teeth and suddenly the knowledge became words.

"I live on the edges," he said, wondering, and there was only a memory of bitterness in his tone. "I will never be entirely at home among the *fianna* or the *filidecht*; in the Otherworld or even in the world of men. You are the center. Without you, I would not know where the edges were at all. But you need me to know the limits of your law."

He drew breath, meeting Cormac's blue gaze with his own, reading the ambition and calculation and truth in that sun-browned face as he had read the tracks beneath the trees. "Against all that lies beyond I will defend you," he said softly. "That was a true offer of service I made you, lord of Temair."

"I do need you—" Cormac's voice had gone hoarse with sudden passion. "If I am to *be* the center, the four fifths of Eriu must be as obedient to my law all the year round as Temair is at Samhain. When I was a boy I wanted to be a hero. Now I want to be a king. They praised my grandfather because he brought peace to the land, and good harvests. I cannot have the *fianna* breaking my peace with their squabblings. When you faced Goll mac Morna I felt like a bone being eyed by two dogs."

As if in answer, they heard the insistent bellow of Goll's horn. Cormac's frown returned, but Fionn grinned up at him.

"*Ard Ri*, I have a way with hounds. Do you make me your *rigfénnid*, and I will find a way to bring Goll mac Morna to heel!"

Cormac's face was still grim. "Fionn, I have not forgotten Tailtiu. But when you speak I hear my dreams. Tame the mac Mornas, and you may call yourself what you will!" His face changed, and Fionn realized that the high king was laughing.

THEY CAUGHT UP WITH THE MAC MORNAS AS THE SKY WAS beginning to release the first few spatters of rain. At the edge of the wood the hounds had surrounded a stag of five tines, gaunted from the autumn's mating battles, but a worthy quarry for a king. He stood now with head a little lowered, breath gusting in moist puffs in the cold air. The dogs had been pulled back, whining, but the men who had taken their places, the mac Mornas on one side and Fionn's men on the other and the Gaels of Cormac's household caught uneasily between, were bristling more furiously than the hounds.

Cormac's glance flicked from one group to the other as he reined in, and he sighed. But Fionn, remembering his words, saw the humor in it suddenly.

"Here's a fine rack of bones to feed your hounds," he said softly. For one moment their eyes met, and then the high king fell to coughing to hide his laughter.

Fionn moved swiftly to Dithramhach's side and some of the tension went out of his own men, but Goll glared balefully. The stag, scenting a change, lifted his head in challenge. Raindrops glittered in the thick hair that covered his mighty neck and along the ridged hairs over his spine.

"Stand back, my lads—" Fionn said softly as Cormac slid off his pony and untied his spear. "This is kingly prey!"

The *Ard Ri* chose his position with care, and Fionn thought that if he had had the training of him Cormac might even have been good enough for the *fian*. The stag, seeing his movement, began to turn; he leaped in the same moment as the spear flew.

Cormac was already rolling away from the slicing hooves as the spear scored the stag's side and rattled away among the leaves. Goll started forward, but as the high king came upright, Fionn tossed him his own spear. The stag whirled away from the mac Mornas, and Fionn's side of the circle bristled suddenly with spears. But Fionn himself leaped to meet the deer, evading the fore-hooves with a lithe twist as he reached for the antlers and jerked, so that the stag was held for just the one moment it took for Cormac to strike him through the heart with Fionn's spear.

The deer fell, thrashing, but Fionn stayed with him, and as they hit the ground he drew his knife swiftly across the beast's throat, holding him as the force went out of his struggles and the life from his eyes with the crimson blood that reddened the fallen leaves.

"*Ard Ri*, it is your kill—" Fionn said softly.

"*Rigfénnid*, it was your spear—" Cormac grinned at him, then whirled at the roar of rage that erupted behind him.

Another spear whipped through the air and Fionn, still kneeling, batted it aside with the same simple, instinctive skill that had saved him at his testing by the *fian*.

"Hold!" cried the high king, but Goll only shook his grizzled head, hefting his second spear.

"I swore to have his life!" growled the mac Morna.
"And you cannot stop me. Samhain is past, and we are
not in Temair!"

Cormac's face changed as he looked around him, seeing the two *fians* facing each other at the edge of the
wood not like dogs, but wolves in the falling rain. His
angry gaze went from Goll to Fionn, and he nodded.
*He has just remembered that we are not in his king-
dom now*, thought Fionn as the *Ard Ri* took one step
back, and then another, to stand with the men of his
own household who had come out from Temair. For a
moment there was no movement but the fall of a last
leaf plucked free by the rain.

"Dithramhach, be still," said Fionn softly without
looking behind him. "This is between Goll and me—"

Goll's second spear came with blinding speed, but
Fionn had seen the beginning of his movement, and
in the same instant was rising, reaching for the spinning shaft, letting the momentum of the spear whirl
him round. He came to rest with Goll's spear poised
in his hand.

"You swore to kill me as you killed my father," Fionn
said clearly as Goll reached for his shortsword. "But
you did not kill Cumhal. . . ." With a disdainful gesture, he cast away Goll's spear.

Goll froze, his single eye glittering. Rain pattered
loudly on the leaves, washing the stag's blood away,
but no one stirred.

"Goll," Fionn continued more softly, "do you recognize the sword that hangs at my side?"

There was a murmur from some of the older men.
Cumhal's sword . . .

"It was lost," said Airt Og. "After the Battle of Cnucha
someone carried it away!"

"Fionnéices took it," said Fionn. "The *fili* who
praised you, and who taught me, and who in the
end tried to kill me as he had killed my father, with
Cumhal's own sword . . ."

"But we fought—" began Goll, rubbing at the ruin of his lost eye as if the memory pained him.

"To a standstill," Fionn agreed. "Until your wounds felled you. I have seen it through Fionnéices's memory. It was then, as you both lay senseless and bleeding, that the *fili* took the sword."

"It was not an act of honor, to kill an unconscious man. . . ." said Airt Og slowly.

"It was not, but the sword avenged it when the *fili* tried to kill me."

"I woke . . . and Cumhal lay dead beside me. . . ." Goll did not seem to have heard. "From my left eye I wept blood, from my right eye tears. . . ." Goll was weeping now, his remaining eye dark with memory, even as the skies wept for pity at the pains of men. "But he was gone. . . ."

"And I am here," Fionn said gently. "Aedh mac Morna, a mistaken oath cannot bind you. Will you, who once loved Muirne, kill her son?"

Goll shrugged and shivered, still struggling with memories, but his hand had slipped from his sword.

"Take up the stag," came the voice of the *Ard Ri*. "Tonight we will feast fallen heroes and new alliances in Temair." Cormac pulled himself up onto his pony and reined her towards the distant hill, where the torches were already beginning to glimmer through veils of rain, and no man disputed his word.

THE SCENTS OF STEWING VENISON AND WET WOOL AND spilled beer filled the feasting hall, but for once Fionn did not mind them, having consumed enough of the high king's mead so that his perceptions were comfortably blurred. The rest of his *fian* were well beyond that state, matching drinks with the mac Morna warriors and toasting a future dim in detail but in outline unreservedly glorious. Even Cormac had shed the slight stiffness that he seemed to feel proved his authority, and was belting out the chorus to an obscene song about a dru id, a herd girl, and a sheep, just a little off-key.

Only Goll still stared morosely at the memories reflected in his drinking horn. His wife had curled up on the feasting couch beside him, though most of the women had left the hall for the relative peace of the *grianan*. She was a a plump, sensible woman with ash-fair hair and fine, freckled skin, and meeting her had raised Fionn's opinion of Goll. Her frown deepened as she saw him watching.

I have not won him entirely, thought Fionn. *Hatred like that carves out a home in the heart. He will be looking for something to fill the emptiness. . . .*

The bawdy chorus ended, and Cormac called for more ale.

"The druid and the sheep!" Fiacail, stretched on a couch on the king's left, was still cackling. "She fixed him!" He peered around at Fionn. "And when will ye fix the druid that's after you, lad? Old Tadg owes you the price of your father's blood. When are ye goin' to Almu?"

The silence around the high king was sudden and absolute. Only Fiacail was still grinning, and it came to Fionn that the old man understood exactly what he had said.

"Almu!" Goll raised his head and eyed Fionn suspiciously. "Are ye blood mad or just crazy? It was to Tadg mac Nuada that I swore to kill you, and I risk my head already, letting you go. At least I've the sense to stay clear of his magics. You'll not maze him with sweet words, *fili-fennid*, as ye did me!"

"You want to claim blood-price from *Tadg*?" Cormac fixed him with a suddenly sobered gaze.

Fionn sighed. Truly, he wanted nothing of the kind, but he supposed it must be faced someday.

"*Ard Ri*, what do you think will happen when my grandfather hears that you are naming me *rigfénnid* of Eriu?"

Silence spread as men sensed the change in atmosphere around the king. Warriors who had been drinking like bound brothers eyed each other with sudden suspicion, and surreptitious glances slid towards the weapons hung on the wall.

"It is me you have been mazing!" Cormac's voice was soft but furious. "When you tricked me into that promise, you knew what it would bring!"

"Cormac—" Once more Fionn pitched his voice to bring ease. "Look around your unburnt hall. Would you be lying here now if you had not made that promise to me? Tadg is a terrible foe, but he did not, or perhaps he could not, protect you from the Otherworld!"

The anger went out of the high king's face and he rubbed his eyes. "It is so," he said wearily, "but if you think a command from me will make Tadg give up his fortress you overrate my power. Almu is yours if you can take it, son of Cumhal, but look for no assistance from me!"

And that, thought Fionn, was a hard admission from a man of Cormac's breed. He had been humbled several times in the past few days, and had taken it remarkably well.

"You are a warrior," growled Goll, "I'll grant it. But you are a fool if ye think a half-fledged *fili* can go up against the druid of Almu. For sure I won't go with you. I have no quarrel with Tadg. The *fians* should be joined, but maybe 'twould be safer if they followed me. . . ."

The high king's gaze came back to Fionn, calculating, but not very hopeful. *He knows me well enough already to realize I'll not roll over for that one*, thought Fionn with a flicker of amusement.

"Have you not?" Fionn ignored Goll's final words. "What about the compensation for your lost eye?"

"It was Luchet's blow destroyed it, and I killed him!" Goll answered furiously.

"Is it compensation to break the blade that wounds

you, and do nothing to the hand that wields it?" Fiacail put in.

"But it was Cumhal who started—" Goll began.

"Not the battle!" the old man interrupted him. "Tadg swore that Muirne had been abducted unwilling and refused the compensation that Cumhal offered him. Tadg wanted the blood of the man who stole his daughter's love. He was the cause of the battle of Cnucha where you lost your eye!"

"Tadg set you and Cumhal against each other . . . ," Fionn added softly. "Tadg broke the *fianna* because it was prophesied that a child of Muirne would take Almu. I am that child, and even Tadg cannot deny what his own arts have said must be."

For a few moments more Goll sat glowering, his blunt features a battleground for fury and fear.

"You might as well go with him," Goll's wife said softly at last. "The old man will be angered enough with you already. Let there be an end to him, and the old feud, at last!"

"Well—" Goll cleared his throat, then glanced up at Fionn and away. "Well, I suppose it will be a fight for the poets to sing about—"

"It will at that," answered Fionn, grinning at him. "Come with me to Almu and it is myself that will be singing, if no one else wants the task!"

He joined in Goll's answering laughter, but he remembered the eagle gaze of the man he had seen in so many visions, and he knew that Goll had been right to be afraid.

"WE'LL CAMP ON THE PLAIN THERE, BELOW THE RISE—" Fionn watched critically as the file of warriors curved off the road and began to trample a new path through the thick grass, mottled with patches from which oncoming winter had leached the green. It had taken them a week to get ready, and most of another to move the combined *fianna* southward. He would have to do something about that when this was over and the lot of them firmly under his hand. A *fian* was not much use if it could not move fast.

There was no question which rise he intended. The Curragh was the largest expanse of grass in Eriu, and the oak-crowned ridge to which he had pointed almost the only thing to break a flat sweep of land that stretched to the line of hills. Once more Fionn found his gaze drawn towards them. Beyond lay the Forest of Gaible, where he had grown up. But the pass that led through them was guarded by a tree-covered hill called the Chair of the Kings, and facing it, the fortress-crowned Hill of Almu. The two peaks seemed innocent enough in the afternoon light that hazed the hills, but even against the glare Fionn could make out the gleam of white walls. Tadg was there, and by now he must know who was setting up camp upon the plain. Sighing, Fionn looked back at the ridge and noted the skein of smoke unwinding above the trees.

"Who lives there?" he asked Fiacail. He knew the land to the west of the hills well, but he had been forbidden to come onto the Curragh in his boyhood wanderings, nor had he dared ask questions of Bodbmall.

"That's Druim Cliadh, the clay ridge—" came the answer, and then, when Fionn still showed no reaction, "Did you not know, lad? The shrine of Brigid is there!"

Fionn's eyes narrowed in speculation. He did not know how the priestesses felt about their bad-tempered neighbor, but their Goddess had shown herself Fionn's friend.

"They'll be curious about us," he said quietly. "I should go speak with them once we're settled here."

"You think maybe they'll help you?" Fiacail laughed, but Fionn frowned, wondering.

FIONN WENT TO THE SHRINE AT SUNDOWN, LEAVING GOLL in command of the *fian*. With the older man he still had to go carefully, but his methods seemed to have worked, so far. Goll was much less prickly when he had work to do, and it was true that there was no one else who could have controlled both the mac Morna men and his own. Dithramhach had been only slightly mollified by being asked to escort him, along with Fiacail.

Dithramhach thought Fionn should have killed Goll when he had the chance. He still did not trust him, and resented the way the big man seemed to be moving into the position of second in command that he had thought his own. It had never occurred to him that Fionn could only become *rigfénnid* through an alliance rather than a conquest of the other *fian*.

Crows flapped heavily homeward across the plain as they turned up the path. The remains of earthworks circled the ridgetop, overgrown with oak trees. Through the bare branches the thatched roofs of buildings could be seen. The scent of wood smoke was borne down by the breeze, and with it another scent that stirred old memories.

Bronze clappers clanked from the neck of the queen-cow as a herd was driven home. It was all so peaceful, and so ordinary; hard even to believe in battle on such an evening, much less in the kind of forces Fionn suspected his grandfather could command. But the path beneath his feet was paved with small reddish stones. Suddenly he knew that if he were to walk around the shrine he would find other pathways, whose stones were gold, or greenish, or blue-grey. A shiver lifted the hair on his neck as he remembered the glowing paths he had seen once as a child in Donait's magic fire.

He held up a hand to halt the others. He understood now why it was the red path that was leading him up this hill. For the past year he had been a man of war, even when he battled Aillén and fought for Donait in the Otherworld. But he would need to be something different for the battle that was coming. Eyes still closed, he took a deep breath, striving to shift his perceptions.

He became aware of the earth song first, so strong he could not imagine how he had shut it out before. He felt the shifting tides of power as the world turned towards nightfall, felt the boundaries of his own body and the forces that moved through it. And now he recognized the scent that had puzzled him. It was the warm sweetness of baking bread—the kind of bread he had eaten in Donait's hall.

"If you're finished napping, somebody is waiting for us up there—" Fiacail's voice in his ear brought Fionn abruptly back again.

A woman in a crimson robe was standing at the entrance to the shrine, watching them. Fionn took a deep breath and led the others up the hill. As he got closer and saw the silver hairs among the russet, like ash in the darkly glowing coals of a forge, he realized that despite her strength, she was not really young. She was looking at him, he thought, as he would look at a youngster seeking admission to the *fian*.

"A blessing on this place and those who serve it," said Fiacail as they reached the gateway.

"A welcome to you and your companions," came the answer. "If you seek us in peace you must leave your weapons at the door. I am called Achtlan."

Fionn had only a sword belt with his knife and his father's sword, and Fiacail his staff, but Dithramhach, who had taken his duty as bodyguard seriously, disarmed in an angry clatter of metal as shield and spear and sword were surrendered and several concealed daggers appeared from hiding places in his garb.

"How do you know the old man has not witched them, living here so close under his eye?" he grumbled as he set the last blade down. "What if there's an ambush waiting in there?"

It was certainly a possibility, but Fionn could see the amusement in Achtlan's eyes deepening.

"Why then, Brother, we'll wrestle them down!" He laid his arm across Dithramhach's shoulders as the other came upright, and after a few moments the other man began to grin back at him. "Trust me. I sense no treachery here," he added softly as the woman gestured for them to follow her.

"I suppose you would know—" his brother began, then fell silent as they came out from among the trees. Within the earthwork, a scatter of whitewashed roundhouses curved around an inner enclosure of holly. Women moved purposefully among the buildings, sparing scarcely a glance for their visitors.

"Put you in your place, don't they," remarked Fiacail. "Reminds me of Bodbmall. There are always nineteen of them here. The sacred fire burns on a hearth inside that holly hedge. But they won't let men inside."

Fionn was still frowning as their guide drew aside the cowhide that covered the entry to the largest of the buildings and gestured for them to go in. Two women sat waiting on the other side of the fire. As Fionn and the others made their greetings, Achtlan took her place beside them.

"So the son of Muirne has come to us," said the oldest. "He has her eyes."

"And his brother, the son of Cumhal," said the third, a thin girl with amber hair who reminded Fionn oddly of Aonghus mac Conail, the *fili* who had befriended him long ago.

"Fiacail mac Conchinn we know of old," the eldest replied. She was bent like an old tree, but the wreath of sweet herbs that crowned her white hair was green.

Fionn was getting tired of being discussed like a bull at a fair.

"Achtlan has given us her name," he interrupted, "or should I be addressing you as Banba, Fodla, and Eriu?"

The thin girl laughed. "Only if you wish to make a claim on the land. But I think that the land has already claimed you. The wise one who sits beside me is Airmedb, and I am Ceibhfhionn."

"Or you can call us Brigid . . . ," the oldest priestess said with a smile that reminded Fionn painfully of Donait.

Fionn's breath caught, for suddenly he did see in each of them a reflection of the Goddess, as one might see a mother differently imaged in each child.

"You may have wondered about the army that is camped in your pastures," he said abruptly. "We have come here to beg your help. Tomorrow we attack Almu—"

"Indeed—but sit down, warriors, you tower over us like trees!" Achtlan smiled. "Here are bread fresh from the oven and milk fresh from the cow. Eat and drink. Before we discuss such grave matters you must accept our hospitality—"

She poured milk from an earthenware pitcher into three bowls as Ceibhfhionn turned back the linen cloth that covered the bread basket and passed it around. The milk was warm and foamy, the bread fine and light enough to make Fionn think himself back in Donait's hall. Airmedb was reminding Fiacail of some joke they had shared in the past while Achtlan complimented Dithramhach on the weaponry he had given up so unwillingly. In moments, it seemed, the other two had passed from suspicion to laughter.

While they ate, Ceibhfhionn took up a small harp and began to play. Fionn felt muscles he had not known were tense releasing. He tried to remember the danger that had brought them to this place, but he had no sense of anything but safety here. Even Dithramhach had lost his scowl, and Fiacail looked younger than he had in years.

Deep within, Fionn felt a flare of anger at being manipulated by women once more. His brother had been right to warn of witcheries, but Fionn knew that it was a magic far older than his grandfather's druidry that held them now. Why would they not let him speak of his need?

He looked from one woman to another until they were all watching him, and then, very deliberately, set his thumb between his teeth and bit down.

The hearth fire flared up between them and the figures of the three women, seen through flame, flowed into one. More radiant than the flame that formed her, stern and fair, Brigid herself looked down at him. She was taller than humankind, but the house that confined them had also disappeared, and Fionn stood now in an enclosure ringed by a holly hedge with his back to the narrow building where they kept the holy things, facing the fire.

As always, when he saw her it was as if no time had passed. He remembered all the visions she had shown him and the choices he had made. And as always, he had no words with which to entreat her, only an inarticulate outpouring of need.

Brigid gestured, and Fionn saw Almu upon its hill. As the light grew, points of brilliance moved around it; he recognized the gleam of spear points and the bosses of shields. His men were attacking! With dreamlike swiftness the battle unrolled before him. He saw the gate breached, then a wave of shadow that brought with it horrors that made even the creatures he had fought for Donait pale. Fionn understood that Brigid was showing him what he would have to face if he attacked Almu; for warriors of flesh and blood such a fight seemed hopeless. But there had to be something he could do!

Despair closed his eyes. When he reopened them, the scene had changed. He was looking down at the clay ridge, but instead of roundhouses an odd building of whitewashed stone stood with the holly hedge behind it. The scene changed, and he knew he saw the unrolling of the years, but still the sacred hearth fire burned, served now by women in black robes.

The building was rebuilt, larger. Men in strange armor marched across the plain. Then, though the building stood, the holly hedge was torn down, the sacred fire scattered, and shadow swept over the world. But it seemed to Fionn that those sparks, tiny, flickering, but never quite dying, were still burning in a thousand hidden corners all over the land.

He stared and realized that the sparks of light formed a pattern. It was the face of Brigid, and there was a question in her eyes. He struggled to answer her.

What do you want? What do you want from me?

The light grew brighter, grew until its intensity was pain. And then, suddenly, it was only fire, and Fionn was looking at the three priestesses through the veil of flame. His lips were still moving.

"What do you want from me?"

The other men looked at him in surprise and Fionn realized that he was weeping.

"Your oath to defend the holy flame . . ." Airmedb replied.

Shuddering, Fionn got himself under control. "Against what?"

"Against all who would extinguish it . . ." said Achtlan.

"Forever . . ." added Ceibhfhionn.

"It will be a short forever if Tadg mac Nuada kills the lad tomorrow in Almu—" Fiacail objected, but they did not seem to hear.

"Since the time of Nemed we have tended the fire that burns in this shrine, counting the long cycles of the moon. The Temples of the Sun have sunk back into the plain, and kings no longer climb the hill of the Chair to claim their sovereignty, but the Goddess remains. Eriu will prosper as long as Brigid is honoured and we maintain her holy flame," said Ceibhfhionn.

"But Tadg has always feared our magic," added Achtlan. "He would be glad to see us gone, but the people love their Goddess, and he can do nothing as long as their faith is sure. Long have we studied his devices, but we cannot leave our circle to use that knowledge against him."

"But we can!" exclaimed Dithramhach. "Give us the spells!"

"A time may come when the people forget us, and Tadg, or one like him, will seek to destroy Brigid's flame," said Airmedb, ignoring him. "We have waited for a warrior who is willing to be her defender. Are you that one, Fionn mac Cumhal?"

Fionn stared back at them. Had he not been, always? Was this any different from defending Donait's hall?

"I will swear," he stretched out his hand over the flame, "by the gods of my clan and kin. So long as I live or am remembered, the flame that wards Eriu will burn."

The fire billowed upward and his companions scrambled back, but to Fionn the flames were a silken tingle across his skin, and their roaring a voice like harpsong that whispered, *"My love for your promise, my fire for your soul!"*

Fionn blinked, feeling as if he had been on a great journey and come home. Even the thought of tomorrow's battle could not disturb him now. He looked at the priestesses.

"Brigid has shown me what magics Tadg will use against us. Tell me what I must do. . . ."

Chapter 8

I N THE HOUR BEFORE DAWN THE PLAIN OF THE CURRAGH stretched away towards the hills like a rolling grey sea. The grass was dew-heavy, soaking shoes and leggings; gorse and broom drenched those who blundered into them with icy showers. Only Bran and Sceolan seemed to be enjoying themselves, bounding joyously ahead of the warriors who marched towards Almu. Fionn thought of grey mornings when he had gone out after waterfowl and longed for the marshes of Gaible when all he had to fear was Bodbmall's sharp tongue and the Liath Luachra's hard hand.

He looked back at the dim shapes toiling after him and sighed. He had hoped to have his men in position before the sun rose. He quickened his pace, passing Dithramhach and Duibhne, saw before him Goll mac Morna's broad shoulders and his helm with the red horsetail streaming down.

"Easy, lad," said Goll as Fionn forged past, "unless you mean to tackle Tadg all alone, I have seen the horrors that guard him through the hours of darkness. We do not want to be arriving there before the sun."

"I know . . ." Fionn sighed and slowed, matching the heavy tread of the older man.

134

Goll turned his head to survey him. "Your father would not have listened. Neither would I, when I was your age!" He gave a grunt of laughter. "Not, mind you, that listening's a bad thing. It's madness enough, being here at all. . . ."

Fionn frowned, trying to figure out if that had been a compliment. From ahead he heard a flurry of barking.

"If those two young idiots have started a hare I'll throttle them—" Fionn began, but already he could see the black blur where Bran stood on guard, and Sceolan was speeding towards him, whining. "Keep the others back—" he said as they came up with the dogs.

"What is it?" asked Goll, stopping the next group with a wave of his spear. "I don't see anything there—"

Nor did Fionn, but the dogs, with hackles bristling, were circling. He was certain now that Tuireann's children had retained their ability to see the things of the Otherworld, and by their movements he could tell where the creature must be.

"The priestesses of Brigid told me Tadg might leave watchers. Watch it, lads—don't let it go—" The dogs settled to a stiff-legged crouch, pointing. Fionn untied the sheath that kept Birga quiescent, slipped it off, and felt the spear shaft quiver in his hand.

"*Thirsty . . .*" came the immediate response. "*Feed me now!*"

"Can you see your meat, gluttonous one?" muttered Fionn, swinging the spear towards that distortion in the grass. Goll looked at him oddly, and then at the spear. "Be ready," he said more loudly. "I'm going in—"

And with that word he was moving, arm swinging in a smooth arc that the spear completed, letting the weapon's own balance determine the moment to set it free.

Screaming, Birga drove down. Suddenly there was a flurry of motion; a sparkle of sickly light flared and a thing like a cross between a serpent and a wolf reared upward, flailing. For a moment they saw it clearly;

then it dimmed and dissipated into the mist, and Birga clattered to the ground. The two dogs ran forward, barking gleefully, as Fionn stepped forward to reclaim his spear.

Birga was humming happily, but Fionn did not hood it again. "I think that Tadg has set some traps for us," he said to Goll. "We'll have to go slowly now. Bran, Sceolan—good lads! Dear hearts, you have done well!" He bent to fondle the hounds' silky ears. "Range ahead of the warriors, my children, and tell me if there are any more!"

Three more of the spectral beasts fed Birga before they reached the foot of the hill. The fourth disappeared before Fionn could cast the spear. For a moment he thought the thing was afraid of him, then the mists brightened, and he realized that behind them the sun was rising in the east of the world. He raised his hand, and the host behind him halted, and through the retreating mists they saw for the first time clearly the gleaming walls of Almu.

"ARE THEY REAL?" ASKED FIONN, STARING UPWARD. IN THE early sun, points of brightness blazed from the bronze-banded leather helms of the men who peered over the wall.

"Most likely—" Goll answered him. "The old man kept a respectable household. Not *fian* warriors, but good enough for the kind of battle we'll have here."

Fionn nodded. An uphill assault against a strongly defended position was not the kind of fighting at which the *fianna* would shine. The ramparts were a smooth slope of timber-braced earth with a palisade and guard platforms spaced along the wall. Below them, the hill fell away steeply on three sides. On the west the slope was easier, but the massive wooden gateway would be heavily defended. His gaze narrowed as he looked back along the wall and he wondered suddenly if he could cut the odds.

By the time the sun was well into the sky, Goll and most of the combined *fianna* were massed before the gate on the *dun's* western side. Fionn, clinging to the northern hillside with a score of his youngest and most agile men, could hear their shouting, and the rhythmic boom as they tried to batter the gateway down. Most of the defenders on the walls above them had disappeared. Fionn hoped that they had gone to defend the gateway. He heard screaming; they must be throwing things down from the walls at Goll's men, but the pounding went on.

Feeling dreadfully exposed on the gorse-covered hillside, Fionn, with his shield buckled to his back and Birga jammed through its straps, scrambled upward.

"Duibhne?" he whispered as they reached the rampart. The boy clambered up beside him, the coiled rope over his shoulder. "Give it your best try, lad—" He gestured at the wall.

Carefully the coil of rope was laid out, and Duibhne straightened, the free end with its iron hook swinging from his hand. Once, twice, the grapple whirled, and on the third swing shot upward, knocked against the wooden logs, and fell back again.

"Again, quickly," hissed Fionn, ducking. "We're not knocking at a door!"

Duibhne's breath came quickly, but already he was gathering the rope back into its coil. A second time he swung, the hook flying outward in a gleaming arc. There was a clunk, hardly audible against the clamor from the gateway, as the hook lodged between two logs. Fionn reached for the rope, but Dithramhach was before him.

"Let me scout for you, Brother—"

Fionn started to argue, but as Dithramhach set his hands on the rope to begin the climb, Fionn saw the rope slacken in his hands. They dodged to either side as the grapple plummeted back again. Laughter came from above and he glimpsed someone moving behind the palisade. No hope for the hook now. As many times as they cast it the man above would fling it down.

"We'll have to climb!" He reached out to the wall, then stopped, feeling a warning tingle in the palm of his hand.

"What is it?" gasped Dithramhach, pulling himself up again.

There was a reason that the druid had felt safe in withdrawing so many men from the palisade. It was the walls themselves into which Tadg had woven his magic. Fionn had been afraid of this, but the lower rampart slanted just enough to make climbing possible, and there was no other way now.

"There's sorcery in the walls. Hang on!" Fionn got a good grip on his daggers, stretched, and struck them through the whitewash that covered the wall.

Agony flared through the blades and into his hands. He heard someone cry out and fall, pulled himself upward, plucked one knife free, reached and struck again. It was like grasping a red-hot iron bar, but working in the smithy had accustomed him to such pains. A spear hurtled down from above and there was a scream. But still he reached and struck and pulled.

A rending crash echoed from the other side of the *dun*. Goll must be almost in, and unless there was some distraction, the moment when he and his men came through the gate would be their most vulnerable. Fionn wrenched his long body upward in a last effort, touched the rough wood of the palisade, and gasped as the pain in his hands disappeared.

A face appeared above him. Steel flared in the morning light, but Fionn's knife was already driving upward. Red gushed as the blade went into the man's throat. He fell, ripping the weapon out of Fionn's hand. In a moment another man sprang up to the parapet to replace him, but Fionn grabbed a log and hauled himself up, slashing with the other knife as he scrambled over the wall.

A kick dislodged the next man, who fell into the one who came after. Fionn freed his spear, and the two warriors who were running along the parapet towards him stopped short as Birga's wicked point swung towards them. He had a moment's glimpse of clustered buildings with dizzying spirals patterning their white walls, laid out as in the drawing the priestesses of Brigid had made in the ashes of the fire, and a cloud of dust from the gate beyond them where Goll was breaking in. Then Duibhne clambered over the palisade, the rope still slung over his arm, with Dithramhach at his heels. As Fionn leaped down from the walkway, Duibhne was looping the rope around a log and throwing it back so that the rest could follow them.

The clamor from the gate crescendoed. Fionn jabbed two-handed at the first warrior who came at him, and at the taste of blood Birga came alive in his hand. He wrenched the weapon free barely in time to knock aside the spears of the next three; almost of itself the spear whirled and spitted them as well. Then Duibhne and Dithramhach were beside him, taking out the other two. Fionn shrugged the Hazel Shield onto his arm, and yelling, they ran around the cookhouse and into darkness.

It must have happened when the gate was breached, thought Fionn as he strove to distinguish friend from foe. A spear came at him and he parried more by instinct than sight, thrust, and felt Birga's satisfaction as its point sank in. He heard curses and the clatter of weapons and Goll's battle cry. From the direction of the gate came barking, and he whistled sharply.

Something huge and dark reared up before him. Shouting, Fionn ducked, and felt wind stir his hair as a swordblade whipped by.

"Is that you, lad?" came Goll's deep rumble, and a fear Fionn had not named retreated once more. "Sorry. Can't see my hand before my face in this murk, even if I had two eyes. What's that wretch done to the sun?"

Fionn jumped as something warm and furry pressed against his legs and a cold nose poked into his palm.

"You had no trouble finding me, did you, lads?" he murmured, and understood suddenly what was going on. "It's a spell," he said to Goll. "Nothing's happened to the light; our minds won't let us see. . . ."

"Did those witch-women give you a spell against it? We'll all be killing each other soon!"

"Call the men," Fionn told him. "Form a circle of shields; make each man give a swallow's nest-call before you let him in."

Goll gave a growl of laughter. An incongruous twitter of bird-song replaced the battle cries as Goll gathered them. It was a signal used among the *fianna* when a scout came in, not easy to learn.

Fionn shut his eyes, trying to remember what Achtlan had said to do.

"Fire blaze in the forge—" words formed in memory. "And might in the mind! Give life to the steel, and light to the blind!" He brought Birga up and around in a symbol that hung glowing in the air. Then he blinked, for though the symbol faded, the spearhead still shimmered eerily. The light had not returned, but objects had a pallid radiance. He could see Goll's blunt features, the flat circles of the shields.

Most of the druid's men were sprawled in the dirt before them. Fionn had parried Tadg's first blow, but his grandfather's malevolent presence was still strong. He scanned the dim shapes of the roundhouses, wondering in which one the old man had gone to ground.

"Dithramhach," he said softly, "we'll scout the first house. You others, be ready to come running if I call. Goll, I want you to divide your people into groups for the other buildings and do the same."

"I'm coming with you," said the older man. "Ferdomhain can lead my men."

Dithramhach was glowering, but Fionn grinned. Whether Goll was coming to protect him, or because he feared to face Tadg alone, he found himself suddenly glad to have his old enemy at his side.

"Stay close together and watch the dogs. They'll see truth that evades our eyes. . . ."

There was nothing in the first building but scattered clothing and gear and a strong smell of old ale. He supposed it had housed the men who lay dead outside, and one more, who rose up from his bed muttering delirious challenges and was instantly spitted on Goll's spear.

Fionn thought at first that the second building was for washing, because of the great tub of water in the center of the floor. Then he realized it must be a wellhouse, though the priestesses of Brigid had not mentioned it. His grandfather would not be hiding here. He turned to tell the others, but the words died, for he could no longer see the door.

There was a soft splash as Goll plunged his spear into the well. For a moment they stood in silence. Then they heard a gurgling from somewhere far below, the smooth surface heaved and began to pour smoothly over the rim.

"My feet are wet!" exclaimed Goll. Liquid was spreading in a darkly shining sheet across the floor. Even as they looked, it poured out more swiftly. Goll splashed backwards, swearing. Suddenly Fionn recognized the odor and gagged. For it was blood in which he was standing—all the blood shed in the world was flooding into the room.

"We can't get out! We'll drown!" cried Dithramhach.

Fionn touched Birga's tip to the dark liquid. There was a horrible hiss of steam and he felt a quiver of pain run up the shaft. Fionn shuddered at the idea of something that could quench even Birga's fires, and Sceolan began to whine.

"I think so too, lad," Fionn grasped the dog's collar.

"Let's get out of here. Come on, show me the way!"

The blood was to his waist now, warm and viscous, and it was growing hard to move. Fionn could still see nothing, but when the dog stopped he jabbed outward, the spear thunked into wood and a spark of light flared long enough to show the latch of the door.

Fionn dodged aside as he stepped through it, afraid the rush would wash him away. But the only thing to emerge from the well-house was his companions, and neither of them had even a wet toe once they touched the ground.

"Well, that was amusing," said Goll, and Dithramhach laughed shakily. "What shall we do now?"

"Try the next one—" Fionn answered grimly, and led them on.

THE SECOND HOUSE THEY ENTERED WAS ABLAZE WITH SUN-light that poured through an opening in the roof. They paused in the entry, squinting into the glare.

"It is a *grianan*—" said Goll, "but where are the women?"

Fionn frowned, for the priestesses had mentioned no women in Tadg's household. Then the light dimmed, as if a cloud had passed across the sun, and suddenly the women were there.

They were all naked, but that was the least of it. The locks that curled on the shoulders of the nearest were writhing serpents, and tears of blood ran from her eyes. Her spindle had a sharp point like a spear, and the wool she was spinning was human hair. The second was old, the bones of her skull stretching the skin, and when she smiled receding gums showed them horse-teeth, yellow as bone. Her pendulous breasts flapped to her waist; her sex was hidden by a trailing mat of nether hair. She was embroidering on a piece of leather, but blood ran each time her needle pricked the skin.

Then the third turned, laughing hideously, and

Dithramhach swore, for this one stared at them from a single eye and stood on one leg, and with a single arm she stabbed the weaving sword between the threads of a loom strung with human intestines, and weighted with the severed heads of men.

"Hail to the heroes!" said the oldest of the hags. "Are they not a fine lot, sisters—see the stout legs on them, and the strong arms!"

"Would you like to lie with me, warrior?" crooned the woman with serpent hair, offering her breasts with sharp-nailed hands. "Am I not what you have always been seeking?" She smiled, and her teeth were fangs.

"Fionn! Touch them with your spear!" whispered Dithramhach. "Make them go away!"

Were the hags real? Fionn touched his thumb to his teeth instead, and shuddered, for his Sight only made the horrible vision more clear. There was only one way Birga was going to make these creatures disappear.

"They do not want you. . . ." the old woman's greasy locks swung back and forth as she shook her head. "Perhaps they fight not from bloodlust, but from greed—"

"Have you brought us skins? Have you brought us wool?" sang the first female sweetly. "It is you who supply fodder for spindle and frame and loom."

"Give me more guts, warriors!" cried the one-eyed woman, and the oldest cackled after her, "Give me the hides of men!"

Gorge rising, Fionn lifted his spear. The one-legged woman swiveled on her foot and fixed him with her single gaze.

"I am the Weaver—" She smiled dreadfully. "I am the Maker of the Tapestry. You have not even looked at it, champion. It is your own life I am weaving. Have you no curiosity?"

Unwillingly, Fionn looked, and saw a tapestry like the ones that had hung in Donait's hall. He saw a boy dressed in animal skins striking a fair lad down; he saw the same lad throwing an old woman into a lake. One scene seemed to melt into another; he saw an older boy standing over the body of a man in *fili's* robes with a red sword in his hand. They were his own deeds, all of them, with the red blood-thread binding them into one terrible image that he could no longer deny. And still the scenes were changing. He saw himself upon a hundred bloody fields.

"Say truly, O men of battle, are we the monsters, or you?"

The spear wavered in Fionn's hand. Goll groaned like a man with a gut wound and turned away. Dithramhach sank slowly to the floor, hiding his eyes. Fionn stiffened defensively, then realized that they were not looking at him. The horror in the eyes of his companions was for themselves.

The hag lifted her weaving sword in a mocking salute, and in that moment he found the resolution to heft Birga again, and throw.

With dreamlike slowness the spear seemed to float across the room. Then the bright point pierced the woman's breast. There was a shriek like the world's ending, and the women, the loom and frame and spindle, and the light itself all disappeared.

"SWEET MOTHER OF LIFE!" DITHRAMHACH EXCLAIMED when they had gotten themselves outside once more. Goll's face was still grim with memory, and Fionn wondered if Cumhal's dead eyes had reproached him from the tapestry. But Fionn did not ask either man what he had seen.

Still shaken, he listened to reports from the other groups as they came in. Most of the buildings had been searched, and they had lost many to horrors real and illusory, but no one had found the druid's lair.

There remained only a few storehouses and the feasting hall.

"Tadg's pride would not allow him to hide behind cabbages," said Goll dourly. "He must be in the hall."

"Let us go with you!" said Reidhe, but Fionn held up his hand. The men had been needed to break into the dun, but he suspected that for what remained, he would have done better alone.

"A small group will move more easily—" he answered, knowing he would not be able to make Goll and his brother leave him. "Watch and ward."

A BURNING STICK POPPED LOUDLY AND FIONN JUMPED, winging to guard. Nothing at all had challenged them as they entered the feasting hall, and he did not trust this stillness. Carefully he poked at the fire and jumped as he glimpsed the blurred outline of a fur cloak wrapped around a figure that might have been a man. Sceolan stiffened beneath his hand, but neither dog made a sound.

"Tadg mac Nuada!" rumbled Goll, "is that you, man, skulking there?"

"Goll mac Morna, is it you who have stained with blood the gate that always opened to you as a friend?"

The voice was as gentle as the whisper of wind in the treetops; clear as the sound of a single drop of water falling into a pool. Fionn felt cold all over. He had been braced to combat illusions of consummate artistry, to meet horrors beyond imagining. But that soft, still voice filled him with a dread greater than anything he had ever known. He understood then that he had been right to spare Goll. This motionless figure in the shadows was his real enemy.

"Dark Druid, come forth to face me." Even a *fili*'s training could not keep Fionn's voice from cracking. He took a step forward, gripping his spear. Tails tucked, the dogs pressed against his legs, trembling.

"Three warriors against one old man—do I dare?" The soft chuckle made Fionn's skin crawl. "Gladly would I have welcomed you, but you have claimed admittance somewhat unkindly. . . ."

"We met your welcomers," Goll spat into the fire, "at the gateway, and on the walls."

"What did you expect, when you came against me in arms? But it is done. Will you be seated, men of the *fian*?"

Fionn tensed as the tall figure stepped into the uncertain illumination of the hearth fire. The druid was leaning on a carven staff, though Fionn doubted he needed it. It was hard to tell what strength might be in that long body, shrouded by the furs. Wolfskin and weasel swung from the old man's shoulders, and fox pelt and fisher, all the cunning beasts of prey. But as Tadg came into the light, it was the sweep of eagle's wings crowning him that one looked at, and the eyes, bright and piercing as the eagle's, that burned from beneath the beak of the bird.

Tadg seated himself slowly, as if he understood how any sudden move would provoke men whose spear shafts trembled with the effort they were making to stay still.

"Goll, Dithramhach stand fast—" This time Fionn's voice was steady. "This challenge is for me."

And now he too stepped into the circle of firelight and caught the moment's widening of the druid's golden eyes. Would Tadg be seeing Cumhal, come back to haunt him? Or, like the priestess of Brigid, would he recognize Muirne's smile?

"Grandfather, I greet you without anger, though little is the love you have ever shown to me!"

Tadg slumped, as if the hatred that had upheld him were draining away. Now Fionn glimpsed the glimmer of the white robe beneath his furry mantle, and a gleam of silver hair.

"What chance did I have, and you filled from birth with tales against me? With lies Cumhal courted and cozened my girl, and with lies the witch-women raised you to hate me."

"You are wrong, old man—" Fionn said bitterly.

"What Cumhal said to my mother I cannot know, but until I was fourteen years old I did not even know my parents' names!" He sat down.

"And was not that the greatest lie of all?" Tadg asked gently. "Did Bodbmall *ever* speak truth to you?"

Not if she could help it! Fionn bit back the words, wondering how the old man had known just what would set the old hurt to aching anew.

"I have grown accustomed to mysteries," he said aloud. "I no longer even care why you sought to destroy your daughter's child!"

"Kill you?" The druid's voice was tremulous with astonishment. "My own blood kin? Is that the tale you have been told?"

"Liar!" Goll interrupted harshly. "You begged me to kill the boy as I sat in this very hall, not seven years ago!"

"You are a fool, mac Morna, trying to deny your own guilt by ascribing it to me!" The druid's dark gaze silenced Goll, and his attention returned to Fionn. "And you a greater, if you trust him!"

"Then let the past ransom the future," said Fionn. "If I am your heir, give me the price of my father's blood and my mother's pain. . . . If you want me to believe you, Grandfather, give me Almu!"

Their eyes met in a silence like the moment before two armies clash, and Bran and Sceolan tried to burrow beneath Fionn's legs, whining. Instinctively, he felt for the grips on his shield. Now, surely, the attack would come.

There was a sound, shocking in the silence. Tadg had begun to laugh.

"My heir? Surely the dun should go first to Muirne if we are talking of inheritance. And why not to her two sons after?" Spittle flew from the old man's lips as he laughed. "Fionn the fool, why do you look so betrayed? Did Bodbmall never tell you that your mother abandoned you? She married King Gléor Lamraige and has borne him two sons. And since she stayed to raise them, I suppose she must love them better than she ever loved you!"

"*Everyone has a father . . . well, a mother, anyhow*—" Boys' mockery stabbed his memory. And then his own reply, "*I am alone. . . .*" Fionn's eyes blurred.

"You are alone. . . ." The soft voice was like an echo. "She did not love you. No one could love you, no one ever will. . . . Alone you will wander forever, and no man will know your grave. . . ."

Dimly Fionn was aware that Tadg had risen, but what did it matter? The hounds growled anxiously as the tall shape moved around the hearth, but Fionn felt the cold of death gather round him.

"Better to sleep than to suffer—" The voice was like music. "Sleep now, sleep safely, my child, and let go of the pain. . . ."

And Fionn nodded, for he heard in that music a long-lost memory.

Words came to him: "*Sleep now, sleep safely, O child of my heart. . . .*" A woman had sung them. He remembered a fold of violet-colored cloth, seen through half-closed eyelids, and auburn hair backlit by the fire. Even then he had recognized her pain.

That was my mother, he understood suddenly, *and it tore her heart to leave me there.* Later memories gave a face to that shape in the darkness, and he knew now why, when he had tended the fire in King Gléor's hall, he had so pitied the sorrowful queen. Neither of them had recognized the other, and if Muirne had borne more children since then, it did not dry the tears she had shed so long ago.

Fionn's eyes flew open. "She loved me!" he breathed. The old man was almost upon him. He leaped to his feet, and the druid staggered back as he shouted, "My mother loved me, old man, and everything you say is a lie!"

The air crackled between them. Tadg swung up his staff, but in the same moment Fionn had raised his shield. He felt the hazel quiver at the force of the magic it was absorbing.

"*I am Hazel, sacred Tree!*" Surely even Goll and Dithramhach must be able to hear its song. Certainly the druid did—he sprang back, glaring.

"Do you challenge me here, on my own ground?" Tadg rasped, as much in disbelief as in anger. In answer, Fionn took a step towards him, and astoundingly, the druid backed away.

"Do you recognize this shield? Do you sense the hunger in this spear?" Fionn came after him. "Your power is all in the mind, isn't it—and since mine has resisted you, you cannot touch me with your petty sorceries."

The druid's gaze swept desperately around the hall, like a badger Fionn had cornered once outside its hole. Fionn had him on the defensive, but he knew that the old man would try to savage him as he went down. Once more he advanced, and the druid skittered sideways, his furs flapping around him.

"Kill him—" muttered Goll, hefting his spear.

"There has been too much killing," said Fionn, and he did not know whether it was pity or revulsion that stayed his hand. "I have no mind to add another panel to that hag's tapestry. Dithramhach, get ahead of him and open the door—"

Hackles bristling, Bran and Sceolan herded the druid towards the entrance to the hall. Fionn heard a mutter like stormwind from outside as the door was opened, but it ceased as the druid of Almu was driven out into the light of day. The old man paused, squinting around him, and fingers fluttered in the sign against the evil eye.

"I give Tadg mac Nuada his life, as he yields to me the fortress of Almu—" cried Fionn, pushing through the door after him.

"I will not—" The druid's cry became a croak as

Fionn's speartip hooked his headdress and flipped it away.

"Your day is done, old man—" Goll's deep laughter rumbled through the air. "Be grateful it's not your head on that spear!"

Trembling with fury, Tadg started to lift his staff, and with a single swift motion, Fionn knocked it from his hand.

"I strip you of your stronghold, and I strip you of your power!"

Birga caught the strap that closed the druid's mantle, Fionn wrenched, and as the leather parted, Bran and Sceolan darted in, gripped the fur in their strong jaws and jerked it to the ground.

The old man glared around him, wisps of silver hair flying in the sudden breeze.

"Do you think so?" he shrieked. "Slay me, and my blood will poison the ground!" He tore at the neck of his white gown, baring a bony breast to the pitiless sun. "Spare me, and you will wish you had killed me when you had the chance!" Wind sobbed in his chest as he drew breath, and Fionn felt a new prickle of fear.

"This is my curse on all these wretches who have followed you! Since you let me live, it is their blood that will water the ground!"

"What other death does a warrior seek?" rasped Goll, but in his voice Fionn could hear the strain.

"My curse on the bitches of Brigid who counselled you," Tadg hissed then, his bony fingers jabbing eastward towards the shrine. "Beyond death my hatred will haunt them, till their sisterhood is scattered like the embers of their stinking fire!"

"Enough!" Fionn found his voice at last. "Begone, old man, and carry your venom into the wild. We have no use for you here!"

He could feel Birga straining towards the old man's chest. Tadg felt it, too, and stumbled backwards, where the warriors were drawing aside to leave an opening.

One reluctant step after another he took through that corridor of bloody shields and pointing spears, towards the shattered gate and the dark sweep of the forest below.

"And this is your grandsire's blessing, Son of Cumhal!" Tadg clung to the gatepost, his voice rising with each word. "Love you shall find, and lose it. As great as the honor you earn shall be the hatred to which it turns. Clan and kin and followers will all desert you, and in your old age you will wander homeless, because you have taken my home from me!"

Then he let go and stumbled down the hill, but the echo of his words seemed to hang in the air long after he had disappeared.

IN THE HOUR AFTER SUNSET, FIONN STOOD ALONE UPON the parapet of Almu. Night was wrapping the world in darkness, but the western sky still held a memory of vanished fires. From the hall behind him came shouts and laughter as the men broached another ale cask. Tadg's storehouses had been well supplied, and his conquerors were glad to drown their memories of the day. But the air inside was too close, the singing too raucous. As if his grandfather's curse had already touched him, Fionn found himself unable to celebrate what he had won.

"No stomach for the ale? Or for your victory?"

Fionn turned in surprise, recognizing the shape of Goll's broad shoulders and the jut of his beard. He had not known the older man could sound so kind.

"Was it a victory?" asked Fionn. "Thanks to you I have all that I fought for, but if you asked me just now I think I would give you the *fian* back again."

"I would not take it—" Goll turned, and his remaining eye caught the last of the light. For a time they stood together in silence, until they heard the first owl among the trees. "Fionn mac Cumhal, do not be doubting your victory," he said then, almost too softly to hear. "You have won my loyalty. Let that content you for now. . . ."

Fionn stared, trying to read Goll's expression in the gathering gloom, and abruptly something that had been frozen by his grandfather's curse was melted by an uprush of pure joy.

"Content I will be"—he reached out to grasp the other man's hand—"if you will come back to the hall with me. Let us show those sots inside how champions of the *fianna* of Eriu hold their ale!"

Interlude

❧

EVEN IN THE FOREST, ONE MIGHT SOMETIMES HEAR what passed in the lands of men. Swineherds took their pigs to the great fairs and came back full of gossip. Charcoal burners heard news from the smiths, who had learned it from the warriors who came to buy their swords. The warriors themselves rode out from their *duns* sometimes to seek the wild boar or the lordly stag, and the little dark men who guided them listened to their words. Even in the shadows of the forest that skirted the high massif of Ben Bulben, the great mountain that looked out over the western sea, one was not quite cut off from the world.

When the high king took to wife Ethne Taebfada, the daughter of the king of Leinster, word came to the people of the forest. And when, having guaranteed peace in the south through treaties with his new wife's relatives, he moved north against his unruly clansmen in the Ulaidh, news of those wars came as well. For a dozen years Cormac was constantly fighting, moving westward to subdue restless chieftains in Connachta once he had the Ulidians under control. Word came of his battles, and of the exploits of the *fianna* who fought for him, and of their leader, Fionn mac Cumhal.

And occasionally word passed back out from the forest. The wandering hunters were the first to notice that smoke was coming from the cave at the roots of Ben Bulben. But no animal would approach the place, and the prickling of the scalp they felt when they neared it was enough to keep the men away as well. The charcoal burners were bolder. It was they who discovered that it was no bogle, but a man who lived there, or perhaps something more than a man, for he seemed older than the mountain, gaunt and bearded, swathed like a shadow in dark robes.

They called him Fer Doirich, the Dark Druid, for he was a worker of magic, able to brew potions of amazing efficacy in exchange for a fresh-killed salmon or a haunch of deer. And for gifts of stoutly woven wool or a well-honed knife, he could set a spell of finding on a staff, or accuracy on a bow. People talked; the stories grew. While Fionn fought in the north for the high king, the folk of the west traded tales of the Dark Druid of Ben Bulben and his strange powers.

"MY THANKS TO YOU, WISE ONE—" THE WOODCUTTER was babbling. "Well I know ye've better things to be doing with Samhain coming on, but three babes have we lost, changed in the cradle by the folk of the mounds for wizened things that did not live till spring. And the little maid my woman bore at Midsummer is as fair a child as one could hope for. If we lose her, I'm thinking my wife will go as well, and that's the truth of it—"

The Dark Druid handed him the sun cross of rowan and hazel withies he had twisted together, making a sharp gesture that stilled the man's tongue. Leaves of betony and wild garlic were woven into the figure, and oghams cut into the wood to empower the spell.

"No being of the Otherworld will pass your doorway while this hangs there," he said harshly. "Now be gone!" Once he had had a daughter, but something worse than the folk of the Otherworld had stolen her away.

"Wise One!" The man ducked his head and waved behind him. "Yonder I have tied the bull-calf we promised you . . . and you wanted news," he added. "They say the *fianna* is going home—the high king has sworn peace with his northern cousins, and Fionn and his lads will be wintering at Almu!" A glance from beneath the druid's bristling brows silenced him, and clutching the sun cross to his chest, he darted away.

"Charms to scare away the Sidhe-folk! Potions for barren women!" The old man's sudden shout frightened the crows that had been perching in the leafless oak tree into awkward flight. "Hedge-magic that any witch-woman could do as well!"

He took a swift step forward and stopped, staring eastward as if his dark gaze could penetrate the trees. "And Cumhal's murdering brat will feast his dogs in my *dun* while I moulder here!"

As his voice sank to a whisper, the crows began to settle back into the branches. The human was only talking to himself. They had heard it before.

The sun was setting red as a coal behind the twisted network of the trees. The walls of Almu would blush like a maiden's cheeks in the last of that light—Almu the fair, his fortress, his home. But no force of arms or magic could wrest it from the evil one who had raped it from its rightful lord. If he wanted to destroy Fionn mac Cumhal, the Dark Druid told himself, the wound would have to come from within.

"When he loves as I have loved he will be vulnerable . . . but whom will he love?" Frowning, the old man turned back to his cave. Samhain Eve was a time between times, when past and future were one. Foolish girls sought to see whom they would marry by sleeping with charms beneath their pillows and watching nuts pop in the fire. Perhaps he could use the power that at this time flowed so freely for a greater magic.

*   *   *

IN THE FOREST THAT LAPPED THE SKIRTS OF BEN BULBEN, barren branches rubbed together in the wind with a sound like scraping bones. The wind was restless, rising and falling in fitful gusts like dust that billows behind the hooves of galloping steeds. But the horses whose hooves raised that Samhain wind were no beasts of this world. It was power that blew through the world at the Samhain riding of the Sidhe, when the ancient mounds gaped open and there were no barriers between Eriu and the Otherworld.

The witch-wind whined about the crags and slid inquiring fingers through the crevices that ventilated the cave. But the aromatic smoke that rose from the Druid's hearth repelled it. Magic herbs were in that smoke—madwort and betony, heyriffe and cleavers and enchanter's nightshade, and the wood of sacred trees burned in that fire. Shrouded in the wet hide of the young bull, the druid's body lay beside the fire, but his spirit roamed between the worlds. . . .

HE KNELT BESIDE THE SACRED SPRING WITH TWIGS OF HAZEL in his hand and drew a circle upon the moist earth with a line dividing it.

"Between the worlds upon this ground . . . between the years by wisdom found . . . to name Fionn's mate these staves be bound!"

Unmoving, he stilled his spirit till all awareness narrowed to the circle on the soil and the staves in his hand. And then, between one breath and the next, his fingers jerked of themselves and the sticks of wood went flying.

A quiver ran through his body, and the Dark Druid opened his eyes. Most of the staves had scattered outside the circle, but four of them lay in parallel lines to the right of the line.

"*Saille* . . . Willow . . ." came the whisper as he let out his breath again.

Then he gathered up the sticks once more. A second time he stilled, and a second time threw. This time only one of the sticks fell inside the circle, crossing the line. "*Ailm* . . . the fir tree . . ." The druid nodded and took up the staves. The next throw brought up the lines for *duir*, the oak and lastly, *Beth*, the white birch, came to his hand.

"S . . . A . . . D . . . B . . ." He paused, the staves still in his hand, for those sounds made a name. *Sadb* was a maiden, the daughter of Bodb Derg, whose hill rose beside Loch Dergdeire on the Sinnan. He was a great power among the Sidhe, big and blustering and a re-knowned warrior, himself a child of the Dagda. Sadb came of high kindred indeed. And she was his favour-ite child.

On any other night, she would have been as hidden as the lands across the western sea, but tonight, all worlds were one. Fer Doirich's spirit rose to the chal-lenge, daring even the wrath of the Sidhe for the sake of his revenge. Grinning mirthlessly, the druid began crafting the spell that would bring her, and moved through the forest like a shadow, cutting lengths of the designated woods and inscribing them with the oghams of Sadb's name.

At the corners of a square he set them; drew a line from one to another to complete the spell. He stood before the trap he had fashioned and then he began to sing.

> "*From ice and fire together twined,*
> *From lonely heart and cunning mind*
> *are spun the spells that spirits bind—*"

Even in the world of men those syllables would have been powerful. Here, they throbbed in the air, but so subtle was the magic that in all of faerie, only one being heard.

"Winter cold and winter chill,
The fire is frozen, soul is still,
In prison fashioned by my will!"

The Dark Druid sang as the stars wheeled across the sky towards dawning. Between the poles a pale mist was forming, white as death, cold as winter. It filled the trap that Fer Doirich had fashioned. And in the last chill hour before the daylight, the maiden came.

One moment the space between the staves was empty; the next, Sadb was there, slim herself as a willow wand, her hair flaming like fir boughs blazing on a fire, and white of skin as the silver birch tree. If the strength of oak was also somewhere in her, the druid could not see. She took a swift step, but the cold within the square was sapping strength and will. Chill mist swirled around her and the flaming glory of her hair began to fade. She lifted her head like a startled doe, staring at him from huge dark eyes.

"Who are you? What do you want with me?"

"It is Samhain," he said smoothly. "Do you not seek to know whom you will love? I know the hero who is destined to love you. . . ." With a druid's magic he began to paint a word picture of Fionn mac Cumhal, with Muirne's beloved eyes and smile, and Cumhal's hated height and frame and hair, and as he spoke, in the grey light that precedes the dawning, Fionn's face appeared reflected in the still waters of the pool.

At first Sadb turned away, but she could not sustain her pose of indifference, and in the end she was staring at the image love and hate had wrought for her, and her pale cheeks grew pink and her breast rose and fell with desire. Her hair had gone completely white now, leached of color by the spell, but she could not see herself, only Fionn.

"Do you want him to seek you?" the druid asked even more softly.

"I do. . . ."

"This *geasa* then do I lay upon you"—his voice rang like a gong—"that Fionn mac Cumhal shall pursue you indeed. To the Forest of Fidh Gaible shall this gateway open, and there shall you wander until he hunts you down!"

As her head came up, lips opening to deny him, the edge of the sun ridged the eastern hills. In that moment, which was neither day nor night, the druid spoke a single word. The scene rippled then like water disturbed by a stone. But as the druid's spirit was jerked back to his tranced body, he saw through the staves between which he had trapped the maiden as through a doorway. The woodland beyond them was that of Fidh Gaible, and the form that came upon Sadb as she went through it was that of a sleek, white doe.

GROANING, THE DARK DRUID THRUST THE STIFFENED FOLDS of the bullhide away and sat up beside the ashes of his fire. The magic was done, and he had only to wait for his trap to spring. And the beauty of it was that even if her kinfolk tried to trace her, all they would find would be winter's chill.

"Perhaps Fionn will kill her," he said as he pulled on his robe and blew at the coals, "perhaps his dogs will hunt her down. Dying, she will regain her woman's form, and he will know that he has killed the only one he could have loved." He grinned mirthlessly and hung a kettle over the fire. "And if he does not . . . if somehow he unravels the enchantment and takes her to be his leman in Almu . . . that will be better still."

"Let him take her!" His voice rang hollow against the stone of the cave. "Let them be linked by love until there is no corner of his heart that does not bear her name. Once I have bound her she can never wholly escape me. At that moment when he possesses her entirely; when he is as happy in her love as I was in that of my girl—then—then I will take her away from him as he took my home from me!"

Chapter 9

IT WAS THE WEEK AFTER BELTANE, AND LARKS DANCED in the sky above Almu. The cattle that the *fian* pastured on the Curragh during the winter had already gone south with the herd boys to spend the moons till Lughnasa fattening in the hill pastures of Sliab Bladhma, and the *fian* was preparing to move out as well. Fionn detoured around a pile of cook pots and stumbled, swearing, over a pack frame that someone had left lying in the middle of the yard. It was high time they were gone.

Slowly the piles of gear that the *fénnidi* would take with them into the field were growing. Fifty bands there were in each division of the *fianna*, with their warriors and their commanders, their *gillas* and their runners and servants, their hounds and packponies, their weapons and supply tents and cooking gear. And for a dozen years all those men had left their winter quarters for the summer's campaigning after every Beltane. And every year, Fionn wondered if he would go crazy by the time they got out of the *dun*.

From the other side of the feasting hall he could hear Dithramhach giving the rough side of his tongue to some fool who had left a horse harness out in the rain. His half brother was not a man to plan a battle or bandy words with kings, but there was none better for handling the day-to-day ordering of the *fian*.

Fionn grinned. According to Dithramhach, the world was mostly populated by fools, and at that moment Fionn found himself ready to agree. It was always like this when three hundred men were getting ready to move. Up at Lough Derg, Goll mac Morna would be facing the same struggle with the third of the *fian* that was under his command. And in the hundred raths around the countryside where the rest were billeted it would be the same. By Midsummer, as always, the transformation from dwellers in houses to creatures of wood and field would be completed. But gods, the confusion while it was going on!

The men had grown lazy in mind and body, wintering indoors. They sent the cattle to the hills to fatten, Fionn thought wryly, but it was the opposite with men. Give them a few weeks to range the woodlands and they would be lean as hounds. Sceolan's cold nose poked into Fionn's palm as if the thought had summoned him, and he ruffled the rough crest that grew along the neck and the arched back of the great white hound as they went along.

"You need the exercise as much as I do," he told the dog, "you've gotten fat lying beside the fire!"

Sceolan growled indignantly, and Fionn laughed. He and his brother had outgrown their puppy fat many years ago. Of the two, Sceolan had grown the fiercer and Bran the more affectionate. Men whispered that they did not grow old, that they were faerie hounds. But that was not entirely true. The children Fionn's sister had given him to foster were only partly of the Otherworld. Though their bodies were those of dogs, they aged at the same rate as men.

And what about me? he wondered. *Have I grown old?* Suddenly unwilling to face the questions that would come at him like spears in an ambush once the men caught sight of him, he turned aside. On the walls at least he could breathe the clean wind. Fionn pulled himself up the notched log that served as ladder, and Sceolan flopped down with a grunt to wait for him at the base of the wall.

A stout walkway ran around the inside of the palisade, interspersed with wooden towers in the Roman style. That was only one of the improvements Fionn had made in the fortress. The walls of Almu were strong, its dwellings adorned with the spoils of a hundred victories. But what of its owner? In a dozen winters as *rígfénnid*, Fionn had filled out, but his belt still latched where it had for the past ten years. Still, at his age other men were building families, not fortresses. Fionn supposed he must have a few children scattered around the countryside. Most of the men did, and some even married. Duibhne's every other word was some tale of his small son Diarmuid. But Fionn had no consort, and Dithramhach was the only man he could call family.

He turned back to the bustle of activity below him. Three hundred men would come running if he blew his horn. Duibhne had left his woman and child without a protest to join the summer hosting, and so had many another. If he had wanted to raise children, Fionn could have stayed with Cruithne and become a master smith. By now he would have had a dozen of them about his knee. He could have become an *ollamh* with his own school if he had finished his training with Cethern. But there were many smiths, and many poets. There was only one *rígfénnid* of all Eriu. Fionn shook his head.

Who am I? What am I? All this is mine—how could any man want more? But I do . . . , he thought, and sighed. *Fiacail could have said what is wrong with me, or stung me out of this despair*. But Fiacail had died the year after they took Almu. Fionn sighed again. *I need to get out in the woods*, he told himself. *It's these walls that are making me so crazy. I need to run free once more!*

A shadow flicked across his hand and he looked upward. Two larks were playing in the sunlit spaces above the *dun*, swooping in ecstatic spirals, as they met and parted and joined once more. A mated pair . . . Fionn felt something within him twist painfully. Donait had almost filled that emptiness within him, but she had sent him away. Was there a woman in Eriu who could make him whole?

He started to touch his thumb to his teeth, willing in the pain of his heart to endure the pain in his head that would follow, and stopped, hand still lifted, at the sound of the lookout's horn.

A cloud of dust was boiling along the road that wound from the west towards Almu. Someone was driving a chariot drawn by two black ponies at reckless speed; through the dust Fionn saw the gleam of a shield, the glitter of a spear. In the road ahead another man was walking. He too was armed, and he walked like a warrior. He turned as the chariot bore down on him; for a moment Fionn thought he meant to bar the way or the charioteer to run him down; then the driver pulled up so that the foot traveller could get into the chariot, and, more sedately, the journey resumed.

A few moments more, and the chariot was at the gates. Fionn heard yelling from within. Frowning, he swung down from the wall.

"And I don't care if you're the high king of the Sidhe!" came Dithramhach's shout. "Unless you state your business, you'll not be coming in." His voice held an undertone of satisfaction, as if he were glad to find a legitimate target for his anger.

"Grey pig in the wood, black crow in the tree—and neither the stag of the *fian* may see—" sang Lomna the Fool, and the men laughed.

"Have some sense, lads," put in Guarire mac Reiche peaceably. "Can't ye see we're buzzing like an overturned hive? An' ye wanted sweet and subtle discourse, ye should have come while we were still settled. Ye'll have to follow us to the forest, now, if ye want to talk to Fionn mac Cumhal."

"Is there then a season for justice?" came the voice of a stranger, deep and furious, in reply.

"Is Fionn hiding in there?" a younger voice chimed in.

"All seasons are good, if the cause is a just one—" said Fionn, stepping around the corner of the stable. "And many a man has sought me who found himself sorry when I appeared."

Fionn's men went abruptly silent, waiting to see what he would do. Fionn looked from one stranger to the other, and smiled. The charioteer stared back at him suspiciously. He looked to be a few years older than Fionn, a powerfully built man in a black tunic richly embroidered, with greying dark hair. The foot traveller scowled. He was younger, short and strong, with a ruddy face and silver-fair hair. The mantle that wrapped him was grey, with a clasp in the shape of a wild boar.

"So then," Fionn said gently, "what is this pressing business that the two of you have with me?"

"I am Aodh mac Ronain, lord of Gabhair!" said the older man, and waited. When Fionn simply stared at him in incomprehension, he added, "Your father killed mine at Cnucha field. . . ."

"Have you come for compensation? I tell you truly, there would not be enough gold in Eriu to pay for all the men Cumhal killed"—he waited for the laughter to subside—"but since at that battle Cumhal himself died, it seems to me that honor should be satisfied."

"Indeed," Aodh said magnanimously. "The compensation I claim is for an infringement upon my own rights and property. Not two days past a band of your men transgressed upon my lands between the two hills of Gabhair and unlawfully killed a buck and three does!"

"Two days past?" asked Fergus the Poet. "Then you have no claim, lord of Gabhair. Though we have not yet taken the field, Beltane is over, and between Beltane and Samhain, all the wild game of the forest and the fighting fish of the streams are the lawful prey of the *fian*. Did a doe drop dead in your dooryard, she would belong to us, not to you."

"Is that the law? Well, it is a bad one!" Aodh cried. "I cry challenge to you, son of Cumhal, for the right to those deer!"

"Your challenge must follow mine," the younger man broke in. "It is on account of a boar's hunting that I have come, and the boar was my father, and it is by Fionn himself that he was slain! I am Conain mac Luachar!"

Fionn blinked, dizzied by memory. He saw once more the boar's blazing eyes and the ridged silhouette of Sliab Muicce against the winter sky. Once more he smelled the stench of its decay. That had been the spear Birga's first kill, the moment when the weapon began to acquire its taste for the blood of the Otherworld.

"The Grey Man of Luachar betrayed his oaths to Cumhal!" Dithramhach exclaimed. "He struck the first blow against him! Whether in man shape or pig, his blood belonged to Cumhal's son!"

Everyone knew that Fionn had slain the boar. He opened his eyes, grateful that he had never told anyone how he also killed the Red-Mouthed Woman, who was the Grey Man's dam. *It was lawful*, he told himself, as he had every time he dreamed he saw the blood running from her jaws. *She was going to kill me!* But there had been no witnesses.

"Lawful or no," cried Conain, "I challenge you!"

"I spoke first. My claim has priority!" Aodh rounded on him.

Fionn blinked, wondering if they would solve the problem for him by killing each other.

"If it's a fight you want," cried Grimthann, "I'll gladly stand my chieftain's champion!"

"And I'll take the other—" Young Suibhne grinned, brandishing his spear.

"Will ye now, and what about me?" asked Dubhtach, but if there was an answer, it was lost as the *fian* closed in around them, baying like hounds.

Instinct brought Aodh and Conain back to back, facing their foes. Fionn looked at the two rivals become allies and started laughing so hard he had not the breath to call off his men. It was Dithramhach who got them quieted finally while Fionn wiped the tears from his eyes.

"There's a fine spirit in you, boys, but my two challengers have the right of it—you cannot take a fight that's meant for me. Yet how can I be fair to the both of you? If you kill me, Aodh, then Conain here will have been deprived of the chance to avenge his father, whereas if Conain is victor, how shall Aodh's honor be restored?" Fionn shook his head sadly, and the *fian*, scenting a stratagem, began to grin.

"But perhaps I can find a solution. Since you are the challengers, it is for me to set the terms of the fight. For you, Aodh of Gabhair, let the contest be in possessions. Each of us shall list his treasures, the winner to set his own forfeit. What do you say, man—is that fair?"

Aodh had begun to grin complacently, and Fionn knew he had found the bait for this one anyway.

"I am a warrior with my own way to make in the world," said Conain mac Luachar sullenly. "It would be no fair contest between you and me."

"Indeed," answered Fionn. "I can see that you are a man of many skills. If you have a talent that is not equalled by one of my *fénnidi*, then you shall claim the price of your father's head from me."

Conain looked around him with a smile that was just this side of a sneer, and Fionn recognized the arrogance of the Otherworld. He nodded, and the *fian* eased back, waiting expectantly.

"So now," said Fionn. "Where shall we begin?"

"I have a hundred milk cows in my herd at home," Aodh answered, "and two bulls to serve them, black as a night without stars."

"Three hundred are the heifers that the *fian* of Fionn has sent to graze in the hills," said Fergus the Poet, "and every one of them the mother of twins. Fifteen red bulls serve them, but a snow white bull rules them all."

"In my barns are twenty horses—" Aodh was not going to accept defeat easily. But the tally of the horses that Fionn grazed on the rich grass of the Curragh was greater still.

In the category of weapons it was really no contest, and even Aodh's list of treasures, which was notable, could not stand against the cream of the spoils that Fionn had taken in a dozen years of war.

"My wife was the pearl of all women," said Aodh then. "She is dead now, but she has left me a daughter, Eargna, who promises to rival Deirdre in loveliness. Eargna is my treasure of treasures, and I have sworn that any man who tries to take her from me will surely die!"

Fionn frowned. Unless one wanted to count Cruithne, the smith's daughter who had been his wife through one long winter almost twenty years ago, he claimed no woman, nor was he sure of a child. *That family I was dreaming about*, he thought wryly as he considered his men, *would come in handy now*! They grinned back at him, confident as children that he would win, and he understood suddenly why he had not needed a family.

"These are my sons—" Fionn waved his hand along the ranks of the *fian*. "Do not I feed and clothe them, praise them when they do well, and correct them when there is need? When a man enters the *fian* he leaves

his birth family, so where shall these look for a father's
love if not to me? Shall one daughter, however beautiful, stand against a host of such sons as these?"

Aodh's weathered features were turning a dull red
as the warriors laughed.

"Aodh, listen," said Fionn gently, "there is no shame.
As well contend with the *Ard Ri* himself in this matter
as with me. I am a lord of treasures, and the one of them
in which you could not even begin to compete with me
is freedom. Wealth we have, but it does not imprison
us. The liberty of the woods and fields and mountains
of Eriu is the true treasure of the *fian*. You look a likely
warrior. Come roam the woods with us, and be free!"

"You want me to join the *fian*?" Aodh's eyes held
Fionn's as the *rígfénnid* nodded, and Fionn saw a spark
kindle there that had likely not been seen since the day
Aodh's father died and laid upon the boy the burden of
his lands, and knew that he had won indeed.

"I am free already," said Conain proudly. "What
temptation will you offer me?"

"Perhaps . . . some worthy opponents?" asked Fionn
gently. "What are your skills, son of Luachar?"

Conain surveyed the assembled warriors. "I can trans-
fix a stag at a hundred paces with a cast of my spear!"
There was a stirring in the ranks of the *fénnidi* and a
grinning, freckled man stepped out from among them.

"I am Suibhne, called the Spear-Bearer, smiter of the
hosts. At the same distance a cast of my spear has gone
through the belly of a man wearing a fighting belt of
hardened leather, and through the man behind him and
pierced the heart of a third." There was a murmur of
agreement from men who had been there and seen it
done.

"I have a sword of blue steel," said Conain, a little
less pugnaciously, "with which I can split a man from
crown to root with a single blow."

"Let Faolchú of the hard-tempered sword come forward," said Fionn.

Faolchú was stout as an oak tree, with corded muscle rippling along his arms. A sword that looked as if it had been forged for a giant was slung at his back, the leather of sheath and baldric shiny from wear.

"In the blink of an eye I have stricken the head from one man, the sword hand from another, taken out the leg of a man standing behind me and sliced open the belly of the man beside him and returned my blade to its sheath once more," said Faolchú.

Conain blinked, but he was still game; a more worthy warrior, Fionn suspected, than his sire.

"I am a swift runner," he said then. "I can cross the Curragh between the time the sun rises and when it stands overhead in the sky."

"Ah, lad, foot-swift Ceallach here is such a runner as would singe your tail." Fionn gestured towards a lean, wiry lad with a shock of red hair. "He can cross the Curragh and return in that much time without even breathing hard. And if you were to call yourself a harper I would call forth our little Cnú Déroil, and if a poet I would set you against Fergus here. Can you beat them all?" For a moment he waited, but Conain was silent, his cheeks flushed angrily.

"I myself am a man of more crafts than you can imagine. When you can defeat all of these, Conain mac Luachar, then you shall fight me," said Fionn. "But this is the compensation I offer you—to come with us and train with our champions. . . ."

"To join the *fian*?" Conain looked like a man trying to recover from a head blow.

"If you cannot defeat our best, neither would you be the worst warrior here. What do you say, men—is he worthy of our company?" At Fionn's wave, the *fénnidi* began to cheer, and this time the color in Conain's face was not from shame.

"The two of you shall serve in Guarire mac Reiche's band—" Fionn reached out to grasp their hands, and at that moment, the lookout's horn blew once more.

"A runner—" the man called down from the gate tower. "Coming fast up the road from the plain! A sprig of broom is thrust beneath his headband, and he carries a reddened spear."

"From Laigin!" said Reidhe. "From the coast," corrected Suibhne, "and coming with news of war." The spearman grinned happily, and a murmur of anticipation rumbled gently through the crowd like the first growling of the guard dogs when they scent a foe.

They stilled, listening to the light patter of footfalls and the hoarse breathing as the runner breasted the last rise. Then he was staggering beneath the gate, and the woman Mongfind pushed through the crowd to offer him a horn of beer.

"Raiders!" the man gasped when he had breath again. "Sixty shiploads! By the markings they came from Alba across the sea—landed just below the headland of Bré. They've burned the raths at Clocha Liatha and Chomhghail and are moving southward. How quickly can you come?"

Fionn realized that he was grinning, and recognized the same look in the eyes of his men. For a dozen years they had been trained for war. No wonder the prospect of a summer's hunting had little power to stir them. There would be no more confusion now.

"By sunset we will be on the road, and near the coast by dawn," he answered, then turned to Conain and Aodh. "Now you shall show us your mettle, my challengers. Follow me and I will give you glory!"

They grinned back at him, but any reply they might have made was lost in the cheering of the *fian*.

THE *FENNID* DID NOT BETRAY FIONN'S TRUST IN THEM. AS the sun slid westward the men marched out through the gates of the dun and down to the Curragh with the shadow of Almu lengthening before them. Only the warriors had been mustered, each man burdened with no more than his weapons and a bag of food. The *gillas* and the servants remained behind to finish the packing, waiting for word to join the *fian* later if the campaign looked like being a long one. Supplies did not matter—the tradition of the *fian* was to live off the land.

When they reached the flat earth of the Curragh they sucked the soft air of early evening into their lungs and began to run, racing the wild ponies across the plain. This pace they kept up until they came to the upper reaches of the Liffe, where they rested and drank from the clear waters that came down from the hills. But the last glow had hardly faded from the sky before they were on the road once more, taking the path that followed the river up into the hills at a steady, ground-eating jog.

It was past midnight when they neared the river's head and turned south and eastward down another track that led towards the sea. Here the wild hills gentled, but their skirts were swathed in thick forest cut by many little brooks, in which it would be easy to lose one's way. It was here, in this last leg in the darkness, that differences in the men's condition and ability began to tell. While the leaders moved on at the same swift pace, the weaker began to fall behind, leaving groups of men scattered along the trail. Night was nearly done before the first of the warriors smelled the soft breath of the ocean, and with it the smoke of the burning of Rath Naoi.

AT DAWN THE WIND CHANGED, AND A CHILL GREY FOG came rolling in from the sea. The blackened timbers of the rath were no sooner glimpsed in the growing light than the mist engulfed them. Sound was deadened; the air came chokingly to the lungs, as if they had wandered into the land beneath the waves.

"In this demon's murk we'll trip over our foes before we find them!" muttered Dithramhach. "Or get lost ourselves . . . I wonder how long it will take the rest of our men to find us?" He shuddered. "Gods, this chill soaks into a man's bones!"

"I did not chase this prey all night to lose it during the day—" objected Ceallach. "We cannot afford to wait for the laggards. We know the raiders are near. If we stop now, they could get clean away!" He disappeared after Dithramhach. From somewhere above the mist that blinded them they heard a raven's call.

Fionn bit back an oath or three. He would have a few things to say to the men about winter training when they were all together once more.

"Fergus," he called, "you're from the coast. Is this kind of fog usual here?"

"Usual enough, though I've rarely seen it so thick. I would be suspicious, though, if it doesn't start to disperse when the sun gets high." His cloaked shape seemed distorted in the swirling mist; Fionn peered closer, and realized that someone else was sheltering under the poet's shaggy mantle.

"Cnú Déroil! What in the name of all bogles are you doing here?"

A twitter of music came from beneath the cloak and a cropped head popped out, grinning at Fionn.

"I've come to play ye into battle, an' ye can find the enemy." The little musician waved the bone flute in his hand. "I'm as tired as any man of you of staying indoors! You did not say, lord, that I must bide in the *dun*!"

Fionn scowled. He had not thought it was needful. Fergus could defend himself, but the musician's only weapon was song.

"Stay with Fergus, then, and both you stick close to me—" he began.

"Look there—" Someone was waving, his form anonymous in the fog, but the voice that of Faolchú. Sand squeaked beneath Fionn's feet as he trotted forward. Through the mist he glimpsed the dim shapes of warships drawn up on the shore. Where were the warriors who should have been guarding them?

"We've found tracks—" Dithramhach reappeared out of the mist, pointing with his spear. "A large band is headed inland, but it looks like another group went back up the coast. And one set of prints are those of a giant."

Fionn frowned. There was a feel to this that he did not like. Was he scenting danger with senses honed by twelve years of war, or was there something at work here that he did not understand?

"Whoever they are, we'll be easy meat if they come upon us scattered from here to Almu. Dithramhach, you can take the lads who are here and go after the main body. I will wait for the rest of our men."

"Brother, I don't like it!" Dithramhach's callused fingers gripped Fionn's arm. "It needs no reading of ravensong to foretell danger! Leave a man to guide the stragglers and come with me."

Fionn's hand closed over his brother's, feeling the strong fingers warm beneath his own.

"The danger is that when those fools do get here they will fall into the sea and drown," he said tightly. "I have a reason for wanting to be here to greet them in person. When I am done with them, they'll wish they had met the foe instead of me!"

"Then we'll all wait," said Dithramhach, "and jeer!"

Fionn shook his head. "That would breed bad blood in the *fian*. And it would be cruel to deny the men who made this run their glory. Go after the raiders, brother. I give them to you!"

Dithramhach shook his head. "I hate the cold," he said glumly. "It freezes a man's courage along with his bones."

"Follow the wartrail, then," said Fionn, smiling, "and maybe you'll find the sun."

In the silence that followed the *fian*'s departure Fionn began to wonder if he should have heeded his brother's words. This fog choked the lungs, thick as some mist of the Otherworld. Far overhead a seabird cried mournfully. The slap of the little waves on the shore was the only other sound. Shivering, Cnú Déroil got out his pipe and tried to play, but the music seemed weak and mournful in the thick air.

They had just gotten a fire going when they heard the crunch of footsteps upon the sand.

"That will be the first of them," said Fergus grimly, and Fionn nodded, readying the sharp-edged words.

From the mist figures were emerging, huge shapes distorted as bogles in the heavy air. Fionn got to his feet, staring. They did not walk like men of the *fian*. . . . For a moment he wondered if they were even men. Then someone gave an order in a language that was not that of Eriu. Fergus gasped and recoiled, and Cnú Déroil dove with a squeak of fright beneath Fionn's cloak and huddled there.

Dithramhach was right, he thought bitterly, *and it's my lads who will be laughing to see me caught flat-footed as any farmer getting his first taste of war.*

Could he fight, or escape them? Before his eyes the shadowy figures were dividing; where one had stood three now menaced them, or was it four? Instant calculations flared through Fionn's awareness. Only surprise could have served them against such numbers, and its advantage was all to the other side. Even his spear and shield were out of reach beside the fire.

He took a deep breath, peering through the mist at his enemy.

"Are ye just frightened, now, or are ye wise?" a deep voice rumbled from the tallest of the figures. "Make no move, an' ye may live 'till we can decide what use ye might be—"

Absurdly, Fionn was reminded of his two challengers. The greatest treasure now was time, and what wealth did he have to purchase it?

The giant figure loomed closer, and he realized it was the man's bearfur cloak that had distorted his outline.

But his height was real. Fionn blinked, gazing upward. The giant was wearing a helm of leather banded with bronze, but the branching horns of a stag had been affixed to it. What warrior would wear such a thing?

"Why should I flee, and I on my own land at home?" he said evenly. "It is for you to say why I should be afraid. . . ."

"I am Laigne! They call me Laigne Mor, and in all of Alba men fear my power. The spirit of the bear serves me; the stag spirit comes at my call!" Even the mist could not mute the laughter that rolled from that deep chest. And Fionn heard a jingling from the charms and amulets sewn to his clothes. "And who, little man, may you be?"

"I have been the Lad of the Skins, and the Child of the Hollow Tree, I have been Demne Mael and Fionnéices as well," said Fionn, thinking hard. Clearly this man was some kind of druid in his own land. It would be foolish to gift him with his true name.

Do I know it myself? he wondered suddenly. *Even now, do I know who I am?*

"And can you give me a reason not to slay all of these persons with one blow?" From the warriors who ringed them came a gutteral echo of the leader's laughter.

Astonishingly, at that moment there came from beneath Fionn's cloak a trill of birdsong. Had Cnú Déroil gone mad? Or had the little musician seen that the only defense they had now was the magic of wit and will? Suddenly words were flowing through him. If he did not know who he was, he must cling to what he had done. . . .

"Wherever I walk, there sounds the music of the Blessed Isles. I have eaten the sacred salmon. I have slain the Boar of Sliab Muicce and the fire serpent Aillén; I possess the crane bag of treasures that speaks to me with the voice of the tides. I have lain with the women of the Otherworld! I know the secret of the Hazel Shield, and the languages of the birds and the trees!" Fionn drew breath. What did all those deeds add up to? He remembered the green path of wisdom that Bodbmall had tried to teach him so many years ago, and realized that in his own way he had followed it as well.

In the mist no one could tell the color of his mantle. Fionn took a step forward, and saw his foe's fingers flicker in a warding sign. He took another, and all around him warriors recoiled.

"I am a druid, and sacred in my office," Fionn's voice rang out, and the air seemed to brighten. "You shall slay neither me nor my people, for the protection of my mantle covers all those who follow me!"

"I shall not attack you or those you shelter. You have my word on it," said Laigne slowly.

Fionn reached for Birga, wondering if Laigne had power enough to sense the magic in it, and at that moment the first of the *fianna*'s stragglers emerged from the woods, calling Fionn's name.

The strangers turned, spears lifting, and Cnú Déroil twittered the birdcall that was the *fian*'s alarm.

"Halt!" cried Fionn, "these men are of my household!" A breath of wind swirled the mist and stirred his hair. The sun was breaking through; already metal gleamed from the harness of the approaching warriors. In a moment the enemy would be able to see his own war gear as well.

"What trickery are you trying!" exclaimed Laigne. "Even in Alba we know the name of the *rigfénnid* of Eriu! My promise was made to a druid, not to Fionn mac Cumhal!"

"I am a druid, brave hero," said Fionn boldly. "No one of all those who have journeyed in the dewy world has surpassed my skill. Man of Alba, your own word binds you to be gone from here, for I shelter all of Eriu!"

Chapter 10

❦

FIONN SLID THE HAZEL SHIELD ONTO HIS LEFT ARM and straightened, swinging Birga toward his foe. He felt the pulse of power as the weapons wakened, but he kept a firm hold on their battle hunger, and on his own. In the sunlight the invaders had lost some of their horror. They were only men, and far from their own land. Even Laigne's horned headdress looked a little foolish in the broad light of day.

"Go now—" he began, but Laigne was not listening.

From the direction in which the *fian* had disappeared came the sound of battle. Fionn heard Faolchú's warcry, and the bellowing of Dithramhach's horn. They were coming this way, so the *fian* must be winning. He grinned wolfishly as Birga began to sing in his hand. It no longer mattered whether Laigne thought he was a druid or no.

"Go while you can, men of Alba! For I tell you, if you do not take ship now for home, your next landfall will be the Otherworld."

Two enemy warriors burst over the bank with mac Reiche right after them; one tumbled bonelessly, transfixed by his spear. The rest of the raiders were on their

177

heels. Laigne's men charged forward to join them, roaring. The truce was certainly over now. Fionn stood his ground with Cnú Déroil and Fergus huddling behind him.

A gap opened in the circle of foes and mac Reiche and Duibhne sped through. Laigne struck down two more of the *fénnidi* as they tried to reach their leader, six others burst past and joined Fionn's defenders. Other *fénnidi* were appearing from among the trees, and above the bank Fionn saw the men of Dithramhach's band. The raiders, caught between their pursuers and the enemy on the shore, were making for the ships, ignoring Laigne's attempts to rally them. Oars splashed awkwardly as the men struggled to get the nearest into the water and away.

"Stop them," said Guarire mac Reiche, panting, "or they'll come back and we'll have it all to do again—"

Fionn nodded. Laigne's oath would hold a great deal better backed up by steel. As men started towards the next ship he moved to intercept them. Suddenly there were plenty of foes. The rest of the raiders had arrived with the last of the *fian* on their heels, and any order the battle might have had disintegrated as they became a single heaving mass of struggling men.

"Get these two to safety," he told Duibhne, nodding towards the poet and Cnú Déroil. No one would knowingly slay them, but flying spears were less discriminating.

An Alban battle cry rang out behind him. Free to fight at last, Fionn whirled, spear whipping forward past the man's guard and into his belly. Fionn ducked as the enemy spear went flying. Blood spurted as he yanked Birga free.

"*Red blood, good blood, feed blood now!*" sang the spear triumphantly. A swordblade banged on the Hazel Shield, and Fionn felt its awareness strengthen ominously.

"Be still," he murmured against the woven wicker,

"stay a shield. Your poison would kill friends as well as foes." From the shield Fionn sensed disappointment, but the faint humming he had heard faded.

Another man appeared before him, spear stabbing downwards. He twisted, and the iron head screeched slantwise across the shield as Fionn uncoiled in a thrust that sent Birga up through the warrior's exposed armpit. The same motion that freed the spear brought its blade slashing across another man's throat. He knew that warriors of the *fian* were behind him, and ahead of him was the enemy. All the complexities that had tormented him vanished as existence narrowed to the stark simplicity of surviving the next blow.

Faces blurred until he saw only one face, which he struck down again and again. It went on, terrible and timeless, until Fionn wondered if he could keep on. The breath sobbed in his breast. Fionn stumbled over a body and nearly fell, tensing against the blow that would take advantage of his mistake and end it. But none came. Blinking, he straightened, but no one faced him. Between him and the sea there were only the dead, their tumbled bodies stirring helplessly as the incoming tide tried to wash the blood from the sand.

Somehow the sun had reached the midpoint of the sky. Fionn squinted across the dazzle of light on waves. Far out to sea, five dark shapes wallowed through the blue waters. Of the sixty shiploads who had come to Eriu, five might make it back to their homeland to tell of the terror of Eriu. Only a few of the wounded foe seemed likely to live long enough to be sold as slaves. But there had been a boy among them, Laigne's nephew. Some of the men were for killing him, or holding him hostage. But there had been too much death here. Better, thought Fionn, to train the boy for the *fian*.

The rest of the Albans, dead or dying, lay all around him on the shore. The fighting was over, but the stink of blood still battled with the crisp tang of the breeze. Fionn had forgotten how sick that smell made him. His arms, grown weak with a winter's resting, ached wearily. Around him, men whose faces were as grimed with blood as his own stared at him in stupid wonder. The rejoicing and the boasts would come later, when they had got over their numb amazement at having survived.

A few steps brought Fionn to the water's edge, and the shock as the clean waves frothed round his feet drove the worst of his sickness away.

"Get the bodies out of the sea," he croaked. "Separate the wounded from the dead and tend them. I want a report on our losses from the leader of each band. Have them choose men to gather wood for the pyres, get some food cooking and carry drinking water from the spring. We won't need it for washing—we've water enough here to get clean!"

Birga's bloody head sank of its own weight until it touched the cold waves, and Fionn felt its ardor dissipate like the brown stain the water was swirling away. He had only to walk forward and the ocean would close over him. The water would cleanse all the blood from his body and wash the aching weariness from his soul. . . . But he stood still, finding what healing he could in the touch of the waves that washed his feet and the soothing murmur of the sea.

He was not aware of time's passing, but the sun had moved a hand's breadth farther across the heavens when Duibhne touched his arm.

"Fionn—it's Dithramhach. I think you should come. . . ."

THEY HAD LAID HIM AT THE EDGE OF THE WOOD, WHERE overhanging branches gave some shade, and they had cleansed the blood from his face and arms. But no cleansing could stop the red stain that was spreading through the cloth Fergus held pressed against Dithramhach's side.

Stiffly Fionn slid the straps of the Hazel Shield from his arm and handed shield and spear to Duibhne to take away. He got himself down on one knee, then the other, beside the wounded man. His brother's skin was clammy to the touch, his breathing labored and slow. He was alive, Fionn thought numbly, but unless they could stop the bleeding, he would not live long.

At his touch Dithramhach's eyelids fluttered. Fionn winced as the other man tried to smile.

"I told you . . . should have stayed . . . with you."

"Be still!" said Fionn desperately as Fergus threw the soaked wad aside and jammed another piece of cloth into the wound. "Save your strength to heal."

Dithramhach drew a ragged breath and shook his head, then seemed to ease. "When we wrestled . . . I'm glad you won. . . ."

Fionn clasped his brother's hand, feeling the answering twitch of Dithramhach's fingers like a parody of the wrestler's grip that had bound them so long ago. Looking down at his brother was like peering into a shadowed pool, the other's face a blurred reflection of his own. And he could feel this other self slipping away from him. His grip tightened, but he could hold only the body, not the soul.

"Dithramhach, you can't give up—"

But the other man's gaze had gone inward. His skin was like dirty wax and cold . . . so cold. Fionn bent over him, gripping his shoulders as if he could send some of his own force into that sagging frame, but he could feel the spirit withdrawing from the flesh in his hands.

I told Laigne I was a druid, but I can only take life, not give it back again . . . , Fionn thought numbly. The breath rasped in his brother's throat, he shuddered, then stilled.

"Brother, I need you . . . ," Fionn whispered into Dithramhach's ear. "Do not leave me alone. . . ."

But Dithramhach mac Cumhal had already gone.

*   *   *

THE *RIGFÉNNID* OF ERIU SAT ALONE ON THE SHORE, WATCH-
ing the smoke of the funeral pyres stain the sunset
sky. They had made one for the bodies of the Albans
with Laigne at their head, and another, smaller, where
the dead of the *fian* lay as a guard of honor around
Dithramhach. Fionn could not recall having felt so
alone since he had lost Bodbmall.

"Drink," said Fergus at his elbow. The Alban loot had
included both mead and ale, and the *fian* was already
making good use of it, drinking to their dead and boasting of their victory.

"If I open my throat to drink, I will howl," said Fionn
bitterly. "And set a bad example for the *fian*."

"Let the *fian* take care of itself. Do you grieve for
him. He was a good man!" said Fergus, holding out
the horn.

"He was my brother," said Fionn. He grabbed the
horn and took a long swallow. "My father was killed
before I was born. I never knew my mother. I spent
only one winter with my uncle, Crimall. I told Aodh
that the *fénnidi* were all my children, but it is not the
same. Dithramhach was the only brother I had!" He
started to drink again and choked as the pain welled
up in him.

"But surely that is not true—" It took Fionn a few
moments to realize what Fergus was saying. "It is the
business of a *fili* to know his chieftain's family. Has
not your mother borne two fine sons to King Gléor
Lamraige? Would it not be a comfort to you to have
them in the *fian*?"

"And get them killed as I did my father's son?" asked
Fionn bitterly.

But he found himself wondering if the two boys had
brought happiness to Gléor's sad-eyed queen. When
Tadg told him Muirne still lived, he had been too
stunned to think of seeking her. And then he had been
too busy, serving the king and building the *fian*.

"It would do no harm to go see them," said the *fili*.
"Perhaps then you would feel less alone."

* * *

BODBMALL HAD SAID ONCE THAT TIME WAS LIKE A RIVer, and though you might try to step in where you crossed before, neither you nor the river would be the same. And though as they journeyed southward Fionn recognized the shapes of the hills and the lie of the land with increasing clarity, the crop-headed lad he had been when last he walked this way was no one he knew.

As he led the third of the *fian* that Dithramhach had once commanded southward, he became ever more certain that it had been a mistake to come. The outcome could only be at best embarrassment, or at worst a kind of pain he had thought himself done with, for both himself and Muirne. But he had announced his intention before all the *fian*, and there would be equal shame in turning back from it. Still, as the slopes of Sliab Eiblinne rose up on their right he found himself wishing they had not disposed of the Albans so completely. He would have welcomed more raiders, or even an incursion from the Otherworld. He would have gone with far more cheerfulness to fight an enemy than he was going to face Muirne. But no appeal came to rescue him, and too soon they turned away from the brown waters of the Siuir and marched up the road towards Lamraige.

Fionn's mother had not even recognized him in the days when he tended King Gléor's fire. He had some excuse, for he had not even known she lived. But Muirne had been too sunk in her own sorrows to know him. What would she think of him now?

And there, up ahead, was the blue gleam of Loch Gaire, fringed with alders and willow trees. As the *fian* approached, a blue heron whirred upward from the reeds and flapped lazily away. Sceolan pressed against Fionn's leg, ears pricking, and he stroked the silky head.

"Not now, lad, not this time—our kinfolk are waiting. Your own grandmother and some uncles not much older than you are, so you must be on your best behavior."

It occurred to him to wonder if Muirne knew that her daughter had survived as well as her son. He might be able to tell her about Tuireann, he thought ruefully, but even a *fili*'s training had not prepared him to explain to Muirne how her grandsons came to be dogs.

THE LONG RAYS OF THE WESTERING SUN SLANTED DOWN through the apple orchard, glowing in the last white petals that clung like a scattering of snow among the new leaves. Fionn trod silently across the thick grass, with his shadow going before him, moving as carefully as if he were stalking some wild thing. And perhaps that was true, for surely the love of the woman he sought there had eluded him more successfully than any animal.

Gléor had greeted him with mixed constraint and pride, his two gangling sons by his side, but without his queen.

"She is in the orchard, lad," the king had told him. "She did not want to greet you before all these curious eyes. Do you go down there and find her; I will give your people a good welcome here."

The earth song surged strongly as he passed beneath the trees, and Fionn realized that he was trembling. Abruptly he understood that his mother had chosen to meet him here because she was afraid. He knew it was so because he was afraid as well.

You can run away after you have seen her, he told himself. *But first you must ask why she abandoned you.* . . . That was it—the ancient wound that still had the power to hurt him as no weapon wielded by man had been able to do. Neither Birga nor the Hazel Shield could defend him against that pain.

And now he could see her, leaning against a tree trunk as she gazed down the valley, wrapped in a fringed mantle the color of old wine. The auburn hair coiled around her head was threaded with silver now. Then, though he knew he had made no sound, she turned.

For a moment she stared, as if dazzled by the radiance of the sun behind him. Then her gaze focused and all the color in her face drained away. She swayed, and he leaped forward to catch her, feeling her tremble, her bones as delicate as a bird's beneath his hands.

"Cumhal . . ." she whispered, "Cumhal!"

Fionn tensed as his gut twisted with a pain he had thought long forgotten. He remembered how he had felt in the days of his early manhood, never knowing if wearing his father's face would win him friends or enemies. But that first moment of confusion before they realized who he was had never been so cruel as now, when the mother whose voice he had longed to hear called him by a dead man's name.

"I am Fionn," he said harshly, "or Demne, or the Lad of the Skins, or any other name but that one! For a whole year I tended your fire and you did not know me—oh, my mother, will you not name me your child even now?"

"I knew you . . . ," she whispered. She was so shaken by weeping, he could hardly hear the words. "I knew you were a son of Cumhal," she said bitterly, "but you were so well grown for your years—I never thought that you could be mine. . . ." Her hands were on his forearms, corded with muscle and traced over with old scars. She gave a little laugh then and released her grip, stroking the fine golden hairs.

"The priestesses of Brigid said that I have your smile," he offered.

"Well, it's little enough smiling I've done since your father died." She shook her head with a twist of the lips that wrenched at his heart. "Especially in those years, when I had no child at all. No wonder, I suppose, if no one noticed a resemblance to me. Ah, lad," she sighed, "it was a pain to look at you, for by your size I thought you must have been conceived in the days when Cumhal was courting me, and though I knew he had always been a man for the women, I did think that while we loved he was faithful to me."

"You never even wondered?" he asked disbelievingly. "You knew how Bodbmall and the Liath Luachra were raising me."

"I heard that the son of Cumhal had won all the contests at the Tailtin Fair, but then he disappeared. Folk said that the men of Clan Morna had killed him. I did send someone to inquire, but neither you nor Bodbmall were anywhere to be found. I thought you were dead—" She looked up into his face at last, her beautiful eyes luminous with tears.

"And so you mourned me even as I sat at your own fireside . . . ," he said wonderingly. It made him feel odd, as if he had seen the ghost of the boy he had been.

"Oh, child, child—"

"Fionn!" He frowned down at her. "Say it—say Fionn, my son!"

Muirne swallowed, and for the first time allowed herself to really look at him, from his strong, high-arched feet to his curling fair hair. "My son," she said softly, "Fionn mac Cumhal . . ."

THEY SAT THAT NIGHT AROUND THE HEARTH THAT HAD once been Fionn's care—Fionn and the most noted of his men with the king's family. Now another lad kept the fire burning, and Fionn had to stop himself once or twice from taking a hand. Sitting here, he was recovering all kinds of memories. Perhaps he should make a tour of the south and west and visit all the places where he had served as a boy. If he revived all of his memories of the youth he had been he might be able to understand who he was now. But for the first time he truly understood the druid doctrine of reincarnating souls that he had learned from Bodbmall. For the person who had been King Gléor's fire boy had been Demne the Wanderer, as gangling and shock-headed as Muirne's two younger sons were now, not Fionn.

"Tell us a tale of the *fian*," said Fearghusa, grinning.

He was shorter than his twin and more muscular, his arms and legs downed already with the beginnings of a pelt of coarse, reddish hair. The other boy, Faobhar, was in all ways lighter and brighter, and yet they had come forth at one birth, like Fionn and his sister. Twins seemed to run in Muirne's line.

"Tell us the story about how you fought the headless men," said Faobhar.

"You must not pester your brother," said Muirne anxiously. "Surely 'tis enough to know that he is a hero without making him relive his battles." She cast a warning glance at Fionn, and it occurred to him that for some reason she did not want them to know.

"Ah, well now," said Guaire, who had not seen the look, or had not interpreted it. "That is a fine tale indeed for a spring evening, though I would not like to be telling it on a night in winter when the wind blows cold around the eaves. It began after the fair at Mag Eala, where Fiachra the king had gifted Fionn with that fine black horse you saw him riding, and our chieftain was keen to try its paces."

Fionn stifled a smile and took another drink from his horn. If a tale must be told, better this one, embarrassing though it might be, than some story of glorious battle.

"On our way back to Almu, we ranged out hunting, and the black horse went so swiftly that of all the *fian*, only the beasts that Ceallach and myself were riding could keep up with him. When evening came we found ourselves in a wild country, and began to look about for some shelter—"

His voice grew softer, and the lads leaned forward to listen.

"Now Fionn looked about him, and saw beyond the crag on his left hand a valley with a great house in it, and firelight showing through its open door. Ceallach thought we should not go down there, for he knew that valley, and he had never seen a house there before. But the wind was blowing cold and we were hungry. So we went down, and I began to wonder if Ceallach had been right on account of the screeching and barking and shouting that greeted us, for a more clamorous, rabbly household I never saw.

"A gnarled, grey-haired churl of a man was their master, with a voice in him like a blacksmith's rasp. He pulled the door off its hinges to let us in, and set us all three down on a couch of hard iron. The log of elder on the fire was so big it nearly quenched the flame, and all in all it was a hard, cheerless dwelling where we had chosen to bide."

"But that was not the worst of it," said little Cnú Déroil. "Tell them about the music!"

Fionn laughed, feeling that if they were in for the story, he might as well tell his share. "When we were seated the grey-haired churl told his folk to rise up and entertain us, but it was no fair youths he had for his singers, nor was it comely maidens. On one side of the room nine severed heads rose up to face us, and on the other side, nine headless bodies. And from the one and the other and the churl their master there came such a shrieking and caterwauling as I have never heard before—"

"The song they sang for us would have wakened dead men out of the clay," said Guaire, "it well nigh split the bones of our heads to hear it!"

"What happened then?" asked Faobhar as they drew breath, grinning.

"Oh, the old man took up his hatchet and went out and killed our horses," said Guaire. "Killed them and cut them up swift as might be and set the joints on rowan stakes around the fire. And we sat watching, amazed to see how quickly they were cooking, wondering what would happen now."

"And when the man brought me my own steed's flesh to eat I refused him, for such meat is forbidden except when it is offered to the gods," Fionn said then.

"And then the lights went out, the torches around the walls and even the embers of the fire," Guaire went on. "We grabbed for our swords, taking up whichever blade was closest as they came at us, the nine headless men and their terrible master. Back to back we fought, Ceallach and Fionn and I, man against man against them all night long until the rising of the sun. And I tell you now that had it not been for Fionn we would have been slain there, so hard was the fray."

"And when the sunlight came we fell down in a hard faint of exhaustion," said Fionn, "for if I fought hard, then Guaire here and Ceallach labored no less manfully. But when we awoke, we found ourselves hale and whole, with not a mark upon us, but the house and the grey-haired man and his headless servants were all gone."

"What about your horses?" asked Fearghusa. "Did you find their bones?"

"Ah, lad, it is the steeds themselves that we found before us, chomping at the green turf in all their health and vigor." Guaire grinned at the boys.

"You're teasing us," said Fearghusa suspiciously. "You said the man killed them."

"Now, lad, why would I deceive you, and the black horse itself outside in your father's yard for all to see?"

The twins looked from one man to another, but Fionn had learned to keep a straight face in his years with the *fian* and did not twitch a muscle.

"You would not have had so hard a fight if we had been there!" Faobhar said finally.

"Will you take us with you, brother, when you go

north again?" asked Fearghusa. "Nothing interesting ever happens here!"

Fionn blinked, and realized then that he should have expected this. Dithramhach had been plagued constantly by lads who came to Almu seeking to join the *fian*. It was another thing that he would have to deal with himself now that his half brother was gone.

But first he had these other half kin to deal with, gazing at him with eyes bright and expectant as Bran and Sceolan when they were wanting a run. He looked at them, for the first time evaluating them as *rígfénnid* rather than as Muirne's son. She had told him that the boys had fifteen winters, which made them old enough to go out with a war band, and certainly they were well grown and healthy, though still with that unfinished look of the young, with a looseness about the mouth and mismatched features, as if they had not yet grown into their bones.

Or perhaps it was the lines of character that were missing. Fearghusa and Faobhar seemed honest and eager, but clearly they had never known hardship. They had never been denied or tested, growing up here under their mother's eye. Fionn would not have wished the sorrows of his own youth on anyone, but he recognized the role they had played in making him what he was. Blood they might share, but in spirit and will were these lads his kin?

In Fearghusa he sensed a wildness that reminded him of the moons he had spent in beast form when he was a child. Faobhar's high spirits were of another kind—in the fairer twin Fionn saw the love of play and laughter that he had so rarely been allowed to indulge. *They are not the best of me, but I understand them*, he thought ruefully.

Muirne looked stricken, but Gléor was frowning thoughtfully.

Fionn nodded at the boys. "If you came to me, I

would have to treat you like any other lads seeking a place in the *fian*. Nor could you expect any favors. If anything, it's a harder testing you would be given because you are my kin."

Faobhar grinned and Fearghusa gave him a truculent stare. *They are young*, he thought. *It has never occurred to them that they could fail.*

"And in any case, I would not accept you against your father's will," he went on, and the two faces turned to Gléor, who sighed and pulled at his beard.

"It is not a decision to be taken over dinner," he said finally. "But it will be considered, if Fionn is willing to have two such rapscallions as you in his company."

Their training was good enough at least so that his word silenced them. But their eyes were as eloquent as a *fili*'s oration, and Fionn knew he had not heard the last of it.

THAT NIGHT, WHEN HIS MEN HAD RETIRED TO THEIR ENcampment in the meadow, Fionn remained sitting beside the fire. It seemed to him that ghosts hovered in the shadows, phantoms more dangerous by far than the headless monsters of Guaire's tale, for they belonged to his own memories. And first among them was the ghost of the boy he had been, lonely, unhappy, by turns truculent and afraid.

He was not much surprised when a breath of air stirred the flames and he saw King Gléor pushing aside the hide that covered the door.

"Have you come to challenge me to a game of *fidchel*?" Fionn's lips twisted as he remembered the long night of play that had ended his time here, when Gléor recognized him as a son of Cumhal and sent him away lest his presence trouble the queen.

"What use—" Gléor smiled. "Even when you were a lad I could not beat you, and I do not imagine that years and experience have lessened your skill. Now it is a deeper game I am involved in, and the stakes are my wife and my sons. . . ."

Fionn shrugged helplessly. "You cannot protect them forever."

"I know it—" the bench creaked as the king sat down. He had grown grey with the years, but Fionn could see strength in him that he had not known how to look for when he was young. Not so long ago Fionn had proclaimed himself the shield of Eriu; in his own way, Gléor shielded Lamraige, but against some powers no shield could hold.

"My sons are young racing colts penned in a yard; they are wolf cubs who have no food but bread. They should have been fostered out long ago, but their mother would not be parted from them, and I had not the heart to insist. I do not know whether it is better or far worse or simply our fate that they should go with you. But I do know that to lose them this way will be far harder for Muirne."

Fionn stared into the fire, his chin resting on his fist; as he turned his head his thumb brushed his lips and sudden awareness flooded through him.

"Everything that is lost will someday be restored, some way—" Words came from that deeper knowledge. "She will not lose her sons. She did not even lose me." And even as the words came, he wondered if one day all the things that he himself had lost would be restored to him.

"I will let Fearghusa and Faobhar come to you," said Gléor, "but not yet. I must let Muirne grow accustomed to letting them go."

He spoke decisively, but Fionn wondered. Some things, in his experience, were best done quickly.

After that they sat for a time in silence. When Gléor rose to seek his bed at last it was past midnight. But the king had not been the only one still waking. When Fionn rose at last to go out to his bed, he sensed something moving in the shadows outside the door and whirled, hand going to the dagger at his side. Then he caught the faint spicy scent of blossoms and realized who was standing there. He reached out and took Muirne's hands. They were cold, and he began to chafe them between his own.

"You are chilled through—why did you not send for me, or come in?" Abruptly the reason came to him. "Is it that you did not wish Gléor to know what you said to me?" He felt her tremble, and freed the folds of his cloak, draping it around her thin shoulders and drawing her against him.

"Fionn, don't take them—don't take my sons!" she said against his chest. "You have already taken so much from me! Your conception cost me Cumhal, and your birth, my father and my home!"

"Men's pride cost you those things, Muirne," he said sternly. "I have enough mistakes to regret in my life, but those griefs, at least, did not come from me."

"You have grown hard," she said, pulling a little away from him. "Will you take my boys that I was never parted from and get them killed in the *fian*? I dared to love them!"

And do you not, even now, love me? he thought bitterly, but that was unfair. He tried to speak soothingly.

"They are a warrior's sons, Mother, and they are nearly grown. One way or another they will leave you, but I cannot tell you how. Sleep now, my dear, and perhaps the new day will bring better counsel." He kissed her, and presently she turned back to the hall, but he knew that she was weeping.

WHEN THE *FIAN* RODE AWAY THE NEXT MORNING ONLY Gléor came out to bid them farewell. Fionn supposed that Muirne had stayed abed to hide her grief, and the boys must be sulking. It was not until the end of the first day's ride, when he surprised his two half brothers helping the *gillas* with the cooking, that he understood that the decision was neither his nor Muirne's.

The boys faced him with stricken eyes, waiting to learn their fate. Clearly they had not expected to be discovered so quickly. But Fionn began to laugh.

"Well lads, I suppose that this is as good a place as any to begin your training. You shall serve your apprenticeship as I did, when I kept your father's fire."

Slowly, as they understood what he was saying, their faces brightened. It was then that Fionn realized that his brothers, like him, had inherited Muirne's smile.

Chapter 11

FIONN SAT ON A LARGE STONE OVERLOOKING THE PLAIN below Almu. It had weathered in such a manner as to make a high seat, and the sun warmed it; since he had discovered it overgrown with creeper a few weeks after bringing his young brothers back he had spent long hours there. That had been almost three years ago. By now, everyone knew that when the chieftain went up to sit on his rock he was not to be disturbed.

Fionn came to escape the constant bustle of the *fian*, the voices of the men and their women, the growls of dogs and the sharp cries of children, the smells of cooking and eating and belching and brewing that sometimes threatened to overwhelm him. Here, on the high stone chair, his restlessness seemed less urgent, and he could almost forget the emptiness within.

He knew something was lacking in his life, but he could not put a name to it, so he tried to be content with the caress of the warm sun upon his skin, and the soothing murmur of bee song among the golden blooms of the gorse below. In most years he and the *fian* would have been away to the woods by now, or off on some campaign. If Dithramhach had been alive, he would have insisted. But peace mantled Eriu, and the harvest

promised to be the best in years. He supposed he would
have to bestir himself and take the men out soon, before
they exhausted the food, but the storehouses of Almu
were well stocked and there was no urgency. That was
his problem—there seemed to be no reason for him to
make the effort to do anything anymore.

His brothers were growing tall. He ought to be content
in their progress. They had not replaced Dithramhach,
but he knew they loved him, and of the love of his
two nephews, who panted beside his knees in the
heat of the day, he had never been in doubt. Long
ago he had been saddened at the idea that Bran and
Sceolan were condemned to live out their lives in dog
form; he had even contemplated seeking some way to
break the spell. But it seemed to him now that perhaps they were the lucky ones. As dogs, they were
content if they had food and exercise and a place by
his side. Fionn scratched Bran's floppy ears without
paying much attention, and got a warm, wet tongue
across his palm in return.

The murmur of the bees and the heat made him
drowsy, and he closed his eyes for a moment and
breathed the sweet, warm air. And suddenly it smelled
of snow.

*The crisp, chill scent of fresh fallen whiteness enve-
loped him. Dark, soft eyes stared, wide and frightened.
He had never seen such eyes, and yet it seemed
he knew them, recognized their dark and promising
warmth, all the hotter because of the surrounding
chill.*

With a slight start Fionn came back to awareness of
the sleepy warmth around him. But that moment of
vision had been so real! He realized now that he had
been dreaming about those dark eyes, full of need and
longing, for the past three nights. Until now, only a
whisper of memory had remained when he woke in
the dawn, a fragment that tantalized him with its illusory sweetness. But whether it was some magic in the

noonday sun, or because whatever spell was on him was growing stronger, he sensed the rest of the vision hovering just beyond conscious awareness.

He gnawed his thumb, tasting the rank flavor of dog, and felt a fragment of poetry writhe along his tongue. Fionn focused his mind, trying to grasp the words as they slipped past.

> *Snow-flower's sweetness now unfold—*
> *Beauty breaks the bonds that hold—*
> *Hawthorne's crown shall conquer cold!*

Fionn blinked, glimpsing snowflakes turning into creamy hawthorne flowers. The blossoming of the thorn trees was the first sign of summer, edging every lane in drifts of white bloom. But it was already summertide, and the world was blooming. Why should he need to support the process with spells? He supposed that the thorn blossoms must be a symbol for something else, but even his thumb's wisdom could not tell him what it might be.

A rustle in the underbrush brought him back to awareness of the world. His brother Faobhar bounded out of the gorse, grinning widely and holding his own lance and Fionn's short hunting spear. "Are you going to sit there all day? We need fresh meat, and you did promise to go hunting with us this afternoon."

The lad, on the brink of manhood, had the breaking voice of his years, deep one moment and high the next. Fionn remembered when his own voice did that, and how it had enraged him. On reflection he realized that almost everything had enraged him when he was that age, and was glad his younger siblings had a different life than his own.

"So I did. Where is Fearghusa, then?" Though the brothers were twins, in temper they were very different. Faobhar loved to talk and asked as many questions as Fionn had when he was still called Demne. Remembering his frustration at the silences of Bodbmall and the Liath Luachra, Fionn tried to answer them. But Fearghusa rarely spoke, never joked, and had not made many friends in the *fian*. Faobhar stayed close to Fionn, but Fearghusa would vanish into the woods for hours and be discovered staring at a badger's set as often as not. Indeed, with his square shoulders and hairy arms, he seemed more like that solitary and rather antisocial beast with each passing moon.

"He is waiting for us at the top of the trail," said Faobhar, "watching the moss grow."

Fionn grinned and got to his feet. The dogs rose with him, thrusting against his thighs and showing their eagerness for the chase with lolling tongues and brightening eyes. He pulled at their silky ears and ran his fingers through the coarser fur on their necks, finding, as always, a comfort in the contact he could not have explained. Faobhar was looking at him with the same expectance as the dogs. Laughing, he rumpled the boy's curly locks as well. Then he reached for his spear and they loped off down the wooded slopes of Almu.

Fearghusa was crouched in the shadow of an oak, virtually invisible to any eyes less keen than Fionn's. His hair lay dark across his skull, and he seemed surrounded by his own silence. At times he could be strangely remote for one still so young.

Fionn had found the rearing of his two younger brothers more difficult than he had expected. Sometimes it was even harder than keeping peace in the *fian*. When the lads got into ordinary boyish mischiefs of the sort he had never known, he found himself wondering what Bodbmall or the Liath Luachra would have advised him to do. He had developed a new appreciation for his foster mothers, but he could not bring himself to be as hard on Faobhar or Fearghusa as he suspected they would have been.

The three men and two dogs moved down the slope of the hill without a sound, becoming shadows among the trees. The bee-borne murmur of the heights faded, but the few birds they heard in the branches below twittered sleepily, as if they were too warm to sing. To Fionn's woodwise ears it seemed almost unnaturally quiet, and he tried to sense if something had disturbed the peace of the forest. The usually active squirrels seemed absent too, and this puzzled him. He paused and took a long breath, remembering another day like this, long ago, when he had encountered an enraged sow and slain her child, seeking praise from his fosterers, and been so sorely disappointed.

There was no scent of pig in the still air. But there was something. . . . He stiffened, nostrils flaring at a chilly whiff like a breath of winter. There was no scent to it, only that deathly *cold*. That was what halted him in his tracks and sent the prickle of danger along his spine. Whatever was in the wood was not of this world.

"What is it?" asked Fearghusa. "Did I miss something I should have seen?" He flushed a little, for he had reason to be proud of his skill as a tracker, and Fionn shook his head.

"Cannot you smell it? That wintry cold that chills the bones?"

Faobhar's eyes widened. "I feel nothing. Indeed, today it is so warm I would fall asleep if we were not on the move!"

Fionn sighed. Even Muirne could not expect him to protect her boys from all the world's perils, but this was different. There was death in that wintry air. He did not like the thought of turning back from danger, but he knew that if he stayed here there was no way he could make his brothers go. On the other hand, if he was the only one who could sense the cold, then perhaps the danger, if any, was only to himself. He sniffed again, but now he could smell only crushed mint and leaf mold and a whiff of drying grass—the ordinary scents of summer in the forest.

I'm getting to be an old woman, starting at shadows, he told himself grimly, and thrust the sense of foreboding away.

They were well into the forest now, and it was time to go more carefully. He lifted his hand to signal to Fearghusa and Faobhar.

Something large and white flashed from a thicket, and the dogs were after it before Fionn could react. Fearghusa and Faobhar charged after the dogs, yelling their excitement, and he had no choice but to overtake them. The noise of the dogs and the faint tread of brogued feet over the floor of the forest rustled in his ears as he lengthened his stride.

The white flash burst between two trees a dozen spear lengths ahead, and Fionn caught a glimpse of soft, arrow-shaped ears and a night-dark and rounded eye. A white deer! It seemed a shame to slay such a rare creature for food, and he lowered his own weapon, hesitating.

But the color of the deer made no difference to the dogs. They scented meat, and as the doe fled, instinct drove them after her. Their deep baying rang through the trees. Faobhar and Fearghusa sprang after them, as excited as Bran and Sceolan. Blue eyes gleamed in the half-light that fell through the leaves; he glimpsed the pulse beat in a sunbrowned throat and remembered when he, too, would have leaped after the deer with no thought for anything but bringing it down.

The white deer gave a tremendous bound into another thicket, but as she disappeared, she looked back at Fionn and a shock of recognition rocked him backward. He had seen those eyes before! His senses swam as he tried to remember; then he felt once more the uncanny cold breath of the Otherworld. Gooseflesh sprang out all over his skin. The deer! The white doe was the focus—she carried faerie with her as she moved through the mortal forest, like an otter, its fur silvered by bubbles, cutting across the current of a stream.

The breeze strengthened; oak trunk and hazel bough were blurred by a glimmering haze. Perhaps it could protect the doe from mortal weapons, but for mortals to see her at all she must be more than halfway into the world of men. His brothers were wholly creatures of earth—what would happen to them if they tried to strike her down?

"Stay!" His voice cracked on the command, but the dogs were barking too loudly for the boys to hear. Fionn sprang into motion, knowing he must overtake the hunters before they caught up with the deer. He felt his heartbeat shake his own chest as he stretched his long legs, running as he had never run before.

From the hazel copse ahead came a flurry of motion; the belling of the hounds changed. Fionn recognized that deep note of triumph and knew that they had brought their quarry to bay.

"Wait! Don't kill her—" he cried, and saw Faobhar's fair head turn, but the dogs were too frenzied to hear. Through the thrashing hazel leaves he could see the deer, her head thrown back and eyes white-rimmed by terror, prisoned by the tangled boughs. He leaped past Fearghusa, knocking the spear aside, and grabbed Sceolan, growling furiously, by his rough mane, for the dogs had gone beyond human words. Sceolan yelped an answer and flinched away, tail between his legs. But Bran's great hindquarters were bunching as he gathered himself to spring.

Fionn leaped for the dog, snarling. His thick-muscled legs closed around Bran's narrow shoulders in a wrestler's grip, and the dog surged against the hold, possessed entirely by his canine nature. They struggled against one another, nephew and uncle no longer, but only dog and man, while behind him the brothers tried to hold back Sceolan. Bran snapped and closed his fangs around the tender flesh of Fionn's calf; pain flared through his body, driving him beyond reason as well.

Fionn felt his thighs clamp together without his will as Bran tasted blood and tried to bite again. He tried to stop the flexing of his thews, but it was too late. There was a tiny popping noise amidst the crashing of their struggle, a sound like green alder wood upon the fire, and Bran's great jaw went slack. The dog went limp and sagged suddenly, hindquarters still twitching. And then, at last, Fionn was able to make his body obey him. He stepped back and knelt, cradling the dog's head as the light dimmed in the shining eyes. Bran could no longer move, but Fionn read surprise and betrayal there.

Blood was dripping from Fionn's leg, but he ignored it. He touched the dog's muzzle, then felt along the throat, his sensitive fingers pausing at the place where his thighs had crushed the windpipe, and tears blurred his eyes. Air gurgled in the ruined throat as Bran's lungs strove to fill, but from the eyes awareness had already fled. Then with a last gasp the breath was gone, and only the little twitches that flicked along the flesh bore witness as the life faded from the limbs.

And then came a moment when Fionn knew that what he held was dead meat, and with a moan he let go of the body and, still staring at it, pulled away. Sceolan lifted his head and began to howl. Fionn turned to silence him, but human words were beyond him; at the sound, the anguish within burst and suddenly his own voice rose with that of the dog in a keen of desolation.

The cry tore through him and rang through the forest. He gasped for breath and felt his skin begin to prickle, looked back, and saw that Bran's black coat was beginning to fade. As he stared, the form of the dog became the body of a lean young man, dark and handsome. For a moment, it lay limp and naked upon the crushed and bloodied ferns, then began to dance with the light of the Otherworld. The brilliance played across the body like a rainbow, then it was gone, and nothing remained upon the beaten bracken except the ashy outline, white and gleaming, of a human form.

Sceolan whined, and the boys edged away, great-eyed with fear. Fionn opened his mouth to explain—but he could not. He had never told them the tale of his hounds, and now it was too late. He drew a ragged breath, then sobbed without restraint. He had smelt death and dealt death before—but this was Bran! His sister-son, entrusted to him, his most faithful companion. Tuireann would weep when she knew. He recalled another summer day and another boy named Bran, slain by a stone from his own quick fingers—so long ago, and yet it seemed like only yesterday.

My fault! Have I learned nothing since then? Will I always be fated to destroy the thing I most love?

After a time the first intensity of sorrow eased and Fionn used his spear butt to help him up from his knees. Blood was still oozing from his leg, but he ignored it. Mongfind could tend it when they got back to Almu, and suddenly he wanted very much to get home, away from the birds that twittered as cheerfully and the sun that shone as brightly as if Bran were still alive. He gestured to the lads to turn back, but Fearghusa pointed over his shoulder, and Fionn turned to look.

The doe! He stared at that exquisite form—the tapered muzzle and delicate legs, the graceful curve of the back and above all the huge, liquid eyes that gazed at him with such entreaty—and saw in it a mockery.

"You are right," he said harshly to his brother, "this creature owes us an honor-price for the death of Bran! What are you?" He turned to address the deer. "Are you some creature of the Sidhe come to amuse yourself by teasing us, or are you an illusion sent to deceive me by some enemy in the Otherworld? You cannot answer—" He went on as the doe's eyes widened and her head sank as if in shame. "But it does not matter, and though this spear is not Birga, I think my own spells are strong enough to send you where Bran has gone!" He drew his hunting knife and scored an ogham of unbinding upon the shaft of the spear.

The breeze carried the scent of the deer towards the hunters, and Sceolan ceased his howling and began to whine. Beneath the musky smell of deer there were other smells—the cold of winter and the sweetness of apple blossom in the spring. It was a stew of smells, disorienting and strange. He shook his head to clear it and began to chant, breathing on the head of the spear.

"By the skill in my hand, by the soil where you stand, truth be revealed where this spear shall land!"

He lifted the spear. The deer took a step back, but did not flee. This seemed even stranger than the powerful mixture of scents, but sorrow was stronger than caution. He drew his arm back to throw.

"Fionn, do not!" Faobhar's cry came at the moment he released it, too late to stop him, but sharp enough to spoil his aim.

Time seemed to slow. In the green sunlight that fell through the leaves, the doe was dazzling. She lifted her head as if to meet the spear, and the great, dark eyes regarding him seemed alive with an intelligence that did not belong to the shape before him—like the human awareness that had lived in Bran's canine eyes. This was no true deer! But he had already guessed that. Then the spear plunged down and scored a line of crimson along the snowy hide. . . .

The deer shuddered, but she did not fall. Nor did she try to flee. But where the magic in Fionn's spear had touched whatever spells surrounded her, there was a wavering in the air and a flicker of rainbow color. White hide and pale flesh wavered in and out of vision.

Fionn moved closer and reached his roughened hand out towards the soft muzzle. The deer seemed to shake its head and turned its face away before he could touch her. Still, he could sense the enchantments that ran along her body. They sang upon his nerves, dark and bright, familiar and unknown.

He closed his eyes, concentrating deeply. An image formed in his mind, the sense of a single thread, leading from the very soul of the deer to his own. But this was no new sorcery—the thing that rocked him back on his heels was the sense of recognition, as if that thread had been a part of him since he first began to know what it was to be a man. But it had never been connected to anything.

Fionn went cold as he realized that he had sought that thread, that connection, in everything he did or thought. He had looked for it in Donait, in Bodbmall, in his uncle, his brothers, his sister and her sons, in Cruithne and the other women he had bedded. He had tried to find it in Fionnéices, then in poetry, in war and revenge. When he had met Muirne in the orchard, he had somehow thought he would find what was missing, and had been disappointed.

It was true, he thought then, torn between rage and wonder. *This sorcery was meant for me. . . .*

The doe stood trembling only a handspan away. He felt the bond tightening between them; the need to draw closer was like a hunger. But his youth had been haunted by admonitions to pause, to think, to hold back, and uncontrolled instinct had already brought him one tragedy today. "*Patience, Demne, patience. Never be hasty when you can do otherwise.*" He could almost hear Bodbmall saying the words. Had he learned nothing in all these years?

The creature who stood before him was as certainly magical as she was dangerous, but was that danger of her own doing, or was she trapped in the same spell that bound him?

Hawthorne's crown shall conquer cold. . . .

The verses that had begun to come to him as he sat on the hilltop sang once more in his mind, and now words were being added, the song of the world slipping in between the words, joining and twining like the thread between them.

Fire and ice, flowing, twisting in endless designs
like the paths he had once seen leading from
Brigid's hall. . . .

Time slowed, then ceased to flow as Fionn tried to discern the pattern of enchantment surrounding the deer, and the nature of the thread that led to her. The spell was unlike any he could remember encountering before, but it was somehow familiar, too—like a stone one ceases to notice because it is seen daily.

He opened his eyes with a sigh and the deer flinched, her sharp little hooves rustling in the grass. Sensitive ears flickered as if she heard the words chasing in his mind. Then, to his astonishment, she took a hesitant step forward and the velvet softness of her muzzle brushed his hand. At the touch, the half-formed verse became intelligible.

"From ice and fire together twined,
from lonely heart and cunning mind
are spun the spells that spirits bind—"

It was a fragile, fleeting whisper in his mind, as elusive as the giggling laughter of Tuireann that he used to hear when he was a boy.

He shut his eyes to shut that memory away and felt a pang in the leg where Bran had bitten him. But slow as that wound was to close, he knew the wound to his heart would take far longer to heal. He stood still for a moment, trying to conquer his pain. Then something touched his leg. It was only the gentlest of pressures, but it left a healing warmth where it passed. His eyes flew open and he jumped back, staring.

The doe looked up at him. His blood showed crimson against her white muzzle, as red as her own blood where his spear had scored her side, and she was looking up at him with an expression he could only call love. Slowly he knelt beside her, stretching out his arms without quite touching her hide. In an instant he could seize that graceful neck and snap it, as easily as he had crushed Bran's. The creature before him must know that. But still she stood, watching him with wide eyes.

> *"When shall this spiral find an end?*
> *When head and heart the soul extend—*
> *When soul and shell in union blend . . ."*

He stilled, allowing all his senses to quest outward, seeking the invisible shape of energy that surrounded and defined the deer; striving to identify its patterning. It was not right. He could sense the enchantment that bound the deer, but he was unable to grasp any portion of it, so seamless was its making.

His spirit's senses were not sufficient. He had to know her physical form as well. He took a deep breath, then reached out and touched his thumb—his left thumb, into which the burning flesh of the Salmon had seared its wisdom—to the bright track of blood on her side. This blood did not burn, but it made his finger tingle. Quickly he set it to his lips.

For a moment he tasted salt and sweetness. Then there was a slight, sickening tug at his soul strings, and a sensation of whirling nothingness expanded within him. For just an instant his feet seemed hooves and his wide brow was crowned with antlers. A trap! He snatched his hands away before it was complete, leaped away from the beast, and discovered he was panting as if he had run the breadth of the plain.

His head was whirling, but there had been something—when he was a child he had tasted the blood of a pig and spent a moon in that form. But though during that time he had forgotten his humanity his human soul had still slumbered within. He looked back at the doe, his eyes narrowing.

"You are a woman," he whispered, "imprisoned by a spell! But by whom, and why do you come to me?"

The deer turned her head and regarded him sadly, then she turned her head away. Fionn drew a ragged breath and looked back at the boys, who were crouched beside a now silent Sceolan, watching him with the avid interest of the young. The wood was utterly silent.

"What are you doing?" Faobhar, always the more articulate of the twins, dared to ask. "Is she dangerous?"

Fionn stared at him, feeling how his heart shook in his breast, how every nerve tingled with awareness of the deer. "Very dangerous," he said gently. "But then, so am I—" Unwillingly, his glance sought the seared grass where Bran had lain. "You must stay still and keep silence. Whatever happens, you must not try to interfere!"

Fionn turned again and extended his empty hand towards the white deer. She stared at him, then took a hesitant step, the bracken fern scarcely rustling beneath her fragile hooves. The air stirred once more, and he could smell the warm animal scent, the cold odor of snow, and beneath it all, the slightly acrid stink of deadly enchantment.

Voices chased through his memory—the plaintive voice of the crane-skin bag that had once been the beautiful Aife, and the enraged voice of his sister, Tuireann, as she had told him of her days as a dog. These were magics of the Otherworld, but he knew there was something about the deer that was deeper and darker than those, something twisted into a dreadful torment. He could sense the pain of the world at this unnaturalness of the being before him, and he could feel the peril to himself in her dark regard. If he had not drawn back when he did, he would have been caught in the body of a beast as surely as he had caught Bran between his thews.

More voices joined the inner clamour now—the ancient voice of Bodbmall and the honeyed tones of Fionnéices, speaking so softly he could not quite capture the words he so desperately needed to hear. Fionn concentrated, trying to grasp the meaning of the murmur within his mind, but the scent of the doe distracted him. His ears began to ring, and a wave of giddiness swept through him, making his belly roil and cold sweat bead on his wide brow. He swallowed hard, catching the tip of his tongue with his teeth, and tasted warm blood.

The deer edged closer, shoulder muscles twitching with terror, but dark eyes trusting. The cold smell of snow intensified. He felt his limbs grow chill and stiffen until he was shuddering with cold. Only the warm metal taste of blood seemed to quicken his flesh as he stared at the deer.

Sceolan made a sudden, low growl, and the icy cold vanished as quickly as it had come. Fionn gasped, only now realizing that the breath had nearly ceased in his straining lungs. His agile mind cleared, and he felt the warmth of the sun touch his flesh through the leaves above.

Winter! The deer was snared in some endless winter, a season of death and cold. He thought again of the verse that had come to him, sitting on the hill. Had those tangled words really risen from his own soul, or were they pieces of another's working?

Abruptly he thrust his thumb into his mouth and tried to banish from his mind all images of whiteness, cold, and death. It was not easy, for the taste of the doe's blood was still on his skin, and now it brought with it the smell of snow, lapping him in waves of cold. He concentrated on the sun, on the golden color and the heat of it, on the smell of earth warmed by its rays, and the rich scent of honey and the bloodred poppies that sprang up each summer in the midst of the golden grain.

Fionn wound all these images into one perfect summer's day, struggling to bind them with words. And gradually he felt his limbs warm, his knotted muscles ease and his skin heat until he was drenched with sweat. And still the heat of his body grew, radiating outward until the deep scent of summer began to drive the chill of death away.

And with the warmth came music, flowing through the silence like the sun melting ice on a spring day. Words rushed out of him on a warm tide of music, a song of summer to drive winter away.

"Summer I summon, sovereign season,
Green-mantled master of love and of music,
Dew stars the dawning, white haze when wind's over,
Covers the valley, then comes the bright sky.
High in the branches, the birds begin singing,
String-music playing, sweet summer is crowned.
Bound silent by winter, the willow once withered
Now hither brings harmony; Summertide, hail!"

The doe was watching him, ears spread wide to catch each tone. Fionn tensed as a shiver rippled through the snowy hide. Was she afraid, or was this something else, like the first tremor when ice begins to break up in the spring? Holding her gaze with his own, he continued his singing, directing the heat that burned within him towards her like a crystal focusing the light of the sun.

"Dales swathed in shade as hilltops in sunshine,
Columbine cloaks the highways, and canopies hedges.

In sedges' green shrine the songbirds are singing,
Bringing lovers to beds in shady green bowers.
Flowers adorn them with freshest of fragrance,
Panting and sighing their music resounds.
Around them the song of birds echoes their crying,
High on the heights, the cuckoo calls clear."

As if they were part of his own awareness, Fionn
could hear birds singing, where before the wood had
been silent. But the sensations he felt within were
more compelling. He understood now that only the
heat of passion could melt the icy spell that imprisoned her, and not the passion of hatred with which
he had wanted to avenge Bran. That way lay madness,
the trap that he was certain now had been set for him,
with the doe as bait to draw him in. But the sweet fire
of love would melt that ice more surely. And love, he
realized, was what he was feeling. It was not a devour-
ing desire that filled him, but an overwhelming urge to
protect and shelter, to let the beauty before him unfold
like a frost-kissed flower opening to the sun.

"Hear now the music, summertide's melody—
Sweet song of love and of life and of laughter;
After the cold comes that chorus, restoring
The forms and the faces distorted by frost."

As he sang, the white deer edged closer, until she
was once more in reach of his great hands. She was
shaking visibly now. The dark eyes were level with his
pale ones, and Fionn could feel the breath of the beast
brush his sweat-salted cheeks.

"The lost one, I summon by song and by sunshine;
Mine is the music that masters the spell—"

The deer swayed towards him. Fionn rocked back
on his heels and nearly lost the last crucial words.

*"Well have I chanted from winter to wake thee,
I break the enchantments by which thou art bound."*

The doe's flanks heaved desperately, then she collapsed into his arms. In that moment, as his strong arms tightened around her, the great heat of his body and his poem seemed to coalesce into a drop of gold that ran from his flesh to that of the beast.

A searing light encircled both animal and man, blinding him as it exploded into the still air. *It burned!* For a moment he was certain he would catch fire like a dry and resinous tree. Then it diminished, and in some distant place he heard a scream of pain, as if the earth itself was scorched by the fiery heat of their joining. His mind staggered at the sound, and he knew dimly that the dreadful spell was returning to its maker.

The swirl of gold around them expanded as the last words left his scalded lips, and the smell of burnt fern filled his nostrils. Then it was gone, and he found himself sprawled on the ground, dazed and aching in every bone, barely aware that the dark eyes into which he was staring now looked at him from the fair face of a woman.

When his mind began to work once more, he gaped. She gave a convulsive shudder, and just as he was beginning to learn the weight and balance of her body, she slipped from his arms. Slowly, Fionn pulled himself upright, staring at the woman who stood before him, her flesh as white as the stones of Aonghus Og's palace, her hair like snow upon the mound. At first she appeared to be without any colour whatever, except for her dark eyes and the silver-ash line of her brows. Then he noticed how red her small mouth was, as if she had been eating berries, and glimpsed the rosy aureoles of her small breasts peeping through the waterfall whiteness of her hair. Mesmerized, his gaze travelled lower, and he saw that the mound of her womanhood was capped with silky snow. For a moment he felt the desire to quench his burning face in that softness. But she was still trembling, and as he saw her gaze flicker around the clearing and back to his face again he found his desire transformed to a need to protect her.

"It is all right, all right, little one," he said softly. "You will be safe with me. . . ."

He held out his hand. The woman studied it for a long time. Then she placed white fingers in his roughened palm. Her hand was not cold as he had feared. Her warm touch reached some deep and empty place within him he had not known was there. He remembered the moment of absolute *rightness* he had felt when he held her, but he knew better than to try to touch her when she was still so afraid.

One of the boys moved behind him; her eyes widened and she took a sudden step towards Fionn. Warmth flared through him.

"It is true, you can trust me," he said softly. "But they will not hurt you. I will not let anyone hurt you—ever again." His heart pounded in his chest as if he had run a great race. He had spoken truly, but even as the words left his lips a great fear followed them. Would he be able to keep that promise, or would he one day bring disaster to this woman as he had done to everyone else he truly loved?

He wanted to clasp her close in his arms and never let her go, but he could sense how fragile was the trust that kept her hand in his. He must not touch her. Fionn felt it with the force of a *geas* between them—no matter how great his desire, he must never touch her until she first reached out to him.

"Do you understand?" he asked her. "Will you trust me with your name?"

The woman did not reply, and he wondered if she was as mute as the deer she had been. Instead, her eyes went to the lads and Sceolan, still crouched among the crushed bracken. The memory of the chase returned then, and Fionn felt once more the rough brush of Bran's coarse hide as he had struggled. His heart slowed, the exultant pulse of his delight fading as he realized how he had slain his nephew for the sake of the slender woman beside him.

The grief rose in his throat, and for a moment he forgot her, cursing his fate. He loved both of Tuireann's children, but Bran had been most dear to his heart. He liked to waken Fionn with a good face lapping, his huge paws on Fionn's bare shoulders, on cold mornings, and was always eager for any adventure. Sceolan was more distant, though his heart was great.

He stared at the outline of a body burnt into the bracken, and knew he had once more paid the price for victory in blood and loss. Fearghusa rose, shifting his feet uneasily, and Faobhar frowned where he still crouched. Both his brothers looked at Fionn with that mingling of awe and mistrust he sometimes inspired in men, even members of the *fian*. He sighed. He had worked so hard to win their love, and now it seemed to have gone in a single flash of golden light.

The woman looked back at him, and he took her hand.

Sceolan got to his feet, threw back his great, shaggy head, and gave a howl that rang through the still trees, echoing across the mountain until the stones trembled and the leaves shook with its violence. And, far away, in the Otherworld, a woman wept.

Chapter 12

THE FEAST OF LUGHNASA WAS PAST, AND THE LEAVES
were turning to gold. Once more Fionn sat in his
stone high seat, as he had nearly every day since he
had returned from the wood with the silent, white-
tressed woman, his brothers, and the dog Sceolan. No
doubt his people wondered where she had come from
and where Bran had gone, but they had not dared to
question him. He stared across the green and tawny
expanse of the plain below without seeing it, reliving
the moment when Bran's form had changed to that of
a boy.

And as he did so, he saw not only the face of his
nephew, but of the first Bran, and of Fionnéices, and
Dithramhach and all the others, staring at him sad and
empty-eyed. Their look did not accuse him, but they
seemed to wonder why they had died. A brown leaf,
stripped from its branch by the wind, sank in slow circles towards the ground, and he sighed.

Fionn felt a small, warm hand on his wrist and
started, for there were not many who could slip
up on him that way. But his flesh recognized the
touch as the hand slid across his palm, fingers curling against his roughened skin. He looked down at a

mass of moon-colored hair. The faerie woman crouched silently beside him, wrapped in one of Mongfind's old shawls, woven in shades of cream and grey. With every touch she became more a part of him, but she herself remained a complete mystery.

Though the woman had not uttered so much as a sound since she had come to Almu, she made it clear that she was used to being cared for. She would wear no cloth with embroidery upon it, nor would she sleep on the skins of beasts or eat of their flesh. There was no anger in her wordless refusals, only a calm he found both admirable and infuriating. At mealtimes she was an island of still whiteness, calmly consuming boiled vegetables or munching an apple, sipping clear water and eating bread dipped in honeycomb, while all around her the *fian* swilled their beer and gnawed on bones. And yet she was not sad—she smiled to see a lark on the wing or the dogs at play, and any babe would still its crying if she so much as stroked its hair.

Her presence filled some great void he had not known was within him, but Fionn could not decide what to make of her. Her stillness challenged him, and so he talked as he never talked before. He spoke to her of Cumhal, his father, and of his childhood with Bodbmall and the Liath Luachra. He told her how his sister had teased him, giggling invisibly, and how she had whispered warnings and saved him, and later, the sad tale of Tuireann's enchantment, which had produced Sceolan and Bran. After two moons, so enormous was the weight of her silence that he began recounting even the tales of his loves, speaking of Donait and Cruithne and the others whose names blurred in his mind.

Today, with the smell of autumn crisp in the air, his thoughts turned to another autumn, when he had been a dog boy in the *dun* of the King of Benntraige, and how the king had discovered his identity and sent him away.

"That was the first time I saw my grandfather, with his eyes hooded like an eagle's and cold as stone." Even now the memory was so vivid he could almost see the old man. "And aged though he was, his mind had talons to grip whatever he could see. He would have had me then if I had not become one with the oak tree."

The woman's slender fingers dug into his palm. "Fer Doirich!"

Fionn nearly fell off the stone. She was staring at him, her eyes huge and dark as if the sound of her own voice had frightened her.

"You can speak!"

"Speak?" She appeared nearly as surprised by this as he.

"Words! Meaning in sounds!" Fionn glared at her, wondering if she had been pretending to be mute all along.

Her face grew intent and her lips parted. She peered cross-eyed at her tongue as she wiggled it. Suddenly Fionn found that funny, and he grimaced to keep from laughing. She glanced up at him suspiciously, closing her mouth. But after a moment, her face relaxed and he glimpsed the swift flicker of her smile that always made his heart skip, as if some rare bird of the Sidhe had strayed into mortal lands.

She touched him. "Hand, finger, thumb, wrist, arm, elbow," she began, tracing her way up his shoulder, entranced, it seemed, by the sheer wonder of the words. "Ear, hair, eyebrow, eye, nose, lips, chin," she continued, brushing his skin lightly. Now he thought he saw mischief in her smile. She started to name her way down his broad chest and flat belly, until her hand rested upon his manhood, which leaped to life at the touch.

Fionn went very still, fighting for control. Did she know what she was doing? She let her hand remain where it was for an instant, then drew back, a faint color tinging her cheeks, the mischief in her eyes turning to wonder as she looked up at him. "I can speak. I had forgotten, somehow, until you spoke of him." Then she shivered all over.

"Who, Lady? Who was the Dark Druid who bound you?"

Her gaze went inward. "His name . . . was in the spell . . . the one who trapped me—Tadg mac Nuada was his name!"

Fionn stared at her, his head whirling. *Tadg mac Nuada? My grandfather?* After Fionn took Almu the old druid had vanished. Surely he must be dead by now! And yet, now that Fionn thought back, the spell that bound the doe did have the stink of the old man's magic.

In those first years Fionn had been constantly braced against it, but aside from nightmares, no attack had come. He had almost forgotten that Almu had not always been his home. But clearly Tadg had remembered. And all these years he had been waiting, plotting. Spite must be keeping him alive! He shuddered, and the woman flinched.

"Do not be worrying—" He reached out to her. "He is my enemy, but he will not touch you here. Those walls are warded against Fer Doirich above all others—" Fionn refused to say the old man's name. "While you are with me or within those walls he cannot harm you!"

Fionn felt his nape bristle, and wondered if he was reassuring the woman or himself. He forced himself to calm and smiled at her. "You have told me his name, but not your own—"

"I am Sadb," she murmured. "Sadb, Sadb, Sadb!" She swayed, arms clasped across her breasts, keening softly.

Fionn gripped her slender shoulders fiercely, raging wordlessly at Tadg, longing to comfort her as she continued chanting, her voice becoming louder until she was shouting into the chill air. The word rang down the slopes, echoing until the world resounded with her name. He felt her hot tears plash on the skin of his hand and could find nothing to say to ease her anguish.

At last Sadb fell silent once more. She slumped against his side. Fionn stroked her snowy tresses gently, enjoying the feel of them, and the sweet smell of her body, clean and warm and womanly. Part of him ached to claim her, but now he felt ashamed that his cruel grandfather had been the creator of her woes. He tried to content himself with the wholeness that her very touch brought him, and that was almost enough.

"I was gathering autumn flowers," she said finally, her voice still raw from screaming. "I remember the smell of the blooms and the earth, and how the sap made my fingers all sticky. But that is all. Surely I had a family, but their names are lost to me." Her silvery brows bent in that lovely line that reminded him of the curved neck of a crane. "I stopped to admire my face in the waters of a lake. My hair was red and my gown was blue and the flowers were as yellow as the sun. There was another maiden, like and unlike me, with hair a darker red, and a gown of green. I heard a sound that made me dizzy and then a mist seemed to swirl between me and the world. I felt myself moving, and when I could see once more I was trapped by the spells scratched into the druid's rods."

"And you know no more? You have no memory of home or kin?"

Sadb took a long, slow breath. "The lake . . . was red. . . ."

Fionn considered her words. If she could not tell him more he must seek elsewhere. Closing his eyes, he thrust his thumb between his lips. As always, there was a rush of images, a freshet that threatened to overwhelm him, a stab of pain that would be a headache later on. He struggled to control the images.

Fionn saw the lake, although he was certain he had never visited the place before, and it was indeed red.

Ruddy hills surrounded the water, whose silt coloured the waters. He knew the place by repute. It was Loch Dergdeire, in the mac Morna lands.

But he saw more than the lake and the hills, and the sight perturbed him. Nestled snuggly on the highest rise was a very ordinary *dun*, but lower down, in the crotch of two hills, there was the unmistakable glow that marked an entrance into the Otherworld. He sighed. Hadn't he had enough trouble with the Sidhe to last him several lifetimes? He had thought Sadb must be of their people, but this confirmed it. He was suddenly grateful that he had been able to control his desire for her. A man who valued his virility did not make a casual leman of a daughter of the Sidhe.

But it was not as a mistress that he wanted her, though every touch set him afire. It was the serenity her presence brought him that he could not live without now. He remembered Muirne, and then his other grandfather, Trenmor, who had run away with the wife of the *Ard Ri*, and wondered if perhaps he might be the first member of his clan to think before he wed.

"Does the name Loch Dergdeire have meaning for you?" he asked.

Sadb's dark eyes widened. "Bodb Derg . . . he is my father! Or he was! Until that man cast his countenance upon me and set his whiteness all around me." She tugged at her hair angrily. "He stole my colour! You must understand—my hair was bright as new copper, and I was vain of it, very vain. This milky stuff pleases me not at all!" Her lips twisted, and Fionn longed to kiss the hurt away.

He resisted the impulse, because he was not certain he could stop at a kiss, and leaned back, thoughtful. Men and gods were jealous of their daughters, and regarded abduction with disfavor. Bodb Derg had the reputation of being intemperate, and he was sure to be angry with Tadg. Fionn was still Tadg's grandson, even though he had rescued the girl. Should he return her to her father or send word? Was it better to risk losing the woman who held his soul in her hands to an outraged father now, or spend the rest of his life worrying about retaliation?

Fionn weighed possibilities long and silently, until Sadb began to eye him anxiously.

"Did you love your father?"

"I was his favorite, and the youngest. I have a sister, Daireann, from his first wife, and I share a mother with my brother Echbel. We were very happy, I think. I was, anyhow. Daireann was always asking for pretty things."

Fionn's heart sank. She had been happy—perhaps she would not want to marry him even if her father agreed. He realized that in the past weeks her wordless presence had filled all the empty places within him. Surely she must feel a link between them too!

"Shall I take you back to Loch Dergdeire and your people?" he said roughly, trying to hide his need.

Sadb stared at him for a long time, as if she knew his doubts and fears. Then she looked down the slope, as if her eyes would pierce the veil of the future. "I would like him to know I still live, though he might not know me as I now appear. Would you let me go?"

"I would take you to your father before the winter comes, if that would please you." As he spoke Fionn felt some shift in the song of the world, as if he had changed the future, and he wondered if he had chosen rightly.

Sadb gave a nod. "That would be for the best," she answered, but she sounded rather doubtful, as if she too knew that something was different now.

IT LACKED A FEW DAYS FROM SAMHAIN WHEN FIONN AND the remnants of his band approached Loch Dergdeire. He had set off with twenty men, his two brothers, and Sceolan. Sadb still shrank away from the dog whenever it drew near, though she was trying to control her fear.

At first they had made good progress, but then a flux had come upon them near Bri Élé, and they were days delayed while first one and then another spewed up a green, vile stuff and shivered with ague.

Fionn had tried all his remedies, but nothing had helped, and finally he himself had succumbed to the strange illness. For nearly a week he had lain on his bed of branches, barely able to summon the strength to roll over and release the hot and bitter stuff that rose from his aching gut. Those who had recovered tried to care for those still sick, and in his rare lucid moments, he wondered if he should turn back to Almu. Was this a natural sickness, or some evil magic?

But half the men were really too weakened to go anywhere. Fionn sent them to rest at the nearest rath, among them Fearghusa, who had lost both weight and strength in a way that frightened him. Fionn's heart ached to see his brother so listless and weary, and felt not for the first time a yearning for a son of his own to rear and watch over.

Thus it was a much diminished party that followed the ruddy shores of the lake with the white-tressed Sadb, now even paler from her bout of illness. Most of the trees around the lake had shed their leaves, so the earth was orange and gold and red underfoot, and deep green from the groves of yew and pine above. The air was hazy with a mist that rose from the water, chill upon their skins. Fionn tried to shake off the unease that increased the closer he drew to Sadb's home. There was something eerie about the lake, and he did not like it.

As the outflow of the lake narrowed into a river once more, armed men emerged from the mist so silently that even Fionn had no warning. They stood waiting, and the *fian* came to a ragged halt. The warriors were well garbed in good woolen tunics of green and fine cloaks of dark brown. Golden clasps shone closing the cloaks, and even at several spear lengths, Fionn could see that the ornaments were the work of a master goldsmith. Their figures wavered, as if they were not entirely in this world. But it was their faces that made him pause, fair with the same accentuated fineness of bone that marked Sadb, the mark of the Sidhe.

No one spoke for a few moments, and then one of the men said, "Who dares invade the domain of Bodb Derg?"

There was a short silence, and then Fionn's heart leaped as he heard Sadb's rare laugh. "How grim you have become, Echbel mac Bodb, since you grew a beard." She ran lightly across the scattered leaves and grasped his hand.

The man stared at her in wonder. "Sadb? Is it you? You wear my sister's fair face, and speak with her voice, but you are. . . ."

"I know, I know." She laid her finger across his mouth playfully. "It was a foul enchantment, and my deliverer is here to bring me home. Echbel, this is Fionn mac Cumhal, who gave me back my voice and helped me find my name when I was lost. Now, stop standing here in the cold with your mouth open, and take me to my father, for I do long to see him." Her voice thinned.

Echbel held her close, and Fionn discovered that even knowing the man who embraced her was her brother, the sight gnawed at his vitals like a shrew.

"Sister, Sister. Welcome home." He spoke the words heartily enough, but Fionn could see his eyes were clouded with doubts as he gazed down at her milky white hair.

AT MOST TIMES, MEN PASSING SID BODBDERG WOULD have seen only a grass-covered mound, though near Samhain, the second-sighted might glimpse, as if through a translucent veil, the outlines of a great hall. But to Fionn and his men, escorted by Echbel with sprigs of hawthorn in their hands, the mist that wreathed the hall was deepened by the swirling smoke of many hearth fires. It smelled of horse and dog and cattle, of food and a sweet, sharp scent that reminded him of Donait's hall. After days in the wild, Fionn found the many odors an assault on his senses.

His stomach clenched uneasily and he wondered whether it were a return of his illness or foreboding, but it was too late to draw back now. The folk of the mound came rushing out to greet them, all fair, laughing faces and bright-colored garments, the sweet jangling of voices, and the deep-toned yammering of faerie hounds. The noise and bustle made it hard to think, but he knew he must be careful. He was still feeling weak from his illness, and so were his men. He did not want to find himself in a fight.

As he followed Sadb and her brother into the wide hall of Bodb Derg, it occurred to him that nowhere in the paths that the Goddess Brigid had shown him in Donait's fair house was this moment predicted. It was a strange sensation to have chosen something even the gods had not foretold. Since he had tasted of the Salmon of Wisdom, he had always *known* which way to turn to pursue his destiny, but the awareness whispering along his nerves, strung to near breaking, seemed to him something utterly new.

A huge man, almost a head taller than Fionn himself, hard-muscled and hard-eyed, rose from beside the fire. His ruddy hair was streaked with silver, and passion had carved deep crevices beside his mouth, but the smoothness of his skin belied the age in his combed and braided locks. His tunic was fine linen and rich with needlework, and the torque around his throat was another masterwork of the goldsmith's art.

From the high seat on the other side of the fire came a woman; she was nearly as tall as the man, and like him in colour and countenance. Her hair was a deeper red, and it gleamed in the hearthlight like silken thread. Her gown of deep green was so embellished with embroidery that it dazzled the eye, and she was weighted with armlets and bracelets in shining gold, with a torque and amber beads about her slender throat, and long earrings dangling beside her braids.

Fionn's gaze swept over her, but not so fast he did not catch the sparkle of interest as she caught sight of him. In other times her look would have pleased him, but now he was indifferent. She was fair enough, but he thought her adornment excessive, and something in the line of her mouth made him uneasy. He put his reaction down to natural wariness and the lingering effects of his illness, and turned his full attention to the chieftain.

"Whom have you brought to grace my hall, Echbel?" The man had a surprisingly light voice, in sharp contrast to his great size. He seemed to know it, and glanced around at Fionn and his men, looking for any smirks of ridicule. Fortunately they were all too glad to be out of the raw weather to insult anybody. Still, he rolled on his toes, as if seeking a fight.

Fionn held back a sigh. He was more weary of contention than he had realized, and wished only to get Sadb's father's permission to return with her to the white walls of Almu and a winter of peace. He was beginning to regret his decision to bring her here.

As Echbel began to answer, Sadb, who had been hidden by broad shoulders and the fall of trail-sodden cloaks, came forward. "Oh, father," she said gravely, but her eyes were dancing, "how stuffy you have become!"

Bodb Derg's eyes narrowed as he studied the small woman moving purposefully around the hearth, disbelief warring with joy. But the red-tressed woman was glaring. Sadb seemed unaware of them. For a moment she looked up at her father, then she flung her white arms around him and buried her face against his enormous chest.

"Sadb? My child, my dearest child?" He wrapped her in his arms. A babble of exclamation filled the hall, much of it delighted, though a few seemed uneasy. It was clear that Sadb was a favorite, and perhaps there were those who were not happy to see her back again. Fionn felt the tug of the thread that joined them—and a flicker of dread that chilled his heart.

HOURS LATER, FRESHLY BATHED AND DRESSED IN CLEAN clothing, the feasting done and the tale-telling past, the company rested on sweet-scented couches. Bodb could hardly bear to let Sadb from his sight, and Fionn found that he could endure the entwining of their fingers only by drinking deeply of the heavy autumn brew.

He struggled to make conversation with his dinner companion, the red-haired woman, Daireann, the daughter of Bodb by his first wife. The longer they spent together, the more uncomfortable he became. With her every motion her many bracelets clashed, giving him the start of a throbbing headache, and she put her hand upon him too often for his ease. There was a look in her green eyes he instinctively mistrusted, the look of a huntress, and her words, through his beery haze, seemed to hold meanings that befuddled his mind even further. He sank into gloomy silence for minutes at a time, only rousing himself out of politeness.

"I will not soon forget this night," Bodb cried out, his clear voice rising above the clamour. "My dear daughter is restored to me, and the renowned Fionn mac Cumhal is feasting at my hearth. What boon would you ask for bringing my dear one back to me? Anything you ask is yours."

Fionn cleared his throat and drew away from Daireann. "I ask nothing but to make Sadb my wife, and to love her until my death," he answered more passionately than he intended. The woman looked at him across the fire and smiled.

A startled silence fell upon the company, and Bodb Derg shook his great head. "Anything but that. Sadb was promised long ago to Len, my goldsmith," he added, gesturing towards the dark man who had been glowering at Fionn since the feasting began. "Besides, my older daughter—"

"Father, I never agreed to marry Len!" Sadb's voice was so shrill that Fionn barely knew it. Her tresses might be white, but the eyes he had thought so gentle could blaze with surprising passion. She pulled her hands away from her father's grasp and set them on her hips defiantly.

"It does not matter. I gave Len my word, in exchange for his arts, and that is that. You may have Daireann, Fionn mac Cumhal. She is the elder in any case, and should be the first to wed. You make a very handsome pair already, and no doubt your children will be strong." Bodb looked very pleased with his solution.

Daireann gave a smile that lacked any warmth, and her green eyes glittered in the firelight. "Thank you, father. You have wisely read my heart's desire, and I accept."

Before Fionn could marshall his spinning wits, his harper Fergus spoke up, his voice weighted with all the multiple inflections of a bard. "Are customs here so different that you insult the famed Fionn mac Cumhal by going back on your word? Fionn has journeyed far to bring your daughter here, that you might know she is well. If you do not fulfill your promise, the lay of Bodb Oathbreaker will be sung at many a hearth."

Bodb Derg's face turned an ugly colour at this threat, and his rather small eyes protruded from his skull. He breathed heavily, glancing from Fionn to Daireann, then to the goldsmith and to Sadb beside him. He looked as stubborn as a boar, and likely as vicious in his anger.

"Take Daireann or nothing! I will not be parted from my Sadb!"

Fionn stood up, shaking off the grasping hand of the red-haired woman, and wondered if Cumhal and Tadg had played out some similar scene over Muirne. He swallowed the hot taste of rage that made the heavy feast feel like iron in his gut, and shook away the lingering fumes of beer that clouded his mind. In his mind he heard a cackle of mad laughter, and knew that somewhere, somehow, his grandfather had known this would happen and was enjoying the whole thing immensely.

He considered his choices for an instant. His handful of men were still weak from the flux. They were some of the finest warriors in Eriu, but they were outnumbered here. The Hazel Shield might have protected him, but he had left it behind with Birga, which was all too well-known in the Otherworld.

Perhaps it was just as well. Fionn wanted Sadb; his soul cried out for her. But what price would he pay? At that moment he felt old and weary of contention and the red path of arms.

Fionn glanced at Sadb and found her great, dark eyes resting on his face with the same desperation she had shown while still enchanted. He did not doubt she longed for him as he longed for her, and wished he had bedded her when he had the chance. She had pulled away from her father, her slim shoulders hunched and miserable, her hands clenched into fists.

Daireann stood up and curled her arm through his, pressing her breast against his side and exhaling a breath heavy with meat and beer. After the sweet breath of Sadb, he had to force himself not to shrink away.

"Do not be foolish, Fionn mac Cumhal. I can give you strong sons and fair daughters," she crooned, her voice honeyed. "My sister is hardly a real woman at all. Her breasts are like acorns, hard and small, and her hips are as narrow as a boy's. I am well favoured and she is . . ."

That was too much. Fionn thrust Daireann away from him roughly, and she fell back onto the couch. "I never saw a less well favoured woman than you, Daireann—not even the Red-Mouthed Woman whom I slew in my youth." He was too outraged to regret his blunt words, and he felt more than saw her answering glare.

Echbel mac Bodb slammed his cup down on a small table, and one leg broke in the violence of his movement. It startled everyone into silence.

"Father, you have shamed us. We have had too much to drink—or too little. This is no matter to be settled tonight. Let us wait until the morning, that our honour might not be stained and no blood shed."

Fergus the poet chuckled. "Most sensible. Your son has a good head on his shoulders, Bodb mac Derg. More drink, and another song." He picked up the harp and struck the strings, and the tension in the hall seemed to lessen. Bodb Derg nodded his grizzled head and sat back down, and the servants began to refill the cups.

Fionn took his place on the couch reluctantly, still angry and frustrated, and Sadb moved as far away from her father as she could. She looked so small and miserable in her plain gown, more like a serving maid than the daughter of a chieftain, and he wanted to hold her against him and tell her she was the most perfect woman in the world. Occasionally she glanced at him and at her sister, and Fionn could almost hear her thoughts. That remark about her breasts must have hurt.

He found his cup in his hand and did not remember taking it. Fionn gave Daireann a baleful glance and noticed her eyes glittering above the rim of her goblet. "I know you did not mean what you said—it was the drink."

"I did not mean what I said? Perhaps."

"Drink, Fionn mac Cumhal, and cool your ire. I spoke out of my heart. When you know me better, you will see that my father is right. I am sorry I said those things about Sadb—it is just how sisters are." Daireann lowered her proud head a little and moved her arms so her bracelets clattered. She seemed anything but genuinely sorry, but he decided to take her at her word. He was too tired for more quarreling.

Fionn gulped a great swallow from his cup and noticed the beer had a slightly oily taste as it slipped into his throat. It was subtle, but unpleasant, and he wondered if the brew was off. Still, it was cool in his mouth. It hit his belly, and fire bloomed within his body. He shook and felt it spread across his torso, then race along his blood, throbbing, until it entered his head with a force like a fist inside his skull.

The hall narrowed before his eyes, then twisted and glowed a ghostly blue. The pillars pulsed and the walls began to close in. There was a dreadful scream close by, and he staggered up, seeking its source in the faces of the guests. As he looked, their startled faces shrank to nothing, and he saw the hall was crowded with great spiders, hairy and shining-eyed. They clacked and began to move towards him.

Seizing a blazing brand from the fire pit, he crouched to fend off the attack, roaring his rage. The spiders seemed to retreat as he swung the brand above his head. The ceiling lowered, threatening to crush him, gleaming green and dripping something red and sticky, and he thrust his weapon at it. The hall was alive, and he was in its belly! He heard shouts of alarm, and several spiders charged at him while others scuttled for the narrowing entrance.

There was a whump above his reeling head, and he heard his name called by many voices, both the living and the dead. He heard Bodbmall's thready voice, and Muirne's rich one; the dry rasp of the Liath Luachra, and the high, piping voice of his sister. Above them all he could hear one most clearly, a sweet voice gone shrill and terrified, crying out in despair. He tried to find that voice, but he could not. Then he smelled the hot stink of blazing wattle, and heard the clatter of golden armlets above the uproar.

He spun around, seeking the ring of metal, and found a great, green spider with many bracelets on its hairy legs. "You!" he roared, casting aside his brand and extending his hands. They seemed to be stranger's hands. His fingers looked like diseased tubers, weak and spongy, but he thrust them at the scuttling spider.

Flesh touched his palms and fingers, warm, soft flesh, smooth and furless. At the same instant he felt a touch on his forearm and saw two small hands encircling his thick wrist. Giddiness swept across him, and the burning within him subsided as abruptly as it had begun.

He looked down and found Sadb clutching his wrist with an expression of terror and determination in her great eyes. His hands, he discovered, were wrapped around Daireann's long throat, the thumbs pressing her torque into the warm flesh.

"Fionn, stop, stop! We have to get out!" A section of the roof fell blazing nearby, and he realized the hall was afire. Guest and host alike were pushing through the entrance, trampling each other in their eagerness to escape. Half the pillars were on fire, and as he tried to order his befuddled mind, one collapsed and fell across the path to the door.

With a grunt he loosed his hold on the sister, tucked Sadb under one arm, and charged at the side of the building with his free shoulder. He felt the wall shudder under him, but it held. There was a terrible cracking noise behind him, and the entire center of the ceiling fell in a fiery crash behind him.

Fionn let go of Sadb, and felt the madness rush back into his blood. Again he heard the dreadful scream and realized vaguely that it was torn from his own aching throat. He felt the fire lick behind him hungrily as he kicked at the wall. He heard the wattle snap as he kicked again and again, until at last an opening yawned. He tore at it with his hands, ignoring the pain, battering the wall with feet and shoulders, gasping for air as the fire consumed the room.

Fionn seized the flash of whiteness that fluttered beside him, felt cool, human flesh, and plunged into the night. He panted while Sadb clung to his side, and felt his head begin to clear. After a moment he heard a clatter, turned, and saw Daireann crawling through the opening.

He bent forward and hauled her up by her ash-smeared hair, until their faces were close enough for ragged breaths to mingle foully. "What did you do to me?" he bellowed as his men grouped around him. He could hear the shouts of the men of Derg summoning buckets to quell the flames and the roar of the fire itself.

Daireann writhed in his grip and clawed at his face. "Nothing," she squealed.

"You poisoned my cup—bitch!"

For a moment it seemed she would deny it. She hissed and spat and cursed while the fire roared behind her, casting a golden light on the smeared faces of those who were attempting to put it out. Fionn could see the grim faces of Bodb Derg and his son, ash-smeared and dark, approaching.

"I only wanted you to desire me, not that milky thing who can only cling to you and whimper. I am Daireann the Golden, and no man can resist me!"

"You flatter yourself," Fionn snarled. Then he thrust her away from him, sending her spinning until she crumpled at her father's feet, whimpering. Bodb Derg looked at her, then at Sadb and Fionn, his piggy eyes glittering in the fire. The old man shifted from foot to foot, glaring at everyone with equal fury.

"Get out!" It was unclear who was meant at first. Then Bodb Derg pointed a shaking finger at Fionn and Sadb. "Get out and take your leman with you! If I ever see either of you again, I will kill you! Curse you, Fionn mac Cumhal, and curse the trouble you bring in your train."

"Father," Echbel protested. "He is not the one at fault."

The old man aimed a fist at his son, catching him across the jaw with a blow that sent the younger man's head back on his neck. "Don't you tell me about fault, you puppy."

Echbel staggered back, then walked away, rubbing his chin, a little blood dribbling from his mouth. "You are a fool, Father, a fool and a man without honor. You never promised Sadb to Len, but only hinted that you might. And if she goes, I go as well," he shouted.

"Then go! I curse the day I ever got you." With that Bodb Derg turned and stumped away into the great shadows of the fire.

Sadb wept. "Fionn, take me home to Almu—take me home!" Her words rang out, and then there was only the weeping of the woman and the crackle of the fire.

The tiny band had covered leagues by the time dusk fell on Samhain, and they were sore and weary. None of Fionn's men complained, and Sadb was so silent he wondered if she had lost her voice again. They found a likely place to camp and settled down to a cold and bitter night in the open. They ate what food they had managed to bring away with them without tasting it, and fell into their cloaks and sleep.

Fionn was drowsing when he felt a cool touch on his injured hands. They were burnt nearly to the bone, and so painful he could not carry his hunting spear, let alone cast it. He opened his eyes and saw the moon rising above the rounded hills, and, in its light, the white woman. Around them, the others were only huddled lumps. Only she was awake, and he, and the moon. She smiled as she gazed down at him, and his heart rose in his throat, full of dizzying joy and desire.

With great gentleness, Sadb drew his hands against her breasts, and suddenly they did not hurt at all. "Are they really like acorns?"

Fionn laughed softly. "They are beautiful, Sadb. I have never forgotten how they looked when I found you first, and I have never stopped longing to touch them."

"Why didn't you?" She sounded annoyed.

"It didn't seem right to just take you, when you did not speak, and after, it seemed less right. I wanted your father's good wishes, and got his curse instead." *Will I ever do anything right?*

Sadb tugged her soiled gown up and drew it over her shoulders. "Touch me now!" Her hair spilled across her shoulders and her nipples hardened in the cold of the night. "I have waited for you so long. Touch me everywhere, Fionn mac Cumhal, heart of my heart."

He was clumsy, both because his injured hands were swathed in herb-soaked wrappings, and because she was so slender and fine of bone he feared to hurt her. She did not seem to notice as she fitted herself against him, lip meeting lip, tongues joining, hands touching. Her cool fingers explored his chest, his flat belly, and went below, waking in him the hot desire of a youth. Her kisses were white moths brushing his skin, until he nearly groaned with the pulsing of his need.

Sadb slipped her legs across him, and he saw her bright smile in the moonlight. "Like this?"

"You are doing fine. Are you sure you've never done this before?"

"I always wanted to, but I never found a man who smelled right. I used to watch my father's cattle and think there must be more than mere mounting and lowing."

Fionn chuckled as she stroked him further. "Smelled right? I stink of sweat and fire."

"From the first taste of your blood, the smell of you, bathed or dirty, has been sweet to me, Fionn mac Cumhal." She lifted herself over him, the softness between her thighs brushing against him, and he could feel the dampness and smell her desire. For a moment she stayed so, looking down at him, then she gave a little wiggle and thrust herself down. He felt the resistance of her maidenhood, but at the contact his own need exploded and he pulled her closer, paying no mind to the pain in his hands, nor to the slight cry she gave as the maidenhead tore. All he knew was the need to join their souls with their flesh. He nearly forgot her pleasure in his eagerness, until she shifted her weight so her breasts brushed his bare chest, and began to slide back and forth.

He moaned deep in his throat, and was answered by her. Sadb moved upon him, enflaming him and resisting him at once, until her body began to tremble. Then she stretched back, driving him up into her, lifting her supple body and sliding against him, panting and almost sobbing as she strove for release. Fionn felt the flutter of muscle around him, then the answering convulsion in his own flesh as all the life in him poured out.

They joined, crying out in their mutual pleasure, as if they had been lovers for years. He heard her gasp and felt the ripple of her completion, and at the same time felt the thread that united them become a band of steel. As their souls became one, he knew that it was not because of the delight he took in her body, great though it was, but because of this link between them, that above all women in Eriu she was the one he must love.

Chapter 13

❦

"*T*HE WALLS OF FIONN'S HOUSE ARE OF LIVING WOOD: *his roof is the sky. . . .*"

The boy's voice was pure and sweet, with the hard clarity of a wild bird's song. Fionn leaned back against the oak tree, watching the leaf-dappling of light on the ground, and sighed in pure content. Almu was a fine dwelling, and never so pleasant as since Sadb joined him there, but he had to admit that only in the forest did he feel truly at home. Strangely, since she had come to him all the malaise that had kept him from taking his men into the field had gone. He missed her painfully, but he had too much energy now to stay at home.

It was odd, considering how he had longed to dwell in a *dun* like other boys when he was living in a hut in the woods with the Liath Luachra and Bodbmall. But they said that you could tell the stag of Fidh Gaible and the eagle of Cnoc Dabilla from any other: man or beast, a creature was shaped by its raising. The forests of Eriu were the true home and the kingdom of Fionn mac Cumhal.

"*The red deer are Fionn's horned cattle, his mead the rushing stream . . .*" sang the boy.

"The lads are shaping well," said Goll, who was

leaning against the tree beside him. Most of the older warriors were off hunting, with young Diarmuid
to act as their *gilla*. Goll and Fionn and a few of the
others had stayed in the main encampment to drill
the boys who had been accepted for training in the
fian.

In the space between the fire pit and the trees Dáire
of Dáirfhinel and Conn son of Feabhal were wrestling,
their sliding muscles dappled by the flickering sunlight
until their shapes blurred and one saw only the shifting
pattern of moving limbs against the leaves.

"Their bodies are forgetting the softness of straw beds
and sheepskins and readjusting to the hard ground,"
said Fionn. As he watched the lads who cheered the
wrestlers or worked on their weapons around the fire,
it seemed to him that there was a new spring to their
movements and a shine to their eyes that he never saw
when they laired within walls.

Goll grunted. "Would that I could say the same! Each
summer it seems to take longer before my bones stop
aching. But I do not complain—" He gave Fionn a quick
glance beneath bent brows, and Fionn saw with a pang
that there was new silver there, and in the other man's
beard as well. "My *dun* is not so pleasant to me these
days that I would wish to stay."

Fionn nodded in quick understanding. Goll's wife
had died that winter, and though the big man did not
lament, he had grown very silent. When they met for
the summer's campaigning Fionn had welcomed him
with extra warmth, but he had not been able to find any
words of consolation. It made him sweat even to think
of such a loss. A fair face filled his vision, framed by
moonpale hair. If anything should happen to Sadb . . .
He shuddered and thrust the thought away.

"You must spend too long at your grieving. When
the summer is over, perhaps we can find a new woman
to keep your *dun*. Dithramhach's daughter Caoinche is
grown now, and I must get her a husband. She should

be a pleasant armful, though no great beauty, and she has a great deal of sense for a young girl."

Goll shrugged, but he did not reject the idea entirely, and for the time being Fionn was willing to leave it there.

There was a shout from the ring of young men surrounding the wrestlers. Dáire had flipped his opponent neatly onto his back and was looking down at him, flushed and grinning.

"Well done," said Fionn as the young man turned to see if he had been watching. Dáire was a big lad with a shock of fair hair who reminded him of himself at the same age. But this boy had come to his training with an uncomplicated enthusiasm that Fionn envied. Of all the young men who were coming to them now, only raven-haired Diarmuid, Duibhne's son, was more promising.

It occurred to Fionn that if Cruithne had borne him a man-child he would have been Dáire's age by now. Indeed, the boy, who had been in his keeping since he had been orphaned at the age of ten, felt more like his own son than young Ferdhomhon, who, according to the crofter's wife who bore him, actually was.

It might have been so, thought Fionn, glancing from Dáire's radiant face to Ferdhomhon's dark frown. He had some vague recollection of having stayed a night once in the cottage of a herder who was out on the hills and ending up in the bed of the wife he had left alone. She had been dark-haired and intense, like her son. In truth it did not matter if the lad were Fionn's son or the crofter's. Believing himself a son of Fionn, he had striven to live up to his father's reputation, and if Ferdhomhon was not the best of the youths who hoped to join the *fian* when they had completed their training, he had earned his place among them fairly.

"My turn next," cried Dubh Droma mac Seanchadh, his red hair flaming as he stepped into a patch of sunlight. "Ferdhomhon, I challenge you, and the winner can fight Dáire!"

"That's well enough," said Fionn, "but you could be wrestling back at the *dun*. When this competition is over I want to see who can run from here to the lake to fetch water without a scratch, and without spilling a drop on the way home!"

"And will you not be leaving us a moment to refresh our sweating bodies in the cool water when we get there?" asked Dáire, laughing.

"If you want the cooks to make you any dinner you must first bring the water," said Fionn, grinning back at him. "Then you can go back and swim as much as you will, and maybe I will join you!"

There were a few sour looks at the prospect of the extra labor, but no one dared to protest seriously. Fionn did not blame them for resenting it—he had complained enough when the Liath Luachra and Bodbmall set him tasks that made no sense to him. But he had complied, from a child's need to please the only two people in his world. These lads could always return to their clans and families—but being here was a privilege, and not a one of them, except perhaps for Miogach of Alba, who still resented Fionn's defeat of his uncle Laigne and all his men, but would have done things that seemed a great deal more foolish in order to stay.

"Look at them," said Goll softly, "like colts in a pasture. I can remember when you were that young, Fionn-lad, but my boyhood is like a memory of another lifetime to me. This is the next generation of Eriu's defenders we are training, who will carry on the tradition when we are gone. . . ."

"Do not be saying such things," said Fionn swiftly. Goll's sorrow must be gnawing at him indeed. There was reason in the older man's words, he supposed, but they found no echo in Fionn's heart. He was no longer a boy, to be sure, but he felt little different from the youth who had eaten the Salmon of Wisdom at Fionnéices's fire. Everyone else got older, but Fionn's strength was undiminished. Especially since he had found Sadb. She had made him young again.

There was a shout from the onlookers as the two wrestlers closed; for a moment Ferdhomhon strained for leverage against his taller opponent. He made up in determination for what he lacked in finesse. He might even win this bout, thought Fionn, watching with interest. But if he did, he was unlikely to beat Dáire. It occurred to Fionn then that a man's sons were not always those of his body, and looking back at his own childhood, it seemed to him that some of Bodbmall's actions made more sense if one realized that more than any of her other fosterlings, Fionn had been like her own child.

"Good throw!" exclaimed Goll, sitting up to see.

Fionn focused back on the wrestlers in time to see the last of a neat cross-hip twist that jerked Dubh's feet from under him and dropped him on the grass.

"The first throw goes to Ferdhomhan," said Goll.

"You'd best get ready to fight him, Dáire," said his friend Dubh Droma.

"Not fair," cried Miogach, ever ready to make trouble, "for the winner of this fight will be exhausted while Dáire goes into the final bout rested."

"You should have sent that boy back to Alba—" said Goll.

"There's a way around that," said a new voice from among the trees. "Let me wrestle Dáire while they are finishing. Whoever wins, both parties to the final fight will be equally tired."

It was not a bad proposal, but that was not why everyone was staring. The voice, light as a lad's but with a husky timbre that bespoke some maturity, was heavily burred with the accent of the western coasts, and it was not a voice that any one of them had ever heard before.

"Come out where we can see you!" said Dáire. "I will not fight with a shadow."

Fionn shaded his eyes as the stranger came out into the sunlight. His bard's training told him the voice was unfamiliar, but he recognized the accent. He had spent two winters among folk who spoke so, learning smithcraft at Lochan's forge. It was not often that lads from so far away came seeking admission to the *fian*.

Nor this time either, he thought in amazement. For as his eyes adjusted to the bright light he realized that despite the sturdy figure and truculent expression, the newcomer was a girl.

"You are staring like so many gaffed salmon," she said, eyeing them warily. "Have you never seen a warrior woman before?"

It was true, thought Fionn, stifling a grin. The boys were gaping, so aware of the firm breasts that pushed against her tunic they had not noticed it was short, and worn over breeches, and that she was leaning on a well-crafted spear.

"It is not unheard of for a woman to join a *fian*. Do you not know that the mother of King Conchobar was a *fennid* for a time to avenge the murder of her fosterers, and so she changed her name from Assa the Gentle One to the terrible Ness? Do you not remember Aiofe and Scathach, who taught battlecraft to Cuchulain?" It was clearly a defense she had rehearsed many times.

"And are you such a one as they?" Fionn asked with some amusement. Despite her womanly curves, the girl's sturdy build gave her as much mass as many of the lads, and she moved well.

"I could be," she said stoutly. "I am a hunter already."

"Lad or lass," Dáire found his voice finally, "we do not take just anyone into our company. You must tell us where you come from, and the names of your kin!"

"Oh, I've no reason to be ashamed of my breed-ing," said the girl. "My name is Lugach. My mother's father is Lochan, a master smith in the West Country." She paused for effect, looking around the circle, and Fionn, warned by the first name, had a moment to brace himself.

"And who sired *you?*" asked Goll.

Unerringly, Lugach's gaze turned to Fionn, who upped his estimate of her intelligence, for there was nothing in his worn hunting garb to mark him as the leader there.

"My father is Fionn mac Cumhal."

In the sudden silence, the fall of a twig seemed loud. A dozen pairs of eyes shifted as one from the face of the girl to Fionn.

It could be true, he thought, as he considered her. Lugach was much taller than Cruithne, though she had the same broad build and shining dark curls. When Cruithne had put her arms around him her cheek lay above his heart, and that fisher lad who had been her other lover was not much taller. If Lugach was indeed his daughter, she had gotten her height from him.

And he could see now that the girl was older than he had first thought her; older than Cruithne had been when he lived in the smith's house as her husband. Bearing children aged most women early, but Lugach was clearly more used to ranging the forest and help-ing in the forge than milking cows and spinning beside the fire.

"Do you think that sufficient recommendation?" said Ferdhomhon bitterly. Clearly he was not pleased to have whatever standing his relationship to Fionn had given him diluted by the appearance of this girl. "We are all Fionn's children here! You will have to prove yourself worthy of our company."

She looked at him scornfully. "What else? Have I not already offered to fight him?" She nodded towards Dáire, whose appreciative grin grew broader.

"I'll roll you in the grass gladly," he said, with a quick look to either side to see if his friends appreciated the double meaning. Then he appeared to remember that this girl was supposed to be Fionn's daughter, and looked at his leader questioningly.

Lugach's rosy cheeks flushed. "Down me in a fair fight, little boy—if you can—for I vow that is the only way you will ever get your hands on me!"

This time the ripple of laughter was directed at Dáire. Then eyes turned to Fionn once more. For a moment he frowned, thinking. The fisherfolk who summered near Lochan's forge were no warriors, but they were deadly with their little knives, and wicked wrestlers. If Lugach had learned their ways Dáire might get a harder fight than he expected. He did not want to shame the boy, but he would do him no service by allowing him to scorn an untried enemy.

"Very well," he said finally. "You may fight. But keep your shirts on!"

By this time, everyone in camp had gathered, and Ferdhomhon's fight with Dubh had been forgotten. Dáire pulled on his tunic, and Lugach laid down the various bundles she had been carrying and tightened her belt. Fionn found himself impressed as she moved into position. Clearly she respected her opponent and was leaving nothing to chance, but she did not appear apprehensive. Dáire, on the other hand, was only too aware of his audience. Fionn understood all the factors that would be distracting him now. For him, it was a matter of pride. But real fighting was not conducted before judges on a playing field. If matters went as he expected, this might be a useful lesson for them all.

There was silence as the two wrestlers circled, though some eyebrows lifted as they saw how fluidly Lugach moved. But she seemed to be in no hurry, and it was Dáire whose patience gave out first. He lunged for her, long arms reaching, and in the same moment she moved inside his guard and with a wriggle that was almost too fast to follow ducked and lifted and sent him flying. There was a stunned silence, followed by a few uncertain cheers.

Dáire got to his feet, scowling. But that first throw had been no fluke. If he had gotten his hands on her she would have suffered, but he never had the chance. Soon enough it was all over, and some of the boys, admiring Lugach's valor, crowded around her, offering shy congratulations. The others followed Dáire, who had muttered an ungracious capitulation and withdrawn in sullen silence. Fionn was sorry to see it, but it might do the lad good to be bested. He had gotten too used to winning.

LATER THAT EVENING, WHEN THE HUNTERS HAD COME IN and were feasting on fresh deer meat, Fionn paused beside his daughter, who was finishing her dinner alone by one of the fires.

"Does your mother still put apples in her stew?" he asked.

She looked up at him with a smile that reminded him suddenly of Cruithne. It seemed to him now that Lugach was probably his daughter as well, though at the time he had not been sure.

"She married Eochaidh, you know, the year after I was born," said the girl, as if she had heard his thought. *Eochaidh*—that was the name of the fisher lad who had been Cruithne's other lover. Fionn nodded.

"He tried to tell me once that *he* was my father, but I didn't believe him." She looked at Fionn in appeal.

"He had reason to think so," said Fionn, remembering the times he had smelled fish oil on Cruithne's skin. "But having seen your spirit, I do not think he could have sired you." He grinned and was rewarded by Lugach's reluctant smile. "You know you will have to be twice as good as the lads, at everything, for them to accept you," he said then.

Lugach gave a short laugh. "When has it ever been otherwise? But I was the boy in my family. My mother only gave Eochaidh a brace of puling girls, and as soon as I could reach the rope I began to pull the bellows for my grandfather in the forge. I am strong, and I am patient. I'll survive."

"I think you will," said Fionn, "If I had known . . ." He shook his head uncomfortably.

"I do not blame you for running away," said Lugach evenly. "I ran away myself." She looked up, and now her expression was not like that of Cruithne at all.

"Well, I would not have known what to do with a little girl, and I do not think you would have grown into a warrior woman if you had been with me."

Lugach nodded, and Fionn felt something within him ease. He had never known how to apologize.

As THE SUMMER CONTINUED, THE *FIAN* SETTLED INTO A pleasant routine, of games and hunting, lying out beneath the stars or building shelters thatched with leafy boughs when it rained. They shifted camp frequently, never staying much more than a week in any location, so as not to hunt out the game. But in summertime, their hunting preserve was the whole of Eriu. They moved from the forest of Fidh Gaible to Loch Ri, and from Benn Leith to Sliab Mourne, marching by day sometimes, singing, and sometimes going by night so silently that folk who glimpsed them hid in their houses, sure they had seen some flitting of the Sidhe.

Once or twice they cleaned out nests of robbers, but the summer had been unusually peaceful, and the worst fights Fionn had to deal with were between the young men, especially those in their final year of training, who were growing increasingly tense as the time for their testing drew near. Lugach worked harder than any, and those who were tempted to think of her as a woman got a painful lesson. Soon the boys were treating her like a sister—all except for Dáire, who could not seem to forget his initial defeat and continued to challenge her.

Fionn would have welcomed some real warfare—an attack by the Albans or even a rebellion—but the best he could do was to divide the men into bands and set them to skirmishing against each other among the trees with blunted spears.

By summer's ending the fian's progress had brought them to the Forest of Brega near Temair. The time had come to find out which of the lads who had been training so hard these past moons were worthy to be counted among Fionn's people, and which would be sent back in disgrace to their clans. This year there was an added tension because the *Ard Ri* himself had come out to observe the testing.

"THEY ARE AS EAGER AS HOUNDS," SAID KING CORMAC, eyeing the runners who were waiting for the shadow of Fionn's spear to reach the stone.

There were four of them, from a field narrowed down from seven by the tests they had already undergone. Ferdhomhon stood too still, tension crackling from every line of his body. Miogach seemed sullen. He had barely squeaked through the previous day's spear toss, and had been heard to protest the impossibility of completing the forest race under the conditions prescribed: without cracking a stick, or disarranging his hair, or taking a blow from the men who would be pursuing him. But every man of the *fianna* had done it, so he got little sympathy. Dáire stood very still, gathering his strength. Of them all, only Diarmuid seemed relaxed, turning to speak to a friend and laughing.

"They are hares," Fionn answered him. "The hounds are waiting in the forest. . . ." The king nodded, but Fionn could tell by the way his eyes swept the trees without focusing that he had not caught the dappling of light on hunting leathers, had not realized which pieces of wood were not saplings, but the shafts of spears.

"This year I won the boys' race at Tailtiu," said the king's son, Cairbre, sneering. It seemed to Fionn that the boy had done nothing but sneer since he arrived, and he was barely civil to his father. Fionn's palm itched. *I would put a different look on his face*, he thought grimly, *if he were under my care*.

"Your son is well grown for his years," he said. "He reminds me of you at that age."

Cormac turned, one eyebrow lifting as if he too were remembering how he and Fionn had first met at the Games of Tailtiu, and how they had been rivals there. Like his son, he seemed old for his years. There was silver in the auburn beard and lines of passion and power graven deeply in the king's brow.

"He is my youngest boy," Cormac said softly, "and perhaps he has been too much indulged. A season with you would knock the pride out of him—"

"Perhaps," Fionn said neutrally. "But it is hard enough for those lads who give themselves to the learning heart and soul. I would not take him unless he desired it above all things." He had taken Miogach unwillingly, as compensation for Dithramhach. He thought now that he would have done better to give him as a hostage to Cormac, or send him back to his father King Colgain in Alba.

The tension in the racers' bodies had increased; their eyes flicked back and forth from the forest to the line of shadow cast by Fionn's spear. And then it was touching the rock, and the runners blurred into motion.

"Where are they going?" The king's little daughter, Grainne, had escaped from among the women and was running towards them. Cormac laughed and opened his arms to her.

"They will run through the forest," Fionn answered, "each of them to a different goal, to bring back the token that has been left there. And all the way there and back again the hunters will pursue them, and any lad who cannot pass through the forest scatheless as a shadow will lose the race, no matter how fast he runs."

"That is not fair!" said the child, pouting. "I want the fast one to win!" She looked to be around six winters old, with a wealth of corn gold curls and a bright, quick glance. Like her brother, she had been spoiled, but in the girl-child that willfulness was still charming. With luck, she would always be able to get her own way with charm.

If Sadb bore me a child, Fionn wondered, *how would it be?* Her failure to conceive had been Sadb's only sorrow. For him, to hold her in his arms through the winter nights was sufficient, but he could see that in the summers, when he was busy with the *fian*, it might be good for her to be training a child.

"They are not running against each other, little one," said King Cormac, settling her on his lap. "But against the forest. It is Fionn who will decide which ones get to stay."

The girl's grey gaze moved from the trees into which the runners had disappeared to Fionn, and he struggled to maintain his gravity as he met that cool, evaluating stare. She would be a wonder of a woman when she was grown, but he pitied the man who had to tame her.

"Are you strong?" she asked, and with equal gravity Fionn nodded. "Are you stronger than my father the king?"

Abruptly the silence grew charged. Cairbre's sullen gaze fixed on him, a shadow of the girl's bright stare. Though Cormac had not moved, Fionn could feel the tension with which the high king was waiting for his reply. The *rigfénnid* sighed. He thought that he and Cormac had worked all this out long ago!

"In the woods I am," he said finally, "but there is no one stronger than your father in the lands of men."

Cairbre's frown deepened, but the answer seemed to satisfy the girl, and he saw a flicker of appreciation in Cormac's eyes.

"Then make the black-haired boy win," said Grainne, looking back at the trees.

It was no use telling her that his hares raced against hunters whose memories of their own testing made them determined that no one who was not as good as they were should be counted among their company. But the real challenge was of another kind.

"In the forest, you win by conquering yourself," said Fionn. "Those who can become one with the forest pass through it like the wind, and neither thorn nor spear will do them harm." The child looked dubious, but even as they spoke part of Fionn's mind had been keeping time. "The first of them should be returning now. In a moment you will see—"

Grainne's eyes widened as the leaves of the hazels at the edge of the wood quivered and a figure appeared, seeming to manifest from the air itself rather than passing through the trees. It was Diarmuid, his fair skin gleaming beneath a light sheen of sweat, and the colours of the painted wand he had retrieved from its hiding place on the other side of the forest glowing in the sun.

Fionn rose, with an effort keeping his features stern. Diarmuid came forward, his own face grave, though his eyes began to dance as he realized he was the first to return.

"Not a hair out of place," said Fergus the Poet, behind him.

Once more the leaves shook; Dáire emerged from among them, and though his face was red with exertion, the braiding of his fair hair was undisturbed. He took his place beside Diarmuid. They waited, while the men who had played hounds began to emerge from the forest behind them. Silently they formed a circle around the two boys. Diarmuid was still grave, but

Dáire, looking past the men to the other folk of the *fian* who had gathered there, saw Lugach among them and grinned triumphantly.

A few minutes more had passed before Ferdhomhon slipped between two oak trees and took his place beside them. But though they waited until the sun had moved another hand's breadth across the sky, Miogach did not appear.

"Men of the *fian*!" Fionn cried at last. "Behold these lads who stand before you—"

He looked around at the circle of faces—at old Goll, squinting with his single eye against the sunlight, at Fearghusa and Faobhar, his half brothers, and at Duibhne, who was grinning from ear to ear as he looked at his son. When he himself had run this race, Duibhne had been one of his pursuers. *Generation to generation*, he thought, *it spirals round*. Mature or young, fair or red or dark, the men of the *fian* were lean as wolves and graceful as deer and it seemed to him that they were all of one lineage. And that likeness extended to three boys who stood before them.

"Diarmuid mac Duibhne and Dáire of Dairfhinel and Ferdhomhon mac Fionn have been tried and tested. What say you, are they worthy of our company?" Fionn cried. But even before the men began to cheer, he knew what the answer would be.

No one mentioned Miogach. It was not until the following morning, when everyone was sleeping off the effects of the night's celebration, that he was found, limping from a gashed leg, and with his hair full of leaves. The king was all for taking him back to Temair as a hostage, but Fionn, who felt a certain responsibility for the lad, gave him a farmstead that was in his keeping and enough gold to stock it with cows. He was buying off his own conscience as well as the boy, and he knew it, but Miogach had no wish to face his father back in Alba, having failed in the *fian*. He was not missed, and soon enough Fionn put the boy from his mind as well.

THE *FIAN* MOVED HOMEWARD AS THE COUNTRYSIDE TURNED to harvesting the bounty of the golden fields. In the woodlands, the red deer, fat from a summer's grazing, were ready for harvest, too, and as they moved homeward, the *fian* did their own reaping, skinning and salting the beasts they killed for a winter supply of meat and hides. When they reached the river Liffe, Goll and his men turned eastward towards Loch Dergdeire, promising to come feast with Fionn at Midwinter and marry Caoinche if she liked him.

In those last days before Samhain, when with each day's travel the shapes of the hills became a little more familiar and it seemed to him that he could almost scent the wood smoke of Almu, Fionn found his spirits lifting. Sadb was awaiting him, and that knowledge sang in his awareness, sweeter and louder than the earth song. Only now, when he knew that soon he would see her, could he allow himself to remember how much he needed her. He could feel the cord that bound them tightening day by day. The rest of the *fian* listened to his cheerful whistling and smiled. He had done his duty by them all summer; it did not matter if love distracted him from his duties now. Soon they would be home.

IT WAS THE WEEK BEFORE SAMHAIN, AND THE FIRST STORM of the season was blowing in from the west. In the light of the setting sun the advancing clouds glowed crimson and purple, edged with flame. But the wind was cold, and the hunters had returned early—all but two of them, Lugach and Dáire.

There were a few snickers when the men realized it, for everyone knew that even though he was now a full member of the *fian*, Dáire still resented the way Fionn's

daughter had defeated him at wrestling. All summer he
had harassed her, but there was little Fionn could do
about it without being accused of favoritism. Most new-
comers to the *fian* got teased about something—their
size or lack of it, an odd accent or a difficulty learning
some skill. Lugach's peculiarity was her sex, and she
had made it quite clear that she wanted no special treat-
ment. For all that she looked like Cruithne, it seemed
to Fionn that his daughter was far too much like him
at the same age—humorless and driven to excel, hiding
her need for love behind prickles that a hedgehog could
have claimed with pride.

Fionn had almost determined to send men out to
look for them when Dáire came in with the carcass
of a young doe slung over his shoulders. He was
limping, mud-smeared, and his face and arms were
deeply scored.

"Hai, lad, what happened? Ye look as if you met a
wildcat out on the hill, not a deer!" The men were
laughing.

Dáire grunted and dropped the deer without answering. Fionn began to frown. He had certainly tangled
with *something*, but those scratches were too broad for
a cat's claws, and not deep enough. Beneath the mud
bruises were forming. The lad had been fighting—He
took a step forward and Dáire flinched.

"Where is Lugach?" he asked softly.

Dáire shrugged, not meeting his eyes. "Out there—
She was all right when I saw her. When she's ready,
she'll come in."

Fionn felt anger rise in him and held it in, remembering Lugach's pride. His first impulse was to back-
track Dáire until he found her, but that would set the
whole *fian* talking. Diarmuid was standing near him,
and Fionn could see the same anger he felt beginning to smoulder in those dark eyes. Duibhne's son
was the best tracker among the younger men. For a
moment Fionn held the boy's gaze, then turned his

eyes towards the shadows beyond the light of the fire. Diarmuid nodded slightly, eased away, and in another moment was gone.

"Clean yourself up," he said to Dáire. "And stay close. I will speak with you later." *When Lugach is found* . . . The words hung between them. *Ah, Dáire, lad, how could you do it?* thought Fionn. *You were like a son to me.*

It was nearly midnight before Diarmuid came in with Lugach limping by his side. She had washed herself already, but she could not hide the darkening bruise on her temple, or the barred marks of fingers on her upper arms. Fionn stood up and she came to a halt before him.

"Did he force you?"

A spark flared in Lugach's dull eyes. "He got lucky. There was a rock to hand, and he stunned me," she answered, touching her brow, "or I would have had his balls."

Fionn felt himself fractionally relieved. Her spirit was intact, at least, if she could talk this way.

"You will have compensation," he said. A *fénnid*'s family could not be forced to pay for his deeds; the gold would come from the treasury of the *fian*.

"What good will gold be if he has gotten me with child?" she said baldly.

"I will make him marry you," Fionn began, but Lugach spat.

"I will kill him if he tries to go into one bed with me. Did you think he loved me?" She shook her head. "This rape was in revenge, because I shamed him."

"Very well. If you bear a boy, I will foster him," said Fionn then. His heart was aching for her, but he knew she could accept no comfort from him now.

"I must leave the *fian*," Lugach told him. "Even if there is no child, they will all know what he did, and others will want to try me. I cannot be on my guard all the time. But if I must go, send *him* away as well. Do not let him remain in the *fian* to boast of how he had the daughter of Fionn mac Cumhal."

Fionn remembered the heartsick look in Dáire's eyes and thought the lad would do no boasting. It seemed to him that Dáire had felt more love for her than he knew, or at least attraction, and had not known his own feelings until the deed was done. But he could not deny Lugach's appeal for justice. Heavily he nodded. "I will banish him."

Lugach turned away into the shadows, swaying a little as she walked, but she would not let Diarmuid steady her.

I have lost her, thought Fionn, *and Dáire, and Miogach*. Of those he had counted as his children at the summer's beginning, only Ferdhomhon remained. And Diarmuid. Trying to smile, he reached out and clasped the young man's shoulder, and as he saw the love in Diarmuid's eyes his heart was a little eased.

Chapter 14

⋙❈⋘

FIONN STOOD ON THE RAMPARTS OF ALMU, LOOKING out over the Curragh as sunset stretched the shadow of the hill across the plain. The winter had been a wet one, with bitter winds, but in the days just past the weather had relented, as if Brigid herself were blessing the world with the promise of spring. The grass whose color sunset's gold was deepening was replacing winter brown with the vivid green of spring. The air that lifted the fair hair that flowed from beneath Fionn's headband was soft. He breathed deeply, and felt a delight that he had forgotten begin to tingle through him.

Where the shadow of the hills lay across the plain, points of fire were flowering as if the sunset had seeded them there. The priestesses of Brigid were leaving their shrine with the wagon where the one of them who had been chosen to carry the power of the Goddess was throned. Before the night ended they would bring Her blessing to each of the raths on the plain.

In the courtyard behind him he could hear the twittering of pipes and the lively beat of a hand drum. The procession would not reach Almu until well after nightfall, but the celebration was already beginning. Children chased each other between the buildings, shrieking gleefully, and some of the younger men were dancing. He wondered where Sadb had got to. All day her mood had been strange, alternating between sullen silences and a febrile gaiety that was as disconcerting.

And Fionn found himself as divided in his reactions, wondering first if he had somehow displeased her, and then, for the first time since Sadb had been his wife, wishing that the winter would end so that the *fian* could take the field. Gazing down at the *dun*, he frowned as he glimpsed pale hair.

"Sadb!" The pitch of his voice carried through the clamor. She paused and turned, looking up at him. This at least had not changed; if he called her she would always hear, and he would always hear if she spoke his name. "Sadb, come up for a breath of fresh air—"

She shook her head, indicating the pile of linens in her arms. "Mongfind—"

"Mongfind can do without you for a little while. Give that to one of the maidservants and come here!"

"Is it commanding me you would be, Fionn mac Cumhal?" Sadb's dark eyes narrowed.

"It is pleading with you I am, heart of my heart—" He bent over the rail, holding out his hand. "For I am all alone!"

For a moment longer she stared at him. Then her expression changed, and very deliberately, she let the folded cloth drop to the ground. Fionn raised one eyebrow, but she was already climbing up the notched log, and he was not about to argue.

"They will be wondering where I am," she said, but she was already turning her head to catch the cool evening breeze.

"Let them. It will be a change from looking for me." He watched her, waiting for the flicker of amusement at the corner of her mouth, and then bent quickly and kissed her.

"You are impossible—" Sadb began, but she leaned

against him as he put his arm around her, and as always when they touched, the balance of the world was suddenly *right* again.

"You do not have to be so busy," he said. "That is why Mongfind is here. Rest, enjoy the sunset—"

"—and entertain you," she finished. "Why not? No one really needs me down there."

"We all need you," he began, and felt her stiffen in his arms. "Never mind—I will *not* quarrel with you, not on an evening when the world is rejoicing in the promise of spring!"

"Wise man," Sadb murmured against his chest. "When you do not even know why—" She fell silent, and though Fionn knew she was still troubled, the vast protectiveness which had been his first response to her surged up in him, and he did not have the heart to press her further. As the sunset deepened, its fiery light was restoring the lost copper brilliance to Sadb's hair.

I need you, he thought. *Your presence makes the evening beautiful*. But even with all a *fili*'s skill, he could not make her understand that if she did not already know. And so he stayed silent, and after a time he felt her tension ease.

Together, they watched the slow fading of the day until the fiery serpent wound up the road to the *dun* and the gates were flung open to welcome the Goddess in.

THE OXEN THAT PULLED BRIGID'S CART HAD BEEN LED away, but the cart itself formed one side of the circle, and the Goddess was still enthroned there on her carved chair. One by one folk came forward with their offerings, a round of cheese, a piece of embroidered linen, a finely tanned skin. The wagon was already heaped with gifts, and others had been sent back to Druim Cliadh. The priestesses would find a use for all of them, for the charity of Brigid was legendary, and there were always many mouths to feed at the shrine.

The gifts the people made were tangible, the fruits of their labor. The gifts the Goddess gave in return were of a different kind. On some she bestowed a smile, and on others a blessing, and to a few, she gave words of prophecy and power.

Fionn waited to offer his gift until the end of the evening, when everyone else had had their say. Sadb was the last to go up before him. He could not hear what she asked as she laid down her length of fine-spun linen, nor the answer, but whatever it was, it made her smile.

He had the wealth now to give gold to the shrine, or cattle, but Brigid liked best the gifts of the heart. He did not wish to give her something that meant nothing to him, or even worse, something that had been looted from its former owner and still bore the echoes of that pain. In past years he had sometimes passed on to the priestesses gifts of honor awarded him by the high king. But this time it was his own work he was giving—a great cauldron of riveted iron, big enough to boil a whole pig or a sheep.

It took two men to bring the thing up, but Fionn, getting his legs well under him and lifting in a single smooth motion, raised it himself into the wagon, grinning at the whistles of amazement and the applause. There was no magic in it—he had not felt the power of the forge goddess flaming through him as he did when he crafted his spear. But it was an honest piece of forge work that Lochan, his old master, would have been proud to own.

"You are still a boy . . ." said the Goddess. "Showing off what you can do."

Fionn looked up at her. This year it was the young one, Ceibhfionn, who was acting as priestess. Her golden hair fell loose beneath her crimson veil. But the voice, and the posture, even the smile, were the same that he had seen every year, whether the priestess was young or old, dark or fair. It was Brigid who dwelt now in that body, filling it with Her essence as the light of a lamp fills a room. And her presence was very like light, he thought as he gazed up into the radiance of that smile, or like the warmth of a fire.

"Lady, I greet you," he said aloud. "May those who come to your table always go away satisfied."

"A good blessing," said the goddess. "And what shall I give you in return?"

What do I need? thought Fionn, gazing up at her. *Wisdom*, the answer came then. *The wisdom to choose the right path for myself and all those who depend on me.*

"Lady, what does the future hold for me and mine?" he asked.

For a moment she looked at him, then she began to laugh. "You ask many questions in one, and those not easy. Even to me, the paths around you seem tangled. Most men walk in ways laid down for them by their fathers, or are driven by need. But you have always had so many choices. Even the gods cannot say what you must do."

Fionn grimaced. He knew better than any the maze of his lifeways. Once it was his elders who had pushed him from one thing to another. These days it was his own nature. He did not need a goddess to tell him so.

"Tell me then, what choices I must make in the season to come."

The figure above him sighed once, and then again, letting the trance deepen.

"I see . . . you have an enemy," she whispered. "A shadow from the past. He is a creature of darkness, and I cannot see beyond the enchantments that veil him. All I sense is his hatred for you. But he works magic against you, and to do so he must set it beyond his own wardings. I see plots within plots, subtle and dangerous. Where you are most certain he would have you doubt, and take from you the thing that you hold most dear. Something of what he has done I can foresee for you—a house is the key to it. Beware of a house, Fionn mac Cumhal—a house with a single door."

She drew breath, shuddering. "That is all I see, child. Do not seek more!"

Fionn nodded and stepped away, frowning. Why had he even asked? Omens and prophecies were often so— as hard to understand as the questions they pretended to answer. And how often it was only after the danger had passed that one understood the meaning of a diviner's words!

As he turned towards the hall, the priestess Airmedb emerged from the shadows beyond the wagon, a small child wrapped in a blanket clasped in her arms.

"Are you not happy with the Lady's gift?" she laughed softly. "Well, never mind. I have another kind of gift for you, altogether more tangible, that I hope you will like well." She pulled back the blanket, and Fionn saw a fair, flushed face crowned with a tangle of flaxen hair. The boy stared back at Fionn with sleep-dazed eyes.

"Take him. He is your own blood, and it is your duty to see to his raising."

Fionn shook his head, for he had touched no other woman since Sadb came into his life, and this boy was scarcely two years old.

"He is none of my getting, though he looks a likely lad. Who bore him?"

"Lugach, your daughter, bore him with great labor and pain. He is weaned now, and she is gone back to the west, commending her son to your care. Will you accept him?"

Without quite knowing how it had happened, Fionn found himself with the boy in his arms. The child was heavier than he looked, but he did not struggle. There was a sweetness to holding that warm weight that Fionn had not expected. He tightened his grip and felt the boy begin to relax against him. He turned to ask the priestess what the boy's mother had called him, but she had disappeared.

"What is your name then, little one?" he said softly. The sober gaze fixed him. "Ma?"

"Ah, my lad, your mother has left you, but I shall find you another to love you. How will that be?" It would never be the same, from his own experience he knew. But he hoped that one day the boy would understand, as he had had to, the necessity.

"A fine boy! Is he yours, Fionn?" came a cry as they emerged into the circle of light. The little boy surveyed the faces around him with a measuring air. He looked like his great-grandfather, the smith Lochan, thought Fionn, in spite of the bright hair. Men lifted their drinking horns in greeting.

Then he saw Sadb, her face blanched as pale as her hair, and stricken as if he had given her a heartwound, looking at him with the child in his arms.

"This little lad is son to my daughter, Lugach," said Fionn loudly, "that Dáire got on her by force, but for all that he is a fine, healthy boy and I am proud to claim him as my kin!"

"Good blood on both sides, then," said Duibhne, and the others cheered.

"Let the lad be welcome in this hall," said Sadb in her soft voice. The stricken look had left her eyes, but she watched the child now with an intensity of longing that Fionn found equally disturbing.

"A fine result to the prank that Dáire played!" said someone softly, and the men laughed.

"Nonsense," said Mongfind stoutly. "A fair, strapping lad is Lugach's son, and he shall grow to be the envy of the *fian*!"

"Will you take him, then, to foster until he is of an age to train?" asked Fionn.

"I will take him and gladly." She accepted the warm armful and bore him off to the women's hall.

"And how does it feel to be a grandfather?" Diarmuid asked him, laughing, and ducked the blow Fionn sent his way.

*　　*　　*

IT WAS DEEP NIGHT BEFORE THE REVELLING ENDED, AND THE priestesses had long ago driven their cart back down the hill. Grandfather he might be, thought Fionn as he picked his way over the still forms of sleeping revellers, but he could still drink the rest of them under the table! He was not even drunk—only nicely lit, as if he had sat too close to the fire.

Fionn was humming softly as he came to the hide curtains that sectioned off the bedplace he shared with Sadb from the rest of the hall. He fell silent as he pushed between them, not wanting to wake her, but as he began to pull off his tunic she stirred.

He slid beneath the sleeping furs beside her and bent to kiss her. Her lips were salt, and he stopped, frowning.

"You have been weeping, love! I did not mean to keep you waiting—" He kissed her eyelids and then her lips once more. Beneath the bitterness they were soft and sweet, and though he had meant to go to sleep directly, he felt the warmth in his blood begin to localize in his loins. She had been his for seven years now, and the touch of her still had the power to awaken his manhood no matter how tired he might be. He kissed her with more power, and felt her stillness begin to turn to yielding.

"That is not why I wept," she said softly, turning a little so that he could stroke down her neck and across her breast. "You are the *rígfénnid*, and you must not seek a woman's arms when you should be celebrating with your men. Indeed, I do understand."

"Why, then?" His hand returned to her breast and began to caress it. She shivered as his thumb found the rosy nipple, and he felt it harden. As well as he knew her body, each time he loved her its wonders became new to him. He moved to the other breast and her breath caught. Fionn grinned in the darkness. He would play her like a harp, he thought, until she sang out with an ecstasy that drove all sorrow away.

"It was Lugach's child," she whispered when he took pity on her and began to stroke her hair once more. "Forgive me. For a moment I thought the boy must be yours. And truly I would not have minded if you had taken another woman when you were away from me—especially since I myself have given you no child."

"Sadb—" he began, "that is not what I want from you!"

"But that is what I want!" she exclaimed. "I hunger for a babe—I think no man can know how it is for a woman whose womb remains empty. It did not matter when I was in my father's house—time means little in the Otherworld. But here it passes so swiftly. I want to feel your child growing beneath my heart. I want so much to give you a son who will be the fruit of our love!"

Fionn held her close, murmuring foolish words into her hair. He had not understood. For him the love was enough. But if his seed was what she wanted, he felt his own body swelling with the need to give it to her. He kissed her, long and deeply, and she returned his passion, her mouth opening to receive his tongue. One hand caught the pale silk of her hair and the other moved across the softness of her belly to the secret joining of her thighs.

Sadb was ready for him, bursting with sweetness like a plum in the sunshine. Her thighs parted easily beneath his probing fingers and she whimpered. Though he had hardly begun to explore the delights of her body Fionn felt the fire surge in his own flesh and knew that he could wait no longer. He lifted himself above her, skin brushing skin with a tantalizing deliberation. Then he found his goal, and felt her welcoming him in.

"Open to me," he whispered, "and I will fill you." With increasing power he moved against her, until he felt a yielding deeper than anything he had known before, as if until now, even with the bond between them, there had always been some part of her that she had kept separate. But there were no barriers between them anymore.

Now all his being focused in a single, glowing core. Beyond speech, words sang in his awareness. "*I give you my life, beloved, and my soul. . . .*"

As if in answer, Sadb moaned, arching against him, and in that moment his own rapture took him and all his passion and power were released in a flood of fire.

WHEN BELTANE CAME FIONN MARCHED OUT HIS MEN IN better spirits than he had known for years. His grandson was growing fast. Fionn called him mac Lugach, after his mother, but many of the men had taken to naming him Gaoine, "the prank," for the manner of his begetting. But despite the name he was a serious child who set about everything, whether it was learning how to run or digging a hole, with a methodical intensity that often brought them laughter.

And as for Sadb, by the time two moons had passed she was certain she was pregnant. In her third month, her belly was not yet rounding, but her breasts, which once she had thought too small, had grown firm and heavy, and there was a radiance about her that filled Fionn with wonder. He had questioned whether he should lead the men out this year—let Goll have supreme command of the *fian*—but she would have none of it.

"I will do very well here with the women," Sadb had told him, "and all the better for not having you here to fuss over me. The child is not due until Samhain, so you will be back when he is born."

And yet, when the *fian* did depart, she wept and clung to him, and Fionn left Ceallach the runner at Almu with orders to come to him if anything went wrong.

*   *   *

THE FIRST MOONS OF SUMMER PASSED WITH NO WORD from Almu, and Fionn was kept too busy fighting to worry, even if he had had more than vague forebodings to trouble him. Colgain of Lochlann was raiding again, this time in Connachta. He had been a thorn in the side of Eriu ever since Fionn had killed his brother Laigne, a vicious fighter and an implacable leader in war. Even his own men feared him, and his name had become a word of terror to the folk on the coastlands.

It was near the Feast of Lugh when they saw the last of the Alban sails disappearing northward. They waited a tenday, but there was neither sight nor word of the enemy.

"They'll have run home to lick their wounds," said Goll, for indeed the *fian* had given the raiders a good savaging. "I'll warrant we'll see no more of them this year."

"We need to do the same," said Fionn thoughtfully. "But not on these coastlands, where between us and the Albans the country has been eaten bare. We should move into the forests east of here."

"How far eastward, I wonder?" asked Goll, smiling. "Back to Almu? You should not be so fearful. My own wife is breeding, too, but do you see me fretting?" Goll had married Dithramhach's daughter, Caoinche, the year before, a sturdy, no-nonsense girl with red hair, and the marriage had prospered.

"For shame, and you a grandsire! One would think you had never begotten a child before!"

Fionn shook his head ruefully. Perhaps he was so anxious because this was Sadb's first time as a mother. Or perhaps it was because with the others, lovemaking had been only a passing pleasure, whereas with Sadb he had shared his soul. With such a conception, could this child fail to be wonderful?

"Mark me, with three months yet to go, Sadb will not want you fussing around her. She'll be big as a cow by now, and feeling it. You'll do far better to leave her alone!"

Fionn sighed. The only one of his women he had ever lived with while she was pregnant was Cruithne, and remembering how carrying had soured her temper, he thought that Goll might very well have the right of it. And so they moved in a leisurely fashion towards the upper reaches of the Sinnan and the rich hunting there.

"HO, FIONN, YOU'LL NEVER GUESS WHO WE FOUND STALK-ing the same deer!" called Faobhar as he came out from among the trees, a haunch of deer balanced on his shoulder. The *fian* had been camped in the Sliab na mBan for several days, for the game was fat and plentiful there. Fionn straightened, the spearhead whose fastenings he had been repairing still in his hand, and his half brother laughed, fair and flushed and eager as a child for a riddle-game.

In general, Fionn was indulgent, but today he found that ingenuous grin an irritation. Smiling in return, he set his thumb between his teeth, blinking at the rush of awareness that came to him.

"Not hard to answer," he said calmly. "It is Miogach mac Colgain whom you have found here hunting the deer—"

Faobhar's eyes widened. "How did you know?"

Fionn smiled enigmatically, for in truth he had no more idea than his brother why that simple motion should give him the power to put together instantaneously so many facts that he might have arrived at by patient reasoning. Now that Faobhar had confirmed his guess the answer was obvious, for Miogach had been trained in the *fian*'s manner of hunting, and the rath he had been given was located somewhere near. But until Fionn touched his thumb to his teeth, he had not known. Faobhar was laughing once more at this evidence of Fionn's magic.

"Well, it is true, and here he is now!"

The rest of the hunting party emerged from the forest with the rest of the deer meat, and Fionn saw that Miogach was indeed among them. Taller and broader than he remembered, and growing into his bones, despite the scraggling black beard, this was undeniably the same boy who had failed the testing of the *fian* two years ago.

The rest of the *fianna* greeted him with a kind of wary courtesy, but Miogach seemed to bear them no ill will. Indeed, that young man had learned, if nothing else, to keep his own counsel. Fionn, who in general could read men's faces as he read the tracks a deer left on the ground, found it hard to make much of him at all.

"And have you done well with the holding that was given you?" asked Goll.

"Very well," Miogach replied. "My cattle fill the meadows and I have adorned my hall with many luxuries."

"Well then, it is surely a great discourtesy in you, lad, not to offer hospitality to the men of the *fian*!" said Conain mac Morna, who was known in the *fian* for loving the pleasures of the table.

"Do you think so?" said Miogach, smiling strangely. "Well, I am not to blame, for surely there has not been a month since I have dwelt there that I did not have a good dinner on my table. And since you have challenged me, I will challenge you in return to accept my hospitality! Two houses I have, one on an island in the river and the other on the shore, and that one is the best of them. Come down to my house this evening and dine with me, Fionn mac Cumhal!"

"Another time, perhaps!—" Fionn began, but Conain shook his head.

"You have no choice, lord. You must go, for he has challenged you!"

"And you will go with me, I suppose—" answered

Fionn, laughing in spite of himself, for Conain was already licking his lips in anticipation. "Very well. Do you come, and Goll, and Dubhtach, and Faobhar, since he brought the news!"

"And what of the rest of us?" asked Diarmuid.

"Stay you here in the forest. I shall not be gone long."

"HERE IS MY HALL," SAID MIOGACH AS THE MEN OF THE *fian* came out from the trees. "This is the House of the Quickentrees, and it is with great care that I have prepared it to welcome you."

The place did indeed appear to be a noble dwelling. The thatching was deep and well bound down, the whitewashed walls painted with figures in ochre and black. Beyond the screen of trees Fionn could see the gleam of water. But he did not have much time to look at it, for darkness was falling and their host was welcoming the men indoors.

Fionn's first impression as he stepped inside was of colour. Surely Miogach must have been doing better than he had thought, for the walls were all hung with dyed and painted linen. Carved benches had been set ready for each man beside the hearth. Servants came forward with basins of water for them to wash in while others carried away their arms. They sat down gratefully, for it was a steep climb down from the hills. A fire was burning brightly, its smoke heavy with the scent of sweet herbs.

"A fair house you have brought us to, Miogach," said Conain. "We look forward to the entertainment you shall give us here."

"Indeed," Miogach answered, "it has been long and carefully thought on. But you must be weary. Do you sit here and take your ease while I go to see that all is made ready." He saluted them and then went out, closing the door behind him.

Fionn looked after him, frowning. There was something odd here that he must ask about when the young man returned. But Miogach had been right—he was very weary, and it was good to sit on soft cushions in a well-built house after so many weeks on the trail. He took a deep breath of the scented air and felt his eyelids drooping. It could do no harm, surely, if he closed them for a moment before the dinner came. The voices of the other men made a soothing murmur around him. Softly as a leaf slipping downstream, Fionn fell into sleep.

In his slumber, it seemed to him he dreamed. People clad in some dark stuff were coming into the hall. Some of them bustled around him—he felt pressure but his senses were so disordered he could not tell what they were doing. But he could see some adding fuel to the fire, and others taking the bright hangings down. How curious, said his dream self. Perhaps he did not really trust Miogach after all. He tried to wake so that he could tell the others, but each breath sent him spiralling deeper into darkness, and after a time he dreamed no more.

When Fionn did open his eyes he thought at first that he was still dreaming. The fire had burned down to coals, and his companions were slumped shadows. But his head was pounding as if he had been at a night's drinking, and the foul taste in his mouth would have wakened a Fomor.

"By all the gods of Eriu," said one of the shadows, "what has come to me?" It spoke in Goll's deep rumble, and as Fionn's head cleared he recognized the shape of the man himself against the glow of the fire.

"Were you sleeping too?" asked Fionn.

"Sleeping! I feel as if the Sidhe have been playing hurley in my head."

"Where is the food?" mumbled Conain drowsily. "To keep us here so long without food or drink is poor hospitality."

"No doubt they are preparing the food in the house

on the island," said Goll muzzily, "and they will bring it when it is done."

"Then it is long in coming," said Dubhtach, "and strange it is that the fire that smelled so fragrant when we sat down now stinks as if a body nine days dead were burning there."

"Here's another wonder," said Faobhar. "The walls that were hung so fair with linen when we came in are now bare logs fastened with hazel withies, and the wind is coming through the cracks, and it is bitter cold!"

Fionn realized that he too was shivering. Though the coals still glowed, the air had become as chill as the grave.

"And though I saw seven curtained doors when we came in here," Faobhar went on, "now I can see only one. . . ."

Fionn blinked, peering through the shadows, and saw that it was true, and a shudder passed through him, for he was hearing a voice out of memory: "*Beware of a house with a single door.*"

"Gods, what is happening?" asked Dubhtach. "I am colder than snow at daybreak!"

"It is my doom," said Fionn in a still voice. "The priestess prophesied this fate for me. Get out, all of you, while you can—"

"We will—" said Conain. He grunted as he started to rise, then swore. "I cannot move!" The others began to struggle, and then Fionn, feeling as if he were still in his dream, tried to move as well.

They were bound, all of them, hand to hand and foot to foot and all parts of them tied to the stout oaken benches, whose posts were themselves set deeply into the floor. The lashings were rawhide, from the feel of them, unbreakable even by the war-trained strength of the *fian*. Strong as the prisoners were, all their striving only made their bonds bite more painfully.

"Put your thumb between your teeth, Fionn, and tell

us what magic has prisoned us here!" said Goll.

"It is the magic that the druid of Benn Bulben taught me that has prisoned you, and only the blood of a king on your bonds will release you," came a voice from the other side of the door. "So here you will stay until my father's ships come rowing up the river, and then he shall pay you for the death of my uncle Laigne and your mistreatment of me!"

"Miogach!" exclaimed Goll. "I said you should have killed him. They have trapped us between them. Why did not we see that his father Colgain turned tail too easily?"

But the only answer was Miogach's laughter, and they could hear it fading as he made his way back to the river.

A sorrow as deep as the Sinnan was welling within Fionn's breast. Whether it was the magic that had been in the smoke or the *geas* of the prophecy, his spirit was prisoned as surely as his body. Was it really all to end here? After all the dangers he had survived, when he was at the height of his powers? Was the good that he had got in his life all that there was ever to be? At the thought that he might not see Sadb again, or look upon their child, a moan of anguish burst free.

"Is it the *dordfhionn* he sings?" whispered Dubhtach. "Then surely our end is upon us." He gulped and then loosed his own pain in a cry of sorrow.

One by one the others joined in, bringing their mouths as close together as they were able so that the deep tones blended in a dreadful harmony. That singing was as sweet as the playing of the pipes when they are lamenting, and more painful, for these sounds came from the deep chests of warriors. Fionn felt all of his pain pass out of him in that song of mourning, and when at last it ended he felt emptied of all emotion.

In the stillness that followed he heard a voice he knew, muffled though it was by the thickness of the walls.

"Ferdomhonn, lad, is that you?"

"It is indeed."

"Take care, and do not touch the walls, for we are imprisoned by black sorcery—"

"What has happened to you?" came a second voice, and Fionn recognized it as Insin mac Suibhne, who had been his foster son. Swiftly, he told them what he knew.

"Sorcery there may be," said Ferdomhonn when he was done, "but I would dare it, if it were not for the great bar and bolts with which the one door into this place is fastened, which is beyond the strength of one man or two to break down."

"Then send word to the *fian*," exclaimed Goll.

"They will come soon enough, when we do not return," said Insin. "But the foreigners might get here before they do, even if we ran. I think we would do better to go down to the river and hold the ford against them. We scouted the riverbank and there is only one place they can get across from the island, and it can be held by two men."

It seemed very quiet in their prison when the young men had gone. After a time it seemed to them that they could hear the sound of battle coming faintly from the direction of the river, but there was no way to tell who had won.

Time crept by slowly. The fire had gone out long ago and the prisoners grew colder and more hungry. But in Fionn a great anger was growing. He could not be meant to die like a hare in a trap after all the dangers he had won through. He strained against his bonds despite the pain, and when he felt the warm wetness of blood on his wrists he welcomed it, for moisture might loosen the rawhide thongs.

Fionn's internal time-sense told him it must be near noon when they heard a scratching at the door. They hoped then that the *fian* had come, but it was only Ferdomhonn, reporting that Insin was dead, though he himself had taken the head of the man who slew him.

"I give you my blessing," said Fionn, "for that was a great deed. But there is no one now between us and death but you."

"Then I will defend you," said Ferdomhonn, and before Fionn could argue, he was gone.

And this time Fionn could not bear not to know what was happening. His body was still prisoned, but there was a way to set the spirit journeying that Bobdmall had taught him to do. On the wall there was a place where the logs had not been chinked and light shone through. Fionn focused on that point of brightness, letting it fill his vision, until it expanded to surround him and he sped through. He did not pause to consider what form he had now, for from the direction of the ford he could hear the clamor of fighting.

The sun shone brightly on the green waters of the Sinnan, broad here, and in places shallow. In the midst of the river was a low island edged with willows. He could see ships drawn up on the far side, and a small house upon the highest point, but every empty foot of the rest of it was crowded with hide tents and armed men.

A dozen warriors had crossed the ford, and Ferdomhonn was fighting them. Fionn saw his strength and his fury and any doubts he had ever had of the boy's paternity disappeared. It was a hard fight but in time the last of the Albans went floating downstream, and Ferdomhonn sat down on the bank, breathing hard and bleeding from a dozen wounds. Those wounds were still red when more men appeared through the trees. As they picked their way carefully across the treacherous footing of the ford, he recognized Miogach, armed now for battle.

"Is that Ferdhomhonn?" called Miogach. "I am sorry to see you here, for in all the time I was with the *fian* you never beat a hound or a dog of mine."

"And what have the rest of the *fian* done to you that

you should turn against us this way? Did not Fionn cherish you like a foster son?"

"He gave me the scraps from his table, and then cast me out. But it is because of the deaths of my uncle and the two brothers of mine that were killed in this year's fighting that I have laid this trap for the *fian*. I have only a few of my father's forces here with me, but before the day is out Colgain mac Teine himself will be here with the rest of them. Leave the ford, Ferdhomhonn."

"Take care," said Ferdhomhonn, "that the vengeance does not turn on you! I bear no ill will to anyone, so long as they do not try to pass. Sorry am I that I did not meet you before my body was wounded and weary."

Miogach did not reply, but rushed upon him with his men, fierce as a hound gone bad that ravages the sheepfold. And once more Ferdhomhonn stood against them, and if Fionn had had a voice in the state he was in, he would have cheered.

But at last Ferdhomhonn began to falter, and the other Albans drew back as Miogach got hold of him by his long fair hair and swung up his sword. Just then someone shouted. Miogach looked up, and in that moment a spear flashed out from among the trees—a long cast, an impossible cast—but before Miogach could turn it struck through his side.

"There is only one man who could have made that throw!" gasped Miogach. But Fionn already knew, even before Diarmuid's raven-dark head appeared from beneath the trees with Fatha panting after him.

"To save Ferdhomhonn!" cried Diarmuid, but Miogach shook his head.

"Nonetheless, for what Fionn did to my kindred he will pay, just as I have taken Fionn himself captive until my father comes—" he said then, and just as Diarmuid reached him he struck and held Ferdhomhonn's head high while the body fell back into the stream.

Diarmuid leaped upon him, and in a few moments, it seemed, Miogach's body was floating after that of the man he had slain. Then the rest of the Albans swarmed forward, and for a while Diarmuid and Fatha were kept as busy killing as ever Ferdhomhonn had been.

But at length even these enemies were dealt with and Diarmuid and Fatha staggered back up the path towards the House of the Quickentrees, weary with the work they had been doing, though most of the blood upon them was not their own. But Fionn's spirit, recoiling, sped faster and snapped back into his body again so abruptly that he cried out.

"Fionn, Fionn! Are you in there?" cried Diarmuid from outside.

"Who is it?" said Conain. "Has that ungrateful whelp Miogach come back to slay us at last?"

"It is Miogach's slayer that comes to us," said Fionn, pulling himself together, "with the head of his enemy under one arm and under the other the head of Ferdhomhonn my son."

Hovering above the fight like a bird, he had been free of human passions, but now that he was back in his body grief filled him—not the self-pity that had sapped his strength, but a wild rage that sparked through his limbs like fire.

"Have we grown ancient in one night, that our children must perish defending us?" said Fionn to the others, and Goll growled deep in his throat and heaved helplessly at his bonds.

"It is no use," said Dubhtach, "for the door is fast, and only a king's blood can release us from these bonds."

"Well I am king of the *fennid*," said Fionn, "and I will be free!" He sent down his awareness deep into the earth until the earth song filled him, and then, as the power rushed back up through him, sang out a Word of Unbinding that he had learned from Cethern. And with that his bonds, softened by his blood upon them, gave way at last.

At the same moment light struck suddenly down among them, and they saw Diarmuid looking down at them through a hole he had made in the thatch above.

Chapter 15

❧

"**F**IONN! STAND STILL—I AM THROWING A KNIFE DOWN to you!"

Through the pounding in his head as his circulation returned Fionn heard Diarmuid's shout and managed to keep from swaying as the weapon flashed by. His hands and feet throbbed with agony, and long immobility had sent his other muscles into spasm. It was several minutes before he could force his body to pick up the weapon, and even so he dropped the knife several times before he succeeded in severing Goll's bonds.

He let Goll release the others, drawing in deep breaths and wondering if he would ever feel like himself again.

"Fatha and I have tied our tunics together. If you stand upon the bench you should be able to reach them and we will pull you out of there," Diarmuid called. "And you had better hurry, for we saw the first of King Colgain's ships coming upriver as we left the ford."

By this time Fionn's fingers were working well enough so that he could grasp the cloth. They pulled him through the hole in the roof and he slid down the thatching to the ground and lay there as the young men brought up the others. Goll was hard for them, for he was a big man, but Conain proved nearly impossible, for despite a day and a night of fasting, his belly was almost too large for him to fit through the hole. As it was, he left a good deal of the skin of his backside on the rafters, so that afterward, the *fian* changed his nickname from Conain the Swearer to Conain the Bald.

"Come," said Diarmuid when they were all on the ground at last. "Once we are in the woods no man of Alba will be able to find us, but we must hurry, for they are very near."

Fionn winced as he got to his feet. "Good. It is time that King Colgain and I made an end." He caught sight of Diarmuid's expression and glared. "Why? Do you think the six of us together cannot hold a landing that you two defended alone?"

Diarmuid's face went carefully blank and Fatha's mouth opened, but after a moment he closed it without having spoken, and Goll began to laugh.

"Indeed, the lad does think it, and to look at us, bent over like old men with the cold of that enchantment still shaking our bones, it is no wonder. But you will see, boy, there is still a blow or two in these arms of mine." Sinews cracked as he stretched himself and started along the path. Conain was still complaining about his backside, but he could hardly hang back when his brother led the way, Faobhar was grinning, and Dubhtach kept the same dour look whether he was sad or happy, so there was no telling how fit he might be.

"At least the Albans will have left us plenty of weapons," said Fionn.

THEY HAD TIME TO COLLECT A GOODLY PILE OF SWORDS and spears before the Alban boats arrived, and Fionn had washed his wounds. But the folk who remained on the island were quick to tell their lord of the disaster, and only some of the boats unloaded their men. The others put out again into the stream and began to beat across the current towards the near shore.

"I don't like that," said Conain. "If they land on this bank they can come up behind us."

"Oh, by then the *fian* will have gotten here surely," said Faobhar. "And thus they will not miss out on the fighting, which they must do if we could only face the foe in small groups as they come across the ford."

"Indeed, that would be a pity," said Diarmuid, grinning in spite of himself. "Let us not kill the men who are coming out to us now too quickly, lest we leave our friends with nothing to do!"

This was all familiar, thought Fionn as he watched the Alban warriors splashing through the water towards him. He had seen it with spirit sight as he watched Ferdhomhonn. But now it was his own feet slipping on the bank whose soil had been churned to mud by the earlier fighting, his own arm trying the weight of an unfamiliar sword. He wished desperately for the Hazel Shield, safe with Birga in the camp on the mountain. The wicker shields of the vanquished had all been smashed beyond repair or gone floating away downstream, but in his other hand Fionn had a sharp spear whose shaft had broken off midway. He planted his feet in the earth he was defending and felt its strength rising within him. Then he ceased to think at all as the enemy came on.

By the time the first wave of attackers had been thrown back Fionn was beginning to wonder if Diarmuid had not been right after all. A night and day such as they had passed were not the best preparation for battle, and his arm was already weary. But downstream the painted boats of the Albans were seeking a landing; it was no good thinking about retreat now. And then he saw among the men coming through the trees at the edge of the island a tall warrior with gold on his helmet and on his shield. He was like Laigne, Fionn thought as the man strode down to the water, but not so massive. And then, with a little shiver of recognition, he realized that he was looking at what Miogach might have become if he had reached his full power as a man.

"Fionn mac Cumhal, where is my son!" cried Colgain.

"His head lies with the head of my own son, whom he killed," Fionn replied. "We are quits now. Go home to Alba, and do no more scathe to Eriu's shores."

The king scowled. "Quits? I do not think so. My brother and my other sons are dead because of you and the *fianna*. I would rather spill your blood than gather Irish gold!"

"Blood you may have," said Diarmuid, "but it will be your own."

Fionn cast a glance back at him and grinned. They had failed with Miogach, but the son of Duibhne, standing knee-deep in the water with his white skin all crimson with other men's blood and the pride of a stag blazing in his eye, had been brought up from birth among the *fian*. He was all that a *fénnid* should be.

My son will be like that, thought Fionn, *when he is grown!* The knowledge came to him with the certainty of prophecy. But would he himself be there to see it? He looked at the warrior stalking towards him and felt every muscle in his body shrieking with weariness. *Diarmuid could fight him*, came a treacherous whisper from within, and Fionn shook his head angrily. Diarmuid could avenge him if he fell, but he might as well offer his neck to Colgain's sword now as ask a boy who had already battled twice as long as he had to fight for him.

He stepped carefully down from the bank into the water and planted his feet among the stones. The water flowing down from above was clean; as it washed the mud and blood away he began to feel strength coming back into his limbs. He bent quickly and splashed cool water over the rest of his body, then scooped up some to drink, his gaze still on his foe.

"You come to your death," Fionn said, rising. The singing of the river filled him, and beneath it the earth song. He took a deep breath of air and the fire in his veins blazed high. "It is Eriu herself who gives me the strength to kill you, but you have no power to draw on, for you are far from your home."

The King of Lochlann snarled and tried to move faster, buffeted by the current, slipping on the stones. Fionn thrust with his spear and the Alban caught it on his shield, pushed the weapon away, and tried to bear him down. But Fionn slid away towards his enemy's sword-side, striking aside his first blow with his own blade and slicing towards his unprotected shoulder. Colgain wrenched himself away, but he was off-balance now.

Now it was Fionn who was attacking, jabbing with his spear. From downriver he heard shouting and knew that the enemy had found a place to land. Once more the king managed to catch Fionn's spear on his shield, but this time the point pierced the hide covering and lodged in the wood beneath. For a moment Fionn strove to free his weapon, while Colgain tried as hard to wrench it from his hand.

Then it came to Fionn that he had only to maintain his pressure to immobilize the shield. And the rest of the Albans might lose heart if he could kill their king. He stiffened his spear arm, holding fast, and began to attack his foe with lightning strokes of the sword. But Colgain's torso was protected by armor of hardened leather, and Fionn's sword was already blunted by many blows. The Alban war cries were louder now; their king heard them, too, and laughed.

There was no point now in hoarding strength—if Fionn did not finish this in the next few moments they would overrun him. Ducking Colgain's next blow, he twisted and jerked suddenly on the spear. This time it came loose, and the Alban, who had been braced against it, lurched forward. Fionn saw the flicker of panic in Colgain's eyes as his foot slipped on a moss-slimed stone.

"Even the rocks fight for me!" snarled Fionn, leaping aside, and as the other man's arms flailed outward, he saw the man's corded neck unprotected, and with all his strength brought down his sword. He felt the jar all the way up his arm as he connected, but the momentum of the blade carried it through. Colgain's head leaped forward as the body sprawled belly-down in the stream.

Fionn made a grab as the current whirled the head by and swung it up by the hair. "Men of Alba," he screamed, "lay down your arms, for see you, I have taken the head of your king!"

But the only reply was a roar of rage. The first of the enemy were already attacking Fatha and Dubhtach at the edge of the landing. Even heroes could not long withstand such numbers if they came from all sides. Fionn flung the bloody head towards the shore and grabbed for the Alban's shield, determined to make them pay dearly for their revenge.

More enemy were pushing through the trees with every moment. Fionn saw Dubhtach fall. And then, as he struggled towards the shore, he heard the wild barking of Sceolan, and the high, skirling war cries of Eriu, and knew that the rest of the *fian* had come at last.

IT WAS SUNSET BEFORE THE BATTLE WAS OVER. THE ENEMY ships provided the wood for the funeral pyres. There had been a great store of food on the island, and a day late, Conain sat down to devour the feast that had been promised him. But Fionn felt too weary for food. There was a painful beauty in the pale flare of the funeral fires against the radiant sky, and in the sweet piping of birds, after the clamor of fighting men. He spent a long time washing himself in the clean waters of the river, surprised to find himself so little scathed, save for the raw wounds left by his bonds.

I am alive! he thought, staring up at the first stars that were piercing the veil of the sky. *I will live to see my beloved once more. I will see our child!* His gaze travelled over the moving waters to the red mud of the landing where so many had died.

Something was moving among the trees. Fionn got to his feet, frowning. They had dealt honorably with the bodies of their foes; no spirit should be walking there. Then the man came out from the shadows, and Fionn saw the shape of him, shock-headed and long-legged as a crane.

"Ceallach!" he shouted, waving. The other looked up, then started across the ford. The man looked, thought Fionn, as if he had run all the way from Almu, and his own belly clenched with fear.

"What is it?" he cried as the runner staggered up onto the island. "Has Sadb gone into labour early?" He could hear the harsh rasp of Ceallach's breathing as he fell to his knees on the ground.

"My lord . . . it is worse than that. . . . She has disappeared!"

THE RAMPARTS OF ALMU GLARED WHITE IN THE HARSH light of noontide when Fionn came home again. Two days had passed since Ceallach had brought him the news, and for most of that time he had been running. Ceallach himself was somewhere on the road behind him, and behind them, Diarmuid and a picked band of the younger men. They were all known for their swiftness, but none of them could become one with the earth song and let it carry him along. But with every footfall like an echo he had heard Sadb's name. Only Sceolan had been able to keep pace with him, lolloping along at the same steady pace and eyeing him with silent sympathy.

There was a part of Fionn's mind that knew he had pushed his body beyond its limits, and that presently he would pay. But not yet, not until he knew what had happened to her. For a breath he paused, squinting up at the fortress. The pointed logs of the palisade that crowned those white walls snarled at the clear sky. He would have matched those ramparts against any foe. But they had not been able to keep his beloved in safety. He moved forwards again and heard once more her name, and with it the questions; Who had enticed her away from its safety? And how, and why?

As Fionn came through the great gates he felt the familiar tingle and knew that the wardings that protected Almu were still there. What power could have snatched Sadb from that safety? Folk fell back before him as if a ghost had come among them. Indeed, he could hardly feel his own body. He tried to croak a question, and Mongfind came bustling forward with a horn of beer for him, clucking anxiously. He knew the liquid was cool and just what he needed, but it had no taste for him. Still, after he drank it he found his parched throat working once more. He looked at the strained faces around him.

"Tell me!"

Some of the story he had heard from Ceallach. Stupid, perhaps, to think that the facts would be changed by hearing them in other words. And yet Fionn listened with fixed attention as Mongfind and Gariv Cronach, the doorkeeper, told their tale.

"She was well, sir, and happy," said Mongfind. "Looking forward to the birth of the child and reckoning the days till you should return. We heard that you had been fighting the men of Lochlann, and that worried her, but she tried not to show it. She kept saying it was only to be expected, that she would not have let a man without courage father her child."

Fionn stared at her. He had felt anger and regret when he faced Colgain. The thing that made him feel hollow with anguish now was fear.

"And then, lord, five days ago, the message came," Gariv took up the tale.

"Who brought it?" asked Fionn.

"An old man with the accent of Connachta. His tunic was torn and he had a bloody bandage round his brow. He stood at the gate and cried out that the *fian* had fought a great battle with the outlanders on the shores of the Sinnan. He said there was no man fit but himself to carry the message, the Albans had so savaged them. He said that you were wounded unto death, lord, and like to die, out of your head with fever and calling her name."

"And so she went out to him?" Fionn's voice had gone flat.

"Fionn, lad, we could not hold her!" Mongfind exclaimed. "She was fair wild with grief and fear, crying that there was no reason for her to stay safe within our walls if you were gone."

"Indeed, lord, she was beyond reason," said Gariv. "But we would not let her go. We invited the messenger to come in, but he swore that a *geas* had been laid upon him to shelter under no man's roof until he should bring the lady to your side, and so he would bide at the gates until he himself died or she should come."

"And that night, when we thought her asleep, worn out by weeping, my lady went out to him—" Mongfind shook her head, unable to meet Fionn's eyes.

Fionn got to his feet. His own eyes felt hot and hard as stones.

"What are you doing, lord?" asked Gariv. "You'll never track them now—it was five days ago!"

"You could not even guard one pregnant woman," he said softly, and they flinched away. "Do you think you can hold *me*? Sceolan!" He whistled, and the dog, who had been sprawled by the hearth, looked up. "I have work for you, my dear one—" The hound got to his feet and padded painfully to Fionn's side. The dog was as tired as he was, thought Fionn, but it was skill, not speed, he needed now.

"It is Sadb we must follow—" He held out a veil of hers to refresh the dog's memory. The hound looked up at him with troubled eyes. "I know, lad," Fionn said more softly. "You are remembering Bran. But surely we paid too high a price to win her to let her be stolen this way! Track her, my lad! Show me where she has gone!"

And so they went out though the gate of Almu—the great white hound and the weary man behind him, and no one dared to hinder him.

No man of Eriu could have followed that trail, not even one of the *fian*. Even for Fionn it would have been hard after so long without the dog. But where the faint outlines of her footfalls had been obscured the hound found scent, and Fionn found traces where scent failed. Of her companion he was less sure, except that the fellow moved fast; for all that he had the uneven, limping step of an old man. And so they passed down the road from Almu, and then, when the fortress was well behind them, into the trees.

Fionn wondered how the man had gotten Sadb to leave the road. Had he told her it was a shorter way, or suggested that they hide from pursuit from the *dun*? It was darker beneath the trees, hard to see the traces, though he was moving now on all fours like a hound. The earth scents filled his nostrils, almost overwhelming in their intensity. But the one scent he was searching for—the flowerlike fragrance that was a part of the woman he loved—he did not find.

It was late afternoon when Sceolan came to a halt, circling in confusion and whining. The slanting light edged every leaf with gold, but Fionn had no eye for beauty. He was staring at the four stakes set in a square in the green turf before him: oak, willow, fir, and a white birch pole. Sadb's footsteps led inside.

The ground here was soft, and the cold stink of magic that still hung about the place had kept any other beast from disturbing it. Fionn shuddered at the deathly chill that smote him as he drew near. He had banished that winter once, and freed Sadb from its spell; he could do so again. But first he must find her.

Fionn could see clearly the marks of a woman's feet: two prints sunk deeply as if she had stopped, wondering, and then a flurry as if she were trying to break free; and then, superimposed on the others, the deep double wedges of a deer's tracks, and not just any deer. Though it was months past the season, the creature that had made those marks was a heavily pregnant doe.

Fionn was still crouched over the hoofprints when the folk from the *dun*, accompanied by Ceallach and Diarmuid, who had caught up at last, found him.

"She is gone . . ." he said dully. "He has changed her back into a doe and from here his spells cover both her tracks and his own. There is no power now that can follow them, neither here nor among the Sidhe."

"Who, lord?" asked Ceallach. "Who could have done such a thing?"

Fionn shook his head. He could not imagine anyone hating Sadb enough to do this—it must be some enemy of his own. But though he knew many who would have been happy to take his head, there was no one who had mastered such powerful magic.

"There was magic at the House of the Quickentrees as well," said Diarmuid, frowning. "Are they the same?"

"The same mind was behind them . . ." said Fionn slowly. Crouched here so close to the earth, many things had become clear. "But the druid who did this was not with Miogach—the only magic there had been done beforehand, to bewitch the drink and the bonds."

"But if you were to be killed, why take Sadb?" asked Gariv.

"This is someone who knows me . . ." Thought followed thought, slow and inevitable as doom. "Someone who hates me, who did not believe Miogach could kill me, even with the armies of Lochlann. This is someone who wants me to suffer before I die. . . ."

"The old man—" said Gariv, who had been one of Crimall's *fian*. "The old druid, your grandfather—could it have been he? He swore vengeance on you for taking

Almu, and you warded it against him. No wonder he could not come inside!"

"*Love you will find, and lose it. . . .*" Tadg's curse echoed in Fionn's ears. *And now Sadb is gone. . . .* The others were still talking, but he had ceased to hear them.

Because of me! the knowledge pounded at his brain. *Sadb is suffering because of me!* Once he had sworn to keep her from all harm, but it had been a lie. If it were not for him, Sadb would be safe and happy—indeed, he thought now that even that first enchantment from which he had rescued her must have been laid with this in mind.

His hands were still stroking the grass, caressing the moist earth where her feet had trod. The scent of earth rose around him, intoxicating, familiar. Fionn had known such intensity once before, as a boy driven beyond humanity by his grief and wounds. He was only exhausted now, but his sorrow was far greater. *Too great for a man to bear*, he thought numbly. *Too great for me—*

Why could these people around him not cease their foolish babbling? Someone laid a hand on his arm, and he twitched away, snarling. They thrust Sceolan towards him, but the dog, understanding better than they did what was happening, hung back, whimpering.

"Come now, my lord. Darkness has fallen and it is time we went back to Almu. You can rest there—"

The words made no sense to him. He could see quite clearly. And why should he want to leave the forest? He bent his head to the earth and rubbed his face against the cool grass, and it seemed to him that antlers weighted his brow.

"Fionn, it is time to go," another voice said more firmly. Hard hands grasped his shoulder, lifting—

And the creature that had been Fionn lashed out, hit someone, smelled blood, and struck again. This was a trap; he had to escape from them! But before him lay the forest. As the men began to close in on him he bellowed again. For a moment they hesitated, and he saw his chance and leaped between them, clearing the lower branches of the hazel copse and bounding onward as swiftly as he could go.

He heard shouting behind him and staggered to his feet on the other side. Did he have two legs or four? He did not know; at this moment he did not know his name. He understood only that pain beyond bearing awaited if they caught him. He gulped air and then began to run.

AT SUMMER'S ENDING ALL THE FRUITS OF FIELD AND FOREST compete in ripeness. As Lughnasa passed and the season drew on towards the festival of harvest, the grain hung heavy on the stalk. But no creature that knew the woods had any need to steal from the fields of men, for the bushes were heavy with berries, roots were storing up starch for the winter, and nuts weighted the branches of trees.

The creature that ranged the Forest of Fidh Gaible knew every hazel copse and stream. Sometimes, swimming in some deep pool, he thought he must be a salmon; for he had memories of leaping waterfalls and the dark, silent depths of the sea. It seemed to him that he knew every curve and eddy of the Boann, and he dreamed of a still pool surrounded by hazel trees. But he could not breathe underwater, and he became chilled if he stayed there too long. And so he crawled up onto the bank and became an otter, losing himself in the joy of sliding down the muddy bank to land with a splash in the stream. He caught fish with swift snaps and ate them, and then scrambled back into the long grass to lie basking in the sun.

One day a bear came down to the water, and, watching that lumbering grace, he thought that perhaps that was his true shape, for like the bear he could walk upright and eat anything. When he was a bear, no other creature threatened him. He copied the swift swipe with which it took fish, and followed it to find where the berries were ripest. But when he tried to dig out a honeycomb, the bees that could do nothing against the bear's thick pelt descended gleefully upon his tender hide. And so he ran off, howling, to soak his stings in the cold stream.

For a time he ran as a wolf in the woods, chasing down rabbits and snatching up small creatures that came down to the riverbank. But for some reason he did not understand, he never went after deer. He marked his territory and patrolled it. When the moon grew full he howled from a hilltop and heard other wolves singing a reply. But when he tried to join the pack they whined fearfully and ran away.

He lay then for a while without motion. But though his body seemed sleeping, in spirit he grew wings and soared into the heavens. He saw Eriu laid out like a tapestry below him—the dark furring of forests, the chequered fields, and the shining serpent coils of the streams. He gazed without fear into the sun and became an intimate of the winds. He learned where to find the warm air that would lift him, and how the flicker of a feather could send him sliding across the sky. He grew accustomed to limitless space, who had spent so much of his life enclosed by thick forest. But after a time, even this freedom became a prison, for he was alone. Need sent him plummeting back into the still shape curled at the base of the oak tree.

The rich scent of the oak mast brought him back to awareness. As he rooted through it in search of acorns, he thought he was one of the pigkind; he had dim memories of having lived in this shape before. He grew drunken on the scents of the forest floor, digging into the moist soil at the roots of trees. He knew without thinking which mushrooms were food for him and which to avoid, and which plants hid tasty roots beneath the surface, however insignificant they might appear. As a boar he could eat almost anything, and he was fierce enough to frighten off most foes. And yet times would come when he wanted something too high up for any pig to reach and found himself stretching up on his hind legs. And then he would see the sun and sniff the wind and feel the need to run sparking through his long limbs.

Need and opportunity drove him from transformation to transformation. He no longer knew what kind of creature he might be. As he experienced the pleasure and pains of each kind his knowledge grew ever greater, until he was not so much a creature of the forest as its soul. The season drew on; days grew shorter and nights cold. In the forest, the leaves began to change their color; the green mantle of the woods grew rich with tawny and crimson and gold.

He moved through the woodlands, at first slowly and then with more confidence, slipping between the trees. At night the meadows drew him, and proudly he stepped through the long grass, his brow heavy with the horns of the forest king. He knew without knowing that there were seven tines to those antlers, one for each of his transformations. He was a king stag now.

In the glens the red stags, fat with a summer's feeding, belled their defiance at all rivals as they guarded their does. The sound of that challenge shocked through every nerve of the king. He felt the hot blood burning within him and leaped to find its source, every movement pulsing with power. Then he scented the rich musk of the does, and his loins throbbed with need for the one he had lost. The stag, roaring, turned to face him, and they fought, sharp hooves tearing up the soil.

And when the red stag lay with a broken neck in a still heap upon the grass, the king stag searched among the does, seeking the white one, the only one he desired. But she was not among them, and after a time he went away, leaving the astonished females to find a new master.

He searched through all the forests during that season of lust and battle when the leaves turned blood red and brown and the moon hung like a golden shield in the sky. But though he challenged a hundred stags and gazed upon ten times that many does, he never found a white one. And as the wind grew colder it began to strip the bright leaves from the trees. He shivered in the long nights and burrowed into the leaves, feeling the white death of winter approaching. Once he had had the craft to defeat it, but he no longer knew the human words from which to forge a spell.

And so the turning of the year brought the world at last to Samhain. The king stag did not know this—he had no way to count the days, but he could sense the gathering of power. Each night as the moon waned another kind of radiance grew, sparking from the leaves and glowing around tree trunks, flowing with the waters and blazing ever more brightly from the hidden roads that crossed the land.

They were not hidden now, not from one with spirit sight, which as the days passed grew ever keener to see the things of the Otherworld. The king stag found himself drawn to those bright pathways, and when he stepped upon them, he felt himself changing once more, but he had no picture in his mind from which to image the creature that he was coming to be. He could only follow those roads which as yet led nowhere, forgetting to eat and drinking only when they crossed a stream. He grew gaunt and pale, if there had been anyone to see, but even those foragers who might have glimpsed him earlier in the season knew better than to wander the woods at this time of year. And so he wandered, a shadow among shadows, until Samhain Eve.

Chapter 16

∼❦∼

A GOLDEN SICKLE MOON WAS CUTTING DOWN SCUDDING clouds still afire with sunset, as if they had been kindled by the Samhain fires that folk were lighting all across the land. They were fires of warding and welcome, to keep the wild powers away and welcome the spirits of dead kinsmen home, bright against stark tree shapes stripped bare by last week's storm. One by one they flared, up and down the land of Eriu, on the hill of Macha in Ulaidh and in Connachta at the mound of Cruachan, before the white gleam of the Brugh na Boinne, near Bri Élé and the Paps of Anu.

At Almu they kindled the fires for the men who had fallen on the Sinnan and wondered if Fionn would be among the ghosts who came to share the feasting. But the creature who had borne that name was not dead, though he could hardly be counted among the living, wasted to skin and sinew and bone as he was, with his hair hanging in ragged locks over his eyes. Nor was he one of the powers of Faerie, though the wild gaze that pierced the tangles might seem as terrible. He existed in a state that was neither Faerie nor the mortal world.

The storm had been violent, precursor of a bad winter to come. The soil was still saturated, and as the temperature dropped, a dank mist began to rise from the ground as if the land itself were kindling with cold fire. The rising wind swirled it upwards as it rattled the branches of the trees. Mist and smoke on the earth and cloud in the heavens drew a veil of mystery across all that was solid and familiar. It was not only the barriers between the worlds that were dissolving, but the world itself. In the *duns*, folk made signs of warding and kept within doors. In the wood, the wanderer whined uneasily.

Night fell and the sickle moon, burnished now the color of white steel, began its downward sweep into the west. The wood was a place of dimly moving shape and shadow. He coughed as the chill air caught in his lungs. But he would not seek shelter. He felt himself as restless as the wind. The woods were waiting; the whole land was waiting. He moved from thicket to meadow and from rock to stream, seeking—something—the same thing that the land itself awaited as the heavens wheeled towards night's noon.

As midnight drew near, the first flicker of light flared through the hazels and up the oak tree. In moments the whole forest was glimmering with pale fire. The wind rose, setting every branch in motion, and the straight track that ran southwestward from the Brugh na Boinne began to glow. At first it was only a pooling of radiance on the ground, but as night deepened the light grew stronger, until a broad swathe of brightness cut through the forest, so brilliant that the trees and rocks that usually obscured it became transparent, as if they were the illusions, and this broad bright track the true reality.

He paced along beside it, desiring that radiance, and yet afraid. He heard a deep murmuring and looked up at the treetops, but though the clouds were scudding across the starpaths, the sound did not come from the wind in the trees. He was near the edge of the wood here, and through a gap in the twisted trunks he could see the sweep of open country to the northward with the shining path laid across it, straight as an arrow could fly. Across the plain a bright haze was flowing; it was from that movement that the sound was coming, hissing like waves on the shore, whispering like wind in the trees, and yet unlike either, for this sound held the murmur of many voices and a sweet silver shimmer of bells.

The creature that crouched at the edge of the wood felt that sweetness like a physical pain. It grew louder, and he opened his throat in a sound that could have come from no human throat, though it held too much sorrow to be an animal.

Now he could see movement within the brightness, shapes of men and horses and other things for which human language had no words. It was Samhain Eve and the Sidhe were riding, on this night, as on Beltane, when the Otherworld drew close to the lands of men. At such times, humans who strayed might be seduced by its beauty, and after a night of revelry wake to find a hundred nights had passed in mortal lands, if they woke with minds still human, or at all. But the being who watched the Sidhe come surging across the plain no longer had a human mind to lose.

And now they were upon him, with a clash and a jangle of bells and shriek of silvery laughter, man shape and horse shape passing through the illusions of boulders and trees. But some of the mounts were horned or fanged, and some of the riders were feathered or glistened with opalescent scales. Pale, red-eared hounds bounded before them, and kelpies and phookas and every kind of bogle lolloped behind. A great crowd they were, as various as a tree full of turning leaves and with a beauty far more unsettling. He drew closer and closer, staring, and cried out, as for a moment he seemed to see among them the pale form of a white doe.

"Sadb!" he cried—he knew that name, though he no longer knew his own. "Sadb!" The last of the wild riders whirled past, and as they went by he lurched forward onto the fairy road.

POWER SURGED THROUGH HIM, AN INTENSITY OF FEELING so great that he cried out in pain, or perhaps in ecstasy. For a moment he swayed, then the vibration of light that was sweeping through his body forced him into motion. With each step it grew easier. As an eagle he had ridden the winds and as a salmon the currents of the stream. To move in this river of light he had only to open himself to the power that flowed through it and run.

Here there was no time, and space was a very different matter than it was in the world of men. As more bright paths flowed into the main track it grew broader, curving now in a great spiral that moved ever more swiftly as it turned towards its core. By the time dawn began to break above the eastern hills of Eriu the faerie riders had passed far beyond awareness of the mortal world. The light, which had once been so blinding, was now a cool luminescence, glimmering through the emerald grass of a land illuminated by the perpetual opalescent gloaming of the Otherworld.

The spiral was still moving, faerie lights swirling on a great meadow surrounded by tall stones. But somehow the horses had disappeared, or perhaps they had simply taken other forms in order to join the dance. The thin, ringing beat of a tight-stretched drum set his feet to moving in a new rhythm; then he heard the piercing silver skirl of piping that would have driven any mortal piper mad with desire, and a golden shimmer of harp song loud enough to be heard through the piping, which was surely magic. It was a music that sang in the blood like honeymead, containing all joy and all sorrow. Between one step and another its magic seized him and he too was drawn into the dance.

"By sound, by sound the sacred round—
By skirling pipe and beating drum,
By whirling feet and harpstrings' hum,
By sound, by sound, our circle's bound!"

He stamped and swayed, drunken on music, forgetting all fatigue.

"By fire, by fire we shall not tire,
By skipping foot and sparkling glance,
By tripping step, we lead the dance,
By fire, by fire comes our desire!"

In the center of the dancing a brighter radiance showed where the great ones of the Sidhe were feasting, but he did not seek to see them. Even the lesser folk, when they did not wear the forms of monsters from men's worst dreams, were beautiful beyond human imagining.

"By Samhain's horn upon the morn—
By lust and laugh and revelry,
By death and immortality,
By Samhain's horn the world's reborn!"

Women fair as flowers swayed, their silken draperies floating around them. No mortal ever had such beauty, and few who walked in mortal lands had ever been so fair. A maiden with hair like the floss of milkweed came twirling by and he reached out to her, but when he saw her face he jumped back—though she was fair beyond human dreaming, hers was not the face he was looking for.

The sweeter the music and the lovelier the dancers, the more poignant became his sense of loss. He made his way through the throng in increasing desperation, turning one way, then another, until he no longer knew anything except his need. Dizzied, he lost the rhythm of the dance and stumbled into a golden-haired female. She cried out, and the dancers eddied away from him. They were all looking at him now, laughing and pointing.

"A mortal! A mortal has come among us on Samhain Eve!" they cried.

"Is it a man or a beast?"

He winced at the trill of faerie laughter.

"Oh my dear, it's a wildman surely, a monster—consider his hair!"

"—and his smell!" another voice replied.

They began to laugh again, still dancing, and he cringed away from their mocking faces and bright eyes.

"Man or beast," a darker voice said then. "It is Samhain, and he is in *our* realm." Now more of the warriors were gathering, pushing past the women, forming a ring.

"Tell us, mortal, how you came here, and why?" That low voice came again. The speaker was a female, very tall, clad in a crimson gown that bared the creamy swell of her breasts. Black hair streamed out on the wind like dark wings. She smiled, and something within him remembered the ecstasy her touch on the soul could bring. He smelled blood and like an echo he heard the screaming of warring men. But he could find no words to answer her.

"What is your name?" Her dark gaze seemed to see into his soul. Some dim, almost forgotten memory told him that he must answer with words of magic.

"I have been a salmon in the stream and an otter on the bank," he said hoarsely, "I was a bear eating berries and a wolf in the wood. I was an eagle on the heights and a boar beneath the trees, I was a stag of seven tines. . . ." His throat closed and he stared around him.

"He is under a spell!" said someone.

"If so, the enchantment is of his own making, for there is no stink of magic about him," the tall woman replied. "The wildman has delivered himself into our hands."

"Mortal blood shall seal the working," a pale warrior said. He reached out and his long fingers brushed the wildman's gaunt arm.

He leaped away, snarling. Had they not heard? He was an animal, and he could fight like one. The music became a battle song as they rushed him, stabbing with sharp, silvery blades. But he had the battlecraft of every beast in his sharp teeth and hard bare feet and his long fingers with their broken nails.

Soon enough they realized their mistake and began to take beast form themselves to attack him. The dark hair of the woman in the crimson gown swirled around her and suddenly a raven was flapping heavily upward, circling the battlefield and encouraging her warriors with blood-freezing cries.

He flowed from one form to another to defend himself, and many of his opponents fell. But there came a time when his breath sobbed in his throat and his limbs grew heavy. More of their blows were landing now, but it did not matter. His real foes were loss and loneliness and pain. He struck out unseeing as the world darkened around him, and only when the ground smacked the breath from his lungs did he knew that he was down. He lay sprawled where he had fallen, dragging in air in tortured gasps. Feathers rustled nearby. He waited for the raven to peck out his eyes.

But it did not happen. As his breath came back to him, he realized that the earth was trembling to the tread of some large animal. With an effort he opened his eyes.

A nobly proportioned white cow with red ears was coming towards him across the trampled grass. The air glimmered around her with a light that seemed to focus in her large, liquid eyes. She came to a halt beside him, and though one of those great hooves could have crushed him, he felt no fear. She looked around the circle and his foes, whether their form was human or animal, drew back. Even the raven, making a rude sound deep in her throat, hopped away.

"*That is well . . . ,*" came words, but he did not think he heard them with his physical ears. "*It is not fated that this man be killed here. He belongs to Me. . . .*"

The great head lowered, and he saw that the cow's horns gleamed like ivory. Her breath was like apple blossom. Then she looked at him, and tears filled his eyes, for he had never seen such love in any creature's gaze.

Or perhaps he had seen it once—recognition teased at his memory. But there was no time to wonder. The cow's large pink tongue rasped across his face, his arms, all the places where his flesh had been bruised and torn, and where it passed, a wonderful warmth spread through his limbs.

Then she moved again, so that the great swinging bag of her udder hung within reach of his hand.

"*Drink, my son, and be renewed. . . .*"

The words were for him now. Her licking had given him strength enough to move his fingers. He closed them on the soft teat and almost at once a thin stream of milk spurted outward, warm on his bare chest and sweet in his mouth, sweeter than honeymead, richer than cream. He gulped as greedily as a child at the breast, and felt the warm honey-sweet tide of life surge through every vein.

He drank until he could swallow no more, then lay back, gazing up at her. Vision pulsed painfully as his body strove to assimilate the energy it had received. The shape of the great cow wavered; it seemed to him that it was compacting and growing taller until a stately woman in a red mantle and a white gown stood there with light raying from her brow. The images of cow and Goddess coalesced and parted in dizzying sequence until all he was sure of was the smile in her dark eyes.

Brigid—Even now he could not speak. But nonetheless She heard.

"Rest, my beloved," She told him then, "and all will yet be well. . . ."

He tried to speak, but it was too much effort. With a sigh he sank back into the warm darkness and knew no more.

"OF ALL YOUR FOOLISH DEEDS, TO TAKE ON THE WHOLE host of the Sidhe with only your teeth and nails was surely the greatest—" The voice was low, sweet, and familiar. "What were you thinking of, Fionn mac Cumhal?"

Despite the mockery in the words, the tone was loving. Fionn stirred, stretched a little, wondering why his ability to do so surprised him, and opened his eyes. Donait was looking down at him, smiling.

"I have not been thinking at all," he said slowly, "since—" he cast back and his face twisted as he remembered—"a little after Lughnasa."

Above him, the interlacing of boughs that formed the roof of Donait's hall was the same as he remembered; if he turned his head he could see that tapestries still hung on the walls. And Donait was beautiful as always, her blue eyes luminous and her hair glistening as if each strand had been spun from living gold.

It was only he who had changed, Fionn thought grimly, gazing down at the hard angles of his body beneath the silken sheet she had drawn over him. Brigid's touch had healed the worst of his wounds, but he was little more than a skeleton, and Donait's beauty aroused not the smallest stirring of desire.

"Brigid—" he whispered, and swallowed, remembering sweetness.

"Indeed," said Donait, "you have friends in high places. I do not think anyone else could have saved you once the Morrigan had claimed you for her own!"

"But why? Why did she make me live?" Fionn shook his head painfully.

"I suppose she must still have a use for you," said Donait a little tartly, "though I cannot imagine what it might be!" She caught her breath, as if she might have said more but had recognized that he could not bear it just now. "Nor will we ever know unless I can put some more flesh back on your bones! You mortals have such little lives—how can you treat yourselves this way?"

That did not demand an answer, but Fionn found that when she asked him to sit up, he was able to move, and after that to get himself from the bed to the marble bathing pool that had appeared with its customary efficiency. And once in the water, he was content to let its healing warmth soak the last of his body's pain. The pain in his soul was another matter. For the moment it was quiescent, but he could feel it waiting like a broken limb for some chance touch to waken once more to agony.

And yet, bathing in the pool did soothe him. When he was done, he felt above all things weary, and it was all he could do to get back into the bed again. He sank down into its softness, and even the warmth of the woman beside him could not keep him conscious anymore.

Fionn slept and woke to eat, and slept again. He could not tell how much time had passed when he found himself fully awake at last, with a twitching in his limbs that made it impossible to lie still any longer. Grief had left him too witless to take his own life, but the life he had been leading in the forest would surely have destroyed him. Still, his body had taken advantage of all the help it had been given in healing. He was still thin, but no longer skeletal, and it had been a very long time since he had had such a sense of well-being in all his limbs.

But without physical pain to distract him, how could he escape the grief that had harrowed his soul? Why did he need clear eyes if he could not look on Sadb? What use were healthy limbs if he could not hold her in his arms? She had so delighted in the feel and mass and scent of his body—her love had given it a new value. Without her, he might as well have looked like a bogle, for all he cared.

Since this body insists on living, he thought then, sitting up in the great bed, *let my mind be the part that fades away. I will desire nothing, think nothing, live only for my senses.* That should not be too hard, he thought then, remembering the intoxicating flavors of the food in Donait's hall.

With that awareness of his states of consciousness that had always astonished him, before the thought was quite done Donait herself appeared, moving gracefully towards him across the polished floor.

"You are awake—" She smiled, watching him carefully.

"Indeed," he answered, "and hungry. Give me some of your apples, Donait, and that wonderful bread."

She was always beautiful, he remembered, but today she was particularly appealing, clad in a gown of pale blue made of some stuff that swirled when she moved and when she stilled, molded itself around her long limbs in graceful folds. Her wonderful fair hair was loose, confined only by a silver band set with pale blue stones. With an artist's eye he could appreciate the wonderful lines of her body, but he realized suddenly that there was one sense he must not allow to waken.

"I think so—" She gestured, and he saw that a table was already set and waiting. Had it been there before? She gave him a tunic of silky white linen to put on, and took his arm when legs that seemed to have forgotten how to bear his weight threatened to betray him before he could reach the dining couch.

He stretched himself gratefully upon it, and Donait settled herself next to him, so close he could feel the warmth of her breast against his arm and the pressure

of her smooth thigh. As she poured milk for him he
drew imperceptibly away. He would eat, and drink
himself senseless if that were possible here, but he
must not even think about that beautiful body. Love
was one pleasure he would know no more.

"Open your mouth—"

Fionn turned, and tears blurred his vision as he saw
a fair hand holding out a piece of bannock. Sadb had
done that—the scent of the bannock was the same—
and as he breathed it in, the sense of smell, oldest and
most powerful of all, swept all the flimsy defenses he
had just been erecting away.

"Get away from me!" Fionn thrust at her and flung
himself from the couch. After two steps his legs
betrayed him and he fell, rolling to a fetal crouch
upon the cool floor. He ground his forehead against
it, moaning Sadb's name.

"Let me go mad," he whispered after a time. "At least
let me go mad if you will not let me die!"

"That will not bring her back," said Donait calmly.
"Will you let your enemy defeat you this way?"

"He already has—" Fionn answered brokenly. "I
thought I saw Sadb in the Riding of the Sidhe, but
it was an illusion. Even the son of the Dagda, her
father, could not rescue her when the druid took her
before. It was my magic that transformed her back into
woman form, but I did not free her—she was released
to be a trap for me!"

"At least you understand that much," Donait said
tartly. "You were always the target, and now you are
letting Tadg destroy you, which is more than all the
hosts of the Sidhe could do! It is not like you, Fionn
mac Cumhal, to flee from an enemy!"

Slowly Fionn sat up, staring at her. "Oh, but it is," he
said bitterly. "I ran away from Bodbmall, and Cruithne,
and the *fian*, and Cethern. And what has my life been
since then but a flight from the *dun* to the forest and
the forest to the *dun*? I am reknowned for my running.

This time it was myself I was running from, and I had almost succeeded, if you and the Goddess between you had not brought me to life again." He shook his head. "But it will do you little good, for it is only the shell of a man that you have got here."

"Do you think so?" She smiled strangely. "Look at the tapestry."

Fionn turned. He remembered trying to count the hangings in Donait's hall the first time he stayed here, when he was still a child. He had never come out with a consistent number no matter how many times he tried. When he defended Donait from the Fomorians the hangings had been different. Looking at them now, he saw that the tapestry of the great Hazel Tree was still there, full grown now, and far healthier than it had been when he saw it before. But he did not think most of the others had been there.

"The life those tapestries are showing is yours, Fionn," Donait said, laughing. "Do you not recognize your deeds?"

He shook his head. He could not believe there was a fault in the work, so it must be his vision that made him see the figures as awkward and the stitching clumsy, the colours crude or dull.

"There," she said, pointing, "is the battle in which you stood over King Cormac to protect him when the men of the Ulaidh had brought him down and then the two of you broke their power."

"Is it truly?" He peered more closely at the cloth. "But it was not quite like that. Goll was there, and the men of the high king's house guard. I only had to hold the northerners for a little while and then we all charged together and mowed them down. That was a good fight," he said, remembering. "We guarded each other's backs like brothers. Cormac is a wolf in battle. I have never felt so close to him as that day—"

"Was it so?" she asked. "And isn't that what the hanging shows?"

Fionn looked again, and now the tapestry was as fair as any of those he remembered. The images were so finely wrought they seemed to move; he recognized the lift of Cormac's eyebrow, and Goll's triumphant grin. He could even identify the shapes of the hills.

"It changed . . . ," he said stupidly, looking up at her.

"It came alive because you remembered it," Donait answered him.

"But you cannot change the past!"

"Can you not? Once a thing is over and done with, what matters is not what really happened but its meaning. The facts are only bare bones. You have bardcraft enough to know that what puts flesh on them is the tale."

"Sometimes," he said sourly, "poets lie." He had heard enough inflated stories about his own deeds to know that. According to the ballads, he and Goll ate ten goblins each for breakfast and rode kelpies into battle, raised up mountains to sit on when they were tired, and dug lakes for bathing pools.

"Will you let yourself be defined by lesser men?" Donait gestured along the wall. "These deeds created you, but you re-create them every time you remember. Tell me your stories, son of Cumhal. In the telling you will learn what matters most to you, and then you will know who you are."

Fionn frowned. He had spent most of his life trying to forget the past, and it seemed strange to intentionally try to resurrect it. But now Sadb was a part of that past, and perhaps in order to understand what she had meant to him he would have to come to terms with what had gone before. Painfully he levered himself to his feet and limped over to the first of the tapestries.

FIONN DID NOT KNOW HOW LONG IT TOOK HIM TO WEAVE the story of his life anew, but by the time he was finished, he was very hungry. There was more on the table this time—curd and honey, loaves hot from the baking and butter to spread on them, greens and nuts and cheeses and every kind of fruit. He ate everything, and when he had finished, his body, at least, felt like something he recognized.

"And do you know, now, what you are?" Donait asked when he lay back at last.

"I am full of food—" He managed a twisted grin. The faerie woman sighed, pleased to see him trying to laugh even as she was exasperated by his evasion. "And"—he took pity on her—"I can see that my life is more than grief for a lost lover, even though there is still a part of me that wants to run howling from this hall."

"And what does this 'more' consist of? In all of your deeds, Fionn mac Cumhal, do you create or destroy? What is it that you do?"

He gazed at the tapestries. "Sometimes the one and sometimes the other. But"—he pointed at the hanging of the Hazel Tree—"more often it seems to me that what I have done is to protect, to maintain the balance. I have guarded Eriu from invasion from other lands or the Otherworld, kept the wilderness from attacking the settled lands, and the men of the *duns* from disturbing the forest. I live on the boundary between them. Sometimes it seems I *am* the boundary."

Fionn looked at Donait sadly. "Have I answered well?" he asked in the tone in which he once had asked how well he had bathed.

"Very well," she said softly. She came to him then and began to stroke his hair, and he closed his eyes.

"Then let me stay here—"

"Are you sure there is nothing left for you to do in the world of men?" Her voice was very still, her long fingers a feather-touch on his brow.

"I am sure only that I cannot continue to be the Shield of Eriu if Sadb is not there."

"Are you thinking that the druid has killed her, then, or do you believe she is here in the Otherworld and that is why you want to stay?"

Fionn felt his flesh turning to stone beneath her hands. "Do you know where she is?" he said in words more terrible because they were spoken softly. He turned suddenly and gripped her wrists. Donait met his gaze without flinching, though he must have been hurting her.

"You know," she said quietly. "Think, Fionn. Remember everything Sadb said to you, and you will know where she must be."

Fionn stared into her blue eyes, but he was seeing Sadb's face made rosy by firelight as she lay in his arms.

"She did not like to speak of it. She said only that she had been taken by a druid and bound by ogham. But he wore black garments, so she knew him to be an outcast. She called him the Dark Druid—Fer Doirich. It seemed to me that only my grandfather could have such power—and be so bitter an enemy." His voice grew hard. "I should have killed him when I had the chance! I made no effort to find out where he had gone to; I did not want to know! It was on the slopes of a mountain that he bound her, but she did not know where. And once she was mine, I did not need to know.

"When I found Sadb, the spells that wrapped her were as cold as the last winter of the world. I recognized the same stink of magic in the place where she disappeared. I suppose . . . if Fer Doirich had killed her, he would have left the body for me. And you say she is not here with the Sidhe. . . . Then she is somewhere that is neither death nor life, suffering an endless captivity—*because of me*!"

"You cannot search every mountainside in Eriu," Donait said softly. "But the son of the Dagda can do that. Once he knows what to look for, he can call on all the spirits of the land to look for Fer Doirich, and when he finds him, I think Bodb Derg will compel the Dark Druid to give his daughter back to him." There was a short silence.

"But not to me . . ." Fionn's voice was leaden.

"You did not part friends—" Donait gestured towards the section of tapestry, which showed Bodb Derg's wrath and the curses of Daireann. "He has already told me I must not harbor you here—and he is a powerful enemy."

Fionn looked at her, and this time it was Donait's gaze that flickered away. "I understand," he said at last. "If Sadb is to be released from captivity and return to the Sidhe, I must take up the Shield once more in the world of men. But she will be well—" He gripped Donait's arm. "She will no longer be suffering!"

"She will be well . . . ," Donait whispered. Abruptly Fionn realized what he was doing and let her go. She sat back, rubbing her arm.

"Forgive me!" He shook his head. "How long have I been here? How long have I been away?"

"It is the seventh Samhain since you disappeared," she said quietly, still not looking at him. "Goll rules the *fian*, but the king has not given Almu a new master, for even now they do not quite despair of you, and each year your household keeps the feast and prays for your return."

"Then I must go to them." As he got to his feet she looked up, and something in her expression made him stop.

"Sadb is lost to you," Donait whispered, "but I am still here . . . and I love you, Fionn mac Cumhal."

"It is love that is lost to me," Fionn said bleakly. "Perhaps that is something that time will heal, though it is hard for me to believe. But I know this, my dear, that if I tried to love you now I would shatter in tiny pieces, and who then would do the work you want me to do in the world?"

"It is so," she looked up at him, smiling tremulously. "Time can compass any transformation. When your healing is done, Fionn mac Cumhal, then you shall return. I have endless time, and I will wait for you. . . ."

Epilogue

I N DONAIT'S WORLD THERE WAS NO SUN TO MARK THE
passage of time, only a slow fading of the light to a
purple gloaming, and a slow brightening to that perpetual luminous silver haze. When Fionn walked through
the mist that surrounded the Otherworld into sunlight,
he blinked, for a moment blinded by the common light
of day. He took a deep breath, and felt a thrill go
through his flesh at the crisp tang of autumn air. It
was not the magical tingle of the air in Faerie, but a
more tangible flavor, compounded of fallen leaves and
wood smoke and the sharpness of approaching winter
beneath the thin, clear warmth of the sun. It made the
blood race through his veins, and muscles unused for
far too long trembled with the need for movement.

With some surprise he realized that what he was
feeling was happiness. The sorrow of Sadb's loss was
like the sorrow of the fading year—melancholy and yet
accepted. Donait had clad him in a close-fitting, sleeve-
less tunic and breeches of tawny leather to match the
season. He moved through the falling leaves like one of
them, finding new vigor in every step. He could hear
wind whispering in the branches, and the calling of the
wild geese as they uncoiled across the sky. Lapped in

the perfection of the Otherworld, he had forgotten the solid beauty of Eriu.

He could see the broad sweep of a high tableland above the treetops, its noble brow jutting westward. From the tang on the wind he guessed it looked over the sea. Memory flickered backward thirty seasons and gave him a name for it—he had come this way when he fled from Cruithne and her father, and folk had called the mountain Ben Bulben. It was no use wondering how he had ended up so far to the west—the Otherworld overlaid that of men strangely, and sometimes the match changed. It did not matter—in a few days he could be home, and he would enjoy the run. Fionn quickened his pace through the autumn woods, rejoicing in each turning leaf and mossy trunk, each stone and stream and blade of grass.

And then, to bring the beauty of the moment to perfection, he heard the piercing sweet summons of a hunting horn and a yammering of hounds. He paused, listening. They were coming his way. Fionn cast about, seeking the trail they must be following.

He saw the trail of a mouse into a crack beneath a beech tree and the track where a sparrow had landed and then flitted away again. He saw old deer sign, crossed by a badger's trail. But there was no new track of deer or boar to explain the hunters' urgency. There was only—he stilled, staring down at the mark that showed clearly in the moist soil by the stream, and his heart began to pound—a narrow human footprint, barefoot, so small it must belong to a woman or a child.

Fionn's skilled glance swept the leaf mold, searching for another trace. He would have to move fast to get in ahead of the dogs. He saw a leaf that might have been turned by a footstep—the quarry, whoever it was, moved as lightly as one of the *fian*. There was another—the hunted was moving faster, the footfalls more distinct as running feet struck the ground. Hounds belled again, from ahead this time.

There were two packs, closing in! Fionn lengthened his stride.

Up ahead someone shouted. Snarls rose above the hysterical yelping that told him the dogs had sighted their prey. He leaped forward, homing in on the sound. Through the trees he glimpsed a flurry of movement. Men were jumping about, spears waving, assaulting the air with shouts and laughter as they urged on the dogs.

"Sceolan, you bitch's son, go after him!" came a cry, and Fionn faltered in midstride, for that was Faobhar's voice he was hearing. He had come upon a hunting of the *fian*!

He burst through the thicket and saw past the tangle of men and dogs a pile of driftwood into which something pale was burrowing. Sceolan was crouched before it, the hair along his spine cresting and every tooth bared as he held the other dogs at bay. A wild hope leaped in Fionn's heart.

"Go on, lads," cried Faobhar, "he cannot stand against you all. Sceolan, give it up—that is our prey!"

"Not so!" Fionn's voice pierced the babble like a well-flung spear. Before they knew he was there Fionn had slipped between two of the hunters and reached the dog. "And Sceolan has done well—" His hand slid along the dog's domed skull as the dog leaped up with an incredulous whine.

The men, on the contrary, were struck to stillness, and the other dogs, sensing something uncanny, fell silent as well. Fionn crouched down and tried to see into the shadows beneath the windfall. He could hear his own heart thumping and the harsh breathing of the creature within.

"Be easy," he said softly. "No one will hurt you!" His eyes misted as he remembered when he had said that before. One small foot was almost within reach of his hand. "Come out now, the dogs are silenced—"

His voice sank to a reassuring murmur, all his being focused on reassurance. There was a small sigh and the foot slid down a hand's breadth as the fugitive began to relax at last.

Fionn grabbed for it and his strong fingers closed. There was a shock of disappointment, for he knew every inch of Sadb's body, and even her slender ankles had never been so small. The leg stiffened as its owner tried to pull free, but Fionn's grip was relentless. He began to pull, and the struggles stilled as the other realized it was useless to fight anymore. Fionn pulled slowly, and little by little his captive was drawn into the light of day.

Not a woman—not Sadb—but Fionn's flesh had already told him that. He saw a boy's small penis and scrotum, a flat, well-muscled belly, and then the face, half hidden by a shock of red-gold hair. The boy's skin was lightly browned all over, as if he had never worn clothing, his limbs scratched and bleeding from his run. The arms were the last to appear, and when the fingers had been forced to let go of the branches to which they clung the boy curled suddenly into a ball.

Sceolan whined gently, padded forward and began to lick his gashes, and after a moment the child uncoiled a little and one dark eye appeared between the golden tangles, widening as he realized to whom that warm tongue belonged.

"You see, he will not hurt you," Fionn found his voice at last. "Who are you, lad, and why are you wandering in the wood alone?"

"And who are *you*," came a rough voice from somewhere in the crowd, "to interfere in the hunting of the *fian*?"

Fionn looked up and saw recognition ripple through the circle of faces around him—an uneasy mixture of awe, joy, and fear that would have been funny if he had had the time to appreciate it just then.

"Well, we should have known, shouldn't we, when the dog let him by," said Dubhtach hoarsely. "Why are you all so surprised?"

"It is Fionn's spirit," whispered Aodh, making a sign of warding. "I told you we should not hunt so near to Samhain Eve!"

"The dog would not be licking his foot if he were not a living man," objected Faobhar.

"But light shimmers around him—"

"He has been among the Sidhe, that is all," said Dubhtach in a strained voice. "And that is no cause for wonder, for hasn't he done it all before?"

"Look—the boy is hungry!" Diarmait said, pointing. Fionn turned and saw that the child was recovering from his fear quickly. He had sat up and was pointing at his open mouth, looking expectantly at the men.

"Then feed him," said Fionn, and saw belief coming into men's faces at the familiar tone of command. He looked at the boy's strong limbs and bright eyes, his belly beginning to tighten with an amazed certainty. Seven years he had been gone—this lad was big for that age, but he himself had always been larger than his years. Was there any way he could be sure?

Trembling a little, he leaned forward and lifted the matted locks from the boy's broad brow. Dark gaze met blue as the child looked fearlessly back at him. Could he see something of Sadb's fine bones in the skull beneath the childish rounding of cheek and chin?

"Oisin—" said Diarmait, behind him. "He is a deer-child—see, there is a patch of deer-hair on his brow!"

Fionn blinked. Looking for shape, he had not seen surface, but it was true. There was a swathe of glistening white hair, wide as the lick of a doe's tongue before she remembered that such licking would doom her child forever to beast form, upon the left side of his brow. His heart began to shake in his breast, and the raw place where the thread of awareness that bound him to Sadb had been ripped away throbbed anew.

"Oisin . . ." Fionn whispered, gently stroking the smooth hairs. He shuddered as something flowed out from him, and the boy turned to stare at him with wide deer's eyes. Fionn's breath caught, for suddenly he felt the link between them and he did not need to set his thumb between his teeth to *know* that the boy was his own.

ON THE SLOPES OF BEN BULBEN, OTHER EARS HAD HEARD the hounds close in on their prey. The dark figure who was hobbling through the forest hurried faster, grinning maliciously.

Though Bodb Derg had forced Tadg to give up the woman, the Dark Druid had congratulated himself that Fionn's son was still within his power. But when he came to the cave where he had been keeping them, the boy was gone. Druid arts enabled him to read a trail as well as any man of the *fian*, but old bones must move carefully. Still, the boy's steps had been aimless—catching him should only be a matter of time.

And then he had heard the yammering of hounds and the deep calling of the *fianna*'s horns. Tadg had searched the skies for storm clouds he might summon to slow them, but the sky was clear. He had almost despaired then, until another thought occurred to him. Fionn was prisoned in the eternal present of the Otherworld. How delightful—how *tasty*—it would be to some day tell the boy how his own son, the offspring of his beloved Sadb, had been torn to pieces by Fionn's own hounds!

That thought had kept the Dark Druid moving briskly even when he began to tire. He pushed through a tangle of hazels, licking his lips in anticipation. Would a well-flung spear pierce the prey before they saw what it was, or would the hounds bring him down?

The clamor ceased suddenly and he paused, listening. He could hear a murmur of men's voices, and dogs whimpering as they will when they encounter something they do not understand. What was going on? He lifted a branch, peering downward. He could see a seething mass of dogs behind the circle of warriors, who stood in unnatural stillness, staring at something, or someone, crouched at the edge of a windfall. Perhaps the dogs had killed the boy already? He moved a little to one side, trying to see.

He saw a man's broad back and the child's leg and foot beyond it. There was no blood, but perhaps the hounds had gone for the throat. . . . The great dog Sceolan stood above him, tail wagging gently. Then the man straightened, and Tadg's gut began to churn as he saw golden hair. But it could not be his grandson, his enemy—Bodb Derg had said that one of the faerie women held Fionn in thrall!

The fair-haired man reached out to draw the boy into his arms, and Tadg saw on both bright faces the mocking flicker of his daughter Muirne's sweet smile.

"Oisin!" the triumphant cry rang through the trees of the forest, through all the worlds. The Dark Druid groaned, for the voice was certainly that of Fionn.

"You are Oisin, and I will raise you to be the greatest of heroes, for you are Sadb's son, and my own. . . ."

The
LENS OF THE WORLD
Trilogy

**Named *New York Times*
Notable Books of the Year—by**

R.A. MACAVOY

"One of the most talented writers
we have working in the field"
Charles DeLint, author of *The Little Country*

LENS OF THE WORLD
Book One
71016-1/$3.95 US/$4.95 Can

KING OF THE DEAD
Book Two
71017-X/$4.50 US/$5.50 Can

THE BELLY OF THE WOLF
Book Three
71018-8/$4.99 US/$5.99 Can

Other AvoNova Books by
Diana L. Paxson and **Adrienne Martine-Barnes**

MASTER OF EARTH AND WATER

Praise for the Chronicles of Fionn mac Cumhal

"A CELTIC FANTASY
THAT COMBINES HEROISM AND GRACE,
it has the austere and mysterious beauty
of a moss agate at the bottom of a clear pool."
Susan Shwartz, author of *The Grail of Hearts*

"SUPERIOR SCHOLARSHIP AND STORYTELLING ...
Diana Paxson and Adrienne Martine-Barnes
have joined the ranks of the
creators of the good stuff."
Chicago Sun-Times

"SPLENDIDLY PACED, ACTION-FILLED,
GORGEOUSLY WRITTEN"
Booklist

"PAXSON AND MARTINE-BARNES HAVE PUT
NEW FLESH ON THE LITERARY BONES
OF THE ENDURINGLY POPULAR
IRISH OUTLAW/POET."
Orlando Sentinel

"A SUSPENSEFUL TALE THAT IS FILLED WITH
MAGNIFICENT DESCRIPTIONS OF CHARACTERS,
ACTION AND SETTINGS."
VOYA

"UNUSUALLY GOOD CELTIC FANTASY ...
THE STORY SINGS"
Kirkus Reviews